D0620409

Odd Fish and Englishmen

Odd Fish and Englishmen

Sarah Francis

An *Abacus* Book

First published in Great Britain
by Abacus in 1996

All characters in this publication are fictitious and any resemblance to real persons, living or dead, is purely coincidental.

A CIP catalogue record for this book is available from the British Library.

ISBN 0 349 10750 5

Printed in Great Britain by Clays Ltd, St Ives plc

Abacus
A Division of
Little, Brown and Company (UK)
Brettenham House
Lancaster Place
London WC2E 7EN

For my family

Acknowledgements

My grateful thanks to Bruce Hyman, for his love, his superlatives, and his unerring support; to Helen Morgan, a true friend and invaluable first reader; to my father and Linda, for never telling me to get a proper job; to my mother, because she 'always knew'; to Leo D'Arcy, for painstaking hours correcting my colloquialisms; to Imogen Taylor, a wonderful editor, instinctively right in her suggestions; to Rebecca Kerby and all in-house at Abacus; and to Angie Torode, friends and family at large, and my cats, simply for being around.

1

It was raining the day Isobel was born. In other circumstances this fact might well have gone unnoticed, but on this particular day it seemed the one thing of which they were all certain: that it was wet. More notable still for their being in the garden at the time, their collective memory of the event was one of umbrellas and wellington boots, of running noses and of blue knees, and it would be a long time before any of them could look out of the window on a wet afternoon and not smile. For Elisabeth, however, these details were rather forgotten, primarily due to the somewhat humiliating experience of lying in the middle of the lawn at four o'clock in the afternoon, her dress around her chin, her wellingtoned ankles securely handcuffed by her knickers, and surrounded by her horrified family. Horrified because not one of them, including Elisabeth, had any notion that she was pregnant. Indeed, it was several minutes before the connection was made, and even then, only Isobel's ultimate arrival, to the cheering tribute of two uncles and a grandfather, settled the matter. And if the situation were not bizarre enough in itself, that it should also be the wettest day on record for almost forty years was perhaps only to be expected.

As in any family in which the males predominate, if only in number rather than status, there is inevitably a certain amount of rivalry in the begetting of the female's attention.

From the very beginning, Isobel was perceived to be special, but by none more so than the three men who had triple-handedly delivered her into this world. Their presence at this miraculous event seemed to each to signify a particular bond with the child, and it was a matter of furious debate for many years to come as to which of them might claim the paternal right. Paternal, that is, in an assumed sense. Who the actual father was Elisabeth never revealed, primarily because she herself did not know, or certainly not by name. And as far as everyone else was concerned, such details were largely insignificant: this way, Isobel would remain here in the family home, idolised by her three fathers and mother, and a surprising ally in the one figure absent from her birth, her grandmother Sadie.

Sufficiently tormented by her own experience of child-birth, Sadie had no desire to share in her daughter's, and opted instead for the slightly warmer option – although no less wet – of her bath. Having observed from her bathroom window the antics in the garden, she made a considered decision to leave them to it, and, as was her habit in times of upheaval or stress, concentrated instead upon the act of drowning. Of course, this was not intended in the literal sense, but was rather a means by which, since a girl, she had found some sort of relief from the monotony of a dry world. She would imagine herself falling, deeper and deeper into the black depths of water, until she had been swallowed up by its nothingness and only oblivion prevailed. No present. No future. No daughter in the garden giving birth to an unexpected, illegitimate child in a rainstorm. Nothing. The practice of this technique had, in the early days, been the only means by which she could survive; since then she had discovered an equally effective capacity for drowning from the inside. A daily dose of the two ensured it to be a rarity that she ever left the bathroom anything less than soaked.

And today was no exception. Isobel's first glimpse of her

grandmother was of a Medusa-like figure, cloaked and hooded in what later were revealed to be the household's entire supply of dry towels, peering down at her from the great height of her slippered feet, and demanding to be introduced. While Elisabeth screamed, hating her mother for so successfully affecting such dramatics, Isobel merely gazed at her. Whether or not she comprehended is a matter of personal opinion, but certainly in the eyes of her aggressor, she had shown admirable courage.

Courage, Sadie imagined, through the haze of her meandering thoughts, was an essential trait even in grandchildren. And she leaned a little closer, until the spokes of the upturned umbrella in which Isobel lay pressed hard against her nose. The child stared back. Her temporary cradle could not have been more suited to the general eccentricity of the occasion, and even the chorus of Elisabeth's outraged wails did little to diminish the appeal of the scene. For Sadie did not intend any harm, despite her proximity: she was merely curious to meet this creature which had come into their home with such floodlike proportions. She felt a genuine affinity with a child born to elemental discord, and for the first time in many years found herself affected by a spirit of less than 12% proof. With sobering reluctance, she stood back. Looking at Isobel was like gazing upon still water: she had none of that peachiness usually associated with babies, but instead possessed a certain translucent calm. Should one move too quickly or carelessly, it seemed she might spill and be lost forever, and that would be unforgivable. And showing a rare sensitivity both to her distraught daughter and her own clumsiness, Sadie resisted an inclination to touch the child, although she felt sure, had she tried, she would be met by that same salty smoothness she herself had always known.

From the outset, Isobel was acknowledged as the core around which the rest of the family might now align itself, as, in her time, Sadie herself had been. Perhaps it was the uncanny air of wisdom which pervaded from her precocious features, or maybe it was simply a projection of their own needs for which she provided a suitable vessel, but a new calm descended upon the household in the succeeding days, and a greater tolerance of one another ensued. Where before there had been isolation and hostility, there was now alliance, linked as they were in the fulfilment of Isobel's needs. The three generations found unity, and as a whole they thrived upon it. That night, as they had stood in the kitchen, four of the five adults still dripping in their raincoats, the other naked except for a shroud of bath-towels, all eyes had fallen on Isobel, and for the first time in many years, they were a family, brought together as one before the peculiar light of this new arrival.

As the days passed, Isobel grew and grew, her face becoming more beautiful by the day, with a clarity which hypnotised all who looked upon her. Her resemblance to her grandmother became rapidly more apparent, despite Elisabeth's denials, and even under the shadow of Sadie's drinking, the glare of their similarities could not be ignored. She possessed that same detached awareness, gliding through the routine of the everyday with a thoughtless acceptance which left those around her wondering that it had ever seemed difficult before. Self-contained and sure, she seemed wholly unaffected by life such as it was offered to her in those first months. Like Sadie before her, she hovered, never quite here, never quite there, and one could not help but question where in fact she did belong. It was only the physical proof of nappies and bedtimes that confirmed that she was present at all, and even then, according to Sadie, this was less than definitive.

Since childhood Sadie had dreamt of a world in which human character aspired to more than history suggested. She longed for the mythical realms of dragons and mermaids, where good conquered evil, and beauty won outright, and she spent many an hour concocting tales of splendour and magicality in which, as heroine, she repeatedly triumphed against the odds. She imagined herself apart, borrowed from another age and another dominion, and she was not afraid to contend that in the face of this other reality, the present was really something of a waste of time. She was caught, she believed, on a divide: on one side was the human, and on the other myth – it was only a matter of chance that she should have received legs rather than a tail; by sheer coincidence that land, and not water, should be her home.

And of course, if Sadie was a displaced mermaid, wrenched from her habitat by the cruel hands of fate, then did it not follow that the same fist had also seized Isobel? One could not deny the similarity of their characters, nor that Isobel had inherited at least something of that intrinsic wateriness individual to her grandmother. Nor could one disprove that the curious lines about the child's stomach were not, in fact, the usual creases of babyhood, but the lingering traces of a scalier past. And yet it seemed Sadie was alone in perceiving such parallels, and quite unsupported in the solutions she saw as necessary. Even at her most lucid, the best Sadie could hope for from her audience was silence, and it was a constant concern to her that they should allow inhibition to cloud their understanding. In particular, she worried about Elisabeth, for as the child's mother, much was dependent upon her.

But Elisabeth's staunch refusal to allow Sadie anywhere near her did not bode well. Elisabeth was, above all, a pragmatist, and had no time for the whims of superstition to which she felt her mother inclined. This persistent round of fairytales bored her, and it was a constant source of irritation that she should repeatedly have to defend her daughter against such fantasies. It was not enough that

Isobel showed a vague likeness. If she was tarred with the same brush she must also be trodden and steamrollered before Sadie would be content. And if this did not suffice, that she should then be branded an outcast, unsuited to the world at large, and in need of particular attention which only her grandmother might provide, was no less than ridiculous. But ridicule, Elisabeth mused, was exactly what one had come to expect from Sadie: gone were the days when one might have taken her seriously, or even paid attention to what she said. Dreams and idealism were all that remained.

Yet for the most part Elisabeth tolerated her mother's eccentricities, if only out of habit. She offered no resistance to the perpetual salt baths, or the insistence upon strands of shells hung about Isobel's cot instead of the more usual mobiles. She had even allowed her to bury the placenta beneath a tree in order to ward off evil spirits, considering there could be little harm in such a practice. It was only when she caught Sadie soaking the nappies in cold water, before fixing them like a fish tail about the child's legs, that she lost all patience, and forbade her to come anywhere near. Had it not been for Isobel's obvious distress at her absence, Elisabeth might have succeeded in such exile. But yet again she was overshadowed, and forced to allow the companionship it seemed both craved. Only this time, Elisabeth insisted, it was to be under the strictest supervision.

Such watched-over periods as they now shared were treasured by child and grandmother alike, and provided a constant source of amusement for whichever family member had been commissioned as observer. Sadie's rather nonconformist approach to childcare had never been in dispute – indeed her children's own experience was proof enough – but she aspired to new heights in her regard for Isobel. For hours they would lie motionless on the floor of the drawing room, staring at the ceiling, and gurgling at one another with untold significance; for whole afternoons they splashed and wallowed in Sadie's huge cast-iron bath at the top of the house, the wrinkles of age providing touching relief to the fleshier plumpness of babyhood; and for days on end they would huddle together, filling the spaces between them with a world of unheard secrets, until they both brimmed with the other. In Isobel, Sadie discovered a whole lease of life, casting off the caution and encumbrance of old, and learning a second time the ease and vitality which was herself. There was once again laughter in the house, where before there had only been bad temper, and life became, as it had not been for many years, unusually important.

Not that life had ever been particularly dispensable, but for Sadie, more than anyone, it had often seemed less worthwhile. Over the years she had grown increasingly dissatisfied with the limitations she perceived around her, and it was only in the quiet moments when she met face to face with the bottom of the bottle that it seemed any of it might have a point. In these tranquil periods, like the time spent drowning in her bathtub, and indeed, often concomitant with such, she found the space and light her immediate environment denied. That this could only ever be a temporary solution goes without saying, and for many years the fraying edges which accompany such cut-offs provided untold frustration, but with practice and determination, she succeeded in surmounting this. The ensuing numbness was in itself of sustaining effect, and it was only the occasional lapse, due to unforeseen circumstances or ill-advised contrition, that suggested it had ever been different. And yet once upon a time it had been entirely different, and although it was largely into the realm of nostalgia that such memories had since been pushed, that fact was never forgotten.

It had taken Joseph a lifetime to accept Sadie's drinking, and even now, he was the first to suggest that, with the right treatment, she might easily be 'cured'. As a doctor, he was perhaps quite justified in making such diagnoses, and yet equally, it was hardly her symptoms which were really at issue. For many years it had been obvious that Sadie was slipping towards this, and yet for many years the fact had been vehemently ignored, in the hope that perhaps, left alone, it might sort itself out. Only when Joseph discovered the linen basket in the bathroom full of empty bottles did he realise the inefficacy of such solutions. Somewhat too late, he attempted to broach the subject with her, pointing out that, in his professional opinion, her behaviour was somewhat unstable, and perhaps they should talk about it further. But to no avail. Both were unpractised in the art of intimate communication, and neither inclined to apply any real effort. In the valley of their individual consciences, the mountains of blame and guilt were too steep. And so any intimations of personal failure or individual loss were washed away upon a river of Irish malt, and only the dregs left to suggest life was less than ideal.

But this was before. The arrival of Isobel on that wet autumn afternoon cast a new light upon the household, and occasioned something in each of them akin to an almost spiritual rejuvenation. This tiny scrap of flesh, with its iridescent skin and lurid eyes, born two months premature and quite uninvited, changed the whole direction they had seemed destined to follow, and incited new determination where before there had been only lethargy. In particular, this applied to Sadie, who temporarily neglected her daily drownings, and Joseph glimpsed anew the girl he had fallen in love with all those generations ago.

2

Joseph had first set eyes upon Sadie from the deck of a funeral boat somewhere off the west coast of Ireland, having just attended the watery burial of his father's oldest friend. Filled with the cluttering associations and memories which inevitably cloak such a day, he was struggling to regain his sense of place, when, out of the green depths which rose and fell before him, he snatched a vision of the most striking and effervescent beauty, here and then gone, that he had ever seen. Not one to exaggerate, nor particularly given to romantic proclamations, Joseph inclined to disbelief, and yet the heat of her image – for it was a woman he had perceived – was firmly etched upon his eye, and wherever he turned, wherever he looked, it was she who filled his sights.

'Did you see that?' He turned to the dead man's wife, who was standing next to him at the bow, and pointed out to sea.

'What? See what?' she replied, with some distraction.

'That . . . girl . . . in the sea . . . just over there . . .'

As he spoke he was aware that he was not making sense, and when his companion once again shook her head, and then moved away to lament her widowhood elsewhere, he was not surprised. But in that split second of gold-green light, he knew he had glimpsed something quite remarkable, and he spent the remainder of the journey leaning over the deck, doubled up in peering curiosity, desperate that he might once again catch sight of such glittering colour. Indeed, had it not been for the concern of fellow mourners, he might well have taken his interrogation of the waters one step further, but a timely hand on his coat tails prevented this, and it was a dry and fractious man who stepped on to the shore and hurried back up the beach to the village. Turning this way and that, to the sea, and then the land, the Englishman formed a comical figure, but the grimaced determination which flooded every feature on his salt-spattered face was no laughing matter. For several hours he stood against the sea wall, staring out at the crashing waves on the horizon, watching for something, anything, that might appease his aching sights. And yet nothing, only white crests and dipping birds and, of course, that still bright reflection of memory.

Eventually, as much due to cold and hunger as to the inevitable despondency, Joseph gave up his vigil, and began to make his way back to the inn, where he and any other alien guest had their lodgings. Determined not to be dispirited, he concentrated instead upon making the necessary arrangements for his impending return to England, and over the next few hours he muddled his way through timetables and bills in order that he might be ready to depart first thing in the morning. He had no qualms about leaving, the focus of his newfound quest largely fixed to his imagination rather than a particular place or time, and he was confident that if she was there, he would find her. For Joseph was a man of fact and purpose. And life, as far as he was concerned, was a matter of engineering and formula. So long as one was concentrated, and the goal clear in one's sights, the rest was purely logistical. Self and not situation, formulae, not fate, ministered to this man's will; and if the sought-for did not show itself at this particular juncture, then he would find it elsewhere.

Having finished his paperwork, Joseph pulled out his bag from beneath the bed and began to sort his clothes into piles, putting some back into his suitcase, and leaving others to one side to change into now. Pulling his shirt over his head, he moved over to the window in order to close it against the evening, momentarily resting his forehead against the pelmet, and shivering for the last time at the bleak grey world which filled the frame. He could just make out the silhouetted figures of two men standing at the edge of the sea wall, where earlier he himself had waited, and he watched as first one and then the other bent to pick up a stone and hurl it into the incoming tide. Following the arc of their arms, his perspective shifted to encompass a further shadow, still and slight, suspended at the water's edge, and with a mutter he considered the foolishness of such wintry paddling. His hand on the latch, he began to pull the window to, when he suddenly paused and looked more closely. Could it be that it was her? No, Joseph rubbed his eyes with his free hand, it was a trick of the light. But what if it was her? Squinting against the bluish deception of approaching night, Joseph watched, transfixed, as the silent form slowly lifted itself from its crouched position, and uncoiled into a singular, serpentine thread, wavering against the horizon like a wisp of smoke.

As he watched, it began to turn, away from the swelling of the sea, and towards Joseph's flattened and smudged regard. It was her. He was sure of it. It was her. He did not know whether to be relieved or appalled, the vision no more rational or credible than it had been earlier. For even according to Joseph's exacting eye, the girl was the most beautiful creature he had ever seen. Wrapped in the gauzy colours of the sea, she seemed to merge into the landscape, until nothing of her was clear except the glow of her hair, which buffeted in the wind like trails of seaweed. He could not take his eyes off her, partly for fear of losing her once again, and partly because he no longer had control over his senses. She glimmered and shone before him, and in the few seconds for which they faced one another, Joseph found himself sinking, hot into cold, flesh into glass, as his rational mind slithered out of his grasp.

Peeling his face from the pane in which it had embedded itself, Joseph threw open the wooden casement to its widest extent, and leaned out, glaring at the motionless figure like a scientist peering at a specimen. She did not falter, only stared in return, and for several minutes, neither of them shifted, until a distant cry, whether bird or human Joseph did not know, caught her attention, and she turned away. Fearful to leave his post and allow her the chance to evade him once again, Joseph contemplated the distance from the window to the street below, and considered his best option was to climb on to the sill and then jump. This was not altogether practical, although neither was it particularly difficult. What it would be, however, was wholly out of character. If there was ever a man fashioned for the use of front doors and formal entrances, it was Joseph: windows were for looking out of, nothing more. And yet here he was, straddling the sill and attempting to manoeuvre his rather ungainly legs into what might be imagined a better position for jumping; for jumping towards a girl who had just begun to walk in the opposite direction. Momentarily disabled, both by his horror, and the reluctance of his left leg to follow his right into this great unknown, Joseph hesitated, the object of his attention disappearing into the mid-distance, and himself quite helpless to prevent it. What to do? Which way to leap? He wavered, straddling the sill, but this was no time for indecision and in a moment of uncharacteristic spontaneity, Joseph threw himself out of the window to land in a clumsy heap on the pavement beneath.

The sight of a figure free-falling past the bar room window succeeded in emptying the inn of its many huddling customers, who promptly rushed outside, still clutching their tankards, to witness this modern day Icarus, dressed only in a vest and with shirt tails gathered about the spectacle, som man, others supporting far more origin, but none providing sufficie acrobatics. Joseph, however, was co figure of whom he had now lost si despair, and writhing to escape the opp en had formed around him, he stretched and like one possessed, until his head was free of the est of limbs, vertical to his horizontal, and he could make out the position where she had last stood. But she was now nowhere to be seen. With the stealth and litheness of a spirit, she had once again escaped him.

'I'm fine. Please leave me alone. I just need a minute to . . .'

Lying back on the pavement, Joseph sighed with exasperation, infuriated by the seeming impossibility of the situation, and irritated by his handling of it. How had he, a respected London doctor, ended up sprawled in front of a public house, surrounded by a babbling entourage, and fretting over the disappearance of a creature he was not even sure existed? He was beginning to wish he had never set eyes upon the girl; had never even come here. He should have listened to his mother and sent a wreath, rather than traipsing across the seas to the back of beyond to bury, or rather drown, a man he had never known . . . and to what end? To suffer mad delusions on a funeral boat, hang around a harbour wall half the day, and then throw himself out of a window? Even if the girl did exist, which was highly unlikely, she could not be worth this.

Joseph sat up once again, his spirits restored by such cynicism, and struggled to his rather bruised knees. But just as he did so a hand on his shoulder held him down, interrupted his thoughts, and, turning to face this intruder, he chilled. For it was her, the very creature which had m to this sorry state. Crouched at his side, poring im like a worried animal, it was her eyes, so distinctly urple, which transfixed him. And while the village looked on, vaguely amused. Joseph lay there oblivious. It was her.

'Hallo.' Gazing down upon this stranger, whom she had watched that morning from the rock, Sadie was fascinated.

'Hello ...' Joseph pushed himself on to one elbow, and gazed at her, the frowning intensity which had first met her softening, folding at the edges, into what was almost recognition.

'How are you? You've taken a bit of a tumble there ...'

'Yes ... er ...'

'But you're all right?'

'Yes ...'

'Great ... well, you'd better be coming with me then.'

She had never met this man whom she now teased away from the fretful crowd, and led along the street to her home, but she did not doubt that she knew him. Or at least, knew of him. Indeed, she had been waiting for him to arrive for years now; watching and planning, with that certainty of faith only the most devout can enjoy; she had even prepared her things so that they might be gathered together at a moment's notice and their valuable time together not wasted. And at last she had been rewarded. At last he was here, stumbling alongside her with careful feet, having seemingly fallen out of the sky like an angel. Was this what he was, an angel? She glanced at him. Certainly he had the face of one, with its gently creasing brow and soft blue eyes, and the wave of nose that seemed to slice his face in half, like two sides of a scale, balanced and weighty. An angel come to deliver her from this sea-soaked world ...

'I'm wondering where you're coming from, so I am,' she began hesitantly, knowing better than to ask such a man outright, 'and I'm thinking it's far and away from this place.' She nodded, as if to reassure herself that such musings were legitimate, and glanced sideways to read his response. But Joseph was silent. She tried again. 'P'raps you came from so far you don't know how to be telling me, is that the truth? You're thinking I'm going to be scared if you tell me, but I promise you, I'm not scared easily, so I'm not. And I've been waiting for you anyway, so you needn't be worrying that I'm not 'specting you, so you needn't.'

Joseph smiled, distractedly, the sense of her words only grazing his consciousness, his mind still hovering somewhere between window and pavement, and he continued to walk on. But the fact that she was waiting for him, that she was ''specting' him, caught his attention, and eventually he paused dreaming, hanging, thanking, long enough to wonder what she meant.

'Waiting for me?'

'Sure. I always knew you were coming, long before I saw you from the rock, so I did. It was just for the seeing, that's all, just for the seeing.'

'So why . . .' Joseph was sorting the idea of predictability into a manageable order, 'so why did you walk away when I saw you this evening? If you were waiting for me, as you say?'

'I didn't.'

'But you did. You looked at me and then you walked away.'

'I didn't. Just 'cause I wasn't facing you didn't mean I was going away. I just wasn't looking straight at you, that's all. I was always there.'

And so Joseph received his first lesson in the complexities of Sadie's presence, or lack of it, and in the learning understood simply to accept. With the merest of wrinkles to convey his confusion, he nodded, shrugged and muddled on alongside. Which was all he needed to do.

'You've got beautiful hands, so you have . . .' Sadie was back to introductions.

'Thank you.'

'Can I . . .' She gripped his fingers tight, deliberating. 'Can I . . .' But she did not continue, and instead pulled his palm towards her bending head, and kissed it lightly, never slowing her step, never doubting.

Joseph trembled, and stared at her.

'"Hands to summon back the tide and beckon in the wind . . ." Who said that?' She gazed at the sea wall which bordered the road, and pulled him towards it, leaning into him as she studied the thrashing waves beyond. 'Maybe it was you?'

Joseph shook his head. No, he was quite sure he had never said anything like that. Quite sure . . .

'Would you have been waiting for me too, tell me?' She held his palm inches from her face. 'Would you have known it was me, can you say?'

Joseph slowed, untangling his fingers from the knot of hers, and shook his head non-committally. He could not bring himself to share in such declarations, even then, and instead he only smiled. Running his thumb the length of her cheek, he could not reassure her he had been waiting for her too; could not admit he had thought her lost long before she had even discovered him; that even now he feared she might disappear at any moment, back to the fleeting waves. He could touch upon such truths only lightly. Much as he might touch upon Sadie herself.

Carefully, Joseph slipped his arm about her shoulder, pulling her to him. She felt soft, silken, as if made of some fabric other than flesh and blood, and he feared that such fragility might not withstand his coarser touch. But it was as if she were warmed by it, her cool becoming fluid within the cup of his hand, melting into him, and as she leaned more heavily against him, it seemed they had always been together. Cheek to brow, nose to eye, soul to soul. Silent. And Joseph understood there and then that he could not let her go. If he must spend the rest of his life chasing her, following her, pulling her, then that is what he would do. There and then, here and now.

They were married within the week, in a ceremony which lasted almost as long as the three days it took to prepare for, and considerably longer to recover from. Nobody was surprised by their haste, except perhaps Joseph, unaccustomed as he was to spontaneity, and if the groom's family were consequently somewhat in absence, there were sufficient relations on Sadie's part to make up the discrepancy. Not least amongst these were her twelve brothers who formed the retinue of best men – the task of choosing between them onerous at the best of times – and under their commanding eyes, it was a rare and imposing event. There was not a pew unfilled as Sadie floated up the aisle, not a decibel untouched as they thundered through the hymns, and not a man present who did not envy and admire Joseph. Only the single line of wizened spinsters, whose rook-like backs and beaking chins are a familiar addition to every such occasion, offered any element of descant: 'She's a knowing wee thing, but she'll ne'er be still, so she won't.' Black heads bobbed along the row, perched and crowing, and rustling elbows tweaked their agreement. 'A proper streel, so she is,' the hissing vowels curling tight around bitter teeth. 'A giddy gibbadaun, if ever there was.' A hat in the pew in front turned round and hushed glaringly, before twisting back into anonymity. One after the other frayed eyebrows rose in dismissal, the gesture sending a small avalanche of dusted powder fluttering into the aisle, before mutterings of 'clatterin' sp'rits' and 'wantin' terribles' once again ensued. But the wall of shoulders which surrounded the subject, and the deafening absorption of her chosen love, barred any notion of doubts or premonition, and as their vows were made such words were washed forever away. And if there was ever cause to remember them, the speakers were by then long dead and buried, and their wisdom but a stray murmur occasionally audible in the wind.

For the two nights and days which followed, the village in its entirety feasted and drank, danced and caroused, until they could feast, drink, dance and carouse no more. Fatted calves were slaughtered in rapid succession, and prodigal progeny appeared from all corners of the earth to join the harangue, and there was not a door which remained unopened, nor an intimacy which had not been rehearsed, by the time the revelling stumbled to its end. On the street and in the pub (for there was really only one of each), in doorways and by waysides, the evidence of the festivities might be found, with bottles and bodies falling in close proximity, and only the most infirm or the most pious providing any uprights to this flattened and rolling landscape. And as the bus which was to take the newlyweds to Dublin rumbled into town, it was to the credit of those few left standing that the roads were cleared, and fatalities both of body and spirit thus avoided.

Although Sadie had anticipated such a departure as this for many years, she had failed to prepare for the wrenching tide of remorse which would accompany it, and only the gentle prodding of Joseph behind her prevented her from turning back altogether. But his hand in the small of her back, and his whispered consolations echoing the voices of her own mind, gradually drew her up the narrow steps into the bus, and squeezed against her as she settled upon the window seat and gazed out upon her gathered family. Central to them all stood her mother, hands on hips, feet spread, and her mouth tucked into a puckering pleat of both pride and concern. Sadie was her youngest child, and her only daughter: it was perhaps inevitable that she should be the first to leave, and yet there is no sparing the ache which necessarily attends. Particularly when it is with an

Englishman. She shook her head knowingly, and pulled her shawl tighter around her as if suddenly cold. For once in her life there were just no words for it, and she sank back, letting her daughter go, and hoping against hope that that would be the end of it. And yet daughters, like bad pennies, have a habit of turning up again, and even England, she was sure, would not keep that one for long. She shook her head once more. The Englishman had his work cut out for him, no doubt about it. And as if they had heard her very thoughts, twelve heads, flanking her on both sides, nodded in agreement. No doubt about it.

Turning away from the nodding, shaking chorus on the pavement Joseph studied his new wife, and he smiled encouragingly.

'This is it then. Are you all right?'

Sadie nodded in assent. Both knew it was a lie, that she was not all right, nor should be, but it required neither words nor expression to convey this, and for the moment it was enough. But as the bus pulled away, and all hands raised in a forest of farewells, a solitary tear slipped unnoticed past its guarding eyelid, to offer its own, trickling commentary on the world it left behind.

3

All her life Sadie had swum against the tide. Where others chose to paddle, to build boats in the sand or castles in the air, Sadie yearned towards the depths, towards the unseen, unchartered waters of her imagination. She was a solitary child, never content in the presence of other children, and preferring loneliness and escape to the void of chattering companionship which it seemed was her alternative. Only when she was on the beach, cradled in the rocking beds of shells and sand, or flooding in and out with the ripples of the waves, did she approach anything of the happiness she dreamed to be her own. She was first person singular, a tale in blank verse, and for the twelve brothers who doted upon her as they never would upon another, she was the very spirit of their soul. Her every whim was indulged, her every impulse satisfied, her every dream a reality. And even on the day she wrenched herself out of their lives and into that of a flying Englishman, they did not begrudge her. For Sadie would never be very far away. Ireland was her home, although she might not know it yet, and she would be back.

Their twelve-timed wisdom, however, was for the moment unspoken, and they returned to their boats without another thought. Sadie might have escaped the nets, but she was still in the water, and, as any self-respecting Irishman will tell you, that is reassurance enough. For Sadie had been born into a world of few boundaries: she had grown up around men who, while they might have lived in the same house, drunk in the same pub, walked the same street till they died, never fixed themselves beyond the next day. Men who ate off newspaper, so as not to buy plates and thereby root themselves; men who drank themselves stupid each night, in a timeworn denial of 'being there' at all; men who lived with their mothers until they lived with their wives, until they lived with the 'Holy Mary, mother of God' they daily invoked to rescue them from both. In short, men who, however long they stayed, however firmly they were fixed, only ever admitted to passing through. That, simply, was their way. And Sadie, the thirteenth born and hence always to be at odds, understood her own existence to be no different. She never grasped the vital differences sisters might have instructed her in, and her mother, with a house full of sons, had long since forgotten that they mattered. Sadie would learn the hard way why home must always be inside the woman, when in a man it is apart, although she would never understand it. And she would suffer a whole lifetime of leavings before the wildness of spirit, which was both inherited and herself, discovered a means to stay.

Sadie smudged another tear into the damp of her cheek, and rested her head against the shuddering window of the bus. She sighed, loudly, and sought out Joseph's hand from beneath the pile of bags and papers on his lap. She did not exactly know what pained her, her mind full of goodbyes and good manners, but it was enough to want to share.

'You'll like London, you'll see. It's not so different from here, and you'll soon feel at home.' Joseph squeezed her scrabbling fingers, his words slicing her back to the present with a sharpness comparable to the grazing edge of metal seating which swiped the back of her knee with every pothole. Absently rubbing her leg, she glanced up at him out of the corner of her eye, and smiled hesitantly.

'Sure I will,' she attempted, the faint tremor of doubt disguised to Joseph's ear by the lilting accents of her Irishness. 'Sure I will.' And she rested her head against his shoulder, and watched as the fields and villages scrolled past the window, fast then slow, blurred then clear, in a myriad of changing colour and shape. Pausing at a crossroads, the tick of the indicator like a metronome measuring time to her thoughts, she found her reflection filled by the glaring features of one of the many statues of the Virgin which scatter the roadsides of Ireland, plaster-grey and luminous. It seemed only polite to stare back. But if she wondered at the significance of such proximate reckoning, it was soon overridden by the greater forces of habit and acceptance, only the faint glimmer of hollow eyes remaining as the bus pulled forwards on to the intersecting road. There were too many icons in Sadie's life for this one to hold any particular value. And too many occasions on which she might be tempted to turn back.

To Sadie's limited awareness, the world was made up of proportionate quantities of water and earth, and wherever one ventured, those amounts would remain the same. As she soaked up her last glimpses of the sea which fringed their route and filled her sights, she did not consider for a moment that this might be the last time she might look upon its mass with anything of the recognition and ownership she had long assumed her right. That in the world there existed places wholly dry and devoid of such salty depths, she could never have conceived. For Joseph it was simply a matter of geography. For Sadie it was an entire history.

In all her eighteen years, she had never ventured further abroad than the neighbouring village, half an hour away by foot, and she was therefore quite unprepared for the six-hour bus ride into Dublin, and for the scenes she would find there. From a world which measured movement in 'trips', she suddenly found herself embarked upon a 'journey', and for all her flightiness and determination to leave, her wings for the moment were held close to her sides. Hands upon lap, head resting upon Joseph's shoulder, she was a passenger, passive and pale, watching as green, then grey, then brown, curled around the length of the bus in a repetitive coil of motion, still amidst its flow. Words had no consequence, for they could not describe the enormity she felt. And thoughts held no weight. The heaviness of inevitability was all she knew, and so she pulled it about her like a shroud, shifting herself deeper into its bulk, and waited for relief.

But relief was to be more a matter of landscape than of any emotional enlightenment, the approach of the city providing terraces and shops where before there had been fields; bricks and plaster where once had been trees. Before their eyes, jagged skylines of chimney pots and washing lines slithered in to fill out the edges, smothering the kissing spaces where horizon met sea beneath the stifling embrace of industry. Even through the thickened panes of glass, she could feel its breath, taste its dust. Sadie was overwhelmed. She had not imagined such places might exist, much less that she would visit them, and she wondered if perhaps her dreams had been misplaced, or certainly, misinterpreted. But her doubts were shortlived, for they had now arrived at the docks where they would take the boat for Holyhead. And before she knew where she was, she was standing on the pavement beside the bus, watching as her past released its handbrake, and eased into gear, forwards and away from her stationary, bag-bewildered self.

'All right?'

'Great.'

'Good.'

And that, as they say, was that. In the light of such mutual understanding, they filed through on to the dockside, Joseph with his array of suitcases, wedding gifts and half-eaten sandwiches – it was impossible to get food past twelve brothers without at least a portion of it being devoured – and Sadie tripping along behind beneath a bundle of shawls and scarves, a single holdall slung across her shoulders. In all fairness, there was hardly the space for the added luggage of conversation, with the shuffle of feet, the chuntering of laden breath, and the unexplained rattling as Sadie's bag swung back and forth against her knees. And besides, there would be plenty of time for that later.

As they walked, Sadie followed the lines of this mulling, swamping world which wove itself around them. This way and that, detached and distracted, people moved without her, their faces a foreignness she had never known before, their passing ominous in its silence. The hours spent on the bus were the first occasion Joseph and Sadie had spent alone together since their meeting, and the unspoken simplicity of it had been welcome. And yet suddenly the distance seemed too complete. She did not know this man. In fact, she did not know anyone here, and from the blankness of their faces, it appeared nor did they know her. Sadie frowned, disturbed by such indifference. And if only to render the situation more comprehensible, she began to nod and smile quite indiscriminately, satisfied if she happened to incite even the smallest glimmer of response, and unnoticing of the less flattering returns. When Joseph paused to change his suit-case from one hand to the other, and to catch the strap of one of the many bags which hung pendulous from his shoulders, she fluttered ahead, like a butterfly skitting from one to the next in the excitement of welcome, careless of where she next dropped. If Joseph was muddled by the stares of embarrassed confusion her passing seemed to invite, he was soon distracted by the greater consideration of finding their tickets, and when he caught up with her at the foot of the gangplank, waving the two pieces of pink paper, her greeting seemed meant for himself alone. Flattered by its warmth, Joseph smiled in return, taking her arm with his spare hand, and guiding her towards the snaking line of fellow passengers.

'Let's find a space by the railings, and you can wave goodbye properly.' Hoisting his load to waist level as they manoeuvred the narrow staircases, Joseph clattered this way and that, already nervous at the prospect of his return, and becoming more English with every elbow. Sadie followed obediently. Wave goodbye? The words meandered in and out of her thoughts, swinging their arms in time to her own, and failing as yet to communicate any particular significance. Wave goodbye . . .

'Wave goodbye to who were you meaning, Joseph?' Sadie's curiosity got the better of her, the possibility that she might have missed some intimate acquaintance come to see them off, despite her arduous smiling, not beyond her.

'To Ireland, silly. Wave goodbye to Ireland. Metaphorically, of course, but I thought you'd at least want to see it one last time.'

'Yes, I do, I will, yes, sure. Mmmm.' And with the further affirmation of her nodding head, up and down, yes, yes, Sadie floated along behind him, watching the crunching of his jacket shoulders as he twisted back to check she had understood, and returning the grin of satisfied acknowledgement with equal fervour. Metaphorically. Now that was a nice word. And she continued to flick it back and forth as Joseph, at last finding a suitable vantage point where they might stand, arranged their bags against the railings and positioned Sadie in between. At this height the wind was much sharper than it had been on the dock, and Sadie was glad of the multitude of shawls her mother had insisted she wear. Bending to catch a stray corner which flapped about her bare ankle, Sadie paused to consider the sturdier woolliness of the legs she had married, and she was momentarily transfixed by the fact that two corresponding parts might be so different. Where she was pale and smooth, he was black and wrinkled, sock and trouser merging together to disguise the identity beneath, and Sadie could not help but wonder what such camouflage was intended to hide. She peered closer, her head now contorted between her arm and shin, and hesitantly fingered the even hem of grey flannel cuff. Joseph stared down upon the top of her head in bewilderment, before reaching down and catching the curious finger in the hook of his own.

'Sadie! What are you doing?' Half-amused, half-irritated, Joseph was unprepared for such intimacies, and failed to share her enthusiasm for show and tell. Still reeling from the suddenness of it all, his saving grace was the fact that they were still strangers, and he intended to prolong the simplicity of this as long as he might. And so he tugged at her finger, denying that either socks or soul should yet be bared, and pivoted her away from him. Sadie gazed at him, her hand limp in his, before, reprimanded, she slowly unfurled.

'Sorry.'

She lifted her head and stared past his profile and out to sea. Unsure of how she had offended, and yet convinced that she had, she considered it preferable, for the moment, to retreat. But as she stepped back into daydream, anchored only by the chain of her finger in his, all thought was deafened by the resonant groan of the ship's horn, bleeding its conch-like battle cry across the harbour, and causing an immediate flurry of excitement across the deck. Sadie turned to Joseph agitatedly. 'Are we away? Is that it? Are we away?'

He nodded in quiet assent, and Sadie turned back to the sea excitedly, watching as the calm waters began to swirl in an eddy of movement, black and white, and the whirr of the engines pulled the weight of the ship backwards and away. Stretching, reaching arms, waving back and forth, were mirrored on either side of the churning lines of the water, and somewhere towards the edge, they stood, two figures, silhouetted one against the other.

And if anyone had been watching, they would have seen the taller of the two reach out, despite himself, and pull the fluid form of the other into him, to kiss her with brief urgency, before translating the gesture into a tousling fondness, cheek upon upturned cheek, arms encircling.

'You're a funny one,' Joseph could be heard to murmur, deep within the curled mass of her hair. 'But I do love you.'

And Sadie sluiced against him, loving him too, and she watched as the ship slowly pulled away from the dockside, and the belt of water in between loosened its buckle and widened into the green-grey girth which was its entirety.

Presuming they would want to rest at some point during the crossing, Joseph had reserved a cabin where he now adventured to leave their bags, Sadie remaining on deck and promising not to move. The wind picked up as they moved further out to sea, the waves thrashed against the side of the ship, and the skies turned from blue to black with frightening speed, but she kept to her word. She did not move. Almost an hour later, she was still there, and Joseph was still wherever he had disappeared to, and, after some deliberation, she decided that perhaps she should try to find him. What if something had happened? Dear God, please don't let him have fallen out of another window . . .

Working on the principle that heavier stones sink deepest, and regarding Joseph as a particularly weighty individual, she decided to start as low in the ship as she could, and she set off down the maze of corridors and stairways, around and down. Looking neither right nor left, her thoughts solely upon descent, Sadie was weaving her way along a narrow carpeted gangway, when a door opened, and a faint voice called out to her, 'Sadie, is that you? I was just . . .'

Sadie turned to find Joseph woefully leaning towards her from behind the shell of an open door, arms outstretched.

'I wouldn't have moved,' she began, 'but . . .'

His faded green face, peering and browful, reminded her of a gargoyle and she hesitated, wondering at the permanence of such a transformation. Joseph shook his head, dismissively, but the action was clearly ill advised, for almost immediately he turned even greener, and jerked backwards into the blank space behind. A cacophony of sorry spluttering ensued, filling the open door, and it was several minutes before the noise died down, and the head re-emerged. 'Did you want to come in? I'll be okay. I'm just a little sea sick, that's all. Do come in, won't you.'

But Sadie had no intention of such recklessness, and she shook her head decisively. 'Carry a fish with you, that's the secret.'

Joseph stared at her, momentarily confused. 'What?'

'A fish. For it keeps off the spirits that're making this hoo-hah, honest to God it does. You'll not be seeing a fisherman in a storm without a fish in his pocket, so you won't. Shall I find you one?'

'No . . . no . . . I'm fine, Sadie, honestly.' Joseph smiled bravely, the very thought sending his stomach into somersaults. 'Just a bit nauseous . . .'

But barely had the words escaped his lips when they were snatched back, and once again Joseph disappeared in a storm of noise. Sadie waited patiently, shaking her head.

'Joseph . . .?' She wanted to ask him if she might go. There was, after all, little she could do except stand and watch him suffer, and what was the point in that? Sufferance, it seemed to Sadie, like all penitential states, was overrated. Far better the 'prick your finger and sleep for a hundred years' school of thought. And she therefore needed little encouragement, when, on appearing to her a third time, Joseph once again insisted she leave him, fishless, as he was, and with barely disguised gratitude she beat a hasty retreat to the upper decks.

The deck was almost deserted by the time she had navigated her way through the winding corridors, the majority of passengers having made their way to the bar or dining-room, with a handful following Joseph's example and disappearing out of sight altogether. The wind swept a coarse path about the darkening skies above, slapping the already intimidated clouds into a frenzy of indirection, and as Sadie watched, the first drops of rain could be seen dappling the swirling waters beneath. Growing in confidence, the drops became pools, splashing on to the blotting paper sea with increasing fervour, and in a matter of seconds all was wrapped in an indistinguishable haze of kicking rain. As if in protest, and unwilling to be outdone, the sea offered its response, waves crashing each against the other like clapping hands, with only the chant of the wind as testimony to the intrinsic order behind such anarchy. Sadie was transfixed, pinned against the railing, and oblivious to all but the raging world before her. The waving fingers of her hair rose to the applause, conducting the storm as it slipped from one movement to the next, and even the most dramatic notes seemed humbled. With her head bowed to the shelf of her forearms, Sadie could close her eyes, and still she knew herself to be present, to be a part of this seething mass where sea met rain, passive and active, and being was the only thing that was. She barely noticed the spray which dressed her from head to toe in sodden relief, nor was she aware of the curious stares of the few remaining passengers as they hurried past her into the warmth, tugging coats and partners about them, and wondering at her recklessness. She was far away from them, thrashing with the waves, chasing with the wind. Apart. Wet. And alone.

4

Night had set in by the time land came into sight some hours later, its inky breadth allowing only the most insistent of lights, sprinkled and blinking along the coast, to direct their path. The wind had died down, and the rain lessened to a mere drizzle, no longer distinguishable from the dampness of the evening, and everywhere the chill hum, always the epilogue to a storm, hung audible and clear. Sadie remained motionless, her sights set upon the illuminated world she saw in the distance, determined that she should see it in all its increasingly visible forms, and fearful that, should she look away, it would be lost to her. As she watched, a trickle of water coursed from her hairline, down the bridge of her nose, to rest, momentarily on her upper lip, before diving to its demise in the soggy regions beneath, and for the first time she took note of just how wet she had become. Looking down at her clothes, she found them drenched, clinging to her like a discarded skin, and she shivered, blowing upon her hands in a facile attempt at evaporation, and wondering when Joseph would be back. A hand on her shoulder, a mouth to her ear, she was soon answered.

'Sadie, you're soaked!'

She nodded, turning to find Joseph, still somewhat jaded, in colour as much as in mood, gazing at her in bewilderment.

'You're soaked to the skin ...' He stared at his hand, damp from its contact with her sleeve, as if in proof. 'Where on earth have you been? How did you get so wet ...?' Trailing off into silence, Joseph peered at her, before moving closer and picking up the corners of her various layers, to squeeze them between his incredulous fingers. Watching the dribbles of water trickle across his wrists like translucent veins, Joseph frowned to himself, before raising his head once again, with a sigh, and looking at Sadie as a headmaster will observe an errant pupil. But Sadie only smiled, her drizzled features illuminated by a suffusing warmth, and her shoulders lifting, sloshing, carelessly. And Joseph had no alternative but to shrug in return, suppressing any further reproach beneath the greater weight of his overcoat, which he now draped about her shoulders, before returning to the cabin to collect their bags.

As he descended, still rather fragile in his bearing, and not yet trusting the warring factions of his body to observe their apparent truce, Joseph was niggled by the fact that Sadie had been so dismissive. It really was irresponsible of her, and he could see that he was going to have to keep a very close eye on her from now on. If he could not leave her alone without her catching her death of cold then there were going to be problems. And especially when there were children to think about. Oh yes, Joseph had it all worked out. Shuffling through his pockets for the key to the cabin, he had the children at boarding school, and Sadie on the seat of governors, giving supper parties every other week and lunches in between, by the time he had even opened the door. Yes, she would have to shape up. He quite forgot that only hours ago he had been celebrating the fact that they were strangers. All he wanted now was to get home; to get his feet back on solid ground, and put the chaos of the past week behind them. It was time, he considered, four days into their marriage, to start living life on a less dramatic (not to mention, drier) level. It was all terribly disconcerting. And if there is one thing an Englishman cannot bear, it is feeling disconcerted.

With a grind the boat hauled into dock, slowly manoeuvring its bulk in a semi-circle of grumbling resistance, and voicing Sadie's own reluctance to end this period of watery transgression. Waiting for Joseph to return, she watched the deck around her fill and then empty as the gathering herds of fellow passengers nudged their way towards the gangplank, and she wondered at her own immobility in the midst of such direction. Unsettled, she shifted her weight from one leg to the other, twisting her foot like a vine about the vertical railing in front of her, and dipping her head to rest it, forehead to knuckles, against the criss-cross of her fingers. Her elbows jutted out at either side like bat wings, purplishly angular beneath the wet fabric of sleeve, and as she inhaled the last few breaths of journey, the shrunken weave of her dress tightened with the effort. It was all so quiet now. Only the mumbling of feet in the distance, muffled and blind, offered any commentary upon their arrival. But even they were fading now, as the roaring wind and the rumble of the engines had faded before them, and Sadie felt herself sinking, disappearing into the silent air around her. With a sigh she tilted her head, eyes closed, and placed her left ear against the cuff of her sleeve, feeling its dampness as a dull warmth, and enjoying the vacuum created by the stopping of this channel. So still. And as the sea lapped against the sides of the boat, rocking it this way and that in gentle lullaby, she once more gave herself up to its whispered reassurances.

She thus heard nothing of Joseph's approach, the clatter of bags and chuntering accompaniment, and even when he reached the upper deck and called out to her to follow him, she was quite oblivious. And so Joseph waited, calling again, this time louder, before dropping the bags in a pyramid at the top of the stairs, and marching efficiently across the deck. Armed with a large red blanket he had taken from the cabin, upon which was inked in bold black letters the name and number of the ship, he was fire to her water, and burning to be off. Home and dry was where he was headed. And for better or for worse, his rather wet wife was coming too.

Four corners of coarse wool broke the curve of Sadie's drooping reverie, and she shot backwards in surprise, sending the unseen Joseph hurtling with her. Her leg still twisted about the railing in front of her, she clutched at the air in an attempt to right herself, but there was no saving her as gravity got the better of both of them, and, dominoes tripped on a wire, they toppled to the deck. Thud. The sea gasped. The wind shushed. And as the chill of the wood seeped through his shirt and back, Joseph, who had taken the brunt of the fall, found himself once again cursing Sadie and her propensity for water.

Crawling to her knees, pulling the blanket with her, Sadie looked down with bewilderment at Joseph, unsure how they had reached this state, and yet reassured by its familiarity. He rather suited horizontals. She moved to touch him, a flush of wet streaking his cheek, but he brushed her away, frowning, and struggled to his feet. Had he been able to gnash his teeth, this would have been the perfect cue, but in the absence of such skills, he settled for the no less threatening tactic of grim silence. As Sadie watched, crouched above the spot where he had lain, he disdainfully wiped his hands against the leg of his trousers, hissing at the blackened stains they left, before folding his arms, tipping back his head, and glaring at her.

'Look at me,' he demanded, in a tone which encouraged quite the opposite. Sadie smiled tentatively.

'What's your problem?' she enquired, curious, her hand against his thigh as she levered him around.

Joseph bristled at the unspoken condemnation, and pushed her off. The subtler elements of peacemaking take longer than four days to learn.

'*My* problem? Nothing! *I* don't have a problem!' Following the curl of Sadie's stare which seemed to suggest otherwise, Joseph twisted around to inspect his back. She watched him passively. The accordion of his neck, as chin creased over collar, reminded her of the pleats left in the sand by a high tide, and for a moment she forgot his angry gestures and saw him smooth and expansive, a shore of strength. But as he twisted further, hand levering shoulder, back turning side, the sand began to crumble, and Sadie giggled as she took note of the wetness extending from his shoulderblades to his calves. Joseph, however, was not amused.

'My God!' He pulled at his back.

Sadie flinched, her smile fading into submission. She did not understand why he was so upset. Men in her world were drenched daily; indeed, if one of her brothers dared to come home without at least part of his person dripping, he was accused of not doing his job. So why was Joseph making such a song and dance? She began to hum nervously, hoping to alleviate the situation.

'One two three four five . . .' She held up her fingers in time to the words, '. . . Once I caught a fish alive . . . six seven eight nine ten . . .' (more fingers), '. . . Then I let it go again.'

Joseph stared at her.

'Sadie?'

She continued, oblivious. 'Why did you let it go? . . .'

She stared back questioningly. Joseph was silent, at a loss for answers. She continued, 'Because it bit my finger so . . .'

Another pause.

'Which finger did it bite? . . . This little finger on my . . .'

With a finger to her lapels and another to Joseph's lips, Sadie bent towards him conspiratorially, and took a deep, whispered breath, 'This little finger on my right!'

With a flick of her shoulders and a flash of her eyes, she thrust his overcoat towards him, and was already half way across the deck and but an echo by the time Joseph had felt even nibbled. Wet and full-fingered, he had no choice but to follow her, pulling bags, sleeves and self after him, and when he eventually caught up with her at the top of the steps, she was no longer singing, and not another word was said.

They were alone as they made their way down the gang-plank and on to the dock, with only the anonymity of stray packing cases littered about in clusters to mark their path. As they walked, Sadie glanced about her excitedly, over-whelmed by this hunching world of bulk and shadow, and straining to make out the forms which lurked within. But with only the streaking lights of trundling engines as they wove from one silhouette to the next, scratching and creaking, and the unreliable arc of the moon as it slipped in and out of the cloud-heavy sky, it was a disaffecting affair, and she eventually gave up to concentrate upon the striding spaces of Joseph's steps as he hurried on ahead.

'Come on, Sadie, we haven't got all day.' He chivvied her, before snatching up his load once again and swinging away. And Sadie gazed after, quickening her pace to match his, breathless with the exertion.

'Wait, will you, Joseph ...' But he was deaf to her, set upon his course, and allowing no sway, and Sadie had no choice but to follow.

The lateness of their disembarking, combined with Joseph's inherent ability to hurry even the most reluctant of processes (including Sadie) ensured their departure from the port to be as swift and painless as their arrival had been convoluted, and within minutes they were seated in the back of a rattling taxi and on their way to a small seafront hotel where Joseph had booked a room. It had been recommended to him by his mother before he had left for Ireland, and he considered her surprise, or possibly her horror, when she discovered that it was for his honeymoon, and not just a convenient stop-over, that he took her up on it. Honeymoon? The word itself made him nervous, and he sank back against the plastic of the seat, and wondered which was worse: the prospect of telling his mother he was married, or that of spending his first night alone with Sadie. At this precise moment neither filled him with any great joy, and he concluded that he should just take it one step at a time. It was important not to rush these matters. And as they pulled up to the kerb, and the driver leapt out to get their bags, he told himself they had all the time in the world for such things. All the time in the world.

'Here we are then.'

Joseph paid the taxi, nudging Sadie as she stood leaden amidst the piles of cases, and nodded towards the hotel. Five storeys of weatherbeaten grey brick. Sadie had never seen a house so tall, nor windows so long, and she was curious to see the size of the creatures who inhabited such places. And did they need so many steps just to reach the front door? Only churches, in Sadie's experience, were allowed such grandiosity, and even then it was to reach the pulpit. She raised an eyebrow thoughtfully, grateful for Joseph's presence as he led her up the steps and knocked on the door: she had never been particularly adept at dealing with higher authorities.

The door opened and they nudged inside, Sadie still gazing at the gaping windows overhead, Joseph trying to hold her upright as she craned towards the sky. A short man wearing tails and an obsequious smile stepped forwards, reaching out with a gloved hand, and Sadie seized it excitedly, holding his fingers and shaking them as if greeting an old friend. Joseph stared at her, his grip upon her arm tightening as at last hers upon the porter relaxed, and he whispered to her to give the man her bag. But Sadie was doing no such thing. 'Me bag? Get on with you, he can get one of his own, so he can.' She glared at the porter's outstretched hand with new hostility, pulling her bag sharply against her stomach. 'That's a fine thing to be asking, so it is. Will you be telling him Joseph? It's a shameful town if they're going round begging other people's property, honest to God . . .'

The porter raised a weary eyebrow, he too looking to Joseph. Joseph smiled apologetically. 'It's all right, Sadie, he's just going to take it to our room. You can give it to him.'

She frowned, watching the little man suspiciously, before stretching towards her husband and whispering, 'But are you sure of that, Joseph? How do you know he will? Maybe—'

'I'm sure, Sadie. Keep it with you if you like.'

The porter, shrugging, began to collect the remaining bags, uninterested in the whims of nervous brides, and disappeared behind a curtain to their left, whistling as doors closed behind him. Attempting to follow, Sadie was surprised when Joseph's hand on her shoulder held her back, and she turned to him in confusion. 'But he's got your bags, Joseph, had we better not go with him, just to be sure?'

But Joseph only shook his head, and before he had a chance to explain, the curtain swung back again and a well-dressed woman in her late forties stepped towards them.

'Very pleased to meet you. I trust you had a good journey.' Her accent was English, her manners likewise, and the fact that this was Wales was immediately forgotten. As, presumably, was Ireland. The woman held out her hand.

Joseph stepped forward, releasing Sadie, and took the proferred hand with receptive warmth, immediately at ease before such formality. Sadie meanwhile remained motionless, shoulder still lifted where Joseph's hand had held it.

'Thank you, it was fine. My wife ...' he was struck momentarily by the novelty of the title, 'my wife is a little tired, that's all. It's been a long day.'

The woman smiled sympathetically, releasing his hand, and looked towards Sadie, puddled at his side. 'Perhaps you would like to warm yourselves a little in the drawing-room before you go up. I'll bring you some tea.' And she gestured towards a door behind them, ushering them through with her well-turned wrist, and smiling yet again. Sadie frowned and followed Joseph, still wondering what had happened to their bags, and feeling increasingly self-conscious about the small patches of damp she was leaving on the carpet. And all this smiling? In Ireland only the deceitful or the mad gave more than a smirk, and Sadie was naturally suspicious of both.

'Sit down, Sadie.' Joseph pointed towards one of the skulking armchairs which hugged the wall of this red, red room, before positioning himself in front of the fire, hands in pockets and sighing contentedly. But Sadie did not want to sit down, both because of the wet which would result, and also because she was afraid that if she did she would never get up again. She glared at the chair. Overstuffed and crimson, she was reminded of a certain priest who had visited school one Easter, and she had no intention of sitting upon that memory's lap. No, she would stay where she was, thank you very much, and she blinked feverishly as the crowding faces of furniture and objects acknowledged her decision.

'Please, sit down.'

It was the woman with the grey hair, back again and carrying a tray loaded with cups and plates, and yes, still smiling. Sadie felt bullied, and all the more determined to remain standing, and when Joseph moved to hold the tray, she quickly took his place by the fire and began to finger the innumerable ornaments, what her mother called knick-knacks, which littered the mantelpiece. Ugly was what Sadie called them, and she shifted them around to hide the worse ones at the back. When she turned back to the room, she found herself the focus of two weary pairs of eyes, one, Joseph's, easily read, the other less so, but both translating as 'don't'.

And so Sadie didn't. She took her cup as invited, and, when she thought no one was looking, hitched her dress a little higher, until the fire hit her bare legs and the tea her stomach, and she began to feel more at home. While Joseph and the woman made small talk in their armchairs, Sadie made big plans in her head, and she was almost sorry when it was time to return her cup to the tray – yes, that was her saucer on the fireplace, she didn't think she needed it – and head upstairs to their room. It wasn't so bad here after all. And she poked out her tongue at the fat red chair just to make sure, pretending not to notice the look of horror on Joseph's face, and instead concentrating on the thick stockinged ankles which now hovered on the threshold.

'It's a beautiful house,' Joseph declared, as they headed into the hall. 'Quite beautiful.' Sadie watched the ankles tip forward at the compliment, and wondered if Joseph was aware of such effects, before looking up and seeing the expression of smug superiority, and realising that of course he was. He made his living out of them.

'Yes, quite beautiful', Sadie echoed, curious to see if the trick would work for her too, but by then they were halfway up the stairs, and her words, however disingenuous, were lost within the thick purple pile of the carpet. And behind them the chairs drew closer to the glowing embers of the fire, relieved of intrusion, and the curtains wrapped a little tighter about the windows, keeping out the evening air like velvet sentries standing guard.

5

At last they were alone.

'I'm real shattered, Joseph.' Sadie lay like a starfish across the bed, her arms flung wide and her head flat to one side. 'Real shattered.'

Joseph smiled, and continued to push their bags, one after the other, beneath the bed. 'I know you are, Sadie. How about if I run you a bath? I think we both could do with one.' And he unbuttoned his overcoat, twisting in front of the wardrobe mirror to get a proper look at the spread of damp which had been slowly turning from a chill to an itch, and congratulating himself on having kept it so well hidden. They did not need their host thinking they were both incapable of keeping dry. One drowned rat was surely enough. The drowned rat to which he referred, however, had no interest in such differentiations, and was staring at him mischievously in the reflection of the mirror. He turned towards her, intrigued by her expression, and, looking from his crumpled shirt to her unfolded body and back again, he was almost spoilt for choice. Almost. But the safety of the known will always win over in the end, and not-quite-nervously, but certainly with a touch of unease, he kept hands and creases to himself and proceeded to re-knot his tie. 'Do I look horrific?'

Sadie hesitated. 'Sure you don't.'

She was not convincing, and Joseph immediately took it to be a yes. 'Ohhh. I knew I did. You should have told me and I'd have changed.'

Groaning, he dropped on to the edge of the bed, and scratched his ear irritably, disappointed by the way things were going, and wishing he might have had more time to prepare. To prepare for what? This.

'Sure you don't.' Sadie repeated the assurance, but the added articulation of her hand upon his back left him cold.

'Well, whatever,' he mumbled, shuffling uncomfortably, and he reached behind and rubbed his back ferociously, just at the point where her fingers had rested. And having started scratching, he could not stop, and as Sadie lay back upon the pillow, taking in the no less vibrant reds of their bedroom, he writhed and elbowed and ouched until Sadie could stand it no longer.

'What's wrong with you, Joseph, fiddling and tickling at yourself so? You're making me itch with all your scratching, so you are!'

'It's this shirt. It's because it got wet.'

'Then take it off, why don't you, or are you wanting to be hurting, you eejit?'

Joseph raised an eyebrow, unused to such aggressive endearments, and was about to defend himself when Sadie hushed him with a laugh. Running the tip of her finger from collar to wrist, (his collar, his wrist), the length of his nearest arm, she began to pick at his cuff.

Twelve brothers had made the mystery of the male body something less of a revelation to Sadie, and while she would not say she had seen it all before – what good Catholic girl would? – she was certainly not going to be bashful. Resting his forearm against her leg as she fiddled with the obstinate cufflink, his hand clamped within the two of hers, it did not occur that she might offend. Indeed, even when, finding it stuck, she lifted his arm to her mouth, and used her teeth instead, impropriety was the last thing she would have imagined herself guilty of.

'You should have buttons, I'm telling you,' she gasped, as at last the cuff was freed, and she looked up at Joseph with the eyes of one who expected better. Joseph nodded, snatching his arm back, and began to remove the second cufflink himself. Unperturbed, however, Sadie set about his tie, and as he shivered nervously he could only hope she did not have to resort to teeth here also. Gripping the cufflinks tightly in his fist, he looked everywhere but at the soft, curling mass of Sadie's bending head: he studied the lamps, the curtains, the crests on the carpet – he would even have read the Gideon's Bible had it been on his side of the bed. And when he finished his survey of nothing at all, he was shirtless, and Sadie was kneeling beside him, folding it into an attempted square, and mumbling something about buttered fingers . . .

'There y'are.'

He sighed, almost relieved. There he was. Sadie looked up at him quizzically, carefully dropping his origamied shirt to the floor, and resting a hand upon the wool of his trousers, just above the knee. Joseph inhaled sharply. Surely she couldn't be thinking to . . . But she could, and indeed would have done, had not the look of terror on Joseph's face discouraged her, and so instead she stood up, balancing upon the mattress, and slowly pulled her dress over her head, tossing it to the floor after the shirt, and not even pretending to care how it fell. And there she was too.

'That's better, so it is,' she murmured, as if her undressing had made their roles more even, and as she lay down once more, this time her head was upon his lap. And where he sat he could smell the salt on her skin, almost taste the fine crust of sea which filled her every pore, and he breathed deeply, holding it, watching her, waiting.

Through the nets of her lashes, Sadie gazed back. She too waiting.

And it was as if the moment was without end, neither of them certain of their next move, and even Sadie, after her show of bravado, suddenly shy. Joseph began to scratch his ear again, and Sadie noticed the Gideon's Bible Joseph had been unable to reach earlier, and although both remained exactly where they were, their minds were elsewhere. Or so they hoped. And when Joseph patted Sadie's shoulder and offered to run that bath he had promised her, she nodded gratefully, and sat up.

They missed dinner that night. Sadie spent almost two hours in the bathroom, and then proceeded to discuss it for at least another forty minutes, unable, she declared, to believe the indulgence of the thing. Never, in all her life, had she seen such a big bath, and if she had ever been lucky enough to have the first run of water, rather than getting the lukewarm dregs after everyone else had finished, then it was not within recent memory. When Joseph eventually made it in there, the floor was awash and every surface dripping, and either there had only been one dry towel in the first place, or Sadie had managed to use all of them, and he knew which was the more likely. He had to shake himself like a dog when he got out, and run back to the bedroom in a bathmat – the one thing, ironically, Sadie had failed to soak – and by that time Sadie was curled up in bed, knees to chin, and fast asleep. Snug as a bug in a rug. And so Joseph climbed in beside her, cupping the convex of her back against him, and watched as the night grew darker beyond the heavy drapes, and Sadie, rising and falling, grew light. She was so precious to him, it was several hours before he was able to sleep, fearful that if he closed his eyes she still might disappear, and he wondered if he would always feel so helpless. But there was something about her, something intangible, which he knew he would always be chasing, something which he would never quite be sure of. Perhaps that was why he had fallen in love with her in the first place. Perhaps that was why even when she half drowned him and everything she came into contact with, he forgave her, for it was just the way she was.

He ran his hand around her back and across her shoulder, pulling her close against him, and whispering in her ear, 'Just the way you are, Sadie, just the way you are.'

And as he spoke she wriggled from just the way she was to just a little further the way she wanted to be, pulling the sheet with her and leaving his still damp back bared to the night air. He let her go, turning on to his other side, but still holding her, and when she woke up in the night and sat up, wondering where she was, he sat up with her, and even managed to retrieve a little of the sheets at the same time, and it was then that they both realised just how it would be from now on. Just how the way they were would be.

When Joseph awoke Sadie was gone, the shadow of her presence replaced by the sharper edges of daylight streaming through the window, and only a small dip in the mattress to suggest he had not been alone. One eye open, he was just wondering where the owner of this shape might have gone to, when the door opened, and Sadie appeared, dressed only in his overcoat, with a precariously balanced towel turban where he had expected to see her hair. In her outstretched arms she carried a bundle of something wet and dripping, which she placed on the window sill, flicking the escaping corners in upon themselves like pastry on a pie, leaving a large circle of damp imprinted upon her front. Turning full circle to face the bed, she found Joseph in the process of sitting up, rubbing his eyes dimly, and she hoisted her overcoat, (or to be more precise, his), up around her waist, and climbed across the pillows, where she knelt at his shoulder, feet tucked beneath her, and pressed an unexpected kiss upon his brow. He looked so nice in the mornings, she was happy to discover, and, tucking the edge of the sheet across Joseph's chest, and smoothing his hair to suit, she launched into an enthusiastic explanation of her day.

'I woke up, Joseph, and the light was so bright, like it was full noon. No mist like home, not at all, no. And outside were cars and people, so many, even more than Dublin. Where they all going? Who are they? I was after running down t'ask them, so I'd be able to tell you when you got up, but the door was locked ... So I did some washing instead ...'

She pulled a strand of red from beneath the turban as proof, fluttering it between her fingers and cheek, and pressing it to her nose.

'Will you look at that, Joseph, it's still all salty, so it is.' She sucked her cheeks in amusement, shaking her head as she tugged the offending hair as if in reprimand.

'And will you see what I've done?' Sadie gestured at the dripping mass lurking on the sill. 'I washed our stuff, so I did, like a proper wife.' The properties of her new role clearly concerned Sadie. 'Like a proper wife, sure. For now you can step out clean at home, and you'll not be fretting about itchy shirts or dirty britches.'

She looked at Joseph proudly, pausing for his approval, and watching as he pushed himself up on to his elbows and stared at the alien bundle. Why on earth would she be washing their clothes when they had to catch a train at ten o'clock that morning? Surely they could have waited until they got home? And he was about to point this out to her when he checked himself: hadn't she just said something about going outside?

'You've been outside?' Joseph twisted his head towards her, carefully sieving each word.

'Outside? No, you eejit, I've been in the bathroom. Why?

Should I have done them somewhere else?'

'No, no. The bathroom is perfect. You washed our stuff? Well done ...' his voice faded away sleepily, still none the wiser. 'But why?'

''Cause they were dirty, and I didn't want you travelling home in duggins, else your mammy'd be thinking I was getting you into bad habits before she even met me!'

Sadie giggled, playing with the thumbnail he had just used to scratch his head, and trying to imagine, as she had done for several days, what to expect of this Lily-creature he had told her so little about.

'Will she like me, d'you think?'

'She'll love you. Even in dirty clothes, just as I do. But we could have just worn something else, you know. These'll never be dry by the time we have to leave, so you really needn't have bothered.'

Sadie looked unnecessarily disturbed by this last remark, and Joseph wondered if he had been too harsh. He knew how sensitive they – and 'they', here, was indisputably women – could be about domestic things, and he certainly didn't want to upset her.

'It was a good idea though. Thank you.' He touched her shoulder reassuringly.

'But I didn't realise we were leaving again so soon ...'

'Don't worry about it, Sadie. It's not important. Honestly, darling, it doesn't matter. Just concentrate on getting yourself together, as we've got another long day ahead of us.'

He settled back against the headboard, having decided he was now awake, and began to plot the various stages of their journey. Culminating with his mother, which was when the strain was really likely to show. Yes, it was going to be another long day.

'But I don't have any ...' Sadie's words hovered above his meandering thoughts, insects waiting to land, and he raised his hand ponderously, swiping what little meaning he could.

'Time? You've got plenty of time, don't worry. The train's not till ten o'clock, and all we've really got to do is get dressed. Don't worry darling. You worry far too much, I can see that.'

Did she? Could he?

There was a pause.

'But I still don't have any.'

'Darling, it's . . .' Joseph reached over to look at his watch, shaking it as if to make sure it was correct, and thrusting it beneath her nose. But Sadie shook her head.

'Clothes.' She raised two flat palms to the ceiling in a gesture of well that's that then.

'What?'

'Clothes.' Louder. 'Clean clothes. Any clothes. I don't have any . . .' Sadie looked at him despondently, shrugging her eyebrows, and leaning back against the headboard. Joseph stared at her, sideways across the pillows, and marvelled that someone could be so cryptic at this time of the morning, when it was for him a trial to be even audible. He moved to stand up, considering it might be less confusing if he were upright, and, pulling the sheet with him, unwrapping it from his parcelled legs, he moved over to the window. Hands crossed behind his back, he peered first at the sodden bundle, and then back at Sadie. Curiouser and curiouser.

When eventually he spoke, he was clearly none the wiser, and the low rumble which crawled along the carpet from where he stood, to clamber up the side of the bed, and hover questioningly at Sadie's shoulder was more theory than threat.

'You have no clothes? Explain.'

Explain? Surely it was pretty straightforward. Self-explanatory, even. Sadie sighed, as if bored by the subject, and stood up. She waved a hand.

'You told me only to bring one bag, so I did, and I didn't have enough room for that sort of stuff, so I didn't. And so

I just brought what I was wearing, but I've made a bit of a mess of that, 'cause now it's all wet, and I've got nothing to wear, so I haven't.'

Grateful for the summary, Joseph shook his head, tapping the palm of his hand against his ear as if to ensure all the facts had gone in, and straightening his back. Let's keep an objective eye on this, shall we. No need to overreact. She has no clothes, nothing to wear, and the train's at ten o'clock, precisely one hour from now. Fine.

'Fine. So what will you wear, Sadie?'

For the moment the question of her clothes was his primary concern, and any interest in what she might have chosen to bring in their place did not occur. Sadie, however, was not so easily diverted, or certainly not on matters she regarded as already hopeless.

'So you don't want to see what I brought instead, d'you not? Are you not wondering?'

He shook his head.

'But you must be interested, surely?'

Nope.

'Well, I'm going to show you anyway, 'cause I want to see them, I do, and you will too.'

Joseph raised his hand. 'Sadie, really, I don't. I'm more worried at this precise moment about what you're going to wear, and about the fact that we've got less than an hour to catch this train. We can save surprises till later, till we're home . . .' Which reminded him of another matter which had been delayed until then. He coughed. 'When we're home we'll sort everything out.'

But Sadie could not wait, anxious to secure Joseph's approval of her prioritising packing, and she had already begun to root beneath the mattress for her bag. Why he had to put them all under here she did not know, but nevertheless, she found it, and with a flourish, waved it at Joseph and sat back down on the corner of the bed.

'Come on, Joseph.'

Torn between stubborn refusal and an easy life, Joseph hesitated. But Sadie had already begun to fiddle with the clasp, and it was clear any reluctance on his part would have no effect other than possibly to delay her still further. And so when she gestured to him to open it for her, he nodded and sat down beside her.

The lock was as inflexible as she was proving, and it took some time just to loosen the key, which it seemed had also received a good soaking the day before and was turning rustier by the minute.

'Is this the only bag you had?' he enquired, more in the vein of, couldn't you have brought a better one, but Sadie merely nodded, for they had been through that already.

Joseph redoubled his efforts, Sadie at his shoulder, tense with excitement as the clasp eventually gave, and, gripping the bag between his ankles for greater leverage, he slowly unbuckled the straps and parted its gums to peer inside.

For several seconds there was silence, punctuated only by the rattle of Joseph's halting breath as he slowly lifted his head. He stared incredulously at Sadie, his expression one of singular confusion.

'Shells . . .?'

She blinked in assent, her violet eyes twinkling with obvious pride.

'Shells . . .' He was lost for words. 'Shells . . .'

He scooped his fist inside the bag, and allowed the tiny multi-coloured corals to trickle through his fingers, before holding out his palm in bewilderment. Sadie reached out a tentative arm towards his hand, and, between finger and thumb slowly nipped a single shell, no bigger than a freckle, and held it up to the light above her head, twisting it this way and that. A faint smile dawned on her face, light filtering through her fingers to fall in slices across her upturned gaze, and for a split second she could have been anywhere. She was certainly, Joseph acknowledged, miles away from where he was sitting – some might say planets, but he would not go so far – and for several seconds he could only watch her. Watch her.

Slowly she lowered her arm and turned to face him, to be met with a stare of such blankness even Sadie was disturbed, and she quickly took his hand, tipping the shells he held into the waiting bag, for fear he would do something silly. Joseph was pale, running his now freed hands through his hair with weariness. There was nothing to be said. And so Sadie said it.

'Beautiful, aren't they? Knew you'd like them, so I did, and I bet you haven't got shells as lovely as these where we're going, so you haven't. Some of them even jangle. Listen.' She carefully selected a couple of the smaller shells, and shook them against Joseph's baffled ears. They did indeed ring – both shells and ears – and he mustered a nod, hoping it gave something of the impression of awe, and yet suspecting that it was closer to that of disbelief. He was right.

'Can't you hear it? Listen.' She rattled the shells once more.

'Yes, yes.' Joseph held up his hand to hers, and whispered his affirmation. 'Yes, I can hear it, but . . .'

And that one 'but' was enough to tell her that however enthusiastic, however understanding, he might strive to be – although right now he seemed neither – he had not got a clue. To him these shells were nothing more than unnecessary luggage; they were the reason they were going to be late for their train, would end up spending the journey in the corridor, and consequently be barely speaking to one another by the time they arrived at Euston. And they were nothing more than that. Even though they sounded like bells when one shook them.

And still they had not resolved the problem of the clothes. There was little option, it seemed, than that Sadie should wear some of his, and without another thought, for time was running out, he found her a soft, collarless shirt, and a pair of grey slacks, with belt-loops, which he dropped on the bed with a 'here'. And that was that. Sadie refastened the buckles of her bag, Joseph quickly gathered together their remaining luggage, wet clothes and all, and between them they muddled their silent way downstairs. If their appearance attracted any attention, it was largely because Sadie kept tripping over her trouser legs, which were several inches too long, (only when they were actually on the train, seatless due to their late arrival, did she think to roll them shorter), and even then they barely noticed. There were far more impinging considerations than a few curious passers-by. Like, for example, Joseph's mother.

Lily, short for Elisabeth, was what many people of that time would have referred to as 'a fighter'. She had lived through two world wars, suffering the death of her parents in the first, and a broken marriage in the second – she married a hero only to discover he preferred saving lives to sharing them, particularly if the victim in question was a lonely young widow called Gloria, two doors down and afraid of the dark – and Lily had not stopped battling since. She had brought up her son virtually single-handedly, changing the locks upon her errant husband and taking the family house as her own, and while her hair had turned grey and her frown set solid in the years which followed, her resolve had only strengthened. Life had not been especially kind to Lily, and as a result she was not especially kind to life. And she saw no reason why it should be any different.

But the last thing she expected when her son returned from the funeral of yet another of his father's war hero friends – she used the terms 'hero' and 'friends' lightly – the last thing she expected was that Joseph would be married.

Had she taught him nothing? She had brought him up to be an Englishman, to be proud, deliberate, and most importantly, controlled, and then he had thrown it all back at her. Behaved exactly the same as his father and run off with another woman without a word. Only worse, because he had run off and then come back again, and she did not even have the pleasure of playing the abandoned martyr, or at the very least, of changing the locks. No, Joseph had let her down, all the more so because he had not told her of the wedding and she had had to find out from that ridiculous Gloria, (a woman to be found at most war-heroes' funerals, for it appeared she had known them all) and that was something she did not forgive lightly.

Joseph was thus at something of a disadvantage when the taxi pulled up outside his mother's Primrose Hill home, and, where he had hoped to gain ground with the tactical strategy of surprise, he found he had already been out-manoeuvred, lucky even to get past the front door. At the sound of his key, Lily was there, hands on hips, eyes on stalks, and he knew from the very first glance that he was lost. And as for Sadie, well, she was doomed long before that. Irish: bad enough; Catholic: worse; dressed in men's clothes: unforgiveable; and effortlessly beautiful: no comment. All of these, added to the fact that she had married Lily's one and only son, and was clearly adored by him, resulted in what Joseph would later explain to Sadie as his mother's insecurity, but which was actually little more than straightforward dislike. While she fussed around her son, tutting at the state of his overcoat, and chastising him for not having shaved, she pointedly ignored the rather fragile looking creature hovering on the corner of the rug. When she announced that she already knew what had happened in Ireland, and that she had no desire to discuss the subject further, she took no notice of the hand which rested itself upon her bristling shoulder and attempted to make amends, and if anything it only encouraged her to further hostilities. Lily was nothing if not unforgiving.

Sadie was confused. She had to pinch herself just to make sure she was still there. And then she had to pinch Joseph, for no better reason than she felt like it. And when Lily finally left them, disappearing in a cloud of smoke from her third cigarette, not only were Sadie's eyes streaming blindly, but her conscience was somewhat adrift too.

'Is she terrible upset with us, Joseph? She doesn't like me, I can tell that for sure, and she's not so keen on you neither.'

'She loves you, Sadie. It's just her way. She's a bit surprised, that's all, and it'll just take her a while to get used to it.'

He cleared his throat with an affectation of dismissal, and hoped he had been convincing.

Sadie shrugged.

'I dunno, maybe we should leave her for a while, and come back when she's feeling a bit better. She's not going to want us around, so she won't, and I'd hate to be getting under her feet.' Sadie gestured towards the door, already retrieving her bag from the chair upon which Joseph had balanced it, and rubbing her heel against the back of her leg impatiently.

'Go where, Sadie? This is home. Where we're going to live. Don't worry, she'll calm down. She might even look at you one day!'

The attempt at humour was met with silence, and it was clear Sadie considered this prospect less than favourable. Joseph put his arm around her, stroking her shoulder, and smiled reassuringly. 'Just don't worry darling. Everything's going to be fine.'

'But live here . . .?'

Sadie's dreams of freedom and undiscovered isles had not taken into account reigning mothers-in-law or family houses. 'Do we have to?'

'Don't you want to?'

'But do we have to?'

'But don't you want to?'

'But . . .'

Sadie's question trailed into nothingness, and she lowered her eyes from the pale of Joseph's and gazed at the pile of suitcases still heaped by the front door.

'S'pose I'd better unpack my things.'

And although they both knew the nature of 'my things' to be nothing more than a bundle of shells, the gesture was not without significance.

'Thank you, Sadie.'

And there the discussion ended. Sadie could not hurt him by claiming the idea of living with the newly-met Lily filled her with horror; and Joseph could not hurt his mother by anticipating such horror and moving out. Loyalties were stretched taut, and generosities, with the exception of Lily, offered as recompense. And while their questions to one another – have to? want to? – remained unanswered, they did learn one thing: while love might be spontaneous, marriage, by its very nature, depends upon planning.

They learnt another thing about marriage that day, and although this second revelation was perhaps less open to generalisation – or so they would have hoped – it was all the more momentous for it. Joseph had directed Sadie upstairs, ostensibly to unpack, and had himself returned to the hallway to fetch their remaining bags, and have a quick word with his mother. Despite his flippancy earlier, he was hurt by her response to his good news, and he wanted to make sure she was all right before he settled in too much and then forgot to ask. Joseph was a man to whom 'All right?' or even 'all right', was largely a solution in itself, and if he overused it sometimes, it was only because it worked so well. And this case was no exception. When Joseph found his mother clattering cups and saucers in the kitchen, and obviously unwilling to discuss the matter in any detail, an arm around her shoulder and a gentle 'All right, Mother?' in her ear were all the words she needed. She could then sit down in the comfort of her kitchen, drinking tea out of her cups, content in the knowledge that Joseph was still her son before anyone else's wife. It was the reassurance and forgiveness of his mother which he looked for, and in this small triumph she rejoiced. All right? She was absolutely fine. And hence the locks remained unchanged, and Joseph could wander after Sadie, content that all was well in the world.

Sadie had indeed unpacked, and when Joseph entered the room which had been his bedroom since he was a child, he found her lying on the bed surrounded by banks of shells which she had strewn at random on every flat surface visible. He did not think the bag could have held so many, and for several seconds he remained on the threshold, wondering if there was some other force at work than Sadie's home-making. But he soon dismissed the idea, still enough of an Englishman to find the prospect of fairies and magic spells quite unbelievable, or certainly in this house, and he eventually concluded it must just be the light.

Of course, the light! That explained everything . . . Why his room looked like an enchanted grotto, and almost unrecognisable to him. Why Sadie, reclined on the bed, looked so beautiful he ached to look at her, and even more at the thought of touching her. And why, when he let go the door and crossed the room he felt so dizzy he had to lie down beside her, and hold on tight just to keep himself horizontal. And of course it was the light which blinded him sufficiently not to care if his mother was downstairs in the kitchen drinking tea, and to focus solely upon the loosening trickle of buttons as he fumbled with Sadie's shirt – which was actually his shirt, and another dimension to the experience altogether; and it was the light which so dazzled as it hit the pale translucence of Sadie's skin, causing him to gasp out loud and close his eyes fast until he could breathe again. And it was the light which allowed him to forget his earlier inhibitions and make love to Sadie with a passion of which he had never imagined himself capable, but which she had glimpsed in his eyes from the very first.

But afterwards, when the bells had stopped ringing and the room had gone dark, and the only thing audible was the hum of his own pulse, Joseph almost doubted whether it had happened at all. Whether such light was not just a dream. Yet when he turned towards Sadie, and saw her lying curled beside him, shells tangling in her hair as her fingers had tangled in his, he knew he could not have imagined such a thing, and for the first time in his life he acknowledged the power of the unknown. And enjoyed it.

6

During the next few weeks 'the unknown' was a frequent guest at the Hill House, as Lily's home was generally referred to, and even the simplest of tasks became a matter for considerable debate. Where to sit; where not to sit; how to eat; how not to eat . . . the list was endless. And every day Sadie was informed (by Lily of course) of yet one more thing she had got wrong; yet one more habit which must be erased from memory, until she was reeling with whys and whens, ifs and buts, and frankly no longer cared. Had she not had Joseph to cling to, she told herself, she would have been on the first boat home. But she did, and so was not, and Lily reigned on.

'Put it there, not there! Mind! Here, not here! And what do you think you're going to do with that? Where . . .?!!'

She could not lift a cup without an eyebrow being raised; could not say a word without an ear being scratched conspiratorially; could not even walk out of the house and into the garden without her footsteps jarring and several heads – she had decided Lily owned at least a dozen, for she rarely met the same one twice – poking around doorways just to check what she was doing. Life was proving a whole new kettle of fish, just as her mother had warned, and Sadie was floundering.

And, of course, the more self-conscious Sadie became, the

more nervous her behaviour. And the more nervous her behaviour, the more susceptible she was to Lily's criticism. For she dropped the cup which provoked the eyebrow, gobbled the words which scratched the ears, and tripped down the steps to the garden right under the noses of the many headed creature which followed her. Which of course only confirmed Lily's original belief. The girl was incompetent.

According to Joseph, however, which perhaps only added to the problem, she was perfect. When he returned to his surgery the week after their return, he was a happy man, and it did not enter his head that there might have been friction between the two women once he had gone. Sadie was a darling, his mother a gem, and himself very lucky. And that was as far as he went. They were a family, and families were united, and so it was easy to dismiss any complaint or upset which greeted him upon his return, for he knew it would soon blow over. As he told his colleagues at the hospital, or the many adoring patients who dared to ask, they were all settling in wonderfully together. Getting married, he confided, was the best thing he had ever done.

Sadie, however, was less convinced. Everything had shifted since she met Joseph, and she could no longer trust herself on even the most inconsequential of matters, fearful of making yet one more blunder to add to the already teetering pile. She even took to breathing in private, finding it preferable to the glaring hostility she met in Lily every time the elder woman found her still alive, and it was not uncommon to spy a rather purple Sadie hurtling around the house with her hand clamped over her mouth. But there was little sanctuary, no matter where she ran: each room had its character stamped plainly across four walls, and nowhere might Sadie find even a corner she could call her own. Until, that is, she discovered the bathroom.

At the very top of the house, lit by a skylight and a single ivy covered window, it had originally been part of the servant's quarters, and was hence never used. Bare walled and bright, it was furnished solely by a huge cast iron bath, rooted at its centre, and a small washbasin hugging to one side. It was the closest place to home Sadie could imagine, and she revelled in its starkness, wallowed in its shallow depths, rejoiced in its solitude. For, such is the hierarchy of English living, even in such servantless years as these, she might rest assured that Lily would never lower herself to intrude upon her here. In the stultifying realms of exile, she had found a space of her own.

Thus, from the very beginning, boundaries were clearly stamped upon the Hill House, with Lily running the main show, and Sadie taking over the vacant spaces above, and for the first few weeks, it appeared it might work. But it was Joseph, out all day and forever on call, who found it intolerable, furious that his much regaled idyllic world might somehow be flawed. This was not at all what he had envisaged by 'family life', and he refused to accept it as such. They must all live together, as one, and if it was difficult at first, it would be worth it in the end. Or so he told himself, when every night he returned to yet another battle; yet another roll of eyes and crackle of warfare as his mother launched one more attack upon his wife. What could he do? It was becoming increasingly difficult to draw the line, and if Joseph had any perspective at all upon the women he left at nine o'clock every morning and did not see again until seven, then it was becoming daily more smudged.

It would be naïve, however, to imagine that Lily, and Lily alone, was responsible for the antagonism which arose and flourished between the two: Sadie had her part to play as well, and even if her contribution was largely unconscious, it was no less irritating for it. For it was Sadie who took three hour baths at one o'clock in the afternoon, and then left towels of all dampnesses strewn around the top floor like confetti; and it was Sadie who changed her mind every week about what she would eat, causing Lily on several occasions to abandon her offerings of roast lamb, or fish pie, in favour of a crisp sandwich with salt and salad cream, or a packet of Crawford's cream crackers; and it was Sadie who still had nothing else to wear but a couple of shawls and Joseph's entire wardrobe of shirts, (she had lost her dress to the rag cupboard the day after their arrival), and who took great pleasure in changing them at least four times a day. (And considering that it was Lily who washed and ironed these shirts, then it was perhaps not incomprehensible that she should resent it.) No, Sadie could hardly be described as easy, and nor, it seemed, would she have wanted to be.

It was at Joseph's request, some two or three weeks after their arrival, and largely due to the state of his considerably depleted wardrobe, that his mother took Sadie shopping in an attempt to find her some new clothes. The period of grace Sadie had been allowed to get used to her new home was coming to a natural end – or rather, he was putting his foot down and forcing that end – and it was time to make some changes. She was, after all, a doctor's wife, and she could not forever be running around in shirt tails, even if she did look rather fetching. No, it was time to take a stand, Joseph told himself; to shine a torch of his own upon the shimmering presences his marriage had illuminated, for they could not make light of it forever: at some point things would have to settle down, and the dim colours of habit be allowed to filter through.

Lily was not exactly thrilled at the prospect of dragging her daughter-in-law along Oxford Street on a Wednesday afternoon, but she had promised herself she would maintain a sympathetic front before Joseph, and she could not therefore refuse. Sadie, however, had made no such promises, and it took a considerable amount of persuasion on Joseph's part, and the agreement in writing that she could choose what *she* liked, to convince her. Or rather, lower her resistance.

Once inside the taxi, however, and weaving towards the centre of town, Sadie relaxed a little, and began to enjoy the adventure of spending Joseph's money on such a whimsical thing as 'shopping'. It was a strange conceit, 'shopping', to someone for whom it had always meant a pound of flour or a bag of sherbet lemons, and Sadie struggled to grasp just what exactly was the point. Why all the ceremony of taking a taxi and driving somewhere? There were perfectly adequate shops at the end of the road, and if not, why did they not just call a man like the one that used to visit her mother in Ireland, who had one of everything and simply took orders? Nothing could quite compare with the excitement of receiving that mysterious parcel, wrapped in brown paper and string and sent from such metropoles as Dublin or Limerick. And even when the contents, the memory of the item chosen long forgotten, turned out to be a pair of black wool stockings, or a too-small jersey for one of her brothers, it did not matter. That was shopping.

And so when the taxi pulled up outside Selfridges, and Sadie was faced with row upon row of gaping dress windows, it was not surprising she was taken aback. To the extent that she jumped straight back inside the car and demanded to be *taken back*. It required all Lily's patience – and she was not exactly overflowing with it – to coax her out on to the pavement, and even then she was disinclined to let go of the car door, much less venture inside. But Lily was adamant, and when she eventually wrenched Sadie off the kerb and towards the shop, it was clearly futile to resist.

Frogmarched through the revolving door, which snapped at her ankles only marginally less than Lily, and into a cage full of people who immediately demanded, 'Where to?', 'Which floor?', Sadie was lost long before they reached the 'Daywear' section. Pulled from one heaving rail to the next,

Sadie knew that if she got out of this alive then it would not be due to good fortune – for that had left her long ago – but rather to her mother-in-law's sadistic ability to make even the most unexpected of tortures an ongoing thing.

As indeed this was going to be, for despite prior negotiation regarding Sadie's ability to choose for herself what she liked, this did not prevent Lily from offering her opinion, and it was soon apparent that the two women could not have been more opposed when it came to taste.

'Green? You can't possibly wear green with your colouring! And don't even think about that fabric – it's far too flimsy. You need a proper, sturdy tweed, something like this ...' And she held up a brown skirt with matching blouse, and waved them in front of Sadie with all the promise of suitability and, well, brownness. Sadie screwed up her eyes and grimaced, observing Lily's choice with all the interest of a bad smell, and returned to her own deliberations. She liked green.

'Well I'm liking this one.'

'You like it? Oh well, it's you who'll be wearing it ... you'd better try it on then, but I wouldn't expect Joseph to approve. He's never been much of a one for green ... But as you will.'

She waved Sadie towards the dressing rooms, but even if Lily's mentioning of Joseph had not dissuaded her, then the prospect of those curtained cubicles and hovering assistants certainly did.

'Can't we just buy it?'

'Not without trying it on. I'm certainly not going through all this a second time just to bring something back because it doesn't fit – or is unsuitable. Either try it on or leave it.'

Sadie left it. She was tired of all this shuffling and elbowing, of the dim lights and endless carpets, and she wanted to get back into the fresh air. Lily, however, had other ideas.

'If you can't find anything you like here, then we'll go elsewhere. Although I can see plenty of things . . . But we are not going home empty-handed, and you are not going to continue wearing out Joseph's shirts. So think hard, and decide what you want. But keep away from green: it's really not your colour.'

Sadie thought hard. And then she walked hard. Back towards the cage, and down the stairs which circled it, and she kept walking until she had found her way out of the doors and was back in the street. Lily was waiting for her, having taken the lift down, and avoided Sadie's meandering detour around the perfume counters in her attempt to leave.

'That's it, is it? Fine, you can explain to Joseph. But I've still got some things to do, so you'll just have to wait here for me.'

And Lily marched back through the revolving doors, heels clicking in unison with her tongue, and Sadie was left to wander up and down the pavement, gazing at the gaudy mannequins propped lifelessly against the windows, and wondering that such a painful experience could be undergone by so many people. As she watched the crowds spilling in and out of the main entrance, and the liveried porter who ran back and forth summoning taxis and carrying boxes, she was glad she was out of it.

'A pack of heathens, the lot of you,' she murmured, resorting to higher authorities as her ultimate defence. And she jangled the handful of shells she had crammed inside her pocket, passing them through her fingers like beads on a rosary. '"Blessed art thou 'mongst women,"' she began, the reassurance of the familiar quick to comfort, and she stared at herself in the reflection of the shop window. '"Blessed art thou,"' she repeated, nodding to the glassy figure she saw there, and when the figure nodded back she considered the matter closed. When Lily returned some time later, bearing socks for Joseph and a variety of gifts for herself, it was a calmer, almost beatific, Sadie she found perched upon the kerb, and, were it not for the unmistakable disguise of shirts and shawls, the elder woman might not have recognised her. Bundling her into a taxi, she pointedly ignored Sadie's chattering welcome, and the journey home was silent but for the rustling of Lily's bags and the fluttering of Sadie's fingers as she blessed herself with every passing church. It was the pattern of the known.

Hence, despite her misgivings, Sadie did indeed live to see another day, although if she had anything to do with it, it was not going to be another shopping day, and when Joseph returned that evening to find yet another shirt missing from his wardrobe, even he knew better than to comment. The silence which met him from the moment he entered the front door, and which remained well into the evening, made it obvious that the day had not been a success – although he had a very nice pair of socks out of it – and it was only when he was alone with Sadie later that night that he ventured to enquire. But Sadie was evasive, muttering sleepily about brown skirts and unsuitable fabrics, and he learnt little more than the fact that apparently green was not her colour. Which was rather a shame as Joseph had always loved it.

'Maybe it wasn't such a good idea after all,' he mused, stroking the pool of her sleeping head as she rose and fell at his side. 'Perhaps we can take a different approach next time.' And, like a man for whom diagnosis is always a form of hit and miss, he settled to deliberate a more suitable solution. And soon.

The trip to Selfridges was but a single wave within a rapidly swelling tide of doubts and recriminations, which was slowly threatening to flood the Hill House, and drown all those who sailed in her. Due to the hours of his work, Joseph remained unaffected by such approaching tragedy, but when for the third night in as many days he returned to find Sadie weeping in the bathroom and his mother stonily silent downstairs, the need to start bailing out impressed upon him. With his usual professional ease he sat the women down and demanded to be told exactly what was wrong.

What was wrong? Where to start? As far as Lily was concerned it was straightforward, but for Sadie the invitation to speak was tantamount to actual confession, and try as she might she could not bring herself to open her mouth. It was only when Lily had spent more than ten minutes telling Joseph how she had wasted a whole day searching for three shirts of his, only to discover them screwed up in the bottom of the dustbin, scorched with the unmistakable wedges of a too-hot iron, that Sadie felt it timely to defend herself. And brushing away any fears that Joseph would be transformed into one of the whispering priests she associated with such soul searching practices, she embarked upon a litany of her own.

'I was only trying to help, so I was. You're always telling me I'm not doing stuff, Lily, so you are, and so I was ironing some shirts to help you. But the mad iron was hissing and spitting like I don't know what, and I only left it for a second to see if it was the plug, or something, and it burnt through all three.'

'How can one iron burn through three shirts at the same time?' Lily pounded. 'You must have left it every time you started a new shirt, and if that isn't stupid, then I don't know what is. Do you learn nothing from your mistakes?'

Sadie gasped at Lily's aggression, and looked at Joseph as if to register the point. But Joseph was leaning back in his chair, intrigued.

'I was doing them all at once, so I was, one inside the other,' she explained, 'for it saves time, and it's what my mammy always did. I wasn't to know your iron got so hot, was I now? It's hardly my fault if it wants to start burning shirts, just 'cause I'm using it, so it's not.' Sadie still inclined to the idea that inanimate objects act independently of the user, and a bad-tempered iron was not inconceivable to her. And if it suited her argument, and denied her fault, then why should she think otherwise? Lily, on the other hand, could think of several reasons why.

'Are you telling me you put three shirts beneath a hot iron, left it there until it had burnt through all three, and expect us to believe it was not your fault? And just for the record, what pressing engagement meant you were in such a rush you had to do all three at once? Or could it be laziness?'

'But that's how my mammy always did it.'

Sadie looked at Joseph once again, feeling increasingly helpless, and this time he responded, placing a hand upon her quivering shoulder, and murmuring, 'But she did have twelve sons to iron for, Sadie. It's a little different.'

'I would imagine there's an awful lot that's different!' Lily again. 'But that cannot be your excuse forever. You never lift a finger about the place. Not in the kitchen – have you tasted any of her concoctions, Joseph?'

She broke off here to glare accusingly at her son, who nodded somewhat weakly in assent. 'Salty' was the word which sprung to mind.

'Exactly!'

The triumph of the unspoken.

'. . . and that's not to mention cleaning, nor, dare I say, washing or ironing. I am supposed to do everything, like some lackey, and just because you married my son you think you can lie in the bath half the day, or wander around the garden half-dressed like I don't know what! Well, it's not good enough, not good enough at all, and if Joseph won't do anything about it, then I most certainly will.'

Her words echoed around the kitchen, bouncing off the lids of saucepans, and chiming dolefully as they hit the swinging mobiles of carving forks and spatulas which hung from the beams above their heads. Sadie shuddered, aware that it was her for whom they tolled, and she shunted her chair just that little closer to Joseph's.

'If you show me . . .' she began, hesitantly, 'if you show me what you want doing, I'll do it gladly, sure I will. But you leave me with a pile of washing and tell me to do it, and then when I've spent two hours trying to get the suds out in the kitchen sink, you tell me you've got a machine for it, and that I've used the wrong soap anyway . . .'

She tailed off, as much due to rising self-pity as the fact that Lily's mouth was opening and closing with such ferocity that she did not dare go on.

'So it's my fault?!' Lily began to splutter furiously, her features blurring into one enraged mass, and Sadie swallowed nervously. Joseph stood up.

'Will both of you please calm down? Is this how you get at one another when I'm out all day? I don't care about the shirt—'

'Shirts,' Lily interrupted grimly, 'three of them.'

'And I don't care for all this bickering. Please, can't you try to give each other a chance, if only for my sake?' He glanced at Sadie, who hung her head apologetically, and then at his mother.

'And please stop smoking so much, mother. It can't be doing any of us any good.'

Lily dropped her cigarette, and sighed loudly.

'You really should try giving up, mother,' he ventured, although now perhaps was not the best time to broach such matters.

Lily scowled, irritated by his high-handed behaviour, and looked away. Her eyes fixed on a spot somewhere beyond Joseph's left ear, her tone only slightly less aggressive than it had been in speaking to Sadie, she demanded, 'So what do you suggest?'

'Well, just try and cut down, mother, that's all.'

'I meant about this.' Lily waved a hand about the kitchen, with particular emphasis as it neared Sadie's crumpling form, and growled once again, 'This.'

Joseph smiled, somewhat indulgently. 'This? Oh, it's obvious. We'll have to get a cleaner, someone to help about the house, and give you both a bit more time to yourselves. I'll see to it tomorrow, and then we can perhaps stop all this palaver, and start behaving a little bit more like a family.'

That magic word: 'family'. Joseph liked the sound of it, and immediately imagined the situation to be resolved. When Lily began to protest, claiming she had never needed help in her life, and did not intend to start now, he simply held a finger to his lips and shook his head. And when Sadie began to wail even more wetly at the thought of another Lily arriving to torment her, and what was more, the potential loss of her bathroom, her one place of retreat, he handed her his handkerchief, and told her to blow. There had been quite enough drama for one day. He had found a solution, and he intended to keep to it. And the solution was Mrs Bradley.

Mrs Bradley, much as one might hope, was a down-to-earth, no nonsense type of woman, whom, it was said, even her husband referred to in the married form. And it was impossible to imagine she had ever been anything less. From the moment she arrived, announcing herself as 'Mrs Bradley-where-shall-I-start', Joseph knew he was on to a winner, and within days her presence had filtered into even the most resistant of camps, bearing as it did the untenable, indefensible weight which being a lifelong 'Mrs' allowed her. She was everything they might have wanted from a housekeeper-cum-mediator-cum-mother-cum-wife. Nothing more, if that is possible, and nothing less.

Of course, Sadie adored her from the very beginning, although the competition for Sadie's displaced affections was hardly considerable, and by the second day of her employment Sadie had declared her the best mother-superior, (superior mother-in-law lacked quite the same ring), this side of the Irish sea. No doubt Mrs Bradley was flattered, but she preferred to keep her alliances ambivalent, and politically refrained from showing any preferences when it came to her employers. (Although had she been pressed upon the subject, a soft spot for Joseph – a man to be mothered if ever there was one – would have been revealed.) No, instead Mrs Bradley concentrated upon restoring the house to some kind of order, assuming that in doing so a similar quality would be communicated to its inhabitants, and in no time at all – or so it seemed to Joseph, although to Lily it was a lifetime – she had shifted and rearranged until the Hill House was barely recognisable.

Not surprisingly, this went down rather badly with Lily, and for some weeks the house shuddered to the constant accompaniment of slammed doors and noisily replaced furniture, as she articulated her complaint within what seemed to her a rapidly disintegrating world. Complaint against all three individuals, but more particularly against the conspiracy which was at the root: marriage. Only when she offered to move out of her room in protest, claiming they might as well have the master bedroom if they intended to take over her house in this way, and they agreed, did she realise that her case was lost. And as she shifted her belongings down a floor, and took up grudging residence in the guest room, which, as Joseph claimed, would be better for her arthritis anyway, she considered she must find another means of revenge. Or if not revenge, then certainly recognition.

With Sadie and Joseph ensconced in the main bedroom, the Hill House seemed closer than it had ever been to a family home, and Joseph was in a perpetual state of excitement, so thrilled was he to be man of the house, and not merely the son. Naturally, he was not so inconsiderate as to dismiss his mother's loss altogether, and he devoted much of his time to making sure she had everything she wanted 'downstairs' (and that she knew she only had to ask if she changed her mind and wanted her old room back) but he was banking on quite a future now, and he was clearly not going to be distracted. And even if the light in this room would never be quite the same as it had been in the first, this did not mean anything more than times had changed, as ever they must, and that things were different now.

One thing, however, which remained the same, was the great void which was Sadie's wardrobe. Since the trip to Selfridges, and the arguments which had resulted, the subject had been tactfully avoided, and Sadie was still limited to a collection of Joseph's shirts, a handful of shawls, and a brown wool skirt generously – or, as Sadie suspected, spitefully – donated by Lily. With the minor addition of two cotton nightdresses which had arrived from Ireland several weeks before, a legacy, perhaps, from the travelling salesman, Sadie was to be seen in little else. There was talk of a possible outing with Mrs Bradley, although this was hardly in her job description, but before that could become anything more than a possibility, the matter was fortuitously resolved.

7

It was Sunday morning and Sadie had woken early. Contrary to her usual practice, she had forsaken her bath in favour of the garden, and was at present standing barefoot on the wet grass, wondering at the bleak November skies and thinking of home. Of Ireland. It was still her home, for sure. Always would be, whatever Joseph promised.

Combing her toes in a semi-circle about her, Sadie was intent upon the swishing blades of grass, water tickling the soles of her feet as she arced back and forth, when she heard a voice call out to her from behind the hedge. Voices without bodies were not an uncommon part of Sadie's day, and as a result she rarely took much notice other than to smile, in acknowledgement that she had heard, as she did now. The voice behind the hedge was unusually persistent, however, and after several more interjections, Sadie was forced to look up, as much in annoyance as in curiosity, and was startled to find herself face to face with the Cheshire Cat grin of a small boy.

''Scuse me, missus, I was wondrin' if I might just hop over your yard, you know, to take me papers next door.' He hoisted a canvas bag into view, and pointed a scrawny finger towards the hedge. 'Saves me time, you see.'

Sadie gazed in wonder, trying to remember if apparitions in the past had spoken quite so chattily, and continued to sweep her toes across the damp grass. Experience had taught her to distrust, or certainly, to ignore, all creatures she had not been introduced to, for you never know quite what they might be up to, and she patiently waited for it to disappear. Everyone knew fairyfolk were a vain lot, and if you pretended not to see them, they always got bored in the end.

‘'Scuse me, missus.’ This particular spirit knew no such philosophies, and simply imagined she had not heard him. ‘'Scuse me, missus!’ The boy hesitated: he always made a shortcut through the doctor's garden on Sunday mornings, saving himself at least ten minutes of walking round, only usually there was no one here to mind him. He stared at the nightdressed girl hovering intently in the middle of the lawn, and considered she probably wouldn't notice anyway. Perhaps he should just run for it.

Hitching his bag on to his shoulder, he leapt forwards, vaulting the hedge with spindling bare legs, and dropped to the other side with a thud. Breaking into a trot, he lurched towards the rockery, behind which the figure stood, and waved cheekily as he passed. Sadie, however, was unprepared for such intimacies, and she leapt backwards, screeching in pain as she landed on an unseen thistle, and clamping a hand to her infidel mouth. Bending to console her foot, she cursed her recklessness: the last thing you should do in situations like this is open your mouth, for they're straight in there, without so much as a please or thank you, and then you never get rid of them. But she had done it now. And she shrugged defencelessly, waiting for the inevitable attack.

But the wee leprechaun, if that is what he was, had frozen. Sadie stared at him curiously, still rubbing her heel.

‘Are you all right?’ he whispered, tucking his bag of newspapers tighter around his middle, his eyes like saucers. ‘Are you poorly or something?’ He cringed away as she straightened up, silently formulating his excuses in readiness for her complaint, and shivering in the chill of the morning. 'I never meant to scare you, I swear I didn't, but I didn't think you'd mind . . .'

Sadie raised a hand to her neck and fingered the small coral crucifix her mother had given her the day she left Ireland. Feeling it there, cool and flat against her skin, she was comforted by the knowledge that, if he was a meddlin' Little Fellow, as she could only assume he must be, albeit the English version, then he could do little harm to her with this at her throat. She lifted her shoulders bravely, looked him straight in the eye, and held out her hand, carefully, because you never know what these creatures have up their sleeve, and gestured to him to step forward. He obeyed.

'Will you be joining me for a cup of tea?' she offered brightly, hospitality appearing the better option, and the boy nodded nervously, anything to appease. 'Step inside then,' and she stepped back to wave him through. 'You might leave your shoes at the door, though, for they don't like mucky prints on the floor, so they don't.'

Overlooking her seeming detachment from the household, the boy did as he was told, and, before he knew where he was, much less who she was, he was seated at the kitchen table, mug in hand, and for all to see a prisoner in this shoeless land.

'Sugar?' Sadie pushed the bowl towards him with her forefinger. Three lumps. She smiled approvingly, tucking her nightdress in between her knees as she bent them to her. Lowering her head, Sadie gazed up at her visitor from shadowed eyes, remembering as she did so that leprechauns were notoriously greedy when it came to sweet things. She reached behind her, holding on to the table as she twisted back, and caught the rim of the biscuit jar, pulling it towards her until she could lift it and send it the way of the sugar. Her visitor grinned, warming to his role.

'Thank you, missus. 'S'not usual I get all this when I'm doing me rounds.'

He dug deep into the caddy, and pulled out a handful of biscuits, which he then began to dunk in solemn succession, before cramming them into his mouth. Sadie was fascinated. Ignoring the reference to rounds, she was flattered by his gratitude, and for the first time felt somehow purposeful in this Lily-fied territory.

'You're quite hungry, then,' she observed, and he nodded ferociously. 'Have you not eaten at all?'

He shook his head.

'Would you want a bit of breakfast, if I fetch it?'

He grinned hopefully, in for a penny, and watched as Sadie, relinquishing her knees, stood up and looked about her.

'Mmmm.'

From this perspective the prospect of 'fetching' something, which inevitably involved cooking, was considerably less attractive, and Sadie was suddenly reminded of the history of such affairs. But then she remembered that this was her day, her guest, and for the moment, her kitchen, and she took heart.

'I'm not too good . . .' she warned, deeming it only fair to share the fact of her incompetence, and as she moved towards the fridge she could not help but wish she had stuck to the biscuits. She would hate the Little Fellow to take her culinary incompetence personally, as it seemed Lily always did, for who knew what revenge he might exact in return?

'You don't mind if it's only a few rashers.' Sadie warned, struggling to keep her head, and she seized a paper parcel from the fridge and quickly closed the door before eggs or sausages might decide to join the fray. Breakfast is a source of great Irish pride, and Sadie could hear the horror in her mother's voice when she heard her daughter had stooped to such a sinful excuse as a bacon sandwich. And she would hear, Sadie did not doubt. But for the moment this inevitable reckoning was brushed aside and, without further ado, she began to rummage and clatter her way towards breakfast. Her guest looked on in silence, having long since given up any hope of delivering papers, nodding dismissively as various objects were held up in enquiry, and wishing every Sunday could be like this.

Such delight, however, was short-lived. Barely had the plates been set on the table, and a second cup of tea solicitously poured, than a click in the hallway announced the arrival of further troops, and as footsteps ticked along the passage, Sadie caught herself regretting they had not stayed in the garden. Lily's appearance in the doorway, fresh from church and bristling with Sunday piety, only emphasised this.

'Well? Good morning?'

If a greeting could sound any more accusing, it would be accompanied by gunshots. Sadie winced.

'Morning to you, Lily.'

'Morning, missus.'

Food, it seemed, had emboldened the Little Fellow's spirits, and Lily was met with none of the hesitant diplomacy Sadie had enjoyed. Which was unfortunate, for if anyone appreciated humility then it was Lily. She turned to Sadie, grimacing, and demanded proprietorially, 'Is my son up?'

Momentarily Sadie faltered, wondering with confusion when Lily had acquired such universal rights, and considering it obvious by the light outside the window that it had been up some time now. But then she realised it was Joseph Lily meant, and she shook her head quickly. Surely that was obvious too.

'I see.' Lily frowned. Oh yes, she saw all right.

Moving to the table, Lily inspected the remains of Sadie's creation, picking up and dropping a slice of bread, with such contempt it was hard to believe it too was without fault. The sight of the bacon caused her to stiffen slightly – if that was possible in such a rigid character as she – and she strode to the fridge and peered inside, already formulating her attack, and wasting no time in its delivery.

'So I suppose we'll just have to do without bacon . . .' The accompanying sigh of but-what-do-you-expect resignation left no 'suppose' about it, and Lily closed the fridge door with firm deliberation.

'Oh, are you telling me you were wanting them rashers? I'm sorry, so I am. I should have been thinking it was Sunday and you'd be wanting it for the pork . . .'

Sadie leant back against the hob, her elbows resting upon its still warm surface, and swung her legs apologetically. Lily's expression suggested it was more than thought that was at fault, and she patted her hair knowingly, before unbuttoning her coat and reaching for her apron, reclaiming her territory.

'Perhaps, Sadie, you might take a cup of that tea up to Joseph. I'm sure all this commotion must have disturbed him by now.'

Sadie bent her head in assent, and, tripping over her nightdress in her haste, did as she was told. Hurrying upstairs, cup in hand, she was tempted to ignore Lily, and leave the cup on the stairs, so she might run back down to the Little Fellow before he disappeared again, but on reflection she considered it better she obey. It was not worth risking Lily's wrath for a second time that day.

Joseph, however, counter to Lily's supposition, was still fast asleep, and Sadie could leave the cup on his night table and tiptoe out again without even arousing a murmur. Making her way back downstairs, she was struck by the fact that both Joseph and his mother should be so impermeable to the charms of such a creature, and for a moment she wondered if it might be something to do with being English. Certainly no one at home would show themselves so inhospitable. And with that in mind, she hurried back to the kitchen, where she found Lily embroiled in battle, vegetable peeler in one hand, victim in the other.

'Where is he?'

Sadie stared at the lifeless mass of potato shavings lying at Lily's hands, momentarily distracted, before she remembered her question, and repeated it, 'Where's he gone?'

'I heard you the first time, Sadie,' replied Lily with acidity. 'He, whoever he was, has gone. We are not running a charity, I might have you know, so I'd appreciate it if you didn't pick up every waif and stray and give them our lunch.'

Another curl of yellow-brown slid off the blade.

'Gone? But he never said goodbye ... He's never gone yet.'

With Sadie it was as simple as that.

'He has.'

With Lily it was no less straightforward.

And so nothing more was said, and Sadie wandered back out of the kitchen the way she had come in. How could he leave without saying goodbye? She kicked her foot against the skirting board of the passage. It was wrong. Another kick. A burst of footsteps alerted her to Lily's approach, presumably to see what the noise was about, and Sadie hurried in the opposite direction, through the hall and out of the back door into the garden. Kicking was far less satisfying when the sound was muffled, and there is only so much damage one can do to privet, but nevertheless Sadie gave it her best shot, before dropping in a heap upon the wet grass – first, of course, checking for thistles – and moaning dramatically. She listened. Nothing. Only the distant clanging of Lily in the kitchen. Everpresent.

With a sigh, Sadie inspected her toes – always her first move in times of stress – stretching out her legs along the grass and flexing her feet at right angles to one another. Her nightdress scrunched around her thighs, she stared at the greenish reflections of her pale flesh, and wished herself far away. But then she remembered Joseph asleep upstairs, with only a cold cup of tea for comfort, and she felt sorry. So sorry she was moved to lie down in penance. And it was here, extended in a line upon the drizzled grass, that she remembered the pointlessness of chasing fairyfolk, or, as they are sometimes called, 'People Outside Us', for they are not a race that likes to be caught. She remembered her brothers' admonitions every time she had begged them to take her out on their boats to search for mermaids, insisting as they did that creatures such as that were only trouble if pestered. And she remembered her own misgivings that very morning, and was grateful she had managed to stay him as long as she had. There would always be voices in the garden, she reassured herself, and having made friends with them once, it would be all the easier next time.

With characteristic acceptance, Sadie hauled herself to her feet and wandered back inside, content in the knowledge that, no matter where she was, she would never be alone. For guardian angels are a universal concept, and in whatever shape or form they arrive, you can be sure to recognise them when they do.

As she re-entered the house, Joseph was coming down the stairs, and they met in the hallway on either side of the cup of tea Joseph was returning undrunk to the kitchen. Kissing her gently on the forehead, he was about to continue when he paused, handed her the cup, and disappeared into the drawing-room. Sadie remained where she was in the middle of the rug, marvelling that one morning could contain so many disappearances, and she was about to run away herself, when suddenly he was back, holding a brown paper bundle in his arms, and grinning broadly.

'I almost forgot. I bought you a present yesterday.' He took the cup and placed it on the hall stand, before leading her towards the stairs and thrusting the package into her hands.

'For me? Jeez, Joseph, you don't want to buy me presents, do you?' Sadie was thrilled, and immediately began to tear at the paper, thoughtless of what might be inside other than the glorious idea of a gift. She shredded the layers of wrapping with a haste only the thirteenth born can understand – unmarked property is always a source of dispute when one is this far down the family ladder – and pulled at the contents, lengths and lengths of it, until she was swathed in a mass of paper and present, and still none the wiser.

'What is it, Joseph?' she mumbled disappointedly, peering at her green armfuls. 'What have you got me?'

Joseph laughed, amused by her despondency. 'It's fabric for a new dress, Sadie. I know you don't like shopping, so I stopped by the store of a patient of mine, and bought you this. I think you'll look lovely in green, even if it isn't your colour, as you say.'

'Not as *I* say, Jose!' Sadie was about to put him right about the source of these shades of wisdom, but the arrival of Lily in the doorway silenced her and she ducked her head back to the matter, or rather material, in hand.

'What do you think, Mother?' Joseph turned towards Lily, inviting her response.

'Not what I would have chosen ... but I suppose it's better than nothing.'

'It's a nice colour, though, isn't it? Sadie isn't sure, but I think she's wrong.'

Sadie looked up, confused as to how she had come to be both unsure and wrong in such a short space of time. 'No, I love it,' she affirmed. 'I really love it. Green as a leek, I'll be,' she added, with a glance at Lily.

Lily proffered what might have been a smile, but which was closer to a sneer, and vanished back to the kitchen the way she had come, taking the cup of tea with her, and throwing an 'I'll get you a decent one, shall I?' behind her as she went. Which could have referred to a number of things, but which Joseph took to be a cup of tea, and followed her diligently. Sadie remained pendant upon the bottom stair, stroking the fringed edges of green, and already devising her creation. That she had never held a needle in her life was at this stage of no consequence, and as she picked up her present and drifted towards the vibrations of the kitchen, where it seemed the morning was destined to be spent, her thoughts of the future were limited to hems and necklines, and she knew nothing of the complications in between.

'Yes, it's going to be a grand dress, so it is, with a zip in the side and no shoulders, and when I walk, it'll brush the ground, like this . . .' She trailed the fabric across the tiled floor of the kitchen, dancing it around Lily's slippered feet, and giggling deliriously. 'I'm going to look a proper streel, in my new dress, so I am.'

Lily raised a disdainful eyebrow: she did not need to understand the meaning of 'streel' to form her own idea about Sadie's imminent 'look', but her pinched disapproval suggested she might. Sadie faltered.

'Well, not streel exactly, for that's not nice . . .' she straightened her nightdress in order to banish any possible accusations of the sluttishness she herself had proposed, 'but certainly, like a proper lady. Yep, that's right, so it is, like a lady.'

Joseph grinned, enchanted by her enthusiasm over what had simply been, as far as he was concerned, the logical alternative to shopping.

'Mind you don't get it dirty in here,' he warned, ever nervous of her sponge-like propensity when clothes were concerned. Lily nodded.

'Mmm. I'd take it elsewhere if you don't want it to get ruined, Sadie.'

Lunging forwards, Lily brandished ominously buttery hands which left little doubt to her meaning, and Sadie edged towards the door with covetous intent. With a sympathetic nod to the waiting parsnips, she fled upstairs, the thunder of her feet drowning Joseph's question as he deliberated aloud what could have happened to their copy of *The Sunday Times* that morning. How was he to know a leprechaun had forgotten to deliver it?

If Joseph was suffering the injustices of the spirit world downstairs in the kitchen, then Sadie knew no less vulnerability in the heights of her bathroom up above. Cursing her inattention during needlework lessons at school, she set about the swathes of green with a recklessness which could not have cried more loudly her need for a little supernatural help. Yanking at threads, teasing at creases, it was soon apparent that dressmaking was not something she was especially cut out for, and when Joseph discovered her on her hands and knees beneath the washbasin, that she needed help was obvious. That it was of a fairy-kind was less so.

'But might it not be better if we ask Mrs Bradley to help you with it instead?' Joseph offered, not convinced by such superstitious dexterity as Sadie promised. 'Leave it till tomorrow, when she's in. It can wait till then, can't it?'

Sadie shook her head violently. 'But night-time, Joseph, is the only time you can get it done properly, for the fairyfolk only come out when it's dark, so they do. My brother Mick swore by them, for they were often in our house after we'd gone to bed, and there was never a button left hanging if they'd been and that's a fact.' She twisted a loose thread hanging from her cuff as if in proof of their absence in these forsaken regions, and frowned irritably.

'If he was here, Jose, if Mick was here now, he'd know how to get my dress made, so he would. You could always rely on Mick if you wanted a stitch on something, so you could.'

Joseph cocked his head. He hated to shatter Sadie's illusions, but he had seen the nimble fingers of the lauded Mick, and it didn't take a qualified surgeon to recognise a skilled needleman when he saw one.

'Has it occurred to you, Sadie . . .' he began, but when her face clouded over, and her frown set into a warning scowl, he hesitated. He did not finish his theory upon the likelihood that such myths were an invention of her brother's in an effort to hide the fact that he was actually quite handy with a bit of thread. Nor that, in certain circles (and the all-male, whiskey-drinking, roughneck fishermen gang to which all Sadie's family belonged was one of them), darning socks and mending collars was not something you bragged about, and hence one would have to limit it to the midnight hours. No, if Sadie wished to believe in benevolent fairies and psychic brothers, as it seemed she did, then who was he to enlighten her? And he left her to continue her search, which had since extended to the linen cupboard above their heads, and returned downstairs, where he made a quick call to Mrs Bradley and arranged to drop off the unmade dress that night, to be secretly returned the next day. Keeping Sadie's faith, it seemed, was as important to Joseph as it was to Sadie herself.

Thus it was that by lunchtime the next day Sadie had her first zipping, scoop-necked dress (Mrs Bradley did not approve of off-the-shoulder), and she did indeed look a proper lady. The final addition of a row of jangling shells around the hem was Sadie's idea, and as she skitted noisily around the upper floors of the house, stopping to gaze in every mirror she passed, she wondered that she had not thought to call on the Little People earlier. Who knew what powers she might have tapped into, and all because she gave a leprechaun a cup of tea.

8

It was around this time that Joseph decided they should give a dinner party. He decided, he invited, he arranged, and he organised. And then he told Sadie. And once he had explained exactly what a dinner party entailed, and given a detailed listing of the likes, dislikes, habits and foibles of each and every guest, Sadie was delighted. Since the encounter in the garden and the creation of her beautiful dress, her confidence in human nature, or at least in its universality with regard to the 'other world', had been largely restored, and she no longer feared the isolation of Englishness. If leprechauns could leap oceans, then so could she. As Seamus, her eldest brother, had advised on the day of her wedding, 'Don't yield to them Saxons, Sadie, just beat them!' – and she intended to do just that. The dinner party was to be only the beginning: just let them see what she could really do when she set her mind to it, Irish streel or no.

Joseph was unaware that the small get-together he was arranging held the significance it did as Sadie's English debut, and he was perhaps a little remiss when explaining to her the type of people he had invited. He failed to inform her that four out of the eight were his mother's age, and of a no less leaden humour; and he saw no relevance in the fact that the other four were all colleagues from the hospital, young doctors with their hearts set upon becoming surgeons. It did not occur to him that Sadie might feel rather out of place, for she had never complained in the past, and he thought only of his own pride in showing off this glorious creature whom he still could not quite believe was his. No, Joseph simply did not realise. And hence when the day of the supper arrived, and Sadie spent the whole day in a state of absolute panic, bathing, doing her hair, hating her hair, re-bathing, re-doing her hair, and so on, she could not have known that there was not a lot of point. That the people Joseph had invited to their first dinner party would barely remember her name, never mind what she was wearing or whether her hair was clean. It was really not their subject.

With Mrs Bradley and Lily in charge of cooking, and having been told, in no uncertain terms, to make herself scarce, Sadie was at rather a loose end as the clock in the hall struck six o'clock and she waited for Joseph to return from the hospital. She was feeling decidedly nervous, despite herself, and she had already raided Lily's make-up drawer twice in an attempt to add that extra something which even now she was not sure she had achieved. If only Joseph was here, he would tell her for sure. But he was not, and she was becoming increasingly fidgety with every ticking minute. Wandering in and out of the hallway, Sadie stood for a while in the drawing-room, studying the trays of bottles and glasses which Mrs Bradley had arranged earlier that afternoon. She had never seen so much alcohol outside a public house, and then she was not sure it had been this plentiful, for the Irish prefer to swallow their drink rather than look at it, and hence a bottle only stays full as long as it is unseen. What restraint she showed then – lining up the bottles side by side, she took just the smallest sip of each, purely out of curiosity, and then a second of the first one, port, simply to confirm it was her favourite. And with what delicacy, when she heard the front door slam and Joseph's familiar whistle echo through the hall, she then patted her lipsticked mouth with the edge of the drawing-room curtain, and hurried out to greet him, keen to share with him the efforts of her day.

Joseph was relieved to find her so calm, having imagined all manner of scenes as possible, and subconsciously delaying his return as a result. It was not that he did not trust Sadie. Of course he trusted her. It was just that he knew how worked up she could get, over the smallest of things, and he saw that their first dinner party could be a prime opportunity to display this. But here she was, calm, collected, and . . . something else. There was something different about her. She looked slightly glazed, but it wasn't that, nor was it the slightly fumbling way in which she had attached herself to his arm. Something else . . . Taking Sadie's hand, he led her into the drawing-room, and poured a small whiskey from one of the bottles she had only minutes ago sampled, before leaning, one hand on the sideboard, and tapping his brow.

'You look different, Sadie.'

Sadie raised her eyebrows enigmatically. 'Do I now? Now why should that be, I'm wondering . . .'

Her voice was soft, playful, and ever so slightly flirtatious. Joseph was none the wiser. Preferring to remain in silent ignorance, he shrugged dismissively, before pouring himself another drop of malt. For reasons unknown to himself, Joseph could never drink a full measure, and would instead persistently drip-splash between bottle and glass until he was satisfied, and although this often meant him standing guard by the drinks tray, it was a habit he could not break. Tonight was no exception.

He tilted the bottle to observe its contents, and then dribbled a thin slither of liquid down the side of his glass, hesitating, concentrating, before placing it back on the side and balancing the cap on top. With a glance at Sadie, who stood before him, watchful and still, he closed his eyes and inhaled, before taking a short swig, and sucking his teeth appreciatively. Sadie nodded in approval of his choice, not to know that it was habit rather than connoisseurship which directed his hand.

''S'good one, so it is. Smooth, with a hint of heather.'

Joseph creased quizzically, her words escaping him, and took another sip.

'Do you know,' he began somewhat absent-mindedly, 'I think I know what it is.'

Sadie waited.

'You're wearing make-up. That's the difference. I like it, I really do.'

Pleased with his astuteness, he celebrated with another tot of whiskey, pausing to affirm that, yes, it was the lipstick, definitely the lipstick. Sadie fluttered her eyelashes in silent acknowledgement, and Joseph shook his head fondly, more paternal than appreciative, before returning his glass to the tray, and making as if to depart. As he did so, however, he noticed Sadie's outstretched hand, reaching for his discarded tumbler, and he paused.

'You would like a drink?' It had not occurred to him to offer.

Sadie nodded. Until she reached out her hand it had not occurred to her to ask.

'Well, then you shall certainly have one.'

Both amused, and a little overwhelmed, by this sudden sophistication – first lipstick, then whiskey – Joseph picked up the open bottle and held it to the glass. But Sadie stopped him, resting a hand upon his, and pointed instead to the bottle of port. He shrugged accommodatingly, searching around for a proper glass, before pouring her a generous measure, and raising his empty hand in salute, 'Cheers.'

'Yes.'

Sadie took a long gulp, grinning from the bottom of her glass, and as Joseph turned to go upstairs, she daubed her mouth once more upon the conveniently hung curtains, and sighed contentedly. Were it not for the jangling of the shells she had sewn into the lining of her dress, one might have thought her most refined, smoothing back the curtains with one hand, patting her hair with the other, and she would have welcomed the adjective. But for the moment the only praise she might enjoy was the burr of applause as the alcohol hit her empty, and unaccustomed, stomach, and she had to make do with that. Pouring herself another mouthful, 'Just a dropeen, for sure,' she wondered at this apparition which faced her from the mirror above the fireplace, and decided she rather liked playing the lady of the house.

Kicking the hem of her skirt into tingling spools about her, she was glad she had overcome her initial doubts about the English, for in the great scheme of things, though they might have bigger houses and wider streets, and an altogether mad way of pronouncing the simplest of words, they were all of a piece in the end. Or so, in her tipsing, rattling, curtain-twitching glory, she was innocent enough to believe.

It is a curious line which divides one man from another, one woman from another woman, and it is not always particularly clear. But that night, it could not have been more patent, and to imagine that 'them and us', or, as it later appeared, 'them and Sadie', were only seas apart was seriously to underestimate the differences between them. Admittedly, by the time the eleven of them sat down to eat, Mrs Bradley serving the first course soup from a heirloomed tureen at the end of the table, Sadie had perhaps had more to drink than she was used to, but could that be all it was?

Lily had positioned herself at the head of the table, with Joseph at the opposite end and their guests arranging themselves diplomatically on either side. Sadie had dashed upstairs just before sitting down to touch up her lipstick, and by sheer default ended up perched in between an elderly man, introducing himself as Humphrey – whose wife (Mrs Humphrey, Sadie assumed) was a close ally of Lily's – and one of the four aspiring surgeons (who failed to introduce himself but was generally referred to as Jones). Neither man was particularly voluble: one through fear of his wife, the other through fear of women in general, and Sadie realised early on that she was fighting a losing battle.

'So you're a doctor, you say. I'm thinking that's terribly bloody, so I am.' Sadie rested her chin upon her finger and thumb, as she had seen the models do in Mrs Bradley's copies of *Woman's Own*, and smiled politely. The young man on her left scowled.

'It can be.'

'Janey . . .'

Silence.

'And you'd like it then?' She was not going to be put off so easily.

'Mmmm.'

'My daddy wanted to be a doctor, so he did. A doctor or a priest, his mammy – my granny, that is – said he had to be. But he ended up a fisherman instead, and all my brothers are the same. Couldn't stand the blood, so they said . . .'

'Mmmm.' He was clearly unimpressed by her attempts at familiarity.

'Poor fish, that's what I say . . .'

'Yes?'

'Yep . . . poor fish with that lot chasing them all day and night. Don't bless the fish till it gets to the land, my daddy always said, but I'm betting those fish are thinking they're cursed, not blessed at all!'

She giggled, nudging him with her elbow, and turned to Humphrey at her other side.

'Don't you think?'

But Humphrey only nodded, and Sadie was left to enjoy the image alone. She picked up her glass and took a gulp, considering how rude they were all being, and wondered if the English always behaved like this. She took another gulp.

Well, she was going to have a good time, whatever, and she pushed her glass towards the middle of the table, gesturing for it to be refilled, and when Humphrey rose to do so, she measured it no less than he ought. Taking it from him with a 'ta', Sadie sank back into her chair, and concentrated for the moment upon keeping him busy.

As the main course was cleared away, and Joseph left the room to open another bottle of wine, Sadie, this long silent, sat up again, and for a second time perused the two men seated at her side. It was all rather a blur, and she squinted giddily, telescoping forwards and back as she tried to find her focus. She sighed loudly. But it was all wind and water, as her mother was fond of declaring when things were going amiss, and she gave in to the flood. Flushed both by the heat of the room and the quantities of wine she had consumed in Humphrey's honour, she seemed quite radiant, and even the doctor sat up straight when she began to talk.

'So you're a doctor . . .'

'Training to be.'

'Training to be . . . And you . . .?' she glanced at Humphrey, who immediately looked towards his wife, clearly the authority on what he was, 'you're . . . married.'

Humphrey nodded, pleased to have got off so lightly.

'So . . .' Sadie paused dramatically, gesturing left and right, and unaware that the whole table had fallen silent and were listening to her every word. 'So, you!' and she pointed her butter knife menacingly to her left, 'you! are a doctor, and you!' the butter knife waved right, 'you! are married.'

The two men nodded.

'And a doctor . . .? A doctor has a difficult job, so he has. My daddy himself said it, so he did. Terribly bloody, so it is . . .'

Her subject nodded. They had already been through this. But Sadie had not finished.

'And married . . .?' She turned to Humphrey with a

flourish, watching his wife as she leant forward warningly. 'Married to ... to Mrs Humphrey, you are!' Sadie opened her eyes wide in mock wonder. 'Now what's that then?' She tipped her head conspiratorially, and in a whisper loud enough to be heard by Joseph in the cellar below, announced: 'Bloody terrible, that is, so I'm thinking!'

Collapsing in giggles, pausing only to flash the squirming Humphrey a smile of sheer purple wickedness, Sadie banged her hand upon the table as she continued to repeat, 'Terribly bloody ... bloody terrible ...' until a rather bemused Joseph wandered back into the room, and the horrified silence which had reigned in his absence was broken.

'More wine?'

'Oooh yes ...' Sadie stopped sniggering long enough to hold out her glass, waving it regally above her head. 'More wine ... a good idea, so it is!'

Joseph moved towards her, but Lily caught him.

'I think coffee might be more appropriate, don't you?' She glared at her daughter-in-law, and stood up. 'I think you've had more than enough already.'

'More than 'nough,' Sadie repeated. 'Oh nooo ...' She turned to Humphrey. 'Humphrey, have I had enough, would you say?'

Humphrey shrugged non-committally, glancing from Lily to his wife, and back to Lily. Sadie tried again, snuggling closer and whispering conspiratorially, wagging a finger towards her mother-in-law.

'Twisting things, she is, all the time ...' Sadie started to snigger. 'Swallow a knitting needle, that one, it'd come out a corkscrew, honest to God it would.' One hand across her mouth, the other tucked through Humphrey's reluctant arm, Sadie collapsed into loud giggles, only quietening when she realised she was alone in finding this amusing. She scratched her cheek uncomfortably.

Joseph, silent throughout, saw his chance to intervene,

and, putting down the bottle of wine, moved towards Sadie's chair as if to help her up. 'Perhaps you could go and ask Mrs Bradley to make some coffee, darling. Would you mind?'

'Nope. Nope, coffee … great …' Sadie nodded, bowing before Lily's glare. She would have asked the man in the moon to make coffee if it meant she might escape from there. And she shrugged, pushing back her chair. ''S'absolutely fine …'

As she spoke, however, the ground beneath her feet began to sway ominously, and in a moment of panic she sat down again, holding on to the table in front of her for support. She could feel their eyes upon her, challenging, but she was unable to move. Staring at her fingernails, Sadie sank her head in her hands, and sighed. She was so tired. So tired. Perhaps if she could just close her eyes for a minute and sleep, she would feel better. But she couldn't sleep here, she knew that, not with all these echoes and open mouths. And not with Joseph and his coffee, for that would really irritate him. She could hear him frowning from where she sat.

'Oh dear …'

Sadie sank deeper into her wrists. She had behaved badly, she knew it. And for the first time in her life Sadie wished herself other than what she was, for she knew Joseph wished it also.

'Oh dear dear dear …'

She rested her head upon the pillows of plate and glass which spread in front of her, opening her eyes just long enough to see Joseph bend down and reach towards her, before falling sound asleep.

'Hell.'

Joseph gritted his teeth and stared at her helplessly, torn between dignity and duty, and not entirely sure which was which. Rather distractedly he began to pull the various pieces of cutlery and china from the tangle of her hair, clearing a space, and then, with a glance at his guests, levered Sadie backwards, tipping her against his arm, and carried her out of the room. As he reached the door, however, he turned back, and with a nod to his mother who sat bolt upright at the end of the table and clearly in a state of some shock, and a smile to the others, he wished them all goodnight.

When they reached the bedroom, Sadie was awake again, lolling backwards against his shoulder, and looking about herself hazily. Joseph lay her down on the bed, pulling off her shoes, and perched beside her.

'Are you all right?'

She considered for a moment, and then nodded, edging herself upright against the headboard, and rubbing her eyes. 'Fine. Just great.' Sadie took a deep breath and held it, lacing her hands across her crumpled lap with sobering piety, before exhaling loudly.

'Go back down, Jose. I'm good.'

But as she spoke, the front door could be heard to slam loudly, and footsteps on the driveway announced it was already too late.

'Don't worry, Sadie, just go to sleep.'

'Oh, Joseph, I'm really sorry, so I am.' She paused as the front door slammed a second time. 'Really sorry . . .' She tailed off, holding her shattered brow in one palm, and reaching to bless herself with the other.

'It's all right, Sadie, darling. I promise you, it's absolutely fine.' He caught her finger as it reached for her heart, and held it to his mouth. 'Absolutely fine.'

'But I'm seeing two of you!' she howled, the proclamation echoing against the four walls and causing a hush in the hall below. 'How can it be fine when I'm seeing two of you! I'm reeling, Jose . . .'

Joseph shook his head. Twice. He blamed himself, of course. He should have kept a closer eye on her, not allowed her to get into this state, especially when he knew she was not used to it. He stroked her tear-stained cheek, and held her as she continued to sob.

'Just try to sleep, darling. It's all going to be fine.'

Through sodden lids Sadie gazed up at him blearily. 'Are you sure?' she whispered.

He nodded. 'Quite sure, you'll see.'

With a sigh Sadie closed her eyes gratefully and, wrapped in her green dress, a smudge of lipstick still smearing her now quiet lips, drifted into sleep. She did not hear him get up and go the top of the stairs to meet his mother as she saw the last guest out, nor the fierce whispering which immediately ensued, in which her name figured more than once, and when he returned some fifteen minutes later to crawl, shirted and tied, into bed next to her, she only grunted welcomingly. He had said everything would be fine, and she believed him.

When Joseph awoke the next morning, however, things were not so straightforward. A restless night, a blistering headache, and the fact that he was still fully dressed, inclined him towards a certain self-pity which his remembered generosity could only exacerbate, and it was several minutes before he could even bring himself to open his eyes. The single refrain of Sadie's 'I'm reeling, Jose' had pinned itself to his memory, and whichever way he turned, whichever way he looked, he heard it. Despite himself he felt decidedly bad tempered. When he discovered he was alone, that Sadie had disappeared leaving only a void of cold sheets in her wake, the blackness of his mood deepened, and he wondered at the lengths to which her disloyalty might extend.

Levering himself out of bed, Joseph hoisted his trousers resolutely, tucking and pulling at his shirt, his hands like spades, until he was one interwoven surface of wool and cotton. He ran a hand through his crumpled hair, glimpsing in the mirror above Sadie's dressing table and pausing only to question if his face had always been so grey, until the memory of Sadie and her absence caused yet another black cloud to settle above his head, and he saw the perpetrator of his pallor. Or rather, he did not see her, which was half the problem, but he intended to find her right now. And arching towards the door, Joseph wrenched down the handle, and flung it wide, before pacing himself out of the room in search of his wife.

When he reached the landing, however, the sound of running water above his head immediately confirmed her whereabouts, and he felt a flicker of relief, quickly to be replaced with the annoyance that he had been led to doubt her in the first place. Like many of his countrymen, Joseph possessed the singular ability to turn any situation into an insult to himself, and as he pounded up the stairs to find her, the cross upon his back weighed heavily.

'Typical,' he murmured, breathless in his haste, 'absolutely typical.' What exactly it was that Sadie was so indicative of he never revealed, but suffice to say, she was guilty. 'She was right, my mother was right!' he declared, as much in spite as in recognition. And with this curse of curses throbbing upon his tongue, he plunged along the narrow hallway towards the crashing water.

The door to the bathroom stood open, and Joseph, having first paused to drop his tie – the matter being formal, but not to that extent – strode forthrightly inside. Glancing about, he was surprised to find himself alone, and as he stepped forwards to turn off the taps, adding carelessness to his list of complaints, he wondered where she could have disappeared to now.

No sooner had he wondered, however, than a rumble in the hallway behind him announced her return, and the door was flung wider still as a thunderbolt of green cloth swept through, hurtling towards the sink. Caught off balance, Joseph held tightly to the taps, but Sadie barely noticed him, his gallowed figure just another obstacle upon her increasingly cluttered path. An obstacle with an attitude.

'Good morning, Sadie.' Joseph reached out an arm to stop her. 'How are you today?'

She stared at him, wild-eyed, and shook her head violently.

'Well?'

Opening her mouth to reply, Sadie was seized with that certain urgency to which the only response is to shut it again. Which she did. But barely had hand clamped it fast, when nausea got the better of her and, falling to her knees, she found herself face to face with the grey-flushed oval of the toilet bowl. For a deceptive, and shortlived, few seconds, Sadie thought genuflection might be enough, but her faith was unfortunately misplaced, and, with a cough and a splutter, it became sickeningly clear.

'So you're feeling better?' Joseph's sarcasm was timed to perfection, his question barely articulated, when Sadie was again flung forwards. She sobbed, patting her mouth with the palm of her hand, and reaching for a towel.

'What was that you were saying, Joseph?'

'I was just commenting on how well you look.'

Even if she had not been kneeling, it would have gone quite over her head. Sadie attempted a smile. 'If the truth be known, Joe, I'm not feeling so good . . . I must be ailing for something . . .' She smiled again.

'It's a hangover, Sadie. ' And he helped her sit up, resting her back against the radiator. 'The best thing you can do is get some sleep.'

Sadie closed her eyes.

'Not here, Sadie, go back to bed!' He stared at her, but she remained motionless. 'Sadie!'

Nothing. Exasperated, he picked up the towel she had

dropped on the floor beside her, and hung it over the side of the sink.

'Stay there then.'

And with that he turned and walked out of the bathroom, suppressing any inclination towards sympathy beneath the greater weight of 'I told you so', and went downstairs for breakfast.

Her legs were stiff when she finally stood up, and it took some minutes for the floor to settle again, and the balances of the room to level out. The light had changed in the time she had been sitting there, and she was struck by the general air of afternoon which seemed to have descended. Was it that late? She had no idea. She levered herself down the stairs and on to the landing, listening for any signs of life, but the house was silent, and she might have been quite alone. She moved to the bannister, and leant over it, peering into the well of parquet hall beneath, and craning to make out the various shapes and faces which huddled together in the darkness. The full moon of the clock stared back at her: just before midday – it was not as late as she had thought.

Her stomach, however, was keeping time to a different beat. Rather unimpressed by the sudden insistence of wood and gravity, as Sadie doubled herself over the bannister, and reached for the stairs, it began to mutter and grumble noisily, and she sank forwards. The jigsaw of hallway beneath quivered threateningly, its many corners flattening and rising up as she pushed against them, and she closed her eyes, breathing deeply in an attempt to thwart the swelling tide of upside-down dizziness which had seized her body.

'O dear sweet Jesus . . .' Sadie moaned pitifully, to anyone who cared to sympathise, but there was only the slow ticking of the clock beneath her, and the rumblings of her own stomach, for company. She was alone. With a whimper,

Sadie leant back, manoeuvring her body floorwards, and started to fumble her way along the bannisters in the general direction of the bathroom. It was a cruel world, she decided, where forgiveness was put at such a price, and in the dark of her folding mind, she determined not to pay it. She figured it was all going to be fine anyway.

When Joseph found her she was curled tight around a plant-stand halfway along the second landing, one hand in front of her mouth, the other clutched to her stomach, and her face even greener than the fern to which she clung. Gathering her up, he stood for a moment, holding her close, before carrying her along the hall to their bedroom. He was angry with himself for leaving her earlier, and was hence all the more attentive now, but when Sadie sat up, leant forward, and was promptly sick all down the front of his shirt, justice seemed to have been done.

'Jeez, I'm sick,' Sadie wheezed, tumbling back against the mound of pillows he had tucked behind her. 'I feel as though my belly's in my mouth, so I do.'

'How's your head, Sadie?'

''S'here, right enough,' she patted her forehead reassuringly. 'Nothing wrong with my head . . . Just hanging over a touch, as you say . . .' She trailed off into meandering silence, contemplating the quantities she had watched her brothers consume over the years, with far lesser consequences than these. She shrugged. 'I'm thinking I'm not one for the beer, so I'm not.' And she pulled at a smile. 'My mammy always said as much, so she did, but I s'pose there's listening and there's knowing, and that's the truth.'

Joseph nodded, feeling somewhat out of place amongst such authoritative memories. 'Well, I'm sorry, Sadie,' he began, 'I shouldn't have let you drink so much, and I certainly shouldn't have left you in the bathroom on your own earlier. I'm sorry, darling.'

'Jeez, you're not the one for saying that, so you're not.'

She paddled her fingers against his wet shirt front, and twisted her mouth comically. 'I'm the one who's for 'pologising round here, causing you all this mess, as I am. Making a hames of it, so I am.'

Joseph waved his hand dismissively. 'Are you feeling better then?'

She nodded, although not altogether convincingly, and he reached for the bowl he had brought from the kitchen, just in case.

'Will you call me if you need me?'

She nodded again. And with a pat, and a shrug, and a carefully aimed kiss to her forehead, he left her to sleep.

Ten minutes later he was back, still repentant, but renewed by fresh hope. A thought had occurred to him.

'Sadie . . .' He nudged her dozing shoulder. 'Sadie, are you awake?'

'No I'm not,' she returned, 'I'm sleeping like you said.'

'Well sit up a second, darling, I want to ask you something.'

'Ask me while I'm lying down, will you? Honest to God, Jose, if I sit up again, there'll be more to me than what you're seeing now, I'm warning you.' She nuzzled deeper into the blankets, and concentrated her whirling thoughts upon the disturbingly difficult task of closing her eyes.

'It's just, well, it occurred to me, Sadie, when did you last, well, when did you last . . . what I'm asking is, have you had a period recently?'

For a doctor Joseph found discussion of 'women's matters' surprisingly daunting. He tried again. 'When did you last menstruate?'

Sadie slowly rolled on to her back and carefully opened a single eye, through which she studied Joseph deliberately. ''Scuse me?' she demanded, an inheritance of closed doors and whispered revelations rushing to meet his question.

'You know, your period . . . the curse . . . whatever you call it?'

'The curse?' Sadie pushed herself upright, nausea for the time being quashed by the more forceful directive of indignation. 'You've not to be calling it the *coirse*,' she admonished, pulling the word across her teeth like chewed leather, 'so you're not. It's a gift, I'm telling you.' Her words burned with the intensity of the much-repeated. 'It's a gift from the Virgin Mary, so it is.'

'Yes, fine, but have you . . .?'

Sadie tipped her head backwards and shuffled her eyes majestically. 'Course, Joseph, the Virgin Mary would not be forgetting, so she wouldn't.'

Joseph sighed, his theory crumbling about his ears.

'Only . . .' Sadie paused to gather her thoughts, 'only I'm thinking she's not knowing I've moved yet. Either that or it's 'cause I'm living with Protestants.'

9

It took some time for Sadie to accept the fact that she was pregnant, and even longer for her to like the idea. Motherhood was not something she had taken account of as yet, and for the first few weeks she felt herself rather intruded upon to say the least. But Joseph's overwhelming excitement, and Mrs Bradley's fervent knitting, and even Lily's attempts at graciousness, eventually brought her round, and she was soon bumbling along with the best of them, making plans for the new arrival, and revelling in the general novelty of the thing. And so while Joseph worried about dates and expectations, about bugs and brainstorms, Sadie concentrated upon simply being herself, and as the months wore on, she discovered just what a liberation this might be. Pregnancy, it seemed, covered a multitude of sins, and Sadie intended to enjoy such blasphemy for all it was worth. She never knew when she might get another chance.

Having never experienced sisterhood in any other form than the Church, which was perhaps not the most enlightened of institutions when it came to women, Sadie found the demands of her new role at times rather isolating. She was a stranger to this secret world of breasts and bellies, in the past having relegated bodies to much the same pile of human experience as confessionals – something one needed to be acquainted with, but which was always better approached in the dark – and the sudden visibility of her most private spaces unnerved her. She became clumsy, where before she had been light; heavy, when once she had soared. 'I'm getting a real lump on me,' she would moan to Joseph, tucking herself behind curtains, or huddling under sheets, and he would smile, forgivingly, and remind her that he still loved her, no matter what she looked like.

'You're beautiful to me whatever size you are, darling,' he would promise, with as much conviction as he could muster, kissing the tip of her nose which seemed the only place he dared touch these days, 'and just think, when he's born, it will all have been worth it.'

And Sadie was left to devise for herself just what 'it' might be. For Joseph, despite his profession, was not a man to whom fathering came easily, or certainly not at this early stage: he felt considerably in awe of the many changes Sadie's body was undergoing, and he was happiest when he might just sit back and let it happen. Let her get on with it, so to speak, until such a time as he might once more have effect, and Sadie could go back to being the girl he fell in love with on the beach.

But Sadie was no longer that girl. Had not been for some time now. And the ballooning forms of her new self only emphasised this. And ironically, or perhaps predictably, it was the man who had transformed her who was the last to notice the loss; and when eventually he did, it was he who was the most bereft. Sadie, as she must, simply carried on.

As the weeks of her pregnancy accumulated, Sadie grew used to the daily metamorphosis her 'condition', as Joseph referred to it, induced, and by the time she was six months gone, she was positively proud. 'Happy as Larry' as she herself declared, although Joseph never found out who *he* was. Her body became an exhibit, forever on display, and she was persistently pointing to one limb or another in appreciation of their change, and demanding everyone else do likewise. She pulled at her shape as a sculptor might pull clay, caressing it, poking it, standing back, scratching her head and marvelling at it, and there was not a day went by when she did not comment, to whomever might or might not be listening, upon the wonder of the thing. It was as if she were the first. As if never before had bellies been used for such purpose, and it was with a grandeur verging on regality that she began to move about the house, a rolling, strolling bundle of births. And it was then, only then, that she came to understand just what it was her mother had forgotten to mention.

'Look, Joseph, look at me now.' She had cornered him on his arrival home from work, and was standing in the hallway, hands on hips, thrusting her stomach into the void. 'I'm getting a mountain on me, will you see.'

Joseph stepped back, turning to remove his coat, and carefully draping it over the chair behind him. He smiled affectionately. 'Almost, Sadie, almost.' He attempted to move past, but she held up her hand, imploring him to stay.

'A proper mountain, will you see.'

Joseph reluctantly lowered his eyes. 'Well, perhaps a hill,' he offered breezily, 'But mountain, I'm not so sure.'

'Feel it, Joseph. Put your hand just here, and then you'll see what I'm telling, for hills don't have volcanoes inside, so they don't. Just feel.'

'That's the baby moving, Sadie,' Joseph instructed, falling back upon the facts of the matter. 'That's all it is.'

'Not a volcano, then?' she whispered, eyes wide in apparent wonder, 'I'm not going to suddenly explode!' She clapped her hands in emphasis and Joseph unwittingly flinched.

'Did I make you jump, Jose, is that it?' Sadie reached towards him apologetically, but when he cringed back a second time, she hesitated. 'What has you so cranky, Joseph? What've I done?' she mumbled, immediately penitent. 'Tell me what I've done, Joseph, that you're scared of me.'

Joseph shook his head. 'Nothing, darling,' he replied, defensively, 'absolutely nothing.' And this was quite true. For it was not what Sadie had done, but more what she had become, that unnerved him, and there were unfortunately few words to articulate this. But Sadie was not giving up so easily.

'Don't you like me like this?' She waved her hands about her stomach, and raised her eyes to meet his. ''S'that what it is? You're thinking I'm all fat and ugly, aren't you. Tell us the truth, Joseph. So help me God, Jose, that's what you're thinking, isn't it?'

Her question had risen to a wail, and Joseph hovered uncertainly as he attempted to calm her. But before he could do so Lily appeared on the stairs behind them, and the intensity of the challenge was momentarily lost.

'What on earth are you doing standing in this draughty hall in just that thin slip, young lady? You'll catch your death, I'm telling you. You have to show more responsibility to that baby, you know.'

Sadie remained where she stood, her back resolutely turned against her barking accuser, and she continued to stare at the wavering Joseph. 'Tell me,' she whispered, 'is that what it is?'

He shrugged, anxious only to escape her, and he glanced past her towards the figure on the stairs, helpless. 'Mother's right,' he began, hoping to change the subject. 'You really should wear more clothes.'

Sadie looked down, studying her billowing nightdress, and Joseph took his chance to slip by, hurrying across the rug to stand alongside Lily, infinitely safer. Slowly uncurling her head, Sadie followed his retreating footsteps, and when she at last fixed him, perched beside his mother and holding tight to the bannister, she was shivering uncontrollably.

'See, look at yourself,' Lily commanded triumphantly. 'You're freezing to death, you silly girl. Get yourself upstairs and put on something more sensible.'

But Sadie was not cold, any more than she was not moving, and when she sat down in a heap against the front door, 'sensible' could not have been further from her mind. So this was what her mother had not told her, was it? That love, and self, and babies, were all all right so long as they were neatly packaged and out of sight. That being a girl, woman, mother, was perfectly fine so long as you didn't try to get noticed for it. Sadie shivered once more. So that was it, was it. Well, she'd see about that.

And hence it was that Sadie, six months pregnant and a lifetime deceived, set upon her quest for self-recognition. The glint of hard-edged individuality which had shone as a child, but which, since leaving Ireland had surfaced only periodically, was to be mined with a vengeance, and Sadie's spade was at the ready. Little did Joseph expect that one 'misinterpreted' silence – as he hastily referred to it – could lead to all this.

All this: the sweep of Sadie's revelations took in both the animate and inanimate, and in no time at all she had secured a grip on the Hill House which was not to be relinquished for many years to come. Even Lily was inclined to retreat, the force of Sadie's presence by the day more desperate, and if Sadie had imagined there was a volcano in her belly, it was nothing compared to the eruptions she effected elsewhere. It began with the salt. Salt here, salt there, streaked across the parquet flooring, scattered across the rugs, until wherever one walked there was an accompanying crunch-scratch as the salt ground deeper. And what was not strewn was gathered in small bowls and deposited in doorways, or arranged alongside the ornaments on the mantelpiece and tables, so that every time Sadie passed by she could take a handful and either swallow or disperse it, depending on her mood. And if salt wasn't enough, then there were the shells, which Joseph insisted had multiplied since their arrival, and which Sadie had taken to stringing from the ceilings and lightbulbs, causing a perpetual jangling, twirling welcome whenever one entered a room. Cockleshells for the drawing-room, mussel shells for the hall and kitchen, and Sadie's own very special bell-shells for the bedrooms and the stairs, for one shouldn't waste their magic on too lowly a location. If Sadie had rattled Lily's nerves in the past, it was nothing compared to the percussional heights she achieved now, and rarely a day went by when one of the house's unlucky inhabitants was not caught hugging their ears and begging for mercy.

But before Sadie might stoop to mercy, she must first perceive their humility, and with all the complaining and threatening her creations had so far engendered, she considered there was some way to go yet. By whom she had been invested with such God-like powers she never stopped to ask, and as any Irish mother would concur, it was better not to, but suffice to say, she took them and she used them, and she was determined to hang on to them. For there is an unwritten law amongst women of six months pregnant, and that is that they must be indulged, left alone, and for the most part obeyed, and Sadie rejoiced to implement this.

Hence, as Sadie grew larger, the chaos which surrounded her flourished with her, and the smaller, less flexible elements of the Hill House were exiled to its outer edges. Lily set up camp in the kitchen with Mrs Bradley, embarking upon a three-month long dissertation upon her daughter-in-law's maternal failings, and Joseph found more and more reasons to keep himself working late. As a result, Sadie's time was largely her own, a fact she articulated by changing all the clocks in the house, so that none were ever correct, and the hour, any hour, chimed from a different room every fifteen minutes. But even this could not allay the sense of hollowness which had set in since that fateful day in the hall, when Joseph had failed to reassure her, and when she had first comprehended the solitude of being herself.

'Jeez, I've made a pig's ear of all this, so I have, and I've not even got a silk purse to show for it, more's the pity.' If Sadie was mixing her metaphors, it was of no consequence, for there was only herself and the privet hedge to judge, and neither party were showing any particular interest. 'I've got a big lump which is going to be landing on me any day now, a husband who lives at his infirmary, and a mother-in-law that's going to be chasing me from here to kingdom come the minute she sees I can run again, sure.' She stared at the mound of her belly, hoping to catch sight of her feet, but as usual they were absent, and her tantrumed kicking went unseen.

Sadie fingered a privet leaf, tweaking it gently in encouragement of some response, but the garden was quiet this morning, as it had been for months now. She had never again set eyes upon the little leprechaun of that long-ago Sunday morning, ignorant of the fact that he had received the sack for his tea-drinking truancy (and had been replaced by a far more diligent individual who would not have dreamed of jumping hedges and taking shortcuts just to deliver newspapers), and the needle fairies had disappeared as definitively as her waistline. For all her salt and shells and time-changing, she could not help feeling the magic had gone out of life recently, and she was at a loss as to how she might call it back.

'Where's it all gone to?' she mused. 'It doesn't just disappear, pooff! without going somewhere, to be sure, but I'm certainly not seeing it round here.'

She pivoted full circle, scowling at the trimmed bushes and manicured beds, and noting that there were few Little Fellows who would want to live in a place like this. 'You don't want all this order and prettiness, do you?' she declared to no one in particular. 'You want a bit of muddle and mess, else how other can you have your fun, God help you.' She shook her head despondently, and Lily, watching from the kitchen window, shook hers too.

'She's talking to the hedge again,' Lily noted, turning to Mrs Bradley at the table behind her. 'She's quite quite insane.'

As if to prove this, Sadie then embarked upon a silent swaying dance around the garden, oblivious to her audience in the kitchen, and intent solely upon summoning up whatever spirit might remain in this barren place. But it was to no effect, and eventually she gave up, dizzy with her efforts, and ambled back inside to scatter a little more debris, and then maybe take a bath.

It was while she was wallowing in the shallows of the bath – it had to be shallow, for so great was Sadie's bulk now that any depth was sent flooding over the rim – that she had her brainwave. She was washing her hair at the time, which was a task and a half, for it involved levering the rest of her so far down the tub that her legs often ended up wrapped around the taps, and hence it was some time before the idea could be be translated beyond anything more than a shampoo-sudded blur. But as soon as she righted herself, smearing the bubbles from her eyes and shaking herself dry, she knew it made sense. If the fairies couldn't live in the garden, then she would build them a home somewhere else. And where better than here, right here in her bathroom? Where better indeed?

She sat up, sloshing puddles of water on to the tiles at either side, and began to formulate her plan. If she collected up all the shells and brought them upstairs, then that would be a start, and then maybe fetched some sand from the pit she had spied in next door's garden ... and then perhaps a few pebbles from the driveway, and a few more bits she was sure she could pick up around and about ... Yes! Once she got started it would be easy.

'Ooh, just wait!' Sadie promised, dappling the palm of her hand along the dripping contours of her belly. 'By the time you get here, we're going to have a whole houseful of the little blighters, so we will, just you wait.'

Thus, when Joseph arrived home that night, he found Sadie perched on the back door step, playing with a heap of gravel, and humming quietly to herself. It was the first time in months she had seemed pleased to see him, and he was grateful for the reprieve.

'Have you had a good day, darling?'

'Look how pretty they are, Joseph, d'you see?' Sadie held up a handful for his approval.

'Lovely.' He nodded, hoping this was not the next pile of clutter which was to hit the newly-created building site of his home. 'Absolutely lovely. What are you, er, what are you going to do with them?'

'Oh, nothing much, no,' Sadie returned, somewhat evasively. 'Nothing much at all.'

And while Joseph suspected that in fact this meant something very much, he did not question her further, for he understood the fragility of her present condition, and until this baby was born he was prepared to put up with anything, if it kept Sadie happy. Stepping over the piles of multi-coloured stones, he left her sitting on the step while he went inside to talk to his mother, and discover for the third day that week that his wife had been talking to the garden. Sadie was thus able to slip by quite easily, her pockets full of chippings, and the only clue that she had been was a thin

Hansel and Gretel trail up the stairs and along the landing behind her, which, along with the salt and the shells, seemed hardly out of place anyway.

Over the next few days Sadie devoted herself to her scheme, spending hours crawling around on her hands and knees picking up shells, and slowly moving everything up several flights where it was ceremoniously dropped in the bathroom. Joseph, of course, was delighted, imagining that Sadie's efforts at tidying were the beginning of a new phase of domesticity, but the subsequent disappearances of rolls of silver foil, Lily's double string of pearls, and several packs of toilet roll, suggested all was not as it seemed. Indeed, when Sadie was caught in the neighbour's sandpit at three o'clock in the morning wearing a bucket and spade and not a great deal else, it was almost worrying. But Joseph continued to tell himself that the end was in sight; that nine months would soon be up; and even when he discovered his prized stamp collection to have been filched from his study, he did not say a word.

And upstairs in her bathroom Sadie continued to cut, stick, balance and hang, arranging and rearranging the spaces of her grotto with ceaseless delight. Chattering away to herself, or possibly to the many spirits and creatures which she held to be there with her, her creativity knew no bounds, her energies still less. It was only when she had been locked in there for two days running, coming out only when a tray was placed outside her door with whichever meal she had failed to turn up for that time, that Joseph decided it was time to intervene. Curiosity, or was it the pull of the conventional, had at last got the better of him, and, dispatching his mother to her sister's in Holland Park for the night, and sending Mrs Bradley home, he decided to get to grips with this once and for all. Little did he know that Sadie had planned to do exactly the same.

* * *

The last time Joseph had ventured as far as the upper floor was the day they discovered Sadie was pregnant, and he experienced a strange sense of *déjà vu* as, drawn by the sound of running water, he climbed the stairs that fateful night. Pausing to catch his breath, he marvelled at Sadie's athleticism, before he remembered that she had refused to come down for two days, and his admiration diminished. Dropping to the step outside the bathroom, he leant upon the door with his shoulder, and called out to his wife, teeth bared against the keyhole, knuckles rapping gently against the wood.

'Sadie, darling, it's me. How are you? Could I come in? I think we should talk.'

'Joseph!' Sadie exclaimed, as though he were the last person she would have expected to be knocking at this time of night. 'Joseph.' And she continued to move about inside the room, her direction ever charted by the scuttling shells and crunching sand which issued in her wake. 'Joseph.'

'Yes, darling, it's me,' he repeated, in a tone one might use when addressing an errant child. 'Do you think I might come in?'

'Well, actually, Jose, I was 'specting someone, so I was, although any other time, honest to God, you'd be welcome, so you would.' Her voice was hushed, pressing through the cracks of the doorway with an almost conspiratorial intent, and Joseph felt moved to whisper in return.

'Don't be silly, Sadie,' he breathed, and then, louder, 'Don't be silly. Who's going to be visiting you at this time of night?' He might have added, 'Who do you know?' but the accusation seemed deliberately cruel, and he refrained. 'Can I just come in?'

Footsteps on the other side heralded her approach, and a sigh just above his ear briefly suggested she might relent. He tried again. 'I just want to talk to you, that's all.'

'But, Jose, I'm telling you,' she hissed, 'I'm 'specting someone, so you'll have to come back later.'

'Tell me who you're expecting then, or I'm staying right where I am,' Joseph demanded petulantly, forgetting for the moment that it was he who was locked out. 'Who, Sadie?'

Another sigh, louder this time. 'Joseph . . .' she began, but then thought better of it. How could she tell him she was expecting fairies? He would never believe her. She shook her head, about to tell him to leave her alone, when it occurred to her that perhaps she was being a little shortsighted. And in the spirit of enlightenment, Sadie reconsidered. 'All right then,' she murmured softly, 'all right.'

Joseph slapped his hand against the step in relief. 'Good girl,' he acknowledged, generously, 'good girl.'

'But you've got to promise not to touch anything, will you? Just look, are you hearing me, just with your eyes.' She waited for his agreement. 'Promise me, Jose.'

Joseph promised.

'Hang on a sec, then.' And she faded away again, just audible on the far side of the bathroom mumbling to herself something about 'no harm in it, to be sure' and wheezing breathlessly. Joseph leant back against the door and closed his eyes, his mind full of mountains and men called Mohammed. He would wait. He had little choice but to. And he listened as Sadie pattered back and forth across the tiled floor, clattering and cranking, and every so often kicking the door to remind him of her presence. He smiled, despite himself. She was worse than ever.

'Nearly there, Joseph,' she reassured. 'Now,' she clapped her hand decisively. 'Now, did you promise?'

Joseph nodded, eyes still closed. 'Yes, Sadie.'

'Well, say it again, so that I can be sure I hears you.'

'All right, I promise.'

'Swear.'

'All right, I swear.'

'Swear on your mother's grave, Joseph.'

'Oh, Sadie, stop playing games and let me in.' He was losing patience rapidly.

Silence. Now it was Sadie's turn to wait.

'All right.' He stood up, growling theatrically, mouth to wood. 'All right. I swear on my mother's grave. Is that enough for you? Now let me in.'

Face to face they watched each other blindly through the blank panels of the door, and then slowly, deliberately, a key grated in the lock, and the seams of wood pulled apart.

'At last!' Joseph stepped forward eagerly, but a low and warning rumble from the thin slice of Sadie which filled the space between door and wall held him back. He smiled apologetically. She frowned.

'Slowly, Joseph. You promised.'

He nodded. And the cracks of colour which streaked the gaps between them trickled deeper as Sadie stretched out her arm, easing the door wider, and stood back. He gazed at her, surprised to find her much the same as the last time he had seen her, and edged forwards to kiss her. She offered him her cheek, twisting sideways so as to manoeuvre him around her belly, before stepping back, hands crossed behind her back, and allowing him inside.

'Well?' Her earlier reticence had been replaced by genuine concern. 'Do you like it?'

Joseph did not move. Dared not. The walls swung back and forth around him, flickering light and dark, and he put out a hand to Sadie's shoulder in order to steady himself. In front of him a brimming bath spilled on to the wastes of shells and pebbles which banked its sides, and all around sandy fingers stroked back and forth in the draught, trailing long golden streaks across the already shimmering expanse of the floor. He gasped. The sense of being underwater was almost suffocating, and he turned back towards the door in search of a little air.

'Well?' Sadie pressed for a response, unnerved by his silence.

'Sadie . . . you've . . .'

As he spoke, a dozen or more mouths opened and closed around him, every turn revealing one more reflection of his incredulous expression, one more fragment of himself. For where before had been blank walls, there were now mirrors and glass, splintering and moulding every surface, almost mocking in their infinity. He moved closer, circling. Mosaics of paper squares, stamps in fact, *his precious stamps*, blistered in between the glass, like coloured tongues poking their disdain, and Joseph reached out to touch one, disbelieving. Sadie dived forwards, raising a hand warily.

'Don't touch, Jose, you swore you wouldn't touch, so you did.'

He nodded obediently, lowering his arm, and continued to gaze around him. His legs felt weak, and he rested against the edge of the washbasin, tilting his head back and inhaling sharply as he observed the pride of Sadie's creation, a plaited net of white tissue woven between the skylight and the wall, a lifting, heaving sail above the splashing length of the bath.

'What on earth . . .?' He stared at the sagging belly of makeshift cloth, strands of which had escaped to straggle soggily upon the still of the water beneath. 'What . . .?'

Sadie grinned, following the direction of his gaze, and pronounced victoriously, 'Toilet roll, so it is. All tied together, toilet roll.'

In between wondering how she had climbed up there to fix it, and why she should have wanted to in the first place, Joseph managed to utter a half-hearted 'lovely', before dropping his head to his hands and sitting down abruptly on the radiator casing to his right. Sadie pored over him, anxiously running splayed fingers through the fallen mop of his hair, and, with as much leverage as her stomach would allow, she bent towards him.

'Are you all right, Jose, will you say, are you poorly?'

He shook his head wearily, still trying to make sense of the spinning walls that flickered around him, and crumpled lower still.

'Joseph . . .' Sadie moaned the word, pulling the 'o' of the first syllable into a wheedling 'oooh' that coiled about his head like a wreath, stifling him still further.

'I need some air, Sadie,' he blurted, and in a single stride rose from the radiator and lunged towards the centre of the room. Before Sadie could stop him, he reached up towards the skylight and began to pull at the catch, pushing aside the folds of tissue, and jabbing viciously. Sadie staggered towards him, pulling at his shirt, clawing him in her desperation.

'Leave it, Joseph, don't be messing . . . please . . .'

'I just want to let some air in. It's so hot in here, I don't know how you can bear it.'

'I can. I can, Jose. So leave it will you?' She pressed her weight against him, trying to catch hold of his reaching fist.

But Joseph only lifted higher, arching away from her, focussed solely upon the skylight, and unhearing of Sadie's pleas. He would later defend himself by claiming it was only to help her, that she would suffocate up there with no source of air, but at the time his reasoning lacked such generosity. He was like a child who has read someone's private diary and then feels disappointed that he has not been mentioned: Joseph felt justified in making his mark when Sadie had so effectively erased him.

'Stop it, Joseph. Just leave it will you? I can do it myself later . . .'

'You shouldn't be doing anything in your present state, Sadie, who knows what might happen!'

Sadie slapped her hand against the rim of the bath, sending waves of warm water churning on to the floor, and kicked her legs hard against its enamel sides. 'He promised not to touch, so he did, he promised,' she whispered, as if addressing some invisible intruder. 'He swore on his mammy's grave, so he did . . . what'll they be saying about that then?' Standing back, she then began to pace back and forth the diagonal of the bathroom, curving around the narrow of the bath, and only hesitating to pull a handful of salt from a pot resting on the sink, which she then crammed into her mouth hungrily. In between thirsty bites she repeated the words, 'swore, so he did, swore,' until her ruminations were but a hoarse whisper. Joseph watched her nervously. From his lofty perspective, hovering astride the taps and clinging to the skylight, her rantings seemed quite ludicrous, and he frowned irritably. Why did she always have to overreact?

'Will you calm down, Sadie,' he demanded, craning beneath the sheets of tissue to allow her the full extent of his scowl. 'Calm down, for heaven's sake.'

But until Joseph was getting down, any such relenting on Sadie's part was unlikely, and he considered his options. Just as he was about to give in, however, and climb down, the catch, at which he had been whittling and niggling all this while, suddenly snapped, and the skylight at last swung open, a gust of air rushing in with an urgency that was almost applause. Sadie spun around sharply, hands flailing wildly, in time to see the cat's cradle of her sail torn from its Sellotaped moorings, a hovering cloud of white, and flap-flutter its descent to land graciously upon Joseph's upturned head.

Silence. Joseph picked at a corner of the knitted paper, extricating it from his shoulder, and dropped it to the floor. Sadie watched, motionless. With the flat of his hand, he made sweeping movements across the front of his jacket, before bending to continue the process upon each of his trouser legs, picking at the specks of white until no more might be seen. Satisfied, he turned towards Sadie and smiled apologetically. She continued to stare, her face an alphabet of potential responses. Somewhere between disbelief and distress, she paused, opened her mouth, and began to scream. At first, it was more the act than the volume which startled Joseph, but as the decibels gathered momentum, even the wind seemed taken aback, slamming the skylight once again shut, and sending yet another wisp of paper fluttering to the floor. Joseph stared at her.

'Sadie?'

She paused for a moment.

'That's better. Now . . .'

But as he spoke, she began to scream once more, louder and louder, until the house rattled with her fury, and even the echoes fought for space. And Joseph was left gesturing inaudibly, a mime artist without an audience to fill in the words, and he knew he was beaten.

'Suit yourself,' he mouthed, which clearly she was going to. 'I'll be downstairs, when you've calmed down . . .' He gestured towards the door, allowing her one last chance for forgiveness, but she was deaf to his charity, and he had no choice but to pick up his pride and run, a flurry of sand and paper skitting in his wake. And only when he reached the hallway, three flights down, did his ears stop ringing, and as he headed straight for his study to check his surgery answering service, he once again marvelled at the volatility of women. He would never understand them.

And Sadie had no intention of being understood. Exhausted by the necessarily aggressive tactics it had taken to remove her intruder, she sank to the floor where she lay for some minutes listening to his distant conversation, and staring at the sky. In the hazing blue of dusk, she could just make out the pencilled outline of the autumn moon, and she was distracted momentarily as she counted the days until it would be full. But her lunar ruminations were of little consolation as she observed the wreckage of her bathroom, and with despair she realised she would never seduce any of the little folk into this noisy garret. If there was always going to be Joseph storming in and out, pulling things apart, how could she ever hope to find sanctuary? She sat back against the curved length of the bath and rubbed her eyes sorrowfully. How indeed. But at least she had made him swear upon Lily's grave: that, she smiled, was something.

10

Never one to dwell on her sorrows for long, Sadie was soon back on her feet and attempting to restore some order to her rather bruised surroundings. The main casualty, it seemed, was the sail – and you couldn't have a ship of all nations without a sail – and she set about knotting and twisting, tying and plying, as the drifting strands were pulled together towards their former glory. So intent was she upon her work, she did not notice the first murmurs of cramp which coiled inside her, and when she stood up to contemplate her efforts, she felt perfectly well.

Hence, it was not until she was balancing astride the bathtub, reaching for the skylight, that the vulnerability of her position really struck her. And struck her hard. For several precarious seconds she hovered between floor and ceiling, like some overblown madonna, convinced that this was divine retribution for her earlier curses, but as the pain seared deeper, hot coals in the fire that was already her belly, she knew it was not so simple. Nevertheless, prayer seemed her best option, and, dropping the sail she had been in the process of resurrecting, Sadie opened her arms to either side, steadying her pendulous mass, and, knees bent, eyes clenched tight, offered herself up.

'Holy Mary mother of God,' she began, for this definitely appeared to be women's business, 'Blessed art thou ... ow!

. . .' the pain struck again, ''mongst women . . . Blessed's . . . umph . . . fruit of thy womb . . .'

Sadie broke off. She was sweating feverishly, swaying from side to side on the pulpit of her bath, and unsure how long she could keep this up. She tried again. 'Holy Mary mother of . . . aaagh!' Her stomach wrenched violently, throwing her forwards until she was only inches from the surface of the brimming bath, and she gasped as she caught sight of the concertinaed reflection which met her there. '. . . God!' The exclamation was as much a cry of anguish as a conclusion to her prayer, but if its morality might at another time have been questioned, right now it seemed to help. For the cramping had suddenly passed, and as Sadie lowered herself to the floor, gulping breathlessly, she wondered why she had never tried it before.

'Jeez,' she murmured, 'You nearly had me that time, so You did . . .' and she smiled wanly as she lay back against the banks of shells. 'I was thinking I was done for, so I was.' Sadie closed her eyes and dropped her hands to her stomach, but as she did so she felt a rush of warm water somewhere between her quivering legs, and as she pushed herself up on to her elbows she gave a moan of despair. 'Dear God, and now I'm all wet . . . wouldn't you just know it . . . I'm flooding, so I am . . .'

There was water everywhere, soaking both skin and sand, and she pulled her skirt higher across her knees. 'I'm drowning . . . drowning in me own bathroom . . .' she mumbled deliriously. 'Sure that's what's to be happening . . . drowning . . .'

Paddling her fingertips in the moat of her thighs, Sadie half-heartedly dabbed forehead, breast and shoulders in a last ditch attempt at submission, but considering she was probably already lost, left it at that.

'Drowning . . .' Sadie stared at the underside of the bath. 'Jeez, I'm really for it this time, aren't I just . . .' and she sank into the bed of debris as the second wave of pain took hold. 'This'll really put the mockers on them, so it will . . .'

But downstairs Joseph, door shut, ears covered, telephone disconnected, was not about to be mockered by anything, least of all Sadie. And, whether by good judgement, coincidence, or sheer paternal instinct, when only seconds later she began to scream his name, he was already halfway up the stairs and hurtling towards her.

When he reached the bathroom Sadie was flat on her back, her rising belly eclipsing all sight of her now tear-stained and sorry features, and only the echo of her 'Joseph, Joseph, Joseph' to assure him that she was still conscious. Inspecting the wrinkling wet of her dress, he smiled to himself, his suspicions confirmed.

'You do make the most of things, Sadie,' he murmured affectionately, the tensions of earlier already forgotten. And bending closer, he pushed the curls of her hair away from her damp face. 'How do you feel? Do you think you can sit up? Darling . . . I said, do you think you can sit up?'

Sadie shook her head violently, and stared at him through a mottled haze of tears. 'I'm drowning, Jose,' she repeated, and rolled towards his hand. 'There's a hole in my back, will you feel.'

Joseph felt, but there was only the softness of her expanded flesh, and he stroked her waist as she continued to lament. 'I can't feel anything, just this big gaping hole, and I know if I tried to reach I'd be straight through to me belly button. Oh Joseph, why do I hurt so much, tell me . . .' She tailed off as another wave of cramps swept over her, and she began to writhe and buck with such distraction, it was all Joseph could do to stop her flipping right over. After several attempts to get her upright, in order to escort her bedroomwards, Joseph accepted that the bathroom was the place, and he cleared a hollow in the dunes of shells and kissed her knees excitedly, before fleeing downstairs to fetch his bag.

Leaving Sadie as he had found her, Joseph hurried from room to room, collecting towels and blankets, and cursing Mrs Bradley's absence – Lily's was a blessing – for he could have done with her help. But he did not realise quite how much he could have done with it until he returned to the bathroom, for, in the short time he had been gone, and by means neither could fathom, Sadie had somehow undressed herself, and was, half-floating, half-drowning, immersed in the lukewarm bath. He panicked, she screamed, and the ever dampening world around them began to flood.

It is often the most momentous of events which are the least memorable, and certainly, for Sadie, this was one such time. Writhing side to side, hands gripping tight to the rim of the bathtub, her only thought was of movement, of keeping the rhythm, and whatever Joseph might have told her, or whatever she herself might have thought, paled beside the urgency of motion. Desperately, devotionally, she gave in to the tides which circled her swirling belly, and with a passivity quite uncharacteristic of the Sadie of the last few months, she simply lay back and prayed. Were it not for the steady rain of tears which coursed her cheeks and dropped, one after the other, upon the puddles of her breasts, one might have thought her quite detached. But she was there all right, and Joseph was going to have his work cut out if he thought of taking her elsewhere . . .

'Leave me alone, Joseph! Noooo! I don't want to get out, I don't want to!'

'All right, all right, you don't have to, but at least let's let the water out! Will you hold on, Sadie!'

He pushed her knees back from their scrabbling descent plug-wards, holding her body with the twisted palm of his hand, and forcing her upright. 'You'll drown all of us at this rate. I need to let some water out.'

He fumbled for the chain of the plug, catching at it despite her kicking, and tugging it free. Immediately the water began to eddy, diving downwards and quickly deserting Sadie's thrashing limbs. She gasped despairingly, and thrust her heel into the plughole like a cork, pushing down hard and grimacing with the effort.

'Stop that, Sadie. Move your leg.'

She glared at him with undisguised defiance, the shimmering wet of her face only serving to emphasise the edges of her temper, and she jammed her foot harder against the enamel. Joseph glared back.

But just as he was about to insist upon the issue, he saw Sadie's face crinkle, scrunching tightly in creases, rivering her tears, and he thought better of it. He placed a helpless hand against her shin, and watched as her head flicked backwards, silent, and her stomach bucked uncontrollably. Water swilled beneath her, slapping against the sides of the bath, flooding the sandy tiles and soaking him.

'Hold on, Sadie, just hold on . . .' Joseph rubbed a wet hand through his already dripping hair, and glanced about himself with what, for a split second, might have been terror. He was unused to such disorder, and wondered if he could hold her off long enough at least to call the midwife. But it was too late for delegation, and he knew it. He took a deep breath. 'Let me just get a . . .'

Towel? Chair? Whiskey? Whatever it was he sought, it never materialised. For barely had he begun to waver, than the waves of Sadie's motion began to bear, and with a rush, and a flurry, and an unheard scream, he found himself looking not at the white of cast iron, which only a moment ago had transfixed him, but at a straining block of colour, bleeding against his dipping wrist. A face. His own. His reflection. He reached deeper, scooping the lines within the open palm of his hand, and easing them upwards, towards the light. Purple and blue, bruising a scowl, two eyes puckered tight beneath a turf of red hair. Joseph hesitated self-consciously.

Glancing at Sadie, he saw her staring blindly upwards, silent now. No reassurance there. And he looked back at the child which lay balanced in the spaces between them. It was quite something, this scrap, this grimace. He ran a finger across its face. And then, as if as an afterthought, he bent to kiss its nose. A flicker of touch. Joseph stared at him with uncharacteristic marvel. Him.

'It's a boy, Sadie!' Revelation had suddenly struck. 'It's a boy!'

Curiously, Sadie seemed rather unimpressed. In fact, she seemed not to hear him at all. Nor the high-pitched howls which accompanied him. Joseph repeated himself, this time louder, leaning towards her and resting the wailing child upon her still rising breast.

'It's a boy, Sadie. Look, look at him.'

But Sadie was fixed upon a spot somewhere behind Joseph's head, and she barely even glanced. He put a hand on her quivering knee.

'Sadie . . .'

There was a sob, and a murmur, and then, as he watched, once again Sadie began to flutter, her body pushing against his restraining hand, her arms slapping against the enamel at her sides with repeated urgency.

'Hell.'

With one hand holding her knees, and the other raised to her breast to support his newborn son, Joseph bent towards the churning waters, gasping as a second wave of colour flooded his open fingers. Twins. How on earth had he not known . . .

'Oh God, Sadie! My darling Sadie, will you see? Twins, Sadie, Sadie look. Twins.' Joseph held up the second arrival, balancing it against his wrist, arms outstretched. It was smaller, this one, but no less fierce, and as he looked from one to the other, and then back towards Sadie, he was lost for words.

'Oh Sadie, Sadie, Sadie . . .'

She smiled wearily.

'So this is who you were expecting, was it?'

And Sadie nodded, simply because it was easier.

Joseph rested his forehead against the cool shelf of the bath, and continued to murmur her name. At the end of either arm a small mouth puckered in chorus, and soon all three were whimpering quietly as exhaustion seeped from them, and the night set in. Only Sadie was silent.

And then slowly, almost inaudibly, she began to sing. Lowering her chin, which throughout this time had been thrust decidedly skywards, she dropped her gaze to the chuntering triangle of which she was the centre, and watched as all three sank towards her. She smiled wearily, causing a further spillage from the pools of her eyes, and she scooped her fingers through the now still waters and caught each to her, cradling sons and husband with the rising comfort of her thin voice. What she sang, Joseph never knew, for the sounds were a blur to him, the words another world. And what he heard, not in this lifetime would he remember. But in between the tremors and the whispers, the echoes and the sighs, even Joseph could see there was a quietness in Sadie, a hovering, and for the first time in hours, months, years, she might have been at peace.

Her pale face glittered in the dim light, and Joseph reached one of his now free hands towards her, stroking the waving seaweed of damp hair behind her ears, running his thumb the length of her creasing cheek. And still she sang. And long after he had prized her foot away from the plughole, and lifted both her and her sons from the gurgling waters, towelling all three with a carefulness he had before never known; long after the singing had died to a tremble and Sadie's voice was little more than a groan; long after the novelty had diminished, and the twins were just another pair of irritable boys, Joseph never forgot how still she had been that night.

11

Sadie was worn out. Shattered to smithereens. For the next few days she did little else but sleep, waking only to feed the two grumbling bundles as and when Joseph or Mrs Bradley delivered them, or to sing the next few verses of whichever lullaby was that day's favourite. Joseph flustered here, there, and everywhere, gathering the twigs and milk-bottle tops of baby paraphernalia necessary to line their nest, and squalking proudly at every given opportunity, be it to his immediate family, or the more detached (but no less grateful for the intimacy) frequenters of his surgery. It was an exciting time, during which, for the first time in many months, Sadie relented in her quest to recreate her homeland, and actually began to settle where she was. She even attempted to make it up with Lily, considering that perhaps they now had a little more in common, but her mother-in-law was not to be so easily seduced, and hostilities remained. Thus for the most part they were happy, and life, revolving around the three-cornered bed to which Sadie retreated each morning, and from where she did not move until Joseph returned home at night with his latest acquisition, appeared at last to have attained a little of that craved-for normality.

With his usual regard for efficiency, over those first few weeks Joseph had made it his mission to write to each and every member of their extensive and extended family, sending cards and photographs, and even in some lucky cases, details of weight loss, feeding times, and the occasional lock of hair. To the extent that not a day went by without the telephone ringing at least twenty times with messages of congratulation, and even Sadie's twelve brothers, who had received individual epistles, despite their shared address, crossed the technological divide and trudged as one to the post office to make the felicitous call. Unfortunately, however, Sadie was sleeping at the time, and Mrs Bradley refused to wake her, and it was as a result of this thwarted attempt at communication – they could, of course, have tried again later, but it never occurred – that they made the decision to visit instead. And because delegation had never been the family's strong point, and it would have taken longer than the trip itself to determine which of them was most deserving, it was agreed all twelve should go. And while Sadie lay singing in her shrinking bed, counting freckles, and creasing tiny fists in an attempt to read their futures, her brothers plotted a distraction all of their own.

It was on a Wednesday they arrived. She remembered this because it was the day Mrs Bradley took the twins out with Lily, and the house was empty. Wednesday was not a perfect day for visiting, primarily because it was the day upon which Sadie felt most heavily the weight of the week, and hence, the day upon which her mood, although for the most part uncharacteristically good during this period, was inclined to drop. Best left to her own devices at such times, it was usually a day for sleeping, or taking long, uninterrupted baths, and she eagerly awaited these precious hours from one week to the next. The telephone was unplugged, the drone of Lily's relentless radio talk shows at last subdued, and any intrusion fiercely discouraged. It was not a day for visitors, much less a band of twelve.

And so when the doorbell rang at midday that particular Wednesday, it was a deserted house which echoed its reply. Even the clock in the hall held its tongue, refraining from the telltale chime which might have signalled life, and upstairs Sadie buried deeper into the bedclothes, cursing intruders and all who met them.

'Jeez . . .' she muttered irritably, 'can't you get a minute's peace round here?' She pulled a pillow across her ear. 'It's like living in a barn, so it is.'

The bell rang again, this time accompanied by banging, and Sadie threw back the sheets and sat up, already sufficiently indoctrinated to know she could not ignore it. She pushed herself up on to all fours, and sat back on her heels, staring at the wall and listening intently. The bell rang once more, prolonged and insistent, and she spun around on the pivot of her knees to stare accusingly at the open bedroom door.

'All right, all right ,' she grumbled, 'I'm coming if you'll just give me a chance.'

Sliding off the bed, she slipped on to the landing and peered over the bannister into the hall below. As she did so she saw the flap of the letterbox rise and fall, as two eyes peered through and then receded. One step at a time she crept downstairs, huddled to the wall, flinching at each creaking giveaway. When she reached the hallway, she paused, staring at the door, and hesitated.

'What if you're a mad cursing lunatic?' she mused, 'I'd better not be opening the door to you then, had I?'

Deciding to play safe, she sidled into the drawing-room, from which window she might study the front step without actually betraying her presence, and, crouching behind the sideboard, she congratulated herself upon her caution. 'A proper little head you're getting on you,' she informed herself proudly, and she glanced about herself with new-found responsibility. The curtains were partly drawn, and the room was heavy in the afternoon light, causing Sadie to hug her nightdress about her defensively, and as she edged towards the window she regretted not wearing a shawl. But she was not going back upstairs now, and with renewed determination she hooked a fold of curtain and slowly curled it back, watching as a shard of weakly sunlight slithered past her hand, to fall lethargically upon the carpet at her feet.

'Well hallooo!' A mouth parallel with her own, wide and grinning.

Sadie gasped, startled. For a moment she could only stare, transfixed by the single opening mouth. Mouths. From nowhere, faces filled the window, nudging and grinning, opening and closing in multiple repeat.

'Hallooo, hallooo, halloooo!'

Sadie stepped back, her hands to her throat, her heart there too, and struggled for breath. 'Halloo?' she stuttered, clearly unrecognising.

'Halloo,' replied at least five, squinting closer towards the dim of the room, and adding, rather cryptically, 'It's Me, Sadie, Me!'

'Me!' She whispered the word, still counting mouths. Eleven ... twelve ... thirteen ... no, she'd done that one already ... twelve ... yes, twelve ... A dozen noses pressed forward to join the mouths, flat against the glass in a galaxy of 'Me's'. Sadie lowered her hands from her throat, and moved forwards. Raising a finger, she ran it from one circled breath to the next, pausing at what she deemed to be the North Star, and tapping gently as a smile began to soften. As if reassured, Sadie stepped back, smoothing her nightdress, and allowing the noses a good look. Simultaneously, the smudges pressed closer, and then away, and thirteen pairs of eyes criss-crossed the glass, taking in details, gesturing relief. Nothing had changed. She was still Sadie. They were still Me.

'How are you?' The North Star took charge, booming through the glass.

'Great, I am. And you all too?'

'Great, just great.'

'Good, that's good.' Sadie nodded approvingly, glancing at each of the mirrored faces in turn, and blinking excitedly. 'Good, good.'

'Might we be . . .' A hand waved vaguely about their collective head, and then pointed inside. 'Might we . . .'

'Oh, yes, yes. I'm forgetting myself already. Oh yes, come in all of you.'

Sadie flustered towards the drawing-room door, loath to take her eyes from the window in case they disappeared, and then shuffled out into the hall. Hauling open the front door, she stood there, the step chilly beneath her bare feet, her arms swirling at her sides like windmills, as two by two her brothers appeared around the corner of the house and flung themselves upon her. Thrown from one to the next in their habitual greeting, this was not the way Sadie usually spent her Wednesday afternoons, and, gasping for breath, watching them as they pushed up sleeves and hunched pockets, she was almost at a loss for words.

'Cat eat your tongue, eh Sadie? There's no tax on talk, do you know?'

It was Seamus, the eldest, and by right the most vociferous. He grinned at Sadie, teasingly, and jabbed a finger. 'Did you lose it to the Saxons, did you? Or is you forgetting your brothers, now you're a proper lady, is that it?'

He chuckled, thrusting his freckling face close against Sadie's, and rubbing her nose affectionately. The salty roughness of his thumb against her skin chafed, and she smiled wistfully, crouching on the stair beside him, and dropping her cheek into his palm.

'I'm not forgetting,' she countered, 'I was just not 'specting yous, that's all.'

'Not 'specting us? Shite, Sadie, are we needing invitations to be visiting you, are you telling me? Do we need to be *wroitin'* when we want to be seeing our Sadie, is that it?'

Sadie faltered, searching for a retort, before Sean, Seamus' twin, younger by five minutes and still struggling to catch up, flung his arm about her shoulders, and spoke for her.

'Jeezus, Shay, you great bosthoon, will you stop!' he chipped, 'Would you be letting nobody get a word in? Begob, it's a wise head that keeps a closed mouth when you're about, so it is.'

'On with you!' Seamus slapped his hand across his mouth in pretended horror. 'You would not be telling me our Sade's getting wise, would you? Is that it then Sade? Are you getting wise on us?'

He lurched towards her, grinning broadly, and stabbed a clumsy finger in the direction of his entourage. 'Well, I can be promising you, here and now, you'll not be getting none of that from this lot, so you won't. Good for nothing, the lot of them!'

As he veered his face closer, Sadie caught a whiff of his whiskeyed breath, and she raised her hand to his mouth, silencing him. 'Has you lot been drinking?' she demanded, looking from one blearied pair of eyes to the next.

'Feck! Might as well tell her lads, so we might.' Seamus draped an arm about his two nearest brothers. 'We have indeed, for it's a long journey, so it is, and we were wanting to wet the babbies' heads properly ... only ...' Turning to Sean, who promptly pulled an empty bottle from each pocket of his oilskin, 'only I think we've already done that, so we have.'

A chorus of dropped heads articulated their apology, and Sadie laughed ticklishly at their affected sobriety, rolling her purple eyes and nodding towards the kitchen. 'P'raps you'd better be following me then,' she announced, 'and you can be leaving your eejity faces where you are.'

All attempts at remorse were immediately cast off, and twelve thirsty grins trooped behind her down the hall, rats to a Pied Piper, leaving their boots where directed in the corridor, and apologising at every turn. Sadie disappeared into the cellar, to return with two bottles of Scotch, and Seamus, instructed to find some glasses, rooted in the cupboards noisily. Those who could, sat down, and those who could not perched on the side and window sills and looked on, wondering at a house which had so few chairs. Seamus distributed the tea cups, and Sadie passed the two bottles, one to either side, and, thus settled, they were off.

'Sooo?' Seamus took a slug of whiskey, and wiped his mouth on his cuff. 'So will you look at our Sadie? Jeez, you're a drip of dishdregs, are you not. Could drown you with a spoon of water, so you could, honest to God! What're they feeding you on, will you tell me?'

Sadie smiled, peering down the neck of her nightdress at the swollen remains of her twin-tubbed body, and raised an eyebrow at Seamus. 'Well if that's not the proof that you've been on the beer, I don't know what is.'

'Get on with you! You're a cure for sore eyes, just as ever, is she not boys?'

Nods and 'sore eyes' all round.

'You're mad the lot of you,' Sadie laughed, 'but it's great to be seeing you again, sure!'

Sean reached for the bottle of whiskey and poured himself another drop, grinning broadly. 'So where's these little fellas we've come all this way to see?'

'Out,' Sadie replied. 'But they'll be back soon, and you'll be staying a while, won't you?'

'Well, if you're asking, we might just, so we might!'

'Course I'm asking. It's grand to see you, so it is, and you can be helping me with the names, so you can.'

'With the names?' Tommy, thus far silent, piped up from the window. 'Now what names would those be, Sade?'

'Not the *babbies*, sure?' Seamus opened his eyes wide, staring at Sadie in horror, all his emphasis thundering on the flat 'a'. 'You're not telling us you've been calling your babbies nothing all this time, God help us, you're not?'

Sadie nodded, unnerved by his excitement.

'Jeez!' Twelve grizzled voices cursed the foolishness of it, and simultaneously took another drink. 'God help us!' they murmured, staring into their cups, 'God help us.'

'What are you all thinking of?' Seamus caught Sadie's arm and pulled her towards his chair. 'How can you be leaving them all this time? If the divil catches you, he'll be whisking them away in no time at all, and who will you tell them he's taken? No names and there's no calling back, d'you hear me now?'

Sadie gazed at him, wanting to tell him that such superstition was laughed at in this household, but her fear, both of his truth and his response, prevented her. And so instead she only shook her head.

'Well, it's done now, and we'll be helping you from here, so we will.' Seamus dropped his cup to the table and reached out his fist for a bottle, both of which seemed to have ended up with Devlin, third born and notoriously heavy handed with his drink. 'Seamus is a must, so it is, for it was your daddy's name, and his daddy's and . . .' he paused, smirking, '. . . and not forgetting it's what they're calling your fav'rite brother, so it is.'

Sadie nodded. 'And the other?'

'Well, t'other you can be calling what you like, I s'pose.' Seamus' helpfulness was sporadic at the best of times.

'Properly, you should be calling the other Joseph, after his own daddy,' Lar advised, leaning forward across the table and giving Sadie the benefit of his toothy wisdom.

Sadie shrugged. It had not occurred to her that the lines of inheritance might also run in that direction.

'He's right,' Sean agreed. ''S'only fair, to be sure. You

don't want the boy always chasing some no good Irishman for his namesake, isn't that the truth. One of them doing it would be bad enough.'

He ducked as Seamus blindly threw a fist towards his twin, and sneaked a swig from the now almost empty bottle as it passed him by.

'Suits me,' Sadie declared gaily, 'Seamus and Joseph it is,' and she padded back to the cellar to fetch another couple of bottles.

It was almost four o'clock when Mrs Bradley returned with the twins, having left Lily at her sister's and strolled back across the park, and the house was quite silent. She wheeled the pram up the steps, and left it on the porch, scooping up the sleeping twins, and closing the door behind her. Presuming Sadie to be asleep, as she usually was at this time on Wednesdays, she was surprised to see her appear out of the passageway to the kitchen, and even more so when, a finger to her lips, Sadie seized the two snoring bundles, and returned the way she had come. Mrs Bradley watched her, fascinated, the flimsiness of her nightdress showing transparent in the afternoon light, before hurrying down the passageway after her and muttering something about a shawl.

Distracted by a low rumbling apparently coming from the kitchen, Mrs Bradley did not notice the barricade of twenty-four matching boots which lined the wall to her left, nor did she spot the one rebel which had broken rank, and which lay in wait for any unsuspecting passer-by; when she fell it was not lightly.

'What on earth ...?' Flat on the floor, she studied her attacker with confusion, wondering how both she and it (or they, for there were twenty-four of them) came to be there. 'Sadie ...'

Sadie pattered back to help her, the twins still oblivious in her arms, her bare feet slapping against the tiles. From her limited position the only word which sprung to mind was 'slippers' and as Mrs Bradley shunted to her feet, she began to chastise Sadie loudly.

'Sadie, you'll catch your death, you will. It's a good job she isn't here to see you . . .' *She*, uttered with such implied reverence, could only refer to Lily.

Sadie turned, her finger to her lips, and shushed fiercely. Mrs Bradley paused, taken aback. 'I was only—'

'Shhhh!'

Mrs Bradley patted her hair self-consciously, and, with the side of her foot, pushed the stray boot back into line. She glanced at Sadie, who was now looking away towards the kitchen once again, and then back at the snaking row of footwear, a growing sense of foreboding tightening with each trailing lace. 'Sadie, for the love of God, what is going on?'

Sadie glanced at the older woman, and then smiled, tilting her head breezily. 'I want you to meet my brothers, Mrs Bradley. Come with me.'

Mrs Bradley heaved a sigh of relief: at least it was only family. She smiled in return, and hurried down the passage after the departing trio.

The low rumble which had caught her attention earlier grew louder with every step, and by the time she had reached the door to the kitchen, it was positively deafening. Clamping her wrists to her ears, she looked about her for the source of such disturbance, but there was nothing there. Until, that is, she looked down. For there on the floor, side by side, head to toe, were twelve snoring redheads, open mouthed and open armed, and their only saving grace the carefully washed stack of cups which drained by the sink. Mrs Bradley gasped.

'My brothers!' announced Sadie, proudly sweeping an arm about their tumbling heads. And, with a baby on either arm, she tiptoed between them, pointing her toes at each in turn:

'Seamus, Sean, Devlin, Denis, Liam, Lar, Jerry, Joe, Paddy, Paul, Mick, Tommy. My brothers.'

Mrs Bradley frowned.

'And . . .' she paused, balancing on one leg between two heaving bodies, 'a couple more wee fellas that you're p'raps not knowing yet, or not knowing by name, for sure, little Seamus,' (she gestured to her left, chin to shoulder), 'and diddy, would you guess? diddy Joseph!'

Sadie extricated herself from the sleeping mass, and climbed back to where Mrs Bradley stood, suddenly subdued. 'I knows you must be thinking they're rude, not standing up or anything, but they've had a long journey, so they have, and p'raps a drop too much of the . . .' she nodded in the direction of the pile of empty bottles. 'But they're no trouble, I assure you. You won't even know they're here.'

And with that Sadie turned and tiptoed out of the kitchen, leaving Mrs Bradley pinned to the wall in horror. She dared not ask if this meant the brothers would be staying; nor even if it was expected they might be waking up in the near future. She merely followed Sadie's example and tiptoed between them, drying the twelve cups and returning them to the cupboard, and then herself retreating upstairs.

By the time Joseph and Lily returned home, very little had changed. The brothers were still snoring, Mrs Bradley was still in shock, and Sadie was still chuntering away about 'no trouble t'all'. Dragging the entire contents of the linen cupboard in her wake, she moved from room to room, regardless of obstacles, making up the sleeping arrangements as she went, and creating beds in the most unlikely of places. Only the newly named twins, little Seamus and diddy Joseph, remained unperturbed, for, like their uncles in the kitchen, they were fast asleep.

12

It was late that night when the brothers eventually awoke, long after Joseph had diplomatically suggested a local boarding house, and even longer since Lily had thrown Sadie's entire wardrobe over the bannisters and insisted she move out there and then, 'and take that rabble with her'. They were oblivious to the tears, tantrums and terrorism their arrival had provoked, and it was to be several days before they discovered that Sadie had a mother-in-law who was now living in Holland Park with her sister, and refused to return until they left. ('She's flittering so she is, in a proper mood, but's no less than the usual.') Also that Joseph had been moved to bribery just to keep his housekeeper from walking out, and would never again feel quite so deserving of her favouritism. Indeed, even if they had been aware of such friction, it is unlikely that it would have affected them: family rifts were part of everyday life in Ireland. That 'she'll come round, to be sure' might have been written in the Constitution.

But if the brothers might ride the storm with such breeziness, Joseph found it considerably more difficult. Since the birth of the twins he had imagined there to be a stability within the household, or more specifically, within Sadie, and he was genuinely concerned about the effects her brothers' presence might have. Only yesterday Sadie and he had been discussing which school the twins would go to, and he would hate for her to be picking up on her brother's socialist views and start fighting him on these things. Added to which, his mother's decampment to West London, for which he knew he would be made to suffer, had more than rocked the boat in terms of loyalties, and he feared to imagine the ructions which were yet to come. Yet he could not deny Sadie her family, and with stoic bravery, Joseph determined to put up with the situation as it was for the 'couple of days' Sadie had promised it to be.

The Irish, however, are infamous for their irreverence in matters of timekeeping, and Joseph soon realised that when Sadie said days, in fact she meant weeks, or possibly even months. At no point, despite her implied reassurances to the otherwise, had she discussed her brothers' departure, much less encouraged it, and without his persistent reminders, it was doubtful that she ever would. For Sadie was in her element: she had her two Little Fellows, as she had taken to addressing the twins, and more charms and superstitions than she knew what to do with; she had a head full of stories, told to her each evening by whichever of the brothers had declined to join the eleven-strong exodus to the pub; she had several pounds of dulse, her favourite seaweed, to keep her chewing for the next month; and she had a sense of belonging such as she had not known for some time. Her only concern was of how this might be prolonged.

'If we were maybe to put a bit of carpet down in the cellar, would that not be the best, then they can be tucking away down there, and you won't know they're even still here, sure you won't. I could be telling them to use the back door when they'd be going out, so as not to wake you with the bell, and I'd make them promise not to touch any of your bottles down there, I would. Ooh, I'm sure that's the best, so I am. Will I be telling them, will I, Jose?'

But Joseph had no intention of letting Sadie's brothers

anywhere near his cellar, much less furnish a basic apartment for them down there, and he would shake his head dolefully, and tell her no, he didn't think it was for the best. And he would still be shaking his head when she returned, hours later, with her next plan, or when the convoy of substitute petitioners staggered in in her place, with nothing that even resembled a plan. The answer was no. When he discovered they had inadvertently trampled his beloved roses in a game of five-a-side (with two referees – 'you can't trust them, I'm telling you'), had drunk every last drop of alcohol in the house, forcing him to keep his whiskey in the car if he wanted a drink before supper, and succeeded in upsetting virtually every neighbour within a two mile radius by the midnight rampages they were inclined to indulge in, the answer, not surprisingly, was still no. Two letters, one syllable, no. He took it no further than this, unwilling to upset Sadie more, and, to be quite honest, finding lengthier debates rather distasteful. But with the assuredness of response the English so pride themselves upon, Joseph knew it was only a matter of time before ample words would spring to mind, and as such he was able to steer politely on. Eventually, he told himself, something would have to give.

Ironically, that something was to be himself, or certainly of himself. For, in the five weeks the brothers were resident at the Hill House – and resident, in this case, suggests less 'guest' than 'inmate', such was the riot of their self-imposed internment – they had ransacked every room, abused every last member of his family and friends, and led Sadie such a dance that her legs would still be twitching long after they had jigged their way back to Ireland. They had been barred from every public house south of Watford, and even the off licences were getting wise to their 'Jeez, I've only got Irish, will you be taking it?' Sadie, with a twin on either hip, became their final hope, an angel of deliverance with two babies and a shopping trolley of whiskey, but even she was starting to attract attention. The final straw, however, was the night of the fire, a night after which the lamest of camels – and Joseph, regrettably, was one such creature – would be hard pushed not to kick back.

The night of the fire was remarkable essentially for its apparent normality. Joseph had arrived home just after eight o'clock, as he did every night, and was sitting in the driver's seat of his Austin 5, headlights on, hugging his single Malt and enjoying a quiet moment to himself, again routine, before he ventured inside. He had just replaced the bottle in the glove compartment by his side, noting that he'd be needing to get the lock mended if the brothers ever discovered this secret stash, when, in the beam of the headlights, he noticed a snail-like trail of soil leading across the gravel and up the steps towards the front door. He paused, curious. Joseph's driveway, like Joseph's life in general, was conspicuous for its sameness, and even during such trying times as these, any intrusion was keenly felt.

'What on earth . . .?' Joseph climbed out of the car and bent down, one hand resting upon the still warm bonnet, the other fumbling for enlightenment.

'What on earth . . .?' he repeated, as, unaware of ironies, he crumbled a handful of wet soil between his thumb and finger, and stared frowningly at the meandering evidence. Following its shaky lead, his eye was led from the front door, and, dropping his bag where he stood, Joseph stumbled across the driveway, over the rose border and into his once beautiful garden. It was early evening, and the light was somewhat deceptive, but this was no cover for the scene of destruction which met his horrified eyes. Everywhere he looked, and Joseph looked everywhere, there were glaring chequers of black earth, gaping like distorted mouths in the once smooth green of the lawn, and everywhere he looked there spelt 'brothers'. Size-fourteen-shoe-size brothers, their names firmly imprinted in the sludging soil, and their numbers under some threat from that booted moment on. He dropped to his knees, arms outstretched before him, and ran his palms across the chessboard of his lawn in a shudder of uninvited acknowledgement. Something, it seemed, had just given.

'Count to twelve,' he muttered. 'Keep calm, count to twelve, and then go inside. There's a simple explanation for this . . . One . . . two . . . three . . .'

Slowly, deliberately, Joseph picked himself up from the wet grass, and, in small, precise steps, walked back to the car. He retrieved his bag, closed the car door, locking it, and made his way up the path to the front steps, his eyes purposely averted from the trail of earth which wound about his feet. Opening the door, he let himself inside, removing his coat and hat and leaving them on the chair by the door, as was his habit. The house was in darkness, only a thin sliver of light showing beneath the door of the drawing-room at the end of the hallway, and for several seconds Joseph stood and listened to the low murmur of voices he heard coming from this direction. They sounded surprisingly sober for this time of night. None of the raucous yelling which usually greeted him. Joseph scowled. It was another attempt to undermine him, he was sure of it; another means of intimidating him in his own home. Well, he'd see about that.

Fixing his sights upon the wavering yellow line which framed the door, Joseph moved across the hall, straightening the corner of the rug as he went, and tutting quietly. At the door he paused, almost inclined to knock, before remembering whose house he was in, and walking straight in.

'Good evening.'

It was a greeting loaded with accusation – and intentionally so – but it fell upon deaf ears. And while Joseph waited, eyebrows raised interrogatively, for some form of response, the room at large continued as before. At large. For all fifteen of them were huddled around the fireplace, apparently watching something, and not one of them was aware of his presence.

'Good evening.'

It was louder this time, more assertive. One of the many bowed heads which circled the hearth flicked back momentarily, nodding, and Joseph found himself almost grateful. He quickly curbed the emotion, and stepped forwards, closing the door behind him. As he did so he became aware for the first time of the unusually pungent smell which filled the room, and as he tried to identify it, he wondered just what all this had to do with the fact that half his lawn had been dug up. But then he realised.

As a second head turned back from the fire, winking its acknowledgement, Joseph glimpsed a shadow of something dark and glistening, lurking to the left of the fireplace, and he edged closer with a stealth the past weeks of invasion had made second nature to him. But the shrouded figure remained motionless, unperturbed by his approach, as were the rest of the room, and he was able to creep so near as to be able actually to touch it, reaching through the walls of ears and noses which formed its entourage, without anyone being any the wiser. Even himself. For it was only when he actually prodded the 'thing', felt it with his own hand, that recognition finally struck home. Or rather, struck garden.

Joseph stepped back. 'My lawn?'

He gasped the words disbelievingly, staring at the leaning tower of turf and trying to make sense of it. Why was the best part of his front garden lying in hacked squares on the drawing room hearth? And why were twelve men, his wife and his two sons crouched on bended knee around it? He could not, would not, should not, even begin to understand. 'I don't understand . . .'

The admission was almost inaudible, but it was these

three words which finally caught flame, drawing attention away from the fire towards the creasing confusion of the speaker.

'What's that, Joe? What are you not understanding?' Seamus turned, grinning at Joseph, and repeated gently. 'What're you not understanding, boy?'

'This!'

'What?'

'This! My garden cut up and stacked against the wall of my drawing-room ... My drive littered with the remains of the said pieces of my garden ... My house ...'

Need he say more? The excess of possessive pronouns made his injury quite clear, and even Seamus was taken aback by the energy with which it was delivered. 'Mmmm ...'

The preponderance was a communal one, humming in spirals that echoed the wisping smoke of the fire, to fade into nothingness. Or almost.

'Mmmm ...'

'Mmmm ... Well, truth is, you're coming in a little sooner than we were thinking, and it's not quite ready for you.' It was Sean, quick to step in where his brother had faltered.

'Ready? Ready for what, might I ask?'

'Of course you might! S'your house, isn't it?'

'Yes!' Joseph rankled. 'Although it seems that some amongst us have forgotten that minor fact. It is indeed my house ...'

'Indeed, indeed.' Several nodding heads offered their agreement.

'Indeed ...' Joseph paused, thrown by such support. 'Indeed it is ...'

'But ...' This time it was Sadie's turn to intervene, piping up from behind a screen of shoulders, and causing Joseph to stretch his already protruding neck. 'But it's actually your daddy's, but I s'pose if he's dead, it might as well be yours.

There's no coming back from where he is, isn't that the truth.'

A chorus of nodding met her declaration, and even Joseph was inclined to agree, despite the inherent motive of her insight being one of contradiction. But so used was Joseph to Sadie's contrariness, he no longer even noticed. Right now it was his garden he was concerned about, and it was time someone provided him with some explanations . . .

'The thing is . . .' Seamus could see a little diplomacy was in order. 'The thing is . . . we were talking this morning 'bout home, and how, at this time of the year, all you can smell is the fires in the houses, and Sade was telling how she missed it all, so she did. So we thought we would be making a fire just like the ones at home, only we were missing the turf, and Sadie didn't know where was a bog . . .'

'So you dug up my garden instead?'

'But it's not the same . . . A nice clamp of turf we were after, but it's not burning anything like . . .' Seamus sighed wearily, clearly disappointed by this unforeseen complication, and he looked at his brothers for ratification. They sighed too.

'And so we can't be surprising you with a bit of Irish firing, as we were wanting. But you'll be glad that at least we found out for you that your garden was badly, all spun out, so it is, and we'll be helping you put it right, if you like. Lar here even said he'd set you some spuds if you fancied, am I right Lar?'

Lar nodded.

Seamus grinned.

And slowly, but most definitely, Joseph began to thunder.

'No . . .' he rumbled. 'No spuds, no Irish firing, no bog, no more. I'm going to my study. I'm closing the door. And you can all . . .' He broke off, gazing from one stubbled chin to the next. 'You can all do whatever you like, but I've had enough of it. I've had it up to here,' and he waved his hand in the smoking air somewhere above his head. 'Enough is enough!'

He peered at Sadie, who remained crouching where she was, meeting her indifferent gaze with a deliberateness she had not seen in him before. Enough. 'I've put up with disturbance, drunkenness, destruction ...' he struggled for another 'd', enjoying this chance for poetics, 'downright and deliberate defiance! ... but I will stand it no more. No more. N. O.'

He had spelt it out quite clearly. What more was there to say? Inevitably, not much. But that did not mean silence. Whether or not there was something to be discussed, there would always be something to say. And Sadie lost no time in making this clear.

'What're you bawlowering at, Joseph? You're getting terribly excited, 'bout something that doesn't matter. Grass'll grow back, so it will. There's no life in that garden any more anyway, not since I don't know when.' She paused as she remembered the leprechaun. 'Your mammy scared it all away a long time ago, honest to God she did.' Nodding conspiratorially towards her brothers, she scowled despondently. 'She'd put the come-hither on the birds in the bushes, that one would.'

'Enough, Sadie,' Joseph commanded, wearily. 'This isn't about my mother.'

'Listen, Joseph.' It was Denis, whose negotiating powers would later make him famous in certain circles. 'We'd not be chewing the rag all night. You've given us a great welcome, so you have, and we'll not be overstaying it, so we won't. Shay was only saying yesterday how's our ma would be getting suspicious if we weren't getting back soon. They'll be thinking we're all drowned, the lot of us. We'll be missing our own wake if we're not heading back, so we will.'

''Tis true enough,' Seamus agreed. 'There's only so long you can be chasing the salmon at this time of year, without them wondering something's amiss.'

Sadie frowned, turning away from the trembling Joseph. 'You were not for telling Ma you were coming to see me?'

A shaking of heads.

'But sure she wouldn't mind? And how can you be chasing salmon in December, tell me?'

'Well, surely you're right, which is why they'll be getting ideas if we're not getting back.' Seamus grinned. 'And as for the old one, well, you know what she's with . . .'

Sadie nodded, waving Joseph away as he tried to return their attention to the matter in hand. 'But you could be telling her, surely to God. She'll not be minding you visiting, she'll not.'

'Maybe as not, but we were not risking her coming too, just to put you straight on yourself. Jesus, she'd have had us here and back again before we even sat down, and to Mass three times in between.' Seamus shrugged dismissively. 'No, we'll be grabbing a fist of salmon and taking them back, and they'll none be any the wiser, mark me.'

'Maybe so,' Sadie conceded, while Joseph, forehead pressed against the doorframe, lamented such maternal absence. ''S'better as it is.'

'Was,' Joseph mumbled. 'Was. Better as it was.'

Sadie shook her head in dismissal, slowly levering herself to her feet. 'Honest to God, Joseph, you wouldn't put a dog out on a night like this, sure you would not. If you'll be calming yourself, we'll be down clearing it up, so we will.'

'I'm perfectly calm, Sadie, thank you very much,' Joseph growled. 'And I assure you I would have no qualms whatsoever about putting even twelve such dogs out on a night like this.' Turning towards the door, he hesitated, gathering himself. 'But I mean what I say. You've got to go.'

Twelve heads bowed as Joseph walked from the room, closing the door behind him. Sadie curled her lip at his departing back, and looked about herself. With murmurs of

'Jeez, what's eating his nibs?' and 'A pity about it, to be sure', the brothers looked with her, and, with a certain amount of jostling, pointing, and general bawdiness, they began to clear the hacked squares of garden away from the fireplace, and one by one return them to the front lawn. Unfortunately, having already tried to burn large chunks of it, any attempt at restoration was patchy, to say the least, and even Mick, famed for his mending abilities, could not smooth this one over. From his study, Joseph watched them. 'No more,' he muttered, as the tribe of twelve stamped up and down in the moonlight. 'No more.'

But as he spoke, 'more' was crouched on the drawing-room hearth and, unaware of such limitations, attempting to burn the remaining evidence. There was mud everywhere, on the tiles, under the grate, on the rugs, and Sadie set about scooping it up and throwing it on to the flames with genuine repentance. She hated to see Joseph in a flap. Reaching across the front of the hearth, she shoved handful after sludging handful into the centre of the flames, dishing the dirt, so to speak, as she lamented Joseph's shortcomings. When this only smouldered, she increased the amount to armfuls, standing, one leg on either side of the tiled hearth, her arms working like cranes, back and forth. And when this failed, she took the packet of firelighters from the log basket, and added them too. 'Now if that's not setting it, then it's not for setting,' she declared, rubbing her muddy hands against the backs of her legs, and she wandered outside to supervise the finishing touches to the lawn.

Not surprisingly, a full box of firelighters was indeed 'for setting', and while Sadie giggled in the garden, watching her brothers return from every direction with a 'borrowed' square to fill in the gaps, the flames began to choke and spatter, throwing off a soupy black smoke that quickly filled the room. Drawn by the draught of the open door, in no time at all the hall and kitchen were similarly darkened, and were it not for Joseph, sensing it was more than bad temper which seeped across the threshold in low, wheedling curls, who knows what might have happened.

'Wonderful, just wonderful,' Joseph cursed, as, throwing open his door, he was met with a wall of thickening grey. 'Set the whole house on fire, why don't you?' he demanded, struggling for breath, and hand over mouth, he rushed from room to room opening windows and propping doors. While the guilty fifteen wafted around the jigsawed lawn, Joseph blew a gale and a gasket inside, and it was a sorry scene which met the rising moon as it peered through the smoke on that memorable night. When the fog finally cleared, and the sea of water thrown upon the grate had begun its long soak into the carpet and rugs, it was not lightly that Joseph took Sadie to one side and reiterated the fact that they must leave. It was a matter of life and death.

Sadie, however, saw it less clearly.

'It's neither right nor lucky, Jose, to be throwing water about the house at this time of night! What would you be thinking of?'

'Sadie, forget the water. I was putting out the fire which you and your brothers started. Would you rather the house burnt down?'

'But Jeez, Joseph, hurling water after dark'll be getting you in all sorts of trouble, so it will. My granny'd have your guts for garters if she caught you, honest to God, and I'm not wondering she might yet—'

'What exactly are you talking about, Sadie?'

'Fairies, Joseph. Drown a Little Fellow and you'll be cursed to high heavens, so you will. Bad luck and fairies, is what I'm trying to tell you.'

'Well fine, but I'm trying to tell *you* that they have to go.'

'Well I'm guessing they've gone, Jose, for if your ma didn't scare them off, then your water would.'

'Sadie, please?' Joseph sighed loudly. 'You know perfectly well I meant your brothers. They have to go.'

'No, Joseph. Not *have* to . . . you would just like them to, am I right?' Sadie smiled at him, and patted his hand. 'Well they will,' she reassured. 'They will go . . . soon.'

'No, Sadie, not soon. Now. Soon is weeks, months . . . Now is now. I won't back down on this Sadie . . .'

She tipped her head to one side and looked at him curiously. '*Huga, Huga, uisce sala.*'

'What?'

'That's what you would be saying next time you're throwing water. It warns the fairies, so it does.'

'For heaven's sake, Sadie! I'm serious. Stop changing the subject and listen to what I'm saying. They have to go. Do you understand me? They have to go. Now.'

Sadie shrugged. 'Sure I understand, but I'm not thinking you're right, Jose. They're going soon anyway . . .'

Joseph glared at her and she shrank back.

'You have to learn that when I say something, I really do mean it. They have to go. Do you understand?'

Sadie gazed past his frowning head, and out of the window.

'Do you? Do you understand.'

Still she ignored him.

'Well they're going. And that's the end of it. Whether you understand or not. Whether you agree or not, for that matter. There are times, Sadie, when you simply have to—'

'Joseph.' Her eyes rolled a weary arc from window to ceiling and back, clearly bored by such didactics. 'Will you stop now?' She shook her head. 'You've had a gob on you like a boiled pike for weeks, so will you just let it rest? They're going, all right. You've said. I've heard you. Honest to God, half the waking world has heard you. They're going.'

'Good.' He turned his back, hurt by her aggression, and

began to pick at the threads of his suit.

'So can we leave it now, sure?' Sadie demanded. 'Will you give up the cranking?'

Joseph raised his shoulders petulantly. 'I just want you to understand . . .' His voice tailed off into silence. 'I want you to understand . . .' He would have liked to say 'me', but he couldn't quite manage it, and instead he swept his hand about the room and simply sighed.

''Tis afterwards that everything is understood,' Sadie mused, with typical passivity.

'Well, you seem to have understanding enough for those brothers of yours . . .' Sadie shrugged, not entirely convinced that she had understanding enough of anybody. 'But I'm not going to argue with you about it. They've got until the end of the week, and then that is the end of it.'

Sadie gazed at him innocently. 'Who's arguing, Jose?'

'So he's wanting us to sling our hook, is he now?' Seamus nodded amiably. 'Well, that's fine, 'tis, 'cause we're not wanting to make trouble. You're great with him, Sade, even though he's an Englishman and likely to be uppity. So don't you worry.'

Sadie gazed at Seamus, tucking her nightdress about her hunched knees, and twisted a smile. Even though he was the eldest, and usually the most raucous of all twelve, there was a softness to Seamus that Sadie clung to, and she ached to let it go. To let any of them go. She looked beyond the bridges of Seamus' shoulders. The brothers sat in folds around her, some on the bed, others on chairs, and two, like bolsters, along the length of the chaise longue Lily had given as a late wedding present. Sadie hated this lop-sided piece of furniture. Always had. But she would hate it even more when there was only herself to see it.

'Maybe he'll be changing his mind, if you all try and settle him . . .'

It seemed unlikely, and Seamus shook his head gently. 'No, Sade, no. He won't be changing, as he meant it. And I'm thinking that's fine, it is.'

'But he was angry, Seamus. He'll be calming, he will—'

'You never for settling, are you Sade?' Seamus laughed, 'You'd be calling the Pope your aunt if it would be getting you somewhere, honest to God you would. Small wonder that Joseph is flittering, so it is ... No, it's time we were away, any means, and if we go now we'll be home for catching the races, that we will.'

The 'races' he referred to was the local Christmas horse-fair, which, for as long as Sadie could remember, had seen the whole village reeling along the sea road and back again, and which was famous for its lack of anything that even vaguely resembled a horse. Usually, the majority of the four-legged competitors were the somewhat out-of-season members of the donkey riding school, sand between their ears, and not a great deal else, who hobbled from start to finish with all the urgency their training amongst three-year-old thugs with ice creams allowed. But it was enough to remind Sadie, for whom last year had been the first time she had ever missed it, that home was a long way away. And that she was here, which seemed yet further.

'Ooooo . . . I don't want yous to gooo . . .'

Sadie sank her head into the cradle of her knees, moaning desolately. Even her toes ached, vulnerable in their extremity, and she clasped her hands in buckles around them, squeezing tight.

'I don't want yous to go.'

All twelve hung their heads.

'I don't.'

Seamus looked up, his expression slurring embarrassment with absolute futility. But Sadie continued to stare at her knees, blinking the comforting smell of sleep that clung to her tired skin, and feeling increasingly weary. She wanted to shout, and yet there were no words. She wanted to kick, but her feet were held too tightly. She closed her eyes.

Tentatively, Mick, tucked behind Seamus, reached out and peeled the fingers from her left foot, uncurling them gently, and tucking the hand into the crevice of her bending legs. Pulling the foot towards him, he began to rub it softly, circling toes, arch and heel in a figure of eight, round and round, his hands rough and broken against the smooth of her skin, murmuring comfortingly. '’S’not so far, you know. You can always be visiting us, and fetching those two babbies with you.' Mick continued to stroke his fingers, back and forth, across the ridges of her toes. '’S’not so far.'

'I know that, but it feels it, so it does. And Joseph'll never be letting me go easy, he won't . . .'

'Sure he will.' Mick shushed her softly. 'You're great with him, likes Seamus was telling.'

Sadie shrugged, looking towards her eldest brother.

'Great,' Seamus offered, as if he did not know what all the fuss was about. And then, pushing Mick backwards, he leant forwards and grabbed Sadie's ankle. 'Bejeezus, what's it mattering with you? It's Christmas, honest to God. Will you stop, the lot of you? We're wanting a hoolie not a wake, surely.'

Sadie flickered hopefully. 'A hoolie, are you saying?'

'For sure. A proper Christmas shindig to see us on our way, do you not think?'

'Jeez, Seamus, you're right. A party . . .' Sadie sat up, looking from one brother to the next as she considered the prospect. 'A proper Christmas dinner, just as you'll be having at home. Only early.' She grinned, and lay back contentedly, reaching out her foot once again to the ever-accommodating Mick, and sighing happily.

'Well, get a wriggle on,' Seamus demanded, nudging Mick away once again. 'We've got lots to be getting on with, so we have.'

'Lots to be getting on with' involved, not least, convincing Joseph that the end of the week was Monday, and hence making Christmas a Sunday, when Mrs Bradley was off and Joseph spent the day with his mother in Holland Park. This accomplished, they were left with forty-eight hours to raise, buy, trim, and swig, the Christmas spirit, and even with thirteen pairs of hands to hurry them, it was not an easy task. Added to which, Sadie insisted it must be kept a secret. She had had more than her fill of the English approach to parties, and she had no desire to repeat the experience. 'Bloody terrible,' was her only admission when Tommy asked about her first experience of London society, and glancing at the twins, whose existence was irrevocably linked with those nauseous first hours, she shook her head warily. 'There's more than one way of drowning a cat,' she informed them, somewhat ambiguously. This time she was keeping to the Irish way.

But while the Irish way might guard against unforeseen births and men called Humphrey, it did not prove particularly effective when it came to more festive details. Decking the halls, without actually *decking the halls*, is not the easiest of tasks, and despite Sadie's insistence that everything be just as it was at home (excepting, for obvious reasons, the peat fires), the secrecy she swore them to was unrelenting. Drown however many cats you need to, she might have told them, but do it quietly.

Eventually, in a moment of inspiration – or was it desperation – the solution was discovered in that old source of refuge, the bathroom. 'Old' is perhaps too harsh a description, for by no means had its importance lessened, nor its significance as the place of Sadie's escape diminished, but it had, since the birth of the twins, lost something of its appeal. She still spent the odd hour here and there, threading the shells, soaking in the bath, but with the brothers to occupy her time, she was less inclined to be alone. And they were not men to be cooped up in the top of a house. Hence the bathroom, in the last few months, had fallen into relative disuse, no longer a shrine or potential fairy glen, but simply what it was, a bathroom, a room for bathing. Until, that is, Christmas came early.

It was Lar's idea. As chief-decorator he was understandably frustrated by the limitations of invisible tinsel and found his undecked halls increasingly dissatisfying. Did it not make more sense to use rooms in which no one ever went, if they wished to stop this particular no one – or, to be more specific, Joseph – from finding out? And was the bathroom not the ideal solution, both for the previous reason, and for the fact that, due to its role as the birthplace of the twins, it already bore a certain spiritual import? (Or it did for Lar, who, at thirty-two, was still the first in line to audition for the role of the Baby Jesus Lying in a Manger in any and every nativity play.) No, the bathroom was the place. Perfect. Now there was only seating to worry about.

Bathrooms, by their very function, are traditionally not places in which there is ever great call for chairs. The odd footstool for reaching airing cupboards, and the fashion for Lloyd Loom, tend to be the most one can expect; anything more would be an invitation to linger in a place where privacy really is the thing. Necessarily, however, such a lack was more noticeable when it came to thirteen adults sitting down – or not sitting down as the case may be – to Christmas lunch. But then, what did chairs matter, when the only table of any consequence was made of planks laid across the rim of the bathtub, and where might have stood candlesticks, instead rose the taps.

And yet it is the small details which make all the difference, and Sadie was not going to be beaten. She even spent the best part of Wednesday afternoon covering crates she had filched from the yard behind the local greengrocers – helped, of course, by her twelve more-than-merry men –

with festive wrapping paper, and ascribing each with its own name tag, so no confusion should result.

'I'm going to be sitting you here, Seamus, if that's all right with you. And I'm going to be putting wee Seamus by your side.'

'Here' was what might generously be taken to be the head of the table, throne-like with its backdrop of mirror and sink, and offering a commanding view along the length of tissue-covered floorboards. Sadie grinned mischievously.

'And I'm going to be 'specting you to keep an eye on them all, so's there's no messing . . .'

'There'll be no messing.' Seamus took his responsibility seriously, straightening his allocated crate, and frowning imperially. Stashing the boxes of whiskey Sadie's last mission to the off licence had secured, he tucked them beneath his seat. There would indeed be 'no messing'.

There was still, however, a mountain of things to be seen to, not least the meal itself. In suggesting Christmas dinner, Sadie had thought only of the eating, and not so much the actual preparation, but as it became clear that one might not exist without the other, certain other difficulties became apparent. For a start, where did one find a turkey in this rose-gardened, privet-hedged country? At home, it was simply a case of growing one's own, or, if this was not viable, of doing a deal with someone else who had done. The eating was all the more memorable when the bird might be referred to by its first name, its flesh all the more tender when one remembered those early days gadding in the back field. But city turkeys, it seemed, knew no such fondnesses, and the creature Sean eventually laid hands on was trussed and plucked to such an extent, if it had been born with rashers of bacon on its back, he would not have been surprised. Dragging it home – turkeys walked to the table where he came from – Sean contemplated this world of plastic wrapping and bags of giblets and concluded that it was a sorry place that bred birds without feathers.

Such regrets were forgotten, however, when it came to the rest of the meal, which was foraged, so to speak, from the same place as the crates: the back yard of the greengrocers. Vegetables grew in the ground, did they not, so was it not sensible to assume that it was from here that they should be picked? And really, it was a crying shame how much people threw out. And so when three of the brothers crept out at midnight, to return, carrots sprouting from all orifices, sprouts no less obtrusive, it was as much an act of salvation, as it was to save money.

'Charity begins at home!' Devlin announced as he bundled the contents of his pockets on to the kitchen table, conveniently adapting the proverb to suit. 'And if you'll fetch me a drop, I'll show you just how!' And he began to scoop his treasures into their designated pans, topping and tailing as he went, and dismissing his two accomplices with the knife-wielding hand that was later to make him a fighter rather than a fisherman. And when, in the early hours of the morning, he was marching up and down the stairs, pans in hand, to hide them in the bathroom, his well-whiskeyed swagger only added to his missionary zeal.

'Thank God they're leaving,' Joseph muttered to himself as he lay listening to the footsteps back and forth outside the bedroom door. 'Thank God.'

And he slunk deeper into the bedclothes, mumbling ingraciously to himself, for Sadie was not talking to him at the moment, nor, it seemed, had any intention of doing so for some time. Ten thousand men trooped their way through the Hill House, with a majority lingering on the landing, neither up nor down, and he was supposed to feel bad for throwing them out? Not a chance. They were leaving. Thank God.

* * *

And still Christmas was a secret. Even Mrs Bradley, who found herself suddenly bereft of anything vaguely resembling a pan or oven-dish, failed to make the connection. Everything was going like clockwork. The places were set, the forks at the ready. Until, that is, they remembered the tree.

'Shite! The tree.'

Lar had been busy decorating the bathroom; Devlin had been concentrating on the food; Seamus had been in charge of removals; and Paddy had been offering advice. This left the other eight – nine counting Sadie – to their own devices. Devices which, it was assumed, included the tree. For Christmas was just not Christmas without a tree, and it was only when the fact that they did not have one was brought to the attention of one and all, that the first shade of doubt was cast upon their plans. How could they have forgotten the tree? How? How? It was everybody's fault but no one's, and someone else's fault but not theirs. And if everyone, no one, and especially someone, did not think of something soon, then Christmas would, in all likelihood, be gone before it had even arrived.

But it was already Sunday. The turkey had been cooked the night before, and was keeping warm on the radiator, and the pans of vegetables were stacked, ready and waiting, in the makeshift bain-marie of the sink. They were already in their labelled places, the Christmas spirits flowing fast, and not one of them relished going out again. But Sadie was adamant. Things must be just as they would be at home. But where would they find a fifteen-foot fir tree – for this was the only size tradition would allow – at this late hour? And there was no way Sadie was going to settle for last year's offering, a silver plastic replica Lily had proffered, not by any means.

Thirteen thwarted revellers stood around the bath-table and stared at one another. Thirteen weary frowns sank on to thirteen gift-wrapped crates, and cursed their thirteen useless selves. They could not bear to look at one another. They had come so far, and now, this one detail, this one silly tree, had beaten them. Simultaneously, all thirteen scowled, shook their heads, and looked up questioningly towards the ceiling, and, by association, towards heaven. God's help, they had each been taught, God's help is nearer than the door. And thirteen pairs of eyes glanced towards the door. Some help. But as they returned ceiling-wards, an idea began to form. Why should it necessarily be a fir tree? And a leaf tapped quietly against the skylight, as if in agreement. Why not any old tree?

And so any old tree it was. Seamus unfastened the skylight, which had remained fixed tight since the night the twins were born, and grabbed the wrist of the trailing ivy which wove along its edges, pulling it into the room. Using string and brute force they then secured it firmly around one of the taps, and closed over the skylight to hold it in place. Fetching the remains of the tinsel which had been used to decorate the room, and adding to it a variety of milk bottle tops, sweet wrappings, and anything else deemed to be festive, in no time at all they had created their very own Christmas tree. One by one, Sadie lit the multitude of thick white Church candles which were placed at intervals along the wall and floors – Lar never explained where he had found them, and it was better not to ask – and, in the fading light of that wintry afternoon in December, Christmas came to the bathroom at the top of the Hill House.

13

Christmas came, and Christmas went. It devoured the lukewarm turkey, battled over the tepid vegetables, and left a scene of such devastation, it was to take Sadie the better part of the next week even to begin to make sense of it. And then Christmas packed its bags, picked its moment, and marched, single file, out of the door and up the street in the vague direction of Liverpool. Twelve turkey-boned thumbs flew a wavering path alongside, and twenty-four weary feet shuffled a reluctant accompaniment. It was a long way home when all there was for comfort was a fistful of wet salmon, and there are few motorists who would be persuaded by this promise alone that they should offer them a ride. But eventually, two by two, progress was made, and by the time Joseph pulled into the driveway, casting a challenging grimace in the direction of the patchwork lawn, they were nowhere to be seen. Only the baldness of the gravel drive – if taking a stone from a place meant one would return, then they would each have a pocketful – indicated that they had been, and gone, and this Joseph could forgive. After all, it was Christmas.

Sadie however, was less magnanimous. They had left her. Left her. Left her. The words swung in loops back and forth, catching at her like straggling tinsel, and she tugged at them irritably. Such disloyalty. It was bad enough that Joseph should throw them out, but that they should actually *leave* was tantamount to downright betrayal. She really had not thought they would. Early Christmases aside, since when did her brothers do anything that was asked of them, especially when the asker was an Englishman? Since never. Since now.

And then it occurred to Sadie that perhaps they were only pretending to leave, that in fact they were just hiding out for a while somewhere nearby. Their well-established poverty would hardly get them further than the Fiddler's Arms, their favourite haunt of the last month or so, and a couple of frozen salmon would not buy ferry tickets. For once the price of fish could have a lot to do with it. Perhaps they were waiting for Christmas to blow over, for Joseph to enjoy this season of goodwill himself, and then they would return. And the more she thought about it, the more obvious it seemed. Of course they would be back. It was purely a matter of time.

In the course of the following days, Sadie gradually, and begrudgingly, returned the variety of borrowed utensils, washed with facecloth and soap in the upstairs sink, to their rightful places, and Mrs Bradley continued to pretend she had never noticed their absence. The puddles of candlewax were scratched and scrubbed until only a few spatters on the flat of the paintwork, and the odd blue scrape where Sadie had been a little too energetic with the butterknife, remained, and the tinsel was bit by bit returned to its box beneath the stairs. The table was dismantled and the crates stacked beneath the bed in the guest room and, as yet another Christmas wheeled around to greet them, there was nothing but the tree, still fixed to the taps and dressed in silver foil, to suggest it had been pre-empted by another. It was the twenty-first of December.

On the twenty-second of December, Sadie announced she was leaving. Or rather, she packed a suitcase, gathered up the twins, and sat on the front doorstep for two hours, which might easily be interpreted as leaving. At one point she got as far as the gate at the end of the drive, but at the last moment lost her nerve, retreating to the step with the added injury of failure, and it took an unwelcome amount of coercion on the part of Mrs Bradley to ease her back inside. It was the shame of the thing. A shame she could, and would, attribute wholly to her husband's lack of love, and which, in years to come, she would remember more than once in their battles, and often to great effect. But at the time all she gained was a chill, and all she impressed upon the others was that, once again, she had been unreasonable. Whereas in fact Sadie felt she had been unusually restrained.

But whether she was drowning cats, pricing fish, or simply doing her own inimitable thing, Sadie would never be as restrained as Joseph would have wished, and hence she would *always* be unreasonable. And the more she was reminded of this, the more it became force of habit; and the more it became force of habit, the harder it was to admit to. Within a week of the brothers leaving, Sadie was kicking and screaming almost as a matter of routine, and it was to be some years before she might deny this with any conviction. But if others found her behaviour hard to believe, this did not sway the faith of the behaved. Not that first week. Not those first years.

'I'm not being difficult, I'm not.'

Sadie pouted defiantly, wrinkling her eyes and fixing Joseph firmly in his place. Which was in the guest room, he had just discovered. She rested her hand upon the armfuls of clothes she had delivered on to the bed, and straightened a lapel distractedly.

'I'm not.'

Joseph stared at her, agog, and struggled to adjust his understanding of 'difficult' to that which it appeared Sadie held.

'You're not?' It was less accusation than genuine wonder.

'No.'

'Oh.'

'No.' If the brothers had to move out for Christmas, then he could too.

'But it's Christmas Eve, Sadie. There's a time for playing games, and this isn't it. I know you're upset, but it has been almost a week now, and I'm getting tired of it.' He cleared his throat, as if to underline the fact that he was indeed weary, and frowned assertively. Sadie shrugged. This was beyond Christmas, as far as she was concerned. Literally. And with that she turned and drifted out of the room, absent-mindedly kicking a roll of socks she had dropped in her evacuation, and muttering softly about 'difficults' he would really know about. This, it seemed, was only the beginning.

But while Sadie plotted her unreasonability, gathering her strategies, marking her attack, the world around her still kept turning. While she moved beds and burnt bridges, sought one family and lost another, life was set upon a course quite apart from her, and it would take more than the displacement of a sock drawer to revoke this. Christmas, this year or any year, was inevitable, and it did not matter how many times she claimed it had been and gone already, it was to no effect. Lily was on the doorstep, prodigal in her return, the silver plastic tree was in the hall, the best crystal was in the drawing-room, and goodwill was to all men. And there was nothing whatsoever she could do about it.

But it was this latter that really irked Sadie. She could cope with the rest, with the fluff and the fussing, and the general festivities of the thing, but the goodwill to all men? That was a problem. She felt neither good, nor willing, and she was quite through with men. If the brothers had not left, she would not be alone. If Joseph had not thrown them out, they would not have left, and she would not have been alone. If the twins had not been born, then the brothers would not have come, and Joseph could not have thrown them out, and they would not have left ... and she would not be alone. The lament goes on. And so did Sadie. What did it matter if nobody was listening; if even Joseph, ousted to the guest room, was unaffected by her tirades? Deaf ears had never been a source of worry for Sadie, and she just shouted that little bit louder. Christmas, she consoled herself wickedly, remembering the horse fair, had always been a time for braying at donkeys.

And so the season was greeted. And so the season passed. Submerged in toys and turkey, mistletoe and mothers-in-law, Sadie spent the majority of the year-long week sulking loudly, her only indulgence being the twins and a plaited length of giftwrap which she taught them to pin upon the rears of any passing beast. By the thirty-first of December the Hill House was a swirling, squealing chaos of unamused donkeys and heckling blindfolds, and it was with some relief that 1961 was ushered in, that they all might forget their battles and begin anew. Pins were confiscated, protective cushions dropped, Joseph returned to the main bedroom, and Mrs Bradley set about organising the household into unbrothered, post-Christmased, glory. Only Lily failed to observe the ceasefire, dropping her Sadie-directed bombshell less than twenty-four hours into the New Year, but how was she to know it would have such repercussions?

They were having lunch at the time, chewing and chatting blithely in their all-too-recently resolved peacefulness, Sadie reflecting upon the sore heads her brothers invariably complained of at this time of year, Joseph considering the sore rump he had never before suffered. The twins were dribbling gravy and watching the windows for passing uncles, and Lily was telling all who cared to listen how glad she was to be back.

'Besides which,' she concluded, 'Rose is moving to Cheltenham at the end of the month, so I could hardly have stayed there much longer anyway. So from now on you're stuck with me!' She smiled self-effacingly, the cracks in her blackcurrant lips all the more pronounced. 'You'll just have to put up with old Lily.'

Lily raised an eye at Sadie and leant across the table for an ashtray, while Joseph embarked upon a profuse and predictable celebration of such good news. It might have been the cigarette smoke, or perhaps even a piece of gristle, which caught in Sadie's throat and sent her running from the room only seconds into Joseph's speech . . . or it might have been the frightening fact of Lily's permanence. But whatever it was, she was not seen again either that day, or for several days afterwards, and even when Joseph opened all the windows and had Mrs Bradley make only salads for the next week, she refused to return. She simply lay around in her bathroom, a squall of nausea, and no matter how insistent Joseph was that it was psychosomatic, the heaving and flushing that went on late into the night would not be told. Eventually, spurred on by the memory of the last time she had run that familiar path from bed to bathroom, mixing-bowl to toilet-bowl, the source, if not the provocation, was revealed. Sadie was pregnant. Despite all her plans to follow her brothers, to punish Joseph, to recruit the twins, and to hell with Lily, Sadie was pregnant. Just when she might be about to set herself free, nature, or Fate, or simply bad timing, reminded her otherwise.

'But it's wonderful news, Sadie! How on earth can you be sad about something like this?'

'I'm not sad . . .' Raising her chin from the floor just enough to make herself heard, Sadie resented such presumptions. She was indeed not sad. She was angry.

'It will be perfect for the twins, a younger brother or

sister. It's important they should learn how to share and interact, and that they should know their mother is not there for them alone.'

Sadie hissed. This was typical of Joseph. Not a clue. They were twins, for heaven's sake! Of course they knew about sharing. And why should they think she was there for them alone? She certainly had not told them so.

'Jeez, Joseph, I'm not sad, all right!' she exclaimed, two smudging tears coursing her cheeks.

'All right, you're not sad.' He waved his arms dismissively. 'You're not sad. End of story. I won't say another word. But at least smile, Sadie, please.'

The snarl she then treated him to was rebuke enough, and he left her alone for what was the fifth or sixth time that week, considering that at least she was predictable when it came to pregnancy. Another few months, he was sure, and everything would be back to normal.

Had he been any less insightful, he would have been completely in the dark. When he suggested Sadie write to her family to tell them the good news, he was quite taken aback by the flood of abuse which met him; and when he asked her if she'd like to leave the twins with Lily and go away for a few days, just the two of them, he genuinely thought she would be pleased. But Sadie was reeling off the walls at that particular time, and the thought of any involvement with the outside world left her cold. She wanted to curl up into a ball and roll away to some lonely corner, until such an inevitable time as they would roll her out again, swollen-bellied and sore, and she could get this over with and go back to being herself. For if her brothers had taught her one thing, it was that freedom is something to be taken, not owed; swallowed, not thirsted for. But right now it was slipping further and further from her grasp.

And so the months of Sadie's second pregnancy were spent largely in a state of prolonged remorse. All her old cravings and foibles returned, and in the case of the salt, many times worse, but the novelty was somewhat diminished, and it became more of a trial than an adventure. This time, rather than revelling in the changes her body underwent, she resented them, and it took more than a few rolls of toilet paper and a stamp collection to make light of this one. Added to which, the twins, missing all the attention they had enjoyed during their uncles' visit, and no doubt picking up on some of Sadie's bad temper, became increasingly difficult to please, and even Mrs Bradley would lose patience, when before she had been so calm. It was a fraught time. And if the immediate concerns of swollen ankles and swelling body parts weren't enough in themselves, then Lily's permanent presence – dearly beloved Lily, whom they had well and truly received – was. It was time to retreat . . .

But if Sadie was intending to retreat to her bathroom, then she was to be disappointed. Inspired by her period of absence, Lily had returned to the Hill House with renewed determination, and her first priority was to clear out the clutter which had accumulated since Sadie's arrival, and assert a little order in the place. Armed with a roll of bin liners and a mop, she stormed the bastion of Sadie's most treasured possessions, and proceeded to shovel and discard with a vehemence that went far beyond the domestic. By the time Sadie awoke at lunchtime the same day, her sleeping habits having become as irrational as her moods, the bathroom was a gleaming void of tiled and enamelled glory, with only a few grains of sand and a couple of shells, too deeply embedded for even Lily's grazing claws to disturb, to mark its former state.

Four bulging black bags stood guard outside the door, and a single, paler one inside, hands on hips, to greet her. And Sadie was beaten, dissolving on to the floor in a heap of unspoken devastations, and unable even to begin to count her loss. When she saw that Lily had also attacked the ivy which laced the one window in the house excused from function; the one window whose view – a knotted green of leaves and stems, through which only the most persistent sun might break – was not bent and manipulated to suit those who looked upon it; when she saw the pile of severed limbs dropped by Lily's avenging secateurs, Sadie knew it was all over. Any hope of restoration, any dreams of new life, were thrown out in the same bag as the now poisoned ivy.

How the tidying of one room could have such dire consequences Joseph would never understand, but when he returned from work that evening to find Sadie huddled half naked in an empty bath, the twins balanced aside either tap, Hot and Cold, and a split bin liner of rescued shells spewing on the floor, he had to acknowledge that it did. His obvious delight at the retrieval of his prized stamps – Lily, it seemed, had been discriminating in her disposals – hardly helped matters, and his attempts to communicate the recklessness of Sadie's behaviour in terms of her 'condition' were received just as badly. When he then pulled rank and asserted his rights as the father of this unborn child, overlooking for the immediate time the more noticeable risk the soap-dished cradles of the twins threatened, Sadie had taken almost more than she could bear. Speaking very slowly, enunciating each word with a carefulness Joseph had not heard in her before, she levered herself up until her head was several inches above the rim of the bath, and looked him directly in the eye.

'Joseph,' she began, in a tone that was almost apologetic, 'Joseph, you're a lovely man, sure, a lovely man, but if . . .' and here she stumbled, a hand rising to her brow as if fearful of her own thoughts, 'but if you don't go away right this minute, and leave me alone, I'm going to scream so loud they'll hear me above the fires of Hell, so they will. I don't want to hear what you're saying, and if you persist in standing there, gabbing at me, you'll be sorry for it, as sure as I'm lying here, you will.' Still whispering, still calculating every syllable, she continued, 'So, if it'll please you, Joseph, lovely man and all, take yourself out of my bathroom and let me be by myself, for if you don't, I'm going to be throwing you out, sure I will.'

Her eyes the colour of overripe plums, heavy and dull, and her skin almost translucent against the scrubbed white of the bath, Sadie had never seemed so fragile. And although Joseph doubted she could barely have thrown herself from the room, much less him, he waived the point and left her without a murmur. He did not hear her when she eventually crept downstairs in the early hours of the morning, depositing the twins in their cot, and climbing noiselessly into bed beside him, but when he woke the next day to find her stretched, ghostly still, along the edge of the mattress, he sensed that something had changed. Where before she had curled, childlike, about herself, now she was stiff; where before she had risen, now she lay cold and bare.

For several days Sadie did not speak, communicating only by means of her shaking head, and pushing away any uninvited advances with the flat-handed inflexibility of a slammed door. Flanked by the twins, her assumed and willing allies, she drifted from room to room, disappearing as soon as anyone else entered, and refusing any moves towards conciliation, be it a more comfortable chair, or, at Joseph's instigation, her mother-in-law's begrudging apology. The slowly expanding edges of her silhouette, as the months of her pregnancy began to show, did little to soften the unwavering rigidity which had come to fix her every move, and even the invariable flush which accompanied this was dimmed. The light had gone out of Sadie, leaving only a dull glow in its place, and the whistling draught which had extinguished it seemed to be growing louder and more forceful by the day.

She did a lot of thinking during this time, perhaps more than she had indulged in in her lifetime, and there was not a corner of her existence, nor a crack in her memory, which was not emptied out and reconsidered. Unfortunately, as is often the case in such savage explorations, there were a number of casualties, and at the top of the list, predictably, was Lily. This was by no means revelatory, and in the shadow of recent events, nor was it incomprehensible, but it did offer an interesting perspective upon those characters ranking a little lower. Most prominent, and perhaps most provoking of these, was God: not any old god, or even this here god, but God-with-a-capital-G, and all the upper cases which surround Him. Such was the nature of Sadie's upbringing, never before had she even wondered at the gaping questions which now haunted her, and it was, ironically, only the very need for sureness which led her to do so now. For Sadie was bemused: in a matter of weeks she had been thrown from paradise into hell; cast out of the promised land she had so lovingly created in her bathroom, and exiled into a wilderness where even curses were invalid – Sadie had never forgotten that Joseph had sworn upon his mother's grave, but reckoning seemed a long time in coming. Added to which her twelve disciples had disappeared into thin air, and her own sacred person was becoming more earthbound by the day. No, if there was a God, then He was working in far too far a mysterious way for Sadie's liking, and it occurred to her that she might just get along better on her own. She thus decided to concentrate upon the more Pagan rites of survival for the present time, if she had not all along, and God was temporarily relegated to the role of general irritant and Lily-baiter. As far as Sadie was concerned, heaven was back up the stairs, first door on the right, and knock before you enter. Her bathroom.

The determination with which Sadie set about restoring this hallowed place was a testament to both her single-mindedness and to the ingrained, and typically Irish, ability to overcome oppression, and then live alongside. The single sack of shells which had lain torn upon the bathroom floor was emptied and rearranged, each salvaged coral counted and revered, and then thrown carelessly to the floor where she liked them best. The shards of glass and mirror so efficiently disposed of had been replaced by one full length tile, taken from the inside of Lily's wardrobe, and under no circumstances to be reclaimed. The stamps were back in place, despite Joseph's protests, and the ivy was being coaxed to grow back. The door was diligently locked, whether Sadie was inside or out, and the key kept, with the crucifix, on a chain around her neck. Nobody, but nobody, was allowed in.

The enforced solitude of Sadie's worship, however, was short-lived, and within a week of her bathroom's resurrection, she had included the twins in her small but honoured circle and discovered that three was a notable improvement. She would climb into her bath, empty or full depending upon her mood, Seamus on one side, Joseph on the other, her belly an island in between, and regale them with a whole history of dreams and myths such as she had forgotten she even knew. She told them of the mermaids which lived beneath the sea, who would tempt fishermen to marry them, and then leave them to drown; she recounted the tale of the man who fell in love with a seal, and had three children by her, all of whom swam away on their tenth birthday. She repeated the story of her own brother, Lar, to be sure, who had got lost one night on his way home from the pub, and would swear to this day that it was a leprechaun that turned him around and kicked him into touch. She told them as much as she might remember, and more besides, and in those early months of this threefold blossoming, a whole heritage was created around which they might grow.

''Cause you'll never forget where you're going so long as you remember where you came from, sure you won't,' she would whisper to them, conspiratorially. 'And you'll never forget where you are coming from so long as you listen to your mammy, and that's the truth.'

But the twins were not the only ones destined to receive the wealth of Sadie's wisdom. As the weeks passed, she relented from her adopted silences, and began to look once more at the world around her with something other than an angry glare. She even agreed to join the family for mealtimes, thus reneging on what she knew to be one of her surest means of provoking Joseph. This did not necessarily imply she took part in those rituals with anything of the enthusiasm which might have been hoped for, but that she was there, however protesting, was enough. And with her newfound self-righteousness in all matters concerning Lily, martyrdom being a particularly effective instrument in battles of conscience, it certainly made for entertainment.

'May the Lord make us truly thankful, Amen.'

Lily lowered her eyes with prayerbook piety, and held her breath as her devotion winged its way above the heads of her listeners. Fingers laced, concentration knit, even young Seamus and Joseph, crammed into highchairs at the other end of the table, were suitably impressed. Sadie, timing the ceremony by the clock above her head, glanced about her with sugared eyes, and demanded sweetly:

'And what are we thanking your God for, Lily, will you tell?'

One hand crested upon the mound of her stomach, the other held spear-pointed in front of her, elbow-deep in cutlery – Lily refused to consider eating without an army of different forks to mark her advance – Sadie was the picture of innocence.

'I beg your pardon?'

'Oh, you don't want to beg, I was only asking, I was. It just seems we're thanking him for something, and I'm wondering what it is. What d'you think?' She smiled, twisting the key around her neck with coy deliberation. 'After all,' she purred, 'He's your God, to be sure.'

Lily stared straight ahead, the only visible effect of Sadie's challenge distinguishable in the growing pallor which had washed Lily's already bleached features, and which promised to extend itself to the room at large if someone did not intervene. And, as usual, someone was Joseph.

'Don't be obtuse, Sadie.'

'Oh, Joseph, lovely man Joseph, I assure you I wasn't being that. Would that be how it's sounding, would it? No, well I was only wondering, that's all, seeing as Lily and me, we have these different gods, so we do . . .'

'Sadie.' More insistent this time, less conciliatory.

'Sure, Joseph, what is it you're wanting?'

'Sadie . . .' With as much warning as he might conceivably imply in five letters, Joseph leant across the table towards her and lowered his voice to a whisper. 'Just leave it and let's eat.' And, turning to Mrs Bradley, busying herself with the twins at the far end of the table, 'It all smells delicious.'

And of course Sadie shrugged, quite happy to do just that. She had made her point, what had become an ongoing and ever-lengthening point, that she neither cared for nor feared the bullying domination of her mother-in-law, or her God, and she had nothing more to say. Until the next opportunity, that is.

It was in the midst of such holy rebellion that Sadie first had the dream. She had started going to bed earlier and earlier, taking her bath with the twins mid-afternoon, and then rarely outlasting their own nightly curfew, which was around six. It was a rare occasion that she was still awake when Joseph got home from work just after eight, and if she was, a grunt and a yawn tended to be the limit of her welcome. Hence, with the exception of the hours of story-telling, the balance of Sadie's energies had largely been tipped towards sleep, and the living that she would normally undergo in the course of the day, shifted to the darker sphere of dreams. Was it then surprising that they should result in the colourful creations they did?

'Jeez!' she would exclaim to Joseph upon waking, stabbing her forefinger into one of the many bowls of salt which had started to reappear. 'I had the queerest dream ever, last night, and if I could only rightly remember it, I'd tell you, so I would.'

Joseph would nod, blearily, having had the benefit of her dreaming most of the night, and the bruises to prove it. 'You should write a book about them, Sadie, for they certainly seem fascinating.'

'Sure, they are, Joseph. And I would, if only I could remember . . .'

But there was one dream in particular, and which would often recur several nights running, the details of which were always crystal clear. It was a dream in which all twelve of her brothers, wearing priest's robes and drinking stout, appeared to her from behind some London landmark, such as Nelson's Column or the House of Lords, and demanded to know why she was not in Confession. In the background of such scenes, she could just make out the sound of bells ringing, and although this often proved upon waking to be Joseph's alarm clock, it did not diminish the significance. She was being called, she was certain of it; only the authority which directed her this time, and she regarded her recent conversion as absolute proof of this, was of human distinction. It was, according to Sadie's interpretation, a definite sign that her brothers were still in London, as she had expected, the clerical dress and allusions to church just a little decoration on the side. Years later she would learn just how unlucky it was deemed to dream of priests, a dozen of them at that, but at the time she was blessed in her ignorance. There was superstition enough.

'I'm wondering,' she began one morning, having devoted the majority of her sleeping hours to chasing Sean and Lar across Tower Bridge, their surplices flailing in the wind like old men's beards, 'I'm wondering if, bejeezus and it could be true, if my brothers never left, God help them, and they're still here, they are.'

She stared at Joseph expectantly. He shook his head.

'No, Sadie. They're back in Ireland, I assure you.'

'But how d'you know, Joseph, will you tell me that? How, in sweet Jesus, do you know?' Eyebrows rising with beetled ferocity, Sadie was already convinced of her greater instinctive power, and as Joseph attempted once more to 'assure' her, she heaped herself away to the twins' room, where she found the reception considerably warmer. And, of course, Joseph knew because he had bought the very tickets, all twelve of them, which confirmed such departure, but there was no way he was going to be telling Sadie that. She blamed him enough as it was.

Eight months pregnant, there was little Sadie could do about finding her brothers for the conceivable future, but this did not prevent her making a series of extravagant, and ultimately inadvisable, plans. With the help of a map, and several rolls of Mrs Bradley's greaseproof paper, she divided the city into bite-sized pieces, detailing the relevant bus routes and landmarks her brothers might frequent, and then put all the scraps of tracing into Joseph's deerstalker hat, and offered them around.

'Many hands make light work, so they do,' she declared, thrusting the confettied brim towards her mother-in-law, and whispering, 'and many heads are even better, so help me it's true.'

But Lily had better things to do with her innumerable assets, and, frowning several frowns, she brushed her away. Mrs Bradley and Joseph were no less amenable, and Sadie was left to reassemble the jigsawed map of her brothers' displacement herself.

'But I'll find them, never you worry,' she muttered from her look-out at the end of the street, 'as soon as I get rid of this lump, I'll be fetching them home to me, that I will, and the hell's with your doubting then.'

The impending birth was thus awaited with impatience, and as the weeks of her pregnancy finally tipped to their conclusion, Sadie became all the more anxious to be free. Her frustration, expressed in the copious amounts of salt she was consuming and the almost blistering temperature of her baths, was regarded as yet another symptom of pre-natal neuroses, and dismissed to the same bone-filled cupboard as her locked bathroom and born-again brothers. And her portentous dreams were sent pretty much the same way. With the exception of the twins, it was generally agreed that Sadie was suffering the delusional effects of physical exhaustion, and when, a week before she was due to deliver, she put herself to bed and refused to get up, nobody disputed the wisdom of this.

'Sleep, and lots of it, is what she needs,' Joseph advised, flicking through his Medical Journal with practised efficiency, 'and she'll be absolutely fine when the child arrives.'

'And let's just hope it's a girl, and only one of them,' added Lily, somewhat disappointed by the development of her grandsons, whose loyalty to their mother was not their most endearing feature. 'A bit of common sense is what this house is in need of, and a little girl would do that nicely.'

Sadie, however, had no intention of bringing forth anything, male or female, to which 'nicely' might be attached, and as she gave herself up to her prescribed week of sleep, she prided herself upon the genetic unlikelihood. With twelve drunken priests in the family – she had decided to allow this imaginative conceit to remain, always enjoying a touch of purple in her dreams – the dubious character of any future offspring was surely a mere formality. As she gaily informed the twins, 'A wild goose won't be layin' a tame egg, to be sure, no matter the gander,' and their subsequent cackling seemed only to confirm this.

14

Elisabeth's arrival was thus something of a surprise. Punctual to the hour, she was born barely ten minutes after Sadie's first contraction, and it was an irritable and rudely awakened mother, still half-asleep and grappling with the bedclothes, that met her.

'He was just about to tell me where he was stopping, the devil he was,' she complained bitterly to the ecstatic Joseph, rubbing her eyes, and looking around her at the shadowy room. 'If I finds all eleven, I shall never catch Tommy now, for he's a slippery fish when he thinks you're not hearing him, holy Mother in Heaven, he is.'

Joseph grinned amiably, ignoring her crumpling scowl. 'I don't think it's such a bad exchange,' he encouraged, and he pushed the neatly wrapped bundle of her daughter towards her. Sadie shrugged, opening her arms and taking the child, but as she looked down upon her, a fading frown her begrudging welcome, she was inclined to disagree. For the face which gazed back at her, alert and somewhat blue, could not have been less reassuring if it had had horns and a long forked tail. Sadie crossed herself quickly, forgetful of her alleged agnosticism, and reached for her coral crucifix, twisted around the back of her neck, only to find the bathroom key instead.

'Jesus, Mary and Joseph,' she shuddered, 'It's your bleedin' mammy, so it is.'

'Sadie!' Joseph exclaimed, horrified as much by her language as her apparent rejection.

'I'm sorry, sure I am,' she muttered, although it was not clear whether it was her language or her daughter she regretted. 'So help me God, I'm sorry.'

The child continued to stare straight ahead, unperturbed by her mother's ill-concealed distress, and when Sadie hurriedly handed her back to her father, she was no less agreeable. Indeed, during these first few days, passed around from pillar to post, as Sadie struggled with all manner of ghosts, living and dead, she barely even flickered. Politeness itself, Elisabeth was her grandmother from the top of her widow's peak to the tip of her toes, and she was hardly going to spoil herself with bad temper. Like Lily before her, she would allow life to do that.

It took several weeks, and a considerable amount of counselling from Joseph, for Sadie to accept the anomaly that was her daughter, and even then she was often to be found hovering in some dark corner, debating the matter. It was not that she was being deliberately difficult, although there were those who thought otherwise, but rather that the turn of events had somewhat thrown her. So used was she to the familiar heather-eyes and red-hair which had patterned every rung of her descent, with even the variety of illegitimate offspring her brothers had unknowingly fathered unable to stay anonymous for long, it was inconceivable to her that she should deliver such a creature. With Elisabeth's flushed pink skin and black hair, her brown eyes and snubbing nose, she was everything her mother was not. And added to which, as indeed her grandmother had predicted, she was niceness personified.

'Jeez, if that child smiles at me one more time, I swear it, I'll weep, so I will,' Sadie would lament, longing for even the faintest of tantrums. 'Surely to the Sacred Heart, she has to give it up soon.'

'It's wind, darling,' Joseph would encourage from behind his newspaper, determined not to rise to her. 'If you'd rather, I'll ask my mother to watch her for a while. You're clearly in no state to.'

Hence the conflict of Sadie's state and Elisabeth's needs came to be, with Joseph a willing accomplice and Lily only too happy to play along too. And before anyone might think to dispute it, the new arrival had been swept out of her mother's reluctant grip and into that of the next generation up.

Thus excused, Sadie could return to the scheme from which she had been so inconveniently distracted: the location of her brothers. Since the birth of Elisabeth her dreams had been worryingly less precise, a fact she put down – in true Joseph-style – to nerves, and when she set off on that crisp April morning, it did not enter her head that she might be wasting her time. Joseph's deerstalker flapping about her ears, a map of Battersea tattooed upon her mind, she was set upon a quest, which, much as in her search for the Little People, would not be given up lightly. 'End of the line,' she declared, leaping aboard the bus, 'and no stopping!'

Had it occurred to her, a letter home to Ireland might have resolved the matter of her brothers' whereabouts far more efficiently than Sadie's more convoluted course, but that had been Joseph's suggestion and as such it was invalid from the start. Besides, where would the fun be in that? And fun, it must be said, was Sadie's prime motivation.

'Now where'll I be starting?' she mused, tripping down the steps of the bus and on to the street, waving to the driver and doing her best to avoid the army of tartan shopping trolleys swarming about her feet. 'Where'll they be hiding at this time of the morning?'

To her left stood Battersea Bridge, gaping and bored, beneath which the Thames churned its lethargic brown body relentlessly on; and over to her right, the power station she recognised from her dream. Sadie hovered between the two, eventually opting for the latter, with its four mast-like grey chimneys, as much because that was the direction everyone else seemed to be taking as through any stroke of premonition. Terraces of mottled brown and red brick snaked off to either side, and every so often one of the troop would split from the pack and disappear into the net-curtained, orange swirled, reaches beyond, until only Sadie and a broad-shouldered man in an army jacket remained. When he too broke away, crossing the road and turning into an adjacent street, she hurriedly followed him, slicing between the parked cars which lined the pavements, and narrowly avoiding an ill-placed lamppost. When she reached the corner where he had turned, however, he was nowhere to be seen. Vanished. Sadie bent down and peered along the kerb, searching for the clunking hob-nailed soles she had followed so diligently, but there was only a riddle of tyre marks and an empty crisp packet, and not a sign of the accompanying legs and jacket. One minute he was there, the next gone. Had there been a likelihood of shamrocks growing in the immediate vicinity, Sadie might not have been so puzzled, but the regrettable dearth of such leprechaun camouflage was well established, and she was forced to search for more human forms of retreat. She looked around her. A bus stop. A dry cleaners. And a pub. As before, she chose the latter. Where better to start a search for her brothers than in here?

Sadie had never been inside a public house before, except as a very young child sent to fetch the men for their tea, and she hesitated for some minutes as she considered her mother's regard for such places. 'Godforsaken dumps, mind what I'm telling you,' she had warned almost daily, flicking a cursory finger in the direction of twelve fleeting backs – thirteen while their father was alive – 'Godforsaken, so they are.'

'But, sweet Jesus,' Sadie shrugged, glancing at the frosted windows above her head, 'is there anywhere that's not?' And brushing the answering picture of Lily and the Hill House far from her mind, she took a deep breath and hastened inside.

As her eyes adjusted to the dim, she glanced about her. The room was smokily dark, with long, low ceilings stained yellow, and walls the texture of bruised peaches. Everywhere she looked, heads were downcast, fixed upon the staring pupils of half-empty glasses, and the conversation rumbled without pause, unnoticing of her arrival. The man she had followed was standing with his back to her at the bar, his arm resting across the shoulder of a younger, stockily-built woman, and as Sadie watched them, they laughed and moved closer together. Music was blasting from a loudspeaker in the corner, and three teenage boys huddled around an ashtray by the fire. Sadie frowned: nowhere, nowhere, could she see her brothers.

She was about to turn around and go out again, when a voice behind her declared, 'What'll you be having, love?'

Sadie spun round, the strings of her hat swinging like the ribbons on a maypole, to find a red-faced woman standing behind her, empty pint glasses dangling from every finger, eyebrows raised. 'Ain't seen you in here before, have we then?'

Sadie followed her as she pushed her way back towards the bar, dropping the glasses on the wood with a rattle, and ducking beneath. 'Have we?' she repeated. Sadie shook her head. 'Well, I always say it's nice to get a new face, I do, don't I Fred?' and she jabbed her elbow into the stomach of a grey-haired man at her side. 'Specially such a pretty one as yours.'

Sadie blushed, her pioneering bravado fading with every second. The woman leant forwards, until the veins of her cheeks glowed luminescent beneath the lights of the bar, inches from Sadie's face. 'So what'll it be?'

'Actually, I was . . .' Sadie cleared her throat as the woman strained to hear above the blare of the music, 'I was looking for me brothers, so I was.'

'Brudders? What're you on about? Say, you're not Irish are you?'

Sadie nodded.

'You're *Oirish*!' her listener repeated, banging her fist hard upon the shelf in front. 'That'll be explaining . . . You want to meet Fred, he's *Oirish* too!' And once again Fred got an elbow in his ribs, as he was pushed towards Sadie's wavering figure.

Fred winked, and reached for a glass from the rack above his head. Whether or not he was Irish Sadie never discovered, for he simply nodded her towards the fire and gestured she sit down. She did as she was told – or at least, as she was nodded – and positioned herself upon a tapestried stool, her bag swinging between her legs, her eyes wide. Minutes later 'Fred' joined her, pressing a tumbler into her hand and winking once again, before shuffling back to the bar and returning to whatever it was he had been doing before.

'On the house,' a voice shrieked from the other side of the room, and when Sadie strained to see who had spoken, the woman with the elbows waved yet another fistful of pint-glasses. 'Seeing as you're new, and that.'

Sadie smiled, and waved back. New. She liked the idea of that. Since Elisabeth had been born she had been feeling decidedly old, ancient almost, and the novelty of being a stranger had dwindled to the insignificance of simply being estranged. But all of a sudden, it seemed she might be 'new' again . . . Yes, she liked that. She liked that a lot.

Taking a mouthful of her drink, Sadie watched the faces and feet of her companions mull back and forth, as doors opened, and stools were seized. Pooling the amber liquid –

'smooth, with a hint of heather' came to mind – she felt curiously peaceful, the rumble of lunchtime voices and the chinking of repeated cheers the closest she had come to sanctuary since her bathroom had been a grotto and the world had been light. She sank back against the stone of the fireplace, tucking her feet beneath the stool, and sighing softly. In the haze before her she saw the man she had trailed earlier lift a thumb from the shoulder of his woman friend and grin; and in the depths of the glass-mountained bar another wink slipped silently from the cracks of Fred's twitching regard. She had not felt so welcome since . . . Sadie gazed at her swilling fingers, curled around the glass, and considered. She had not felt so welcome.

She did not finish her drink, eventually abandoning it to the perch of the mantelpiece and scurrying a retreat just as the bell above the bar began to ring. Loath to leave, but knowing better than to be caught in such places, such *godfersaken* places, when Church is in, she dared not linger after the first toll, and as she meandered back along the nameless streets to where she hoped she would find a bus, she was reassured by the genuine piety of the thing. In those few solitary hours, while she had failed to trace her brothers, she had discovered a certain togetherness, a certain congregation, which as yet England had not shown her. The ringing of the bell seemed only confirmation of this. Whichever god it tolled for. And as Sadie ran to catch a hesitant bus she saw waiting at the traffic lights, she knew it was only a matter of time. The signs were there, and somewhere, somehow, so were her brothers.

It took an age for the bus to crawl the long, traffic-clogged way back across the bridge and towards home, and by the time Sadie staggered across the drive of the Hill House, her head was pounding and her legs felt weak. The 'hint of heather' had got her again. She flung herself up the stairs, oblivious to Lily's glaring demands of 'What time do you call this, young lady?' and 'Oh, so you're here are you?' and immediately began to run a bath. Wrenching off her coat and dress, along with Joseph's hat, which she kicked towards the door, she sunk herself into the steaming water, closed her eyes, and promptly fell asleep.

Her next attempt, a week later, was closer to home, the 'lucky dip' approach having been put to one side for the moment, in favour of 'Better the fireside you know', and she was considerably more hopeful. After all, would not her brothers too keep to the place they knew? But while the experience was no less pleasurable, the welcome no less warm – most thought she must simply be waiting for someone, so plied the trade – and the solution to 'What'll it be?' notably easier, her questions were received with no more success than before. Twelve red-haired Irishmen were not something one forgot, and the certainty with which heads were shaken in all three of the bars Sadie visited that day was disillusioning to say the least. Yet she would not give up, and in the course of the next few months she covered the ground from Maida Vale to Mile End with disciplined persistence. 'I'm looking for something,' she would announce upon ordering her single Jameson's, and if she no longer insisted that this 'something' was her brothers, her search was no less poignant.

In time Sadie's quest was to narrow considerably, the list of possible hide-outs shrinking to a couple of places in nearby Belsize Park, and the Fiddler's Arms at the top of the hill. She no longer silenced the bar with her interrogations, nor threw herself upon unsuspecting redheads in the hope that they might be family, and instead she began to look upon her visits as purely part of her weekly routine. Along with her baths, of course, her hours with the twins spinning tales, and her brief but frequently traumatic involvements with Elisabeth. Which was another mission altogether. For even if the progressive-thinking Joseph could forgive Sadie her afternoons of freedom, her daughter, under the vigilant direction of Lily, could not, and it was thus Sadie had her second lesson in what it was her mother had forgotten to tell her: a daughter, when she knows herself to be one, is trouble.

'If,' Lily pronounced, as Sadie crept through the front door one Wednesday evening, the word ringing from her lips like a death toll, 'if you spent as much time with your daughter,' she paused, 'your daughter, Elisabeth, as you do going out ...' another pause, during which it was hoped Sadie might fill in where 'out' might be, '... then everyone would be better off.'

Sadie closed the door quietly behind her.

'And if ...' Lily began again, but her daughter-in-law's raised hand silenced her momentarily, and she held fire, chin hoisted defensively, as she awaited her excuse. Sadie, however, only wanted her to be quiet, and had no intention of further discussion, and she slowly began to remove her shoes, intending to go straight to bed. Lily bristled. 'And if ...' But once again she was silenced as a thud at the top of the stairs announced the arrival of her grandson Seamus, head first, down the stairs, hands working like brakes in front of him as he hurtled towards the rug. Lily stood back, the clause to her second 'If' realigning itself no less speedily. 'And if you were at home with your sons, instead of gallivanting, then they might have a better idea of how to behave!'

Sadie raised her head, considering the unlikelihood that she might teach her sons anything Lily would approve of, just as Joe, never far away from his twin, appeared from the back garden, a flurry of leaves and mud skittering in his wake.

'Jeez, will you look at the pair of you,' Sadie laughed, holding out her hands as they slithered towards her.

'Will you look at yourself!' Lily demanded, refusing to be ignored.

Picking the foliage from the creases of Joseph's knitted suit, Sadie leant against the door and pulled the twins close, pointing as one by one the leaves were carried off on the edge of draught which slipped beneath the mat. 'Will she look at herself, I wonder now,' she murmured, and two pairs of eyes blinked at her in a wonder of their own. 'Will she never.'

Sadie hauled herself to her feet, a hand upon each of their wise heads for leverage, and smiled sweetly at her aggressor. 'This daughter of mine,' she began, 'and where might she be, in this hour of need you're thinking she's suffering?'

Without another word Lily strode off towards the kitchen, and Sadie, assuming that to be the end of it, began to climb the stairs. But Lily was back almost immediately, Elisabeth tipped against her shoulder, and Sadie reluctantly halted where she stood and waited for them to join her.

'Oh, I can see she's suffering something terrible, I can,' Sadie observed, Elisabeth's smiling face now parallel with her own. And she bent towards the child, affecting a closer look. As she did so, however, Elisabeth opened her mouth and began to scream, her mother's Jamesoned breath (or could it have been Lily's pinching fingers?) clearly a source of great pain. Sadie stared, perplexed, at the wrinkling, angry face of her daughter, and bent closer still.

'Now do you see?' Lily demanded, triumphantly, 'Now do you understand what your behaviour is doing to your children?'

'Holy Mother in Heaven, my behaviour? I've been out, one afternoon in I don't know how many that I stay in, and it's behaviour? Jeez, woman, you don't know the meaning of the word, sure you don't.'

'I know,' Lily announced, into her stride now, 'I know it means neglecting your children while you drink yourself into a stupor.' She stiffened, her hand to Elisabeth's head, as

Sadie stepped forward with not a little menace. The twins, still fixed upon the mat, looked on in delight.

'Stupor?' Sadie growled. 'I've had two drinks, that's all. I'll show you stewporrr . . .' She pushed the word through her teeth like grit through a sieve. 'I'll show you what I mean by—'

'I've seen it all already, Sadie,' Lily retorted, smugly, and began to descend the stairs, Elisabeth all the while shrieking.

'So help me God, you've seen nothing!' And Sadie turned around, thundering after her, 'Nothing I'm telling you.'

Grabbing her shoes which lay unlaced by the door, Sadie nudged the twins aside, and, slamming the door behind her, swept out of the house. She ran down the drive, across the garden, over the hedge, along the pavement, and up the hill to the Fiddler's Arms, all the time her shoes dangling from her fingers like useless puppets.

When she reached the Fiddler's Arms, however, Sadie stopped. The windows of the pub were bathed in light, and she could see dark shadows moving back and forth inside, trays of swilling glasses held aloft like flaming torches. The low rumble of afternoon conversations had been replaced by a higher pitched, more constant, squall: how could she, Sadie, become a part of that? She hugged her coat about her, edging from one foot to the other, and shivered in the chill night air. It looked so different in daylight. She could slip unnoticed through the side door, tuck herself into a quiet corner with her drink, and simply look on; listen. She didn't even need to talk to anyone, for watching was company enough, and so long as she had her not-quite-empty glass, they left her alone. Sadie sat down upon the edge of the kerb and dropped her head in her hands. She had said she would show Lily, but what would she show her?

The door behind her opened gratingly, unleashing a rush of music-laden din which wrapped itself around Sadie's crouching form. She shivered. The Hill House, for all its hostilities, was better than sitting here. Or, at least, in places it was. She should go back. Slowly, deliberately, she began to pull at the laces of her shoes, knotting tight bows around her fingers and thumb, before tucking them, left to the left, right to the right, into the pockets of her coat. Standing up, she then began to walk back down the hill, her toes pale blue in the moonlight, the gentle slapping of her soles upon the tarmac her only companion. Defeated? She shook her head. Merely a temporary retreat.

Joseph's car was in the drive when she reached the house, and so she skirted around the side, through the garden, and entered by the back door. The kitchen was in darkness, but Sadie knew where she was going, and she quickly felt her way towards the back cupboard, where the keys were hung, vine-like, beneath the shelf. Fumbling until she found the spidery thread of the one to the cellar, she clutched it in the ball of her fist, and edged noiselessly into the hallway, feeling along the wall for the smooth panel of the door. Without another thought, she unlocked it and let herself through and down the steps. There was a light, but she ignored it, waiting instead for her eyes to adjust, and as she lay herself back against the yielding stairs, smudging into the shadows, she felt somehow reprieved. Sufficiently so to justify the full bottle of whiskey she then wriggled from its horizontal perch above her head, and into which she poured the well of her troubles until late that night.

Sadie's retreats underground became, after that evening, her salvation. Relatively sporadic, and generally traceable directly to Lily, she might flee here whenever the screams in her head threatened too loudly, whenever the space that she had carved for herself began to pinch. She discovered a silence here, a stillness all the more precious because it was secret, and, should she ever be forced to account for her absence, she would simply say, 'Out.' And to Sadie's mind, this was indeed true: she was out – out of their hands, out of their grips, out of their control. Free. Had she known the price of such freedom, she might not have seized it so readily, but on that first night, her pumps stuffed deep in her pockets, she believed her funds to be more than sufficient.

The years passed and the patterns set. Gradually, where Sadie was, or might be, lost significance, and only when she was actually present, eating at the same table, talking the same talk, were her whereabouts of interest. 'Are you with us?' Joseph would enquire solicitously, 'Can you keep up?'

And Sadie would nod distractedly, wrenching herself away from her daydreams just long enough to acknowledge the question. 'Sure I am, don't you know, right up there and flying!' Then, with a flick of her tail and a flutter of her wings she was back in the purple and reds of her imagination, leaving Joseph smiling in her slipstream, glad of the fresh air.

Absence, in time, becomes a reassurance in itself. But while Joseph might be happy to sip such half-measures, others were not. In particular for Elisabeth, whose discipled attachment to her grandmother would always leave her somewhat parched, Sadie's flightiness during these early years was a source of profound recrimination. Through the eyes of Lily the child learnt to see her mother as nothing less than a monster, and on the few occasions they were alone together, Elisabeth would thrash and bellow with such ferocity, it was good for neither party to prolong the intimacy. She was unrelenting in her judgement; inexorable in her punishments. Barely old enough to carry herself, Elisabeth bore the weight of the world, and the leadenness therein would remain with her for the rest of her heavy life.

Sadie, of course, would hear none of it. Martyrs were of their own making, as far as she was concerned, and she had no intention of being held to account for her daughter's saintliness. ''Tis a wedge from itself splits the oak tree,' she would mutter, when the latest accusations of maternal neglect were read out. 'I'll not be twistin' twigs, so I won't.' But for all such leafy philosophies, the facts remained the same: the only splinter in Elisabeth's side was her mother.

As the years passed, the splinters became needles, and the needles, stakes. By the time Elisabeth was four years old she was a walking fire-hazard, and even Sadie found her woodenness wearing. The twins had started school the previous September, the house resounding with their newfound independence, and Sadie, in between ferrying them to and fro, searching for her brothers, and drowning in the basement, found herself thrown towards her daughter with unnerving regularity. Try as she might, without the ever-provocative alliance of her sons to distract, escaping the screeches of her disapproving daughter became daily more difficult and, in the shallows of her own creation, Sadie began to flounder. She tried to make amends, to introduce Elisabeth to her bathroom, to share with her the stories the twins had devoured, but already tainted by the sourness of Lily, Elisabeth spat them straight back. Sadie tried again, offering Elisabeth her shells, teaching her to swim in the wide-bottomed tub, but once again her efforts were scorned, the glare of past neglect and future absences always that little brighter than the immediate. And eventually Sadie gave up.

'I'm wasting my time, Joseph,' she shrugged, wringing out the remains of the last ditched attempt at a swimming lesson from the wastes of her dress, 'for she wants me nowhere near, so help me God. She's got a head on her, so she has, that would fight the angels in heaven, it's true, and I would not be knowing what to do for the right, I would not.'

And Joseph, who did not know either, simply shrugged in return. But something would have to give, as it always did, and he sat back, bracing himself, for it could only be a matter of time.

Joseph's passivity, however, was deceptive. He would only wait so long, only accept so much. When a particularly vicious attack by Lily sent Sadie beneath the stairs for almost a day and a half, his subsequent discovery of an entire bottle of Glenfiddich, guzzled and washed up beneath the wine racks could not go unmentioned, resulting in a row which then sent her back there for a further night. When yet another of his treasured malts was found shipwrecked under the washbasin in Sadie's bathroom, likewise he made his feelings known. Yet this seemed only to make things worse. Sadie felt all the more isolated, the thunder of their three accusing faces deafening the quieter reassurances of the now largely absent twins, and life felt all the more unfair. And fairness to the Irish, like free speech to the Americans and the National Health to the English, is a right that will be fought for tooth and nail.

'You're not being fair!' Sadie might be heard to scream from one end of the house to the other. 'You're not being fair!'

'Life isn't fair, Sadie,' Joseph would reply, acid in his moral rectitude. 'Life isn't fair.'

But the tides were changing within the Hill House: the wind was picking up and the timing of things were increasingly uncertain. The fish began to swim in ever tighter circles as they strove to maintain their indifference, and the waves kept coming. Until one day, one ordinary, unremarkable January day, they were cast right out of the water.

'What on earth are you doing there?' Joseph stared at her in bewilderment. 'Are you all right?'

Sadie dared not move. She frowned a little harder, and sunk a little lower, her knees straining against the worn green of her dress and sending a shimmer of bells rattling around her bare ankles.

'Sadie.' Joseph tried again. 'Darling, why are you sitting

on the front step when there's a frost on the ground?' No answer. 'And why, more's the point, did you call me home in the middle of surgery? You know I have responsibility to those people, and everyone's running at least half an hour late now.'

'Sorry,' Sadie gasped, her apology muffled within the creases of her folded arms, 'but . . .'

Joseph eased himself on to the step beside her, and lifted her chin towards him. Her face was pale, threadbare, like silk so finely woven that it is almost transparent, and her eyes were dull. 'What is it?' he murmured, cupping his hand around her cheek. 'What is it?'

Sadie shook her head, feeling for his fingers and pulling them to her mouth, as if by doing so she might communicate her thoughts without the obstacle of words. Her own fingers were cold, curled knots upon her open palms, and no less articulate.

'Please, Sadie, what is it?'

With an effort Sadie dropped his hand and turned towards him. 'I called you . . .' she began, but the words trickled away into the spaces between them.

Joseph nodded. 'You called me . . .?'

'I called you . . . I called you . . .' Sadie took a deep breath, 'because . . . because . . . she's dead.'

Joseph nodded. 'She's dead?' He was a priest coaxing confession. 'She?'

Sadie fell forwards. 'O Jesus, it wasn't my fault, I swear, it just happened. She was standing there ranting, picking at me, and waving . . . and then she . . . she just fell over, dead as a doornail. Pfloomph.' Her mouth trembled. 'Pfloomph. Just like that.'

Joseph stared at the hinge of her wrist as she gestured the fall, and then slowly, deliberately, he eased himself to his feet. Hand on the doorframe, he paused, tilting his head back and forth in tiny, flickering moves, as if trying to make sense of its contents, before turning towards Sadie.

'You should come inside,' he murmured. 'You'll get cold sitting there.'

Elisabeth was waiting for him on the landing as he climbed the stairs, her normally still features a muddle of fidgeting shapes, and when she took his thumb to lead him into her grandmother's room, he could feel her trembling.

'Wait here, darling,' he soothed, but Elisabeth was fixed to his side, grim and unhearing, and she only held tighter, drawing him on.

Mrs Bradley shuffled nervously from behind the door, standing back to allow him past, and as Joseph entered the curtained and suddenly hollow room, he was a child again, no older than Elisabeth, terrified of what might be lurking in the shadows. Edging towards the bed, an outline of grey against the slithered black of his closing mind, he wanted to cover his eyes and run, in the blithe hope that not seeing might also mean not true. But then there she was, weighted before him, calm and peaceful as she had never been in life, and most definitely, as Sadie had so succinctly put it, dead as a doornail.

Elisabeth never forgave her mother for Lily's death. In her five-year-old wisdom she had the proportions of the event quite clearly established, and no amount of medical evidence to the contrary would sway her. Her mother had killed the person she loved most in the world. End of story. Her mother was guilty.

Except, of course, it was not the end of the story, for Elisabeth was but five years old, and had many more yarns to spin with her mother before that chapter of her life would be closed. A fact which perhaps made the situation even worse, for there is nothing to needle a child like the knowledge of its childishness; nothing to provoke conflict quite like the desperation to grow up. Sadie might be guilty,

Lily might be dead, and life might be unfair ... But what could Elisabeth do about it? She was but five years old.

In this respect, Sadie could have been deemed to have the upper hand. 'She's a child,' Joseph would sigh, when, only hours after Lily's death the doors began to slam and the walls come tumbling down. 'Leave her alone, she's a child.' And so Sadie continued to do just that.

'We have to get through today, and then put this behind us,' Joseph advised tremulously, on the morning of Lily's funeral. 'If we pull together as a family, we can do it.'

Sadie nodded obediently, trying to ignore the volley of scowls her daughter was hurling across the table at her. 'As a family, sure.'

'That's right.' Joseph patted her hand gratefully. 'It won't be the same without her here though,' he added, rather nonsensically as far as Sadie could see, for they wouldn't be here, draped in black and staring mournfully at the sausage rolls, if Lily was. 'But we'll be brave, won't we?'

His congregation of four nodded, bravely.

'And we'll be a family?'

More nodding, although somewhat less convincing. Bravery was a doddle, but family took more practice. Especially when the sum of its parts didn't quite add up.

Sadie had never been to a funeral before. Her eyes wide, her nerves jangling almost as loudly as the two keys and the crucifix – the cellar had since been added to her collection of faiths – she pleated herself against Joseph's suited arm and did not let go until the curtain had dropped and the audience filed out.

'So where's she going now?' she whispered, Lily still very much in the present tense for Sadie.

'To be cremated.' Joseph continued to stare straight ahead.

'Cremated? You mean, burnt?' Sadie gasped. 'They're

going to burn her behind there?' She pointed to the waving curtain through which Lily had recently disappeared, her voice rising incredulously.

Elisabeth let out a loud wail, pulling against her father's other arm, as the smell of her grandmother's burning flesh began to fill her sniffling nostrils.

'Of course not,' Joseph growled, glaring at Sadie. 'Of course not,' he repeated, gentler, to Elisabeth. 'Of course not,' he insisted a third time, just for himself. And they sidled out of the mahogany pew and followed the snaking trail of fellow mourners out of the chapel and back to the Hill House, the twins charging ahead, Joseph and his manacled wife and daughter staggering behind.

Sadie always maintained, even many years later when such retrospection was but a drop in the ocean, that the day of the wake was when it really started to go awry. The sight of so many crow-black faces, she claimed, beaking through the house, their yellow eyes greedy with sufferance, simply unbalanced her. It reminded her of her wedding day, of the squawked denials from the back of the silent church, which she had pretended not to hear, but which were sealed in her memory regardless; and it reminded her of her own someday death, a subject with which Sadie had never been particularly comfortable.

'So I had a drop of the hard stuff, as my daddy always called it, just to ward off the divil and let him know I would not be coming just yet, I would not. And then I felt a touch drowsy, and I thought, I'll lay down for a while . . .'

A while became an hour, and an hour slipped into two. Joseph noticed her absence, but he dismissed it, too submerged in his own suffering to wonder at hers, and it was late in the afternoon when she was at last discovered, fast asleep in the guest room and snoring loudly. Indeed, had it not been for the sound effects, it would have been considerably later that she was found, for the twins had taken it upon themselves to bury her, bundling the variety of capes and scarves they had been handed by the black-clad mourners, one after the other on top. An umbrella for her pillow, a bottle of whiskey for her sins; when the first of the guests trundled in to reclaim their belongings, Sadie was not at her best. Her pounding skull, coupled with the glare of her abstemious audience, made any attempt at explanation rather pointless, and so she merely hugged her bottle tighter, mouthed a silent sorry, and once more closed her eyes.

'But sure we'll be dead soon enough, so we will,' was the last they heard of her, and nobody could dispute the logic in that.

The spirits were out in force on the night of Lily's death in more ways than one. When Sadie finally escaped her cloakroomed bed, and stumbled upstairs to seek further redemption in her bathroom, she found the mirrored tile she had taken from Lily's wardrobe in two daggered shards upon the floor. So certain was she that it was a sign from beyond the grave, a tit-for-tat retort to the curse she herself had exacted from Joseph upon his mother (the possibility of an angry, five-year-old fist, did not occur to her) and which had since come true, that she spent the rest of the night on her knees in the empty bath begging for forgiveness. Uncertain to which God or gods she should devote herself, she settled upon a general sacrifice all round, and there was not a body more castigated, nor more charmed, than Sadie's hazing form in the dim of that January night. A bottle of sherry she had smuggled upstairs several days before was offered up with similar generosity, and as the clock in the hall struck midnight, Sadie skipped the light fantastic from one world to the next with the best of them. Angels and devils, witches and wizards, she plummetted from cloud to broomstick and back again, and when the next morning Joseph caught her dancing along the landing with an empty bottle she insisted to be her wand, he could only hope that this particular spell wore off.

Unfortunately, however, it was only beginning to wear on. If Sadie was correct about one thing, it was that after Lily's death it was downhill all the way. Perhaps it was the loss of what had been a declared force of reckoning from the moment Sadie set foot on English soil; or perhaps it was the fear that, without Lily, Joseph's dependence upon herself would be so much greater; or perhaps it was that she had actually become rather fond of her. (She had been known to mutter, in her weaker moments, what a 'grand ol' stick' her mother-in-law could be.) But whatever the reasoning or theories behind it, and there were many of them, the fact remained that Sadie, far from finding redemption on a mirror-shattering cloud of glory, would henceforth be lucky if she even saw the crack.

A.L. After Lily. In the beginning there was light. Lots of it. Following the funeral, the curtains were thrown open, and, at Sadie's insistence, the wallpaper in every room torn down and replaced by paint. Tapestry lampshades were ousted in favour of thin paper globes, and lights were left burning day and night. By the end of two weeks, if Lily's spirit had any intention of staying on to haunt them, then it would have needed a strong pair of sunglasses and a considerable depth of projection to do so. Even blind ghouling was out, for the daily rearrangement of the furniture, with the added disappearance of certain unfavourables, meant the dead were not the only ones caught between worlds, and the helpless cry of 'Where am I?' had a particularly human resonance.

Joseph showed himself surprisingly tolerant of such poltergeistery, and for some weeks it was almost as if he did not notice. 'Grief,' Mrs Bradley supposed, as he ambled past the bonfire of Lily's belongings Sadie had constructed in the hall. 'Clueless,' mused less charitable observers. But Joseph's passivity was perhaps his saving. When he left the house in the morning, his only desire was that it would be there when he returned that night, without too noticeable a scar to mark the passing hours, and if that was so, then he was happy. What Sadie did, or did not do, in the intervening hours was her own business, and experience had taught him that it was better that way. Moving furniture was the least of his worries. Far better than her old habits, chasing around London searching for brothers who were probably exiles across half the Western world by now, or sitting in a cold, dank cellar – he had known for some time now that this was where she disappeared to – thinking up who knows what schemes. If the odd chair or table lamp was his only trouble, then he was a lucky man. There was a lot to be said for a certain detachment within a marriage. Mutual respect, and so on.

The same clichés were somewhat lacking when applied to fatherhood, however, and it was this which eventually brought home to him the extent to which Sadie had let herself, and everyone around her, go. In the past he had chosen to overlook the rather tempestuous nature of Sadie's relationship with her daughter, tracing it to a simple clash of character, or an unfortunate, albeit two-way, dislike. But since his mother had died, it had become intolerable. The child had shut herself off entirely, from both the living and the dead, and it was becoming increasingly difficult to know what to do with her. When a five year old screams every time a female member of her family is mentioned, role models can prove rather an elusive influence, and Joseph would hate for Elisabeth to rely solely upon himself. The responsibility was vast.

No, what they all needed, he decided, as for the second time that week Elisabeth locked herself in her bedroom and refused to come out, was a holiday. Sending Mrs Bradley down the road to the locksmith, and the twins upstairs to keep an eye on their mother, he wandered up and down the hall deliberating his options. Home or abroad? Complete break or mild fracture? While Elisabeth picked the wood-chips from the wallpaper, bored by the lack of effect, and Sadie bribed her sons to fetch her a bottle of vodka from the cellar, Joseph balanced patience and patients as he plotted their reprieve. A holiday. Just what the doctor ordered.

'If you could go anywhere, Sadie, where would it be?' He threw the question at her from the driveway that very evening, having seen off the locksmith, and calmed a thwarted Elisabeth, and in the meantime spotted his wife hanging from the once ivy-covered bathroom window. He did not know she now spent most of her day here, picking the leaves and calling to strangers, finding it preferable to the more demanding intimacies of lower realms.

'Anywhere 't'all, do you say?' she demanded gaily.

'Anywhere.' Anywhere except Ireland he might have added, a country irrevocably associated with bad falls and drunken uncles. 'Anywhere at all.'

'Ooh, now let me think now. For sure, I've never been to America, nor never to Japan, or China too . . .' She gazed skywards for inspiration. 'And I've never been to the moon, tho' my mammy was always saying I'd be raving at it before I was done.' She giggled, and as she rearranged the vodka bottle which she had tucked inside her dress, Joseph wondered at her good spirits.

'Well, apart from the moon,' he suggested, craning to see her as she briefly disappeared out of sight, to return, wiping her mouth distractedly. 'Where else?'

Sadie grinned, leaning dangerously far across the ledge, her hair falling like kelp around her face. 'You know where I'd really like to go, what I'd really like to see?' she declared. Pausing while Joseph shook his head, she appeared to reconsider a moment, before proclaiming, in a whisper which seemed a part of the wind itself, 'I'd like to see the rolling hills, so I would, the *real* rolling hills.'

And so Joseph took his wife, his daughter, the twins, and the Axminster carpet under which he habitually brushed his worries, to the Lake District. He stood Sadie on a roadside, and in between the roar of passing caravans, quoted Wordsworth, and Coleridge, and any other source of lake-land reference, and showed her her hills. Sadie nodded, missing the real part; and the twins thumped Elisabeth, missing their friends; and Elisabeth screamed, missing an ally; and Joseph got back in the car proudly, missing the point. It was the longest two weeks of their collective lives. (And they were not collected easily.) But at least Joseph had tried, and at the time, that was an achievement in itself. Much like the hills, which soon turned out to be more real than Sadie imagined.

'Well, now we've seen them, let's get a closer look by climbing one,' Joseph announced energetically, as they slipped in behind a traffic jam of holiday makers and trawled into Windermere. 'Everybody out!'

With Sadie trailing begrudgingly at the back, the twins causing chaos amongst a group of Italian tourists up ahead, and Elisabeth perched loftily upon her father's shoulders and happiest of them all, they began the long, exhausting hike Joseph had planned for them. 'Step on, Sadie! Hurry up at the back!' Joseph balanced on rocks, wavered on stream-sides, hollered from hillocks, as Sadie cursed and sweated her soul behind.

'I'm coming, will you hear, I'm here, am I not . . .' she groaned, rubbing her ankles, hitching her sleeves. 'Some kind of holiday this is, honest to God. I might have known: offer you the birds in the trees and then tell you to go get them yourself! Surely to the Sacred Heart there must be more than this . . .'

As indeed there was. Breaking for lunch at a small hotel

beside one of the many indistinguishable lakes Sadie chose to forget the names of, there were two double vodkas more. While Joseph drank orange juice, and the children melted ice pops, Sadie drowned her aches in the best way she knew.

'Do you really need that?' Joseph demanded, as she sailed back to the bar for another one.

'Yup,' was the only answer he heard.

'Oh,' was the only one he gave.

But Joseph was not finished yet. In the same breath as they wheezed back down the hill that afternoon, they were then ferried straight on to a rowing boat, handed a bamboo pole with a plastic net pocket spindling the end, and taken fishing.

'Fishing?' Sadie mocked. 'Begob, Joseph, you'll be catching nothing more than tiddlers with a bit of rubbish like that, do you know.'

'Tiddlers is okay.'

'Pah!' Encouraged by her double vodkas, very little was okay with Sadie.

'Just wait and see. Now take an oar, Seamus, Joe . . .'

Sadie waited. And she saw. For ten minutes they spun dizzy circles as the twins mastered the art of rowing, and then for a further twenty they sat in the middle of the tourist filled lake and listened to a man on the side screech numbers, as the other boats were called in. Elisabeth caught the first 'sprat' as Sadie referred to it disparagingly – 'a brat with a sprat!' amused her no end – but Sadie insisted it be thrown back for it was bad luck to keep the first of the catch. Elisabeth tantrumed, Joseph placated, the twins declared mutiny upon an innocent raft of schoolchildren, and Sadie felt sick.

'I want to go in now,' she decided, indicating the bank and hauling herself across the bow to check their number on the outside of the boat. 'That was us he was calling, just then, Jose. Time to go back.'

'No it wasn't, Sadie. We've got another half-hour at least. Just sit down and enjoy the view, will you?'

'Jeezus, Joseph, if you don't take us in, I tell you, I'll be throwing up lunch, so I will.'

'You didn't have any lunch, Sadie, apart from half a pint of vodka,' Joseph hissed, turning away from the children as if to protect them from such facts. 'Which is probably why you feel sick.'

'Take me in, Joseph,' she repeated.

'No, Sadie,' he refused.

'Take me in.'

'No.'

All four faces were turned towards Sadie, curious for her response to such unusual defiance on Joseph's part. She glowered, furiously. And then without another word she unlaced her shoes, took off her cardigan, and stood up.

'Suit yourself,' she shrugged, and dived straight over the side and into the water. While Joseph and the children, and several hundred others on both land and lake, gawped in horror, she swam lazily back to the shore. The man shouting the numbers silenced long enough to haul her out, and with a smile to the crowd, she scooped up her skirts and dripped her way back to the hotel Joseph had left their bags at that morning. When the others returned shortly after, chastened and churlish, she was tucked up in bed, surrounded by hot water bottles, and room service running back and forth every ten minutes. The mini-bar had been set to with a vengeance, and several trays of tea testified to the medicinal benefits of hot toddies.

'Are you quite happy there?' Joseph wanted to know.

'Over the moon!' Sadie grinned, opening another miniature bottle and pouring it into her tea cup. 'Over the moon 'n' back again. I always said I'd get there in the end.'

And that was about as far as Sadie did get for the remainder of the two-week holiday. When Joseph asked her to join them for dinner, she claimed she was 'as happy with a tray here, if that's all right with you'; and when the next day he suggested a less strenuous itinerary of a stroll around Keswick and an ice-cream or two, Sadie had the distinct sense that she might be getting a cold, and thought she'd better stay in bed. With the mini-bar. And room service. And the three abandoned plastic nets which were to be an endless source of amusement.

And so Joseph left her to it. When they returned from their various excursions to find her sailing the high seas with a pirate chambermaid commissioned to 'shiver her timbers' with three bamboo poles affixed to her left leg, (the remains of the fishing nets made perfect stage props) or walking the plank along the window ledge, smuggling the contents of the minibar in the room next door into her own diminishing stash, they knew better than to challenge her on this one. As Joseph said, not without a certain regret, it was everybody's holiday, after all. Even when he had to carry her back from the hotel bar at two o'clock in the morning, when she'd sworn she was just nipping down the hall to the bathroom, Joseph refrained from argument. Since Lily's death, the fact of being a 'family' seemed the most important detail of all. Smaller, less categorical aspects were for the most part dismissed. Besides, they'd be home soon enough, and then things would be back to normal. Whatever that might be.

And hence, much like the house that remains standing, or the life that isn't fair, because they survived the two weeks at all, the Lake District was considered a success and Joseph booked them into the same hotel for the following year, and the year after that, and the year after that. Until it was just another two weeks within the annual decline, and the real rolling hills were just another item on Sadie's growing list of dreams.

15

Sadie's disappointment at finding her real rolling hills to be little more than gentle mounds (or certainly according to Joseph's guidebook), while never articulated, proved to be instrumental in her behaviour over the next decade. She could forgive the absence of the Little People, for she was sure they had more important places to be than here; and she could rationalise, albeit reluctantly, her missing brothers, as Joseph had hardly made them welcome; but the betrayal perpetuated by her very landscape? That was unforgiveable. She began to question everything, both actual and remembered, forever doubting whether this shape or that would be the same this or that by tomorrow; forever shifting and insisting everyone else shift with her. Before they knew where they were, life was a circle around which they all kept turning, hands held, Sadie in the middle, ringing the rose as she fell down, got up again, fell down, got up again. Any bruises which resulted were daubed and then dismissed; any scars ignored. For what could any of them say? As far as Sadie was concerned, the music had stopped long before.

Living alongside such faithlessness can be rather a strain. The twins, whose early introduction to the realm of fantasy had provided them with more than enough causes to devote themselves to, gritted their teeth and battled on. But Elisabeth, denied such imaginative release, felt only delusion: she had been promised fact and formulae, and had instead been given a freak. Mothers were not what they ought to be, Elisabeth concluded, and being a daughter was a drag.

Joseph did his best to alleviate the situation by, whenever possible, distracting from it. Hence, he would send the twins to yet another boy scout's meeting in yet another tin hut, and Elisabeth he would package up and take with him on his rounds. The surrogate mothering she received from the grateful ill easily compensated for the growing insufficiency of home, and she soon came to consider the flood of cups of tea and devotionally baked biscuits as by far the surer option. She even began to tell certain of the more regular patients she loved them, which was seen to be terribly sweet, and years later she would be reminded of the indiscriminacy of such proclamations with an embarrassing regularity. A regularity that somehow overlooked the fact that she had meant it.

Each of them – with perhaps the exception of Joseph, who had been brought up being told it is bad manners to ask, and one should wait until one's offered – were thus set upon their individual pilgrimages in search of something more. Sadie, because older and therefore not as nimble as she used to be, was the first to admit she might not make it, but that was some way down the line, and by then it was too late. The mirrors on the wall, the fairest judge of all, had already assured of that.

Disposing of Lily's broken tile had not been easy, the threat of seven years bad luck only adding to Sadie's reluctance to meddle in such matters of the spirits, and it took almost two years before she eventually got around to throwing it out. Wrapping the two slicing shards in a bundle of newspaper, and dropping them in the dustbin, she hoped, throwing salt over her shoulders with abandon, that that would be the end of it, but when the mirror she replaced it with met the same fate, she quickly reconsidered and left the wall bare. She had never liked what she saw anyway.

From then on Sadie adopted the less revelatory measure of a bottle. Made from glass, and just as gloating, it nevertheless allowed a certain blurring at the edges that was instantly preferable, and Sadie kept this one up for quite some time. The green versions were her favourite, which might have accounted for the quantities of gin she took to consuming, and the black of a full bottle of stout best of all, although this never prevented her drinking it. In short, rather than looking she began to only see, and when even this became unreliable, she sat in the dark.

But it was the dryness of these blackening hours which really disturbed her. She could contend with thirst, for this was only a temporary condition, but she could not bear the feeling of sheer aridity which took over her body the rest of the time. For however many baths she took, however much liquid she drank, the scratch and scrape of drought remained. Her skin was like paper, and her hair, once a shimmer of colour, was dull and wasted, dried out seaweed which crackled to the touch. Pots of cream and lotions littered every surface of her bathroom, promising everything from rejuvenation to the removal of blemishes, but nothing could bring back her old wateriness, nothing could restore her glow. Joseph put it down to the amount of salt she still insisted upon eating, and which she had even taken to putting in her bath, and he suggested a higher intake of saturates in her diet instead. Handing her a bottle of cod liver oil, he advised two teaspoons daily, and sardines for lunch, but she found the taste so disgusting she had to wash it down with a notably bigger dose of whiskey, and hence lunch never even happened. That was the last time Joseph intervened. After that Sadie was left to her own remedies, and it became a regular sight to find her perched upon the kitchen table, saucepan in hand, working upon her latest concoction in which Mrs Bradley's cooking sherry invariably played a leading part. But no matter the ingredients, no matter the conviction, it was to no avail; she was impervious from her hot head to her cold feet, and there was nothing anyone could do. Least of all Joseph. Love, it seems, blinds even doctors.

Elisabeth, however, failed to share such passivity, and in the course of her mother's long-term drift into obscurity, proffered several solutions, including divorce, adoption and straightforward abandonment. She hurled abuse and she hurled bottles, careless of where either might fall, and she made it her God-given mission – or could it have been Lily-given? – to spread both the word and the evidence of her mother's drunken gospel. But when Joseph arrived home from work to discover Elisabeth in the middle of the front lawn, eight years old, clutching a half-empty bottle of vodka, and shrieking malevolently, it seemed she might have taken such a calling a step too far. It was the conclusion any anxious parent would have jumped to, and when Elisabeth then began to wail and heave with an abandon bordering on the evangelical, it was not surprising he responded as he did.

'Where is your mother? Where is your mother?' he ranted, seizing Elisabeth by the shoulders and shaking her violently, as if to free her of an evil spirit – which further explained his interest in Sadie's whereabouts. 'Where is she? And what has she done to you?'

This last pleased Elisabeth no end, and she saw little urgency, for the present time, in informing him that Sadie was having a lie down upstairs, and she, Elisabeth, had simply been pouring the vodka down the gutter, not drinking it. And so instead she shrugged.

'Inside!' Joseph was panicking now, and he threw Elisabeth over his shoulder, and charged through the front door. Once there, he continued to shake Elisabeth, while she, rethinking the wisdom of her previous ambiguity, attempted to convince him that, really, she was quite all right.

'All right? All right?' Joseph howled. 'Half a bottle of vodka is not all right! We've got to get it out of you!'

'But I'm all right, I . . .' Elisabeth's teeth, arms, legs, rattled as Joseph's desperation increased, and any hope of explanation was deafened beneath the chatter.

'Salt then!' he declared, and he wrenched Elisabeth towards the kitchen where he began forcefeeding her salt-water by the gallon. If there was one thing guaranteed to turn Elisabeth's stomach, it was salt, such were the inevitable associations it had with her mother, and within seconds she was retching the contents of her empty stomach in every direction. Mrs Bradley looked on in horror. Not only at the effect upon her clean floor, but also at the fact that it was obvious neither child nor parent knew what was going on. Joseph ranting and Elisabeth screaming for all she was worth: somebody had to do something.

The somebody Mrs Bradley intended, however, was not the somebody who then arrived, jangling down the passageway and swaying to a halt in the mouth of the door. Rudely awakened by the ear-splitting screams coming from the kitchen, her head already pounding after a particularly drenching morning, Sadie was as incoherent as those she should have been helping, and as a result her presence only exacerbated the situation.

'Will you maybe keep it down a touch, will you?' she mumbled, 'I was taking a rest, to be sure, and Jesus himself would not be sleeping through this racket, so he would not, so . . .' She watched, bemused, as the three figures before her turned as one and glared at her. She stepped back.

'Hallooo?' She raised a conciliatory hand towards the trio, whistling the greeting with an airy hesitation. Elisabeth continued to scream. Joseph continued to shake. And the salt water continued to spill in ever greater waves across Mrs

Bradley's kitchen floor. Curious, she edged closer, stretching each foot tentatively before her, when she noticed the half-full vodka bottle resting upon the table. She bent to pick it up, holding it to the light as if to verify its contents, and then tilting its neck to her squinting eye and peering inside. She took a small, evaluative, sip. So rare was it to find such bounty, she doubted it could be for real. She took another sip.

'Don't you think you've had enough already?' Joseph's voice was hard, cutting cold against the warmth of the vodka and causing Sadie to splutter short her salute, and look up.

'I beg your pardon?'

'I said, do you not think you've had enough already? More than enough?'

'Beg pardon?' she repeated, unused to such overt challenges, and wondering if she had missed something. 'Enough?'

Joseph shook his head disbelievingly. 'Do you have any idea . . .?' He pointed from the groaning Elisabeth to the sea of the floor. 'Do you?'

She smiled disconcertedly. Clearly not.

He was about to elaborate when the subject of this 'any idea' herself, having remained gratefully silent throughout their exchange, decided it was time to intervene. With a howl that was three parts genuine and the rest largely attention-seeking, Elisabeth began to rock violently from side to side, clutching her salty stomach and sobbing even saltier tears. Joseph pointed at her as if in proof. Sadie stared back unimpressed.

'Do you see what you've done?'

'What I've done? But I've just this minute walked through the door, so I have. I don't think you can be 'cusing me of doing anything, I don't.'

'Tell her where you found that,' he demanded, turning

towards Elisabeth, and pointing towards the bottle of vodka, still flush to Sadie's chest.

There was an ominous silence, during which Elisabeth contemplated her options, standing as they were on either side, glaring. 'In your bathroom,' she admitted, having judged her father to be the surer of the two in terms of allies.

Sadie froze. 'What did you say? In my bathroom?'

She advanced towards Elisabeth, and brought her clear, insoluble features within inches of her daughter's crystalised face. Joseph put a protective arm around the child's shoulders and squeezed reassuringly, but his gesture was nothing in the glare of Sadie's. 'You were in my bathroom, were you now, little miss? And what exactly did you think you were doing there?' Memories of Lily hurtled to the forefront of Sadie's mind, and she frowned harder. 'Well? What've you got to say for yourself, madam?'

'Be quiet, Sadie.' Joseph lifted Elisabeth off the table, and carried her out of the kitchen. 'For once, just be quiet.'

And Sadie, because there was nothing else she could be, was.

Three people were isolated that day. Joseph, by his disappointment; Sadie by her silence; and Elisabeth by an emotion she neither wanted nor understood, but which was nonetheless felt. As they went their separate ways, Joseph disappearing to his study, Sadie disappearing, via the cellar, to her bathroom, and Elisabeth just disappearing, because nobody ever noticed where she went anyway, not one of them thought to look back. All at odds. All slowly working even.

The Hill House accepted such disparity with ease, the natural boundaries of rooms and walls unnoticing of more territorial claims, and as time went on such divisions were barely seen. The twins were similarly accommodating, always open to the challenges of a new conflict, a new war, and they crossed the lines from one zone to the next with vigour. 'There's never any winners in life!' Seamus would shriek. 'You just got to keep fighting!'

In addition to their uncles' profound sense of justice, the twins had also inherited a remarkable physical likeness, their bouldering shoulders and starfish hands frequently convincing Sadie, in her hazier moments, that it was one of her brothers home to visit her. They would thunder in and out, red hair blazing, wreaking havoc wherever they happened to stop, and happily rejecting any attempt to regulate this abandon. Their mother, of course, was right behind them in this, often in body as well as spirit, but Joseph could not tolerate it. 'Calm down, both of you!' he was forever insisting, withholding pocket money here and scout outings there, but the twins only ever grinned.

'We're just boys, me and Shay!' Joe would retort, playing his father at his own diminutive game. 'Just boys havin' fun!' Which was exactly what Joseph wanted to believe.

The twins were not the only ones going wild, however: Elisabeth had similarly decided upon a more 'off the rails' approach, driven as she still was by the steam of unexpressed emotions, and she lurched through the early years of her teens with runaway speed. Long since having rejected the hours visiting patients with her father, she now sought a different focus for her attentions, and they, in their multitude, sought her. For while her family might not cherish her, Forms V and VI of the local Grammar School certainly did, news of a maiden in distress sure to send more than one knight off to polish his armour. Hence, Elisabeth careered out of childhood at around the same time as her mother was collapsing back into it, although the irony, like so much else during these years, was well and truly lost.

Sadie's descent was figured most symbolically by the exchanging, at Joseph's instigation, of their double bed – the bed in which Elisabeth had been born – for two singles, and his subsequent gift of an embroidered hot water bottle when she complained of the cold. He was tired, he claimed, of being woken up every hour by Sadie's frantic dreaming, or, on the nights when she slept too heavily for dreams, of listening to her snore. Separate beds would solve this, and, to be quite honest, he did not know why he had not thought of it earlier. Sadie was not so impressed.

'But you never used to mind me dreaming, to be sure you didn't,' she urged, watching their mattress disappearing down the stairs. 'So what's changing, God help us, what's the difference now, will you say?'

Joseph shrugged. 'We're not as young as we used to be,' he offered lamely.

'I am, to be sure I am!' Sadie proclaimed, her hands rising to cover the paper of her face. 'I am.'

'Maybe so,' Joseph reflected. 'But it won't hurt,' he waved towards the new beds, 'it won't hurt just to try them, will it now?'

But it did hurt. Sadie hated the loneliness of sleeping alone, even when she knew Joseph was only an arm's length away, and her restlessness became even more pronounced than before. 'This wasn't how it was supposed to be,' she murmured, winding herself up in the bedclothes and kicking the hot water bottle on to the floor. 'This wasn't it.'

Unfortunately, however, it was indeed 'it', just as Sadie was now 'her', Joseph, 'him', and the remainder of the household simply 'them'. With the dividing of the beds came an even greater dividing of the loyalties, and Sadie, in particular, opted to have none at all. She spoke to no one, unless absolutely unavoidable, and made a point of exercising her independence from the family at every possible opportunity. The enforced solitude of a single bed served only to justify the many exiles she had indulged in over the years, her drowning and her drinking, her sanctuaries and her searches, and Sadie rose up, forgiven. 'Redeemed!' she informed the world from the pulpit of her bathroom window. 'Now, let me tell you all, I'm going to hell a happy lady, so I am!' And she raised her bottle and drank to such futures with the grace of a true penitent.

Hell, Sadie had decided, was the safest bet as far as homecomings were concerned, and she spared no more thought for the rolling hills of past inclinations. Pulling her world tight about her, sinking to its deepest depths, she prepared herself for its imagined torments by a concerted and disciplined enactment of them in the here and now. For several months the Hill House shook with her damnations, quivered beneath her fiery glares, and almost razed itself to the ground when she began her infernal chantings. It became indeed a hell on earth, and in the best interests of all who lived there, souls were rapidly evacuated until a later date, and only the shells and the bodies lived on.

Not surprisingly, such bodies gradually began to tire of the perpetual roasting they were subject to in Sadie's domain, and set off upon a search for eternal life all of their own. Joseph found his in the continued giving out of pills and sympathy, the primrose path of such benevolence a delightful deviation. And Elisabeth, hers, with the ongoing giving of herself, likewise a pleasure. The twins, however, took a different tack, and forged their way forward by more demonstrative means, heedless of popularity or risk, and, like their mother, discovered a genuine direction for themselves in hell-raising. If there was a protest, they were there, protesting; if there was a march, of any sort, anywhere, the twins were marching. When, for the third time in a month they were delivered home in a police car, charged with 'disorderly behaviour', and Joseph locked them in their room until further notice, it was a matter of minutes before they were down the drainpipe and off again. There was, it seemed, no stopping them, and no matter how many times Joseph sped to this location or the other, hoping to catch them and bring them home before the police did, they were not discouraged. They were their mother's sons.

And Elisabeth, like it or not, was her mother's daughter, a fact she made more than clear all those years later in the garden. The expanding girth and persistent stomach upsets which Joseph, ever the naïve father, put down to puppy fat and too much junk food, revealed themselves on that wet Autumn morning as a far greater presence than a couple of oversized sweaters and an elastic waistband could hide. With a 'disorderliness' she could be proud of, she unleashed a little of her own creativity upon her doubting family, and, as they would later all agree, it was her finest moment. Like Sadie before her, the 'spirits' were clattering and the 'wantins' terrible, and gone was the little girl with the grandmother's face and the nice smile. As her screams and curses buried themselves in the heavy English soil, and the privet huddled closer, pale in the light of the impending arrival, even Sadie, glancing out of her bathroom window, was impressed. Who would have thought it of Elisabeth?

'Happen she's not such a tame egg after all . . .' Sadie sank back into the bath, and closed her eyes, allowing the water to seep over her until she was a flattened surface of colour. 'Hatching out all over the place, so they are.'

16

It was several hours before the commotion outside ceased, hours during which Sadie lay quietly in her tub, watching the patterns of dusk chalk their shapes upon the skylight above her head, and the rain continue to wash them away. She forgot all about the bottle of whiskey she had balanced between the taps at her feet, and it was only upon drying herself, rubbing at her feet and suddenly noticing her toes as more than a distant blur, that she was reminded of the lapse. Hurriedly setting this right, she wrapped herself in the customary half-a-dozen towels, and shuffled her unsteady way downstairs.

The hall was in darkness, the pale hands of the clock her only illumination, and as Sadie pulled her robes tighter, a train of damp towelling puddled in her wake. She shivered. At the end of the passageway into the kitchen, she could just make out the edges of a flickering yellow light, and she hurried towards it, suddenly cold, suddenly outside. As she entered, she saw her daughter sitting in front of the fire, wrapped, not dissimilarly to herself, in a bundle of shawls and blankets, her head tipped back against the wall, her legs draped across the hearth. She was staring straight ahead, her thoughts buried in the flames, and her hands twitched nervously upon her chequered lap.

Sadie coughed. The three shadows which had been

lingering by the window, gazing out, looked around, smiling peaceably, and then turned back. Elisabeth remained motionless, only the nervous dance of her fingers admitting her consciousness. Silence.

Sadie coughed again. And a small voice somewhere near the fire coughed in return. Sadie narrowed her eyes, pulling at a corner of damp turban which had fallen across her ear, and tucking it resolutely to one side. Slowly bending down, she peered beneath the table in front of her, palms clutching modestly at her many flapping wings, knees knocking on the tiles like knuckles on wood. She was bemused. Where was it, this creature. She groped to her feet, swaying, looking from the backs of the three men by the window, to the burning passivity of Elisabeth, and then down, upon her own cloaked confusion. Had she dreamt the scene in the garden? She wrinkled disappointedly.

As she turned to leave, however, Elisabeth, her eyes still fixed upon the fire, raised one of her hopscotching hands and gestured to her to wait. 'Don't you want to meet your granddaughter?' she demanded, her voice barely a whisper, her features challenging despite their profile.

Sadie shuddered, unprepared for such a sudden shift of generations, and she instinctively shook her head, her mind clamping shut as an army of Lily's galloped into view. To her side, Joseph twisted to face her. 'You should,' he murmured, but it was unclear to whom this obligation was due.

Sadie shrugged, losing another layer of disguise in the process, and nudged towards the corner of the fire, where the axes of Elisabeth's wavering finger and Joseph's nodding authority met in a single glowing light. And there, still tucked inside the upturned umbrella nobody had thought to remove her from, was Isobel.

'Hello, Isobel.' Sadie put a hand to the wall and hung there, poring down upon the rain-stained child, and remembering another Isobel, her grandmother, a woman famed and feared for her ability to summon a storm by swilling rainwater inside a clay bowl, and who, to this day, was invoked whenever a boat went down. 'Hello, Isobel.'

'She doesn't have a name yet,' Elisabeth murmured, 'I haven't decided.'

But Isobel was Isobel, and after that first evening they never thought to call her anything else. For once they were agreed, and as they balanced precariously around the wheeling cradle, it was to be the beginning of many such tolerances. And although they continued to watch one another, or, more specifically, watch Sadie, there was a hopefulness in their eyes which had before been quite absent. When Joseph later carried Elisabeth upstairs, leaving the twins to keep an eye upon their mother, he did not mind that they were not there when he returned, nor that Sadie was now crouched upon the hearth, Isobel huddled tight to her breast. He simply sat down at the foot of the table and watched her there.

Joseph did not intend to fall asleep, or certainly not fully dressed and sitting at the kitchen table, but the excitement of the afternoon combined with the warmth of the fire after the chilling damp of the storm lulled him, and it was almost morning when he raised his head and found himself alone. The flames had died down long since, and the sky outside the window was opal in the spidering light of dawn, but as he staggered to his feet, tugging at the belt of his raincoat, he was strangely comforted by such coolness. It restored a tranquillity, an order, to the memory of the previous day, and allowed it all to settle somewhat. And there was nothing Joseph liked more than to get things settled.

Stumbling out of the kitchen and up the stairs, Joseph hovered outside Elisabeth's room, listening, before continuing on towards Sadie's bathroom, as he did most nights, to coax her down to bed, and hoping she had had the good sense to take some blankets. But the room was empty, the bath a pool of white, and any fleeing spirits – with the exception of an empty bottle of whiskey pendant upon the taps – nowhere to be seen. He frowned. Backing out again, Joseph hurried down the stairs, his raincoat crunching louder with every stride, and threw himself into the dark of the main bedroom.

'Sadie . . .' he hissed, feeling around for the lightswitch. 'Sadie, are you there?'

No reply. He fumbled around the foot of his own bed, and reached the calculated three or four feet to find Sadie's.

'What the . . .?'

His waving hand measured the air, up, down, left, right, but not only was Sadie evading him, the very furniture seemed to have disappeared too. He struggled back towards the door, once again patting the wall for the light, but just as his fingers seized upon the edge of the casing, a sigh from the other side of the room distracted him.

'Sadie?'

Joseph flicked the switch and the room was swamped in orange light. Blinking at its ferocity, he waited several seconds for his eyes to adjust, staring at the floor, and then looked up. The two beds had been pushed together, the side table which usually separated them up-ended on the floor, and the covers and blankets from each had been stripped. Moving closer, kneeling upon the edge of the bare mattress, Joseph found Sadie huddled on the carpet at the far side, a mound of pillows and sheets, snoring lightly.

'Sadie . . .' He prodded her gently, but the wail which went up was different from Sadie's usual roar, and as he lifted a corner of the eiderdown, he found Isobel tucked into the curve of her grandmother's stomach, and frowning fiercely. 'Sadie . . . wake up.' He nudged her shoulder, pulling back the web of sheets to find her pale and towel-less. 'Will you wake up.'

Sadie opened an eye, and rolled her head towards him,

catching at the array of folded back edges and once again covering both herself and Isobel. She smiled. 'Hello.'

'Sadie, what are you doing?'

'Sleeping,' came the obvious reply.

'But on the floor? Why are you lying on the floor, and why is Isobel with you?'

'Who else would she be with, honest to God?' Sadie demanded quietly, slipping a hand beneath the cover and stroking the unseen child.

'With her mother, of course!'

'But . . .' Sadie paused, reflecting upon this fact, and, deciding she could not contest it, instead winked. 'But she likes it with Sadie, so she does. Sleeping like a log, she's been, so help me, snoring like a boozer, isn't that the truth.'

'Sadie,' Joseph sighed, dropping his hand to the bed upon which he perched, 'Sadie, it was you who was snoring, I heard you. And Isobel, however much she likes it with her granny,' Sadie winced at such a title, 'should be with her mother, with Elisabeth.'

Reaching towards the swell of Sadie's waist, Joseph lifted Isobel free, teasing away the grappling fingers which held her, and gathering her against his waterproofed front. Isobel let out a howl, Sadie adding to it with a series of 'See!'s and 'Will you look now?'s but Joseph was already halfway down the landing, and ignoring both. Depositing his find safely in Elisabeth's arms, and waiting only to make sure both parties were aware of the other, he then returned to the bedroom to discover Sadie elevated from her previous position, and coiled across the crack of the two divans. Gathering the covers from the floor, he spread them over her, and then, gratefully extinguishing the light, climbed in alongside. They could move everything back to where it should be in the morning.

The morning, however, saw no such restorations: Sadie was up and running a bath what seemed only minutes after

Joseph had at last fallen asleep, and when he next surfaced, she was sitting astride him, whispering in his ear and dangling cups of tea in all directions. She was so full of energy, he could not bring himself to condemn her for the night before, and when she offered toast to go with the tea, he cast caution to the wind and declared he'd love some. While she rattled off downstairs to set fire to a few appliances and probably electrocute herself in the process, Joseph leant back against the single pillow he had managed to wean from her sleeping grip, and rubbed his brow. He hated it when she started drinking first thing in the morning.

But the only liquid to have passed Sadie's lips that day was a sip or two of tea, and several unintentional mouthfuls of bathwater when she was washing her hair. She didn't feel like drowning today, preferring to keep her sights clear when the outlook was so promising, and although it had been some time since she had risked such surface encounters, Sadie was not nervous. She shuffled around the kitchen, this world she had defected from years ago, opening cupboards and drawers at every turn, and refusing to be beaten. Somewhere here was a packet of matches to light the stove; somewhere a grill pan; somewhere a packet of butter. Where? She did not know they had switched to electric around the time Lily had died, and that a timely toaster now reigned where the grill pan had burnt; and she was certainly unaware of the recently discovered perils of butter which assured nothing less than margarine would be found in this health-conscious household. If she intended to keep up such sobriety, she would have a lot to learn.

Elisabeth did not descend until almost lunchtime, her eyes bruised, and her skin possessing that particular crumpledness that suggests it has been left out in the rain too long – as indeed it had. She moved slowly, every step an effort, and when Joseph held out his arms to take Isobel, she gladly relinquished the child.

'How do you feel, Lizzie?' Sadie was sitting atop the shuddering washing machine, swinging her legs, and gazing towards Isobel.

Elisabeth watched her with astonishment. Her mother had not been downstairs before suppertime for longer than she could remember, and she had never invited conversation then. 'Fine,' she stuttered. And then wondered at the untruth. 'Actually, no, I feel bloody awful.' She sat down roughly on the same chair by the fire she had occupied the previous night. 'Bloody bloody awful.'

'Elisabeth . . .' Joseph wheedled, seeing no reason for such expletives.

'Bloody, bloody, bloody . . .' Sadie chuckled, heels thudding against the side of the vibrating twin tub, 'bloody, bloody . . .'

She broke off, reaching towards Joseph with outstretched arms, and nodding to Isobel. Elisabeth cringed. 'Give her to me, Daddy . . .' she pleaded. 'She . . .'

But Joseph shushed her reassuringly, nodding his head with an authority he usually reserved for discussing senile patients. 'She'll be all right, trust me.'

He wagged a finger at Sadie to get down from her spinning perch, but she brushed it aside, and lifted Isobel towards her, laughing delightedly as the child began to jiggle up and down with her.

'For heaven's sake, Daddy!' Elisabeth hauled to her feet, her expression pained, but he only smiled. 'Daddy!' she insisted, forcing him to turn around. 'Please.'

'Yes, sorry.' He stepped towards Sadie, resting a hand upon her trembling knee. 'Sadie, get down from there if you're going to have Isobel. Please. You're making Elisabeth nervous.'

Sadie glanced at him, a glint in her eye, and then across at Elisabeth. 'What a proper pair they look, honest to God,' she whispered, her nose to Isobel's cheek. 'Can you see what a pair of old women they are, can you? Jeez, what would you be doing with them, will you tell me, what?'

Elisabeth scowled, unhearing, and clamped her hands to her hips with a matronliness far disguising her fifteen years. Joseph shifted uncomfortably. 'Just get down, please.' He held out a hand, offering his help, but if Sadie was going to relent, it would be under her own steam.

'Twitter, twitter, twitter,' she chuntered, walking her hips forward to where she might slide off the tub. 'Twitterin' on an' on, that's what they're doing, so it is.' And she dropped to the floor, babe in arms, and looked about her brightly. 'Happy, the lot of you?' she demanded, and with a grin to her applause-less audience, she turned and waltzed out of the back door and into the garden.

When Joseph eventually caught up with her she was standing beneath the bay tree at the far end of the lawn, and crooning gently to the rocking Isobel. Putting what he hoped to be a commanding hand upon her shoulder, he eased her around, intent upon chastisement, but the tear-stained face which met him left the words stuck in his throat.

'Darling . . .?' he mumbled, the intimacy ringing hollow in its strangeness. 'Darling, what is it?'

Sadie shook her head, light bouncing off the pale coral of her cheeks in waves. 'I don't know,' she murmured, her tone suggesting such validations to be insignificant. 'I don't know, sure.'

Isobel lay beneath the waterfall of Sadie's tears, her eyes wide open, apparently unnoticing of the rivers of damp that were collecting about her. Joseph delved in his pocket for a handkerchief, tying it about her like a surplice, and with his cuff dabbed the source, Sadie's eyes.

'Darling, you must know what's upsetting you?'

But Sadie did not know. She could not articulate what it was to look upon such stillness as Isobel and feel only one's own fractiousness; she could not explain how she felt when she read the lines of her own life in the as yet unlived smoothness of this child; she could not contemplate such waste as she perceived when, in the mirror of her granddaughter she saw only the greying weariness of herself. And so she wept instead, allowing the wash of salty tears to speak it for her.

Sadie continued to weep for almost a week, only interrupting her lament in order to eat or sleep, and even then maintaining a certain translucent wash. Elisabeth was convinced she was drinking some dangerously potent cocktail, and spent the best part of two days turning the house upside down in a search for her mother's new hiding place, but to no avail. If Sadie was drinking, as she vehemently denied, then she was showing unusual care in concealing it. Joseph kept well away: while he sensed something different about Sadie's repentance this time, her record thus far was not convincing, and he refused to be drawn into her battles if she was then going to give up halfway through. The twins, however, would be drawn into anything, and hence were their mother's righthand men – or, at least, one was right, the other took her left side to equal it out – always there with a box of tissues, an ever-broadening shoulder, and, when they could secure her, Isobel.

It had not taken Elisabeth long to realise the power Isobel allowed her over her family, and she was swift to exercise it. After the initial shock of motherhood had worn off, and she began to understand the element of possession that was necessarily attached, she grew covetous of her daughter's waking hours, and imposed a severe timetable upon those who wished to share them. 'She's my daughter,' she was frequently heard to exclaim, 'so I'll say what she does, and with whom,' and because nobody dared risk their position as a 'whom', they conformed. For the first time, it seemed, Elisabeth was a player in this house that had always sidelined her, and she took to the field like a true professional.

'Team spirit,' Seamus would grumble, himself always the first to show unity. 'You can't keep her all to yourself. And after all, I'm as much her Dad as anyone, so I've got rights.'

But 'rights' had never been an especially popular argument for any of them, and Elisabeth refused to be swayed. 'Whim' was by far the preferred means of reckoning, and even in this she was not overly generous. If there was one thing she had inherited from her mother, apart from her ability to draw a crowd with her curses, it was a wholehearted submission to the power of the spirit. Only in Elisabeth's case, rather than the heavenly or bottle-shaped versions Sadie had always worshipped, that spirit was the never-to-be-broken, all consuming armour of Self.

'If you can't help yourself, who can you help?' became her favourite, and much repeated, saying, with the emphasis more upon 'and if you can't, leave me alone anyway', which naturally underlies the proverb. And 'If you want a job done properly, do it yourself', incidentally a great belief of Lily's, which also might be read as 'so don't ask me'.

Such exclusivity extended not only to the day-to-day matters upon which her family sought to intrude, but also to the subject of Isobel's father whose identity remained a secret. There was really only Joseph to whom it was ever of any importance, but when his casual, and occasionally authoritarian, approaches were met with stony silence each time, defeat was soon contended and Elisabeth's solo right as parent acknowledged across the board. Should any of them later think to challenge this, it would be surreptitiously.

At last the dam of Sadie's tears dried up, and it was once again possible to hold a conversation without forever pausing to mop the floors. Her return to the land of the living, in whatever form, was quickly absorbed into the routine of the everyday, and as the weeks went by, it was as if she had never been away. Her abstinence of the first few days appeared to have been kept up, and although her thirst had by no means abated, an hour or so spent with Isobel was guaranteed to quench it at least part way to being bearable. That her regard for her granddaughter should have become as desperate as it did, was thus hardly surprising.

'Please, Elisabeth, I swear to God, just for an hour . . . half an hour . . . ten minutes . . .? Surely to the Sacred Heart you can spare her that long, can you not?'

Elisabeth would glance at her watch and consider the proposal before, more often than not, declaring no, she couldn't spare her actually, and wandering away. Perhaps she was testing her mother? Or maybe simply paying her back for the years of denial Elisabeth felt she herself had suffered: years spent creeping around the house, and going out to play, because you never knew if it was a good day or not; years spent angry, when all she wanted was to be nice. Why, after all that, should she 'spare' anything?

If Isobel became a means of bargaining, or, potentially, of revenge, she was none the worse for it. Unaffected by the moods and inclinations, wet or dry, of those around her, she drifted in and out of the various clutches which made up her world with rarely a murmur. Not that she was passive: she could tantrum and paddy with as much conviction as the rest of them; but rather she was peaceful. The conflict which so divided her peers appeared to have worn itself out by the time it reached Isobel, and she embodied the very same singularity for which they had each fought so determinedly. For Elisabeth, and the twins also, this was simply a matter of character, and they failed to link Isobel's sense of being with anything of their own. But for Sadie it was a reminder of a loss, her own loss, and as she gazed upon Isobel, she saw just how complete it had been. When did it happen? When did the floating in the shallows of the sea, the basking upon the shell-encrusted rocks, turn into the drowning, rotting nothing it was today? When did the singular fall apart into all these tiny pieces?

When it happened, however, was soon dismissed in favour of the surer unanswerability of how. How had such containment become isolation? How had the thrill of being alive, being filled by her world, degraded to mere survival, living at its lowest ebb? And after how, came where, and after where, who, and after who, who next? And if all the other interrogatives were met with a blank, at least this last was clear: who next? Isobel, of course.

Sadie's subsequent spiral from quiet anxiety into deeper and deeper desperation was rapid. No longer could she gently plead with Elisabeth for her granddaughter's company, but rather she felt compelled to demand it, a matter of life and death, and she would rant and rave until it was given. And having thus secured it, every moment, every precious spill of time, was held up to the light, shaken, blown upon to reveal its colour. No more the walks in the garden, the paddling in the bath, for these were activities anyone could share in; it was the uninvited, the intrinsic, with which Sadie was concerned, and she set about a teaching of this with a vengeance born of her own regrettable truancy.

Isobel loved every lesson, from the tinkling shells which were wound about her legs and arms, to the softness of the sheepskin rug Sadie used to imitate the seals; from the cool slick of the oil which was smeared upon her 'tail', to the tickle of sand as they buried themselves. Every day they climbed inside the boat of Sadie's bath, rub-a-dub, and sailed to a new and more exciting world which it was promised could be hers; every day they swam the tide of discovery, flailing to get home before they were missed, and tomorrow's outing suspended as punishment. Isobel was three months old. What part of Sadie's instruction she might or might not have understood was left to the individual to judge.

Elisabeth, it need not be emphasised, was indignantly dismissive. She resented her mother's meddling, and distrusted its effects. When Isobel was returned to her after an afternoon with her grandmother, laughing and exhausted, she chose the latter as her focus and complained that Sadie was irresponsibly 'overdoing it'. On other occasions, when the child was calm and serene, she accused her mother of failing to stimulate her. She decided to follow them when they disappeared, watching for the slightest eccentricity, the smallest abuse of Elisabeth's iron-fisted rules, and when, on the very first day of spying, she watched Sadie knot wet towels about her daughter's legs and dangle her above a full bath to teach her how to dive for shells, she lost all control. Storming along the landing, screeching blue murder in language just as colourful, she vowed never to let her mother near Isobel again.

'As soon as they come out of there,' she pledged, 'then that's it. Finished. I'm not going to have my daughter growing up like her! Finished. Over.'

Locked together inside the bathroom, Sadie was at a temporary advantage at this point, and she considered the possibilities of 'that's it' with grim evaluation. But even Sadie knew she could not keep Isobel hidden in a room whose only escapes were a linen cupboard and a full bath – and experience had taught Sadie the crippling effects of both if indulged in for too long a period of time. No, they would have to come out and face 'it' for what it was.

And face it they did. By the time Sadie had made up her mind to descend, Joseph had been called home from work, the twins from college, Mrs Bradley from the kitchen, and they were each lined against the back wall of the drawing-room, nodding frantically to Elisabeth's every demand.

Sadie's entrance, complete with the now tail-less Isobel, was a relief to all of them, but the onslaught which ensued, involving not only faces, but hands, fists and feet to boot, proved less than welcoming.

'Sadie, is this true?' Joseph demanded. 'Were you drowning Isobel in the bath just now? Were you?' He paused, struck by the absurdity of such a question, and glanced towards Elisabeth.

She nodded. 'Drowning, Daddy. Drowning.'

Sadie laughed. 'Holy Mary Mother of God, I wasn't drowning the mite, I was teaching her how not to, so I was. Drowning, would you not be knowing, takes more practice, so it does. She'll not be doing that for years, surely to God you knew that.'

'Don't be flippant, Sadie,' Joseph accused, 'this is serious.'

'I can see it is, so I can, with the great long mouths you're all having, honest to God, I can see.' She bent her head to Isobel and suggested she take note of this also. 'Then you'll know when to start your drowning,' she encouraged, 'when you've had a few of these growling at you!'

The twins sniggered, and simultaneously swung their alliance towards their mother. The odds might be against her, but her strategy was by far the more deserving.

'She's right, you know, Da, you do look a miserable lot!' Seamus whooped, sticking a forefinger in either side of his mouth and grinning grotesquely. Joe did the same.

'Stop it!' Elisabeth screamed, and the fingers quickly moved from mouth to ears. 'Stop it! You're as bad as she is. None of you, none, is coming near my child again.' She launched across the room and grabbed Isobel to her chest, knocking Sadie backwards, and causing a landslide of persons and furniture in all directions. Isobel, assuming it to be time she gave her opinion on the matter, let out a wail of such pitch and fury, if anyone had wanted to continue the debate it would have to be in writing, for no further word was audible. As they each picked up their arguments and fled, the thunder of feet muffled to a mere patter, it was clear that any drowning to be done, while it might indeed involve Isobel, was to be of the more verbal 'out' variety, than any more watery interpretation.

Nevertheless, Elisabeth had her way, and from this day on Sadie was refused her previous hours alone with Isobel, and limited to the occasional supervised twenty minutes here and there. She was allowed no higher than the first floor landing, and no further than the bay tree at the bottom of the garden, and should she even dream of getting the child either wet or oily, then even these allowances would be denied. Sadie was distraught, the ever popular 'But that's not fair' making a howling comeback, and even Isobel seemed to find the situation rather a bore. Both child and grandmother became listless, washed up upon the banks of Elisabeth's stipulations, and within weeks of the 'compromise', as Joseph diplomatically referred to it, being put into play, what new light there had been seemed to have turned decidedly dull.

'She's pining, so she is,' Sadie observed, when for the third time in a month Isobel had come down with a cold. 'She's wanting to return to the sea, to be sure, and if you're not letting her go, so help me God, you'll be losing her for good. She'll sneeze herself right out of your hands, honest to God, she will.'

'Don't be ridiculous,' Elisabeth scorned, smearing Vic's vapours across Isobel's wheezing chest. 'Go fill your own mind with such rubbish, but if you're thinking of filling my daughter's, don't bother.'

Sadie leaned forwards and dangled a string of shells above Isobel's stomach, watching as the child's red and watery eyes followed them from side to side, and murmuring incoherently.

'Mother, go away,' Elisabeth warned. 'Just go away and take your witchcraft with you.'

'Fair enough,' Sadie complied, 'But you'll be calling me back again soon enough, sure you will, for you can't make a rope out of sea-sand, honest to God, no.'

And with that she wafted out the door, leaving Elisabeth all the more convinced of her mother's insanity, and Isobel noticeably frayed.

17

She had, Sadie maintained, no choice but to leave. Even much later, when Isobel was a grown woman with children of her own, Sadie swore it had been an act of mercy, of desperate salvation, and to her dying day she would defend her flight. Fishes swim with the tide, she intoned, and this one was going out.

It was raining the day they left, and the skies outside the bathroom window were heavy with premonition. Sadie watched as Elisabeth, buttoned to her chin in bright yellow mackintosh, hat pulled tight around her ears, clattered in and out of the back door with armfuls of soaking nappies rescued from the line, and willed her to look up. But Elisabeth was set upon more earthly pursuits, and as she splashed across the kitchen where Isobel roasted by the fire, she could not have known that upstairs Sadie was filling a suitcase with shells and gathering for the off.

'I hate this weather,' Elisabeth grumbled, dropping the squares of sodden terrycotton into the tumble drier. 'I hate this weather.' And only feet away Isobel swilled the contents of her bottle in ever faster circles, as the thunder crashed and the sky lit up with white.

Sadie waited until Elisabeth disappeared into her bedroom to change, and then, locking the bathroom door, she crept downstairs, suitcase under her arm, and into the kitchen. Wrapping Isobel in her shawl, and tucking the bottle inside, she took a last look around and then she was out the back door, through the gate, and down to the end of the street before Elisabeth had even removed her socks.

'We're away!' she whispered to the silent Isobel. 'We're away, so we are.'

They took a taxi from outside the Fiddler's Arms, windscreen wipers cutting a vivid arc, and made their way around Regent's Park and out towards the West, all the while Sadie whispering their freedom in ever increasing excitement. 'I want to be going home!' she had instructed the driver upon sitting down, and he, establishing the whereabouts of this, had recommended Heathrow Airport.

'Will you be flying alone, miss?' he enquired, eager to pass on a few tips from his own experience, but her horrified 'Flying? Jesus, Mary and Joseph, I'm not to be flying, am I?' quickly dissuaded him. You got some odd ones coming out when the weather was bad, he noted wryly. Flying indeed.

Arriving at the airport, Sadie rooted in her suitcase for the wad of money she had taken from Mrs Bradley's housekeeping pot the night before, and handed him a crumpled handful of one pound notes and cockleshells, before dragging herself, Isobel, and the said shells through the door to the check-in. Joining a queue entitled 'Passengers Without Tickets' she waited patiently for her turn.

'Where will you be travelling to, madam?' the desk clerk politely wondered.

'Ireland,' Sadie declared.

'So that will be Dublin?' the clerk offered.

'Dublin?' Sadie exclaimed, her eagerness to reach her destination overlooking the details of the actual journey. 'Jeez, yes, Dublin, I s'pose.'

There was a flight just after midday, in an hour and a half, and Sadie, refusing to give up her suitcase to the baggage controllers, was despatched to the departure lounge until her gate was called and she could board. She sat down next to a group of middle-aged businessmen, and fingered the edges of Isobel's shawl distractedly. The digital numbers of the clock above her head shuffled towards noon, dropping out of sight like a magician's cards, and Sadie wondered at the likelihood of her own disappearing having been discovered yet. Quite high, she supposed.

High indeed: Aces, Kings, and the Jokers are wild. When Elisabeth returned to the kitchen to find Isobel gone, she immediately assumed Mrs Bradley must have taken her, but when the innocent kidnapper, polishing the silver in the sitting-room, denied all knowledge, it was clear that Sadie was up to her old pranks. Charging up the stairs, cursing her mother's defiance from every door and keyhole, Elisabeth was less than surprised when she reached the bathroom and found the door locked and the occupants silent. Sadie was always so predictable.

'Well, you'll have to come out sometime,' she philosophised, throwing herself on to the step, 'and I'll be waiting for you when you do.'

Elisabeth waited there for six hours, her feet wedged to the wall of the landing, her back bolt upright against the door, and it was not until Joseph arrived home later that afternoon and opened the door with the spare key he had had secretly cut for just such an occasion, that the cause of their interminable silence was discovered. The bathroom was empty, even the shells gone, and who knew where Sadie could be by now?

Dublin was where. After a short flight during which Sadie was pinned to her seat, and Isobel was almost nailed down with her, they touched down at Dublin airport to the welcome applause of an Irish jig over the tannoy, and a shimmering rainbow over the tarmac. Sadie climbed down the steps, her pots of gold held tight beneath each arm, and took her first look at Ireland in almost twenty years.

'Blessed Mary,' she murmured, 'I'm home, so I am. At long last I'm home.'

Not quite, however. When she eventually emerged from the grasping hands of Customs – 'They're shells, bejeezus, what do you think they are?' – and leapt on board the first bus she saw upon leaving the Arrivals lounge, it did not occur to her that it might not be going where she was. Sadie's experience of public transport in Ireland, albeit twenty years ago, was that a bus went once a week, and in one direction only, and it surprised her to learn that this might have changed. When she informed the driver of the village she was heading for, he gave her the special look Dubliners reserve for such ignorant exiles as she – a look which says '*Chroist!* Ya might have been away, but you're still a *culchie!*' – and suggested she get off at the Busaras office down the street and ask there. Sadie did not appreciate being classed as a tourist, but considering her position, she swallowed her pride and did just that.

A bus, she was informed, would be going on Tuesday (today was Friday) but if she took that she would have to change twice, and the connection on the third leg of the journey was not always reliable. Alternatively, she could wait until Thursday when there was a bus straight through, but if Thursday was the last day in the month, which it was, then there would not be one. Of course, she could always take the train, although she would probably have missed the one today by now, and then get a bus the last few miles. 'Its whatever's suiting you, dear, sure it is, but I would be hurrying you now, as I'm closing for lunch ten minutes ago, I am.'

Sadie stared disbelievingly as the curtain was drawn across the smiling, unhelpful face of the woman behind the desk, and dropped her head to Isobel's cheek. 'What's suiting,' she confided, 'would be getting us home before next Thursday. That's what would be suiting, surely to God . . .'

A man in the queue behind her, similarly disappointed by the timing of the CIE's eating habits, tapped her on the shoulder. Sadie turned around. 'I'd be trying the train, sure I would, they's always running behind on Fridays, without fail, honest to God, and you might as well.' He nodded to the curtained desk. 'Better than waiting here, would you not say?'

Sadie nodded gratefully. 'Might as well,' she echoed and, gathering shawl and shells, she trundled out on to the street in search of a station.

'Heuston or Connolly?' the first passer-by she launched herself upon demanded.

'Jeez, there's more than one, you're telling me?' Sadie sighed, feeling increasingly thwarted.

'South or North then?' the woman demanded.

'Jeez, I don't know . . . West, I'm guessing, though since when it mattered, surely to the Sacred Heart, I just . . .'

'Heuston then,' her advisor proclaimed, and promptly walked off. 'And good luck to you,' she threw back, with not a little sarcasm.

Heuston, then, it was. Sadie flagged down a taxi, repeated the wisdom, and braved the driver's curses at the other end when she had only English sterling to pay him with. To the rumbling echoes of a much rehearsed Nationalist spirit, she fled platformwards to discover that, yes indeed, the train for Galway, which it turned out was the nearest main station to home, was running late.

Joseph failed to inform the authorities of Sadie's disappearance until noon the following day, a Saturday. Her devotion to her granddaughter was, they agreed, the greatest guarantee of both their safety, and anyway, Sadie was only doing it for badness. She would be back, repentant, in a matter of hours, so why make an issue of it? Why play into her hands?

'You know what she's like, Elisabeth ... this is just her way of making sure we don't forget her. Isobel will be absolutely fine, you know she will. Just let your mother have her moment, and then we'll sort it out.'

'You always forgive her,' Elisabeth accused, incredulous. 'Why do you forgive her when she never deserves it, never? Why do you let her get away with this?'

'I don't,' Joseph defended, weakly. But he did. He knew he did. It was just something he couldn't help. 'I just don't want us to overreact to this, that's all.'

'You mean you don't want to show her for what she is.'

'No, Elisabeth.'

'Yes. Same as always. Pretend she's fine, and hope it'll all go away. Until the next time, and the next time ... Well, all right, if you want to think that, okay. But as soon as she gets back with Isobel, then I'm leaving. I've had enough of this stupid family, I'd rather be by myself.'

'Elisabeth, please ...' Joseph sat down at the table beside her and attempted to take her hand but she snatched it back and continued to stare past him towards the door. He sighed. 'Elisabeth, don't shut yourself off—'

'Hah!' she returned.

And he knew that door had slammed long before. One more successful bid for exclusion.

Sadie did not return in a matter of hours. Nor did she return the next morning. Joseph went off to his Saturday clinic with a heavy heart, and at lunchtime he called the police. Predictably, they claimed there was little they could do until Monday, and because it was 'in the family' so to speak their hands were pretty much tied, but if he had thoughts as to where she might have gone, they'd do their best. Where she might have gone? Up until making the telephone call, Joseph had disallowed the prospect that she might have gone anywhere. Where she might have gone? He drove home, the question ringing in his ears, attacking him in every screech of tyres, every blare of car radio as he waited at traffic lights. Where she might have gone? But she wouldn't have gone anywhere, surely. Not without telling him first.

'I don't know,' Elisabeth offered. 'One of her brother's maybe? She was always going on about visiting them somewhere around here. Didn't one live in Battersea or something?'

'No,' Joseph sighed, 'that was all in her mind.' Elisabeth raised an eyebrow knowingly. 'Her brothers are all in Ireland, or were the last I knew.'

'Maybe she's gone to Ireland then,' Seamus suggested, picking at the edge of the window ledge with his nail. 'Maybe that's where she is.'

'No,' Joseph repeated, sighing a second time. 'She'd never have gone all that way. Not with Isobel with her.' Elisabeth raised the other eyebrow. 'At least, I don't think she would . . .'

The train pulled into Galway station at just after eight o'clock that evening. It had stopped at every conceivable town, village, or watering hole along the length of the five-hour journey, and it now seemed as relieved as Sadie to have at last reached its destination. As she stepped on to the platform, the rain beat like marbles upon the corrugated roof, and she shivered, cradling Isobel close, and searching around her for a trolley, porter, anything, to relieve her arms of the two leaden weights they had carried since London. But there was nothing. Following the pencilled arrows towards the ticket office, kicking paper cartons and sweet-wrappers as they blew about her feet, she thought she must be at the end of the world.

No. But it was nigh. The ticket office was closed, the

room in darkness, and only the distant ringing of a telephone from deep within suggested there might once have been life. A flaking board of timetables to her left had been recently revamped with the broad, anonymous strokes of a local graffiti artist, and even if there was a bus, which the emptiness of the station seemed rather to discourage, then she would not have known it anyway. She moved towards the exit, dragging her suitcase behind her, but as she approached a gust of wind blew the wooden door open, and she saw the rain had become sleet, and she turned back. She dropped to the floor, resting upon the case, and put her head in her hands. There seemed to be nothing else she could do. As if in sympathy, Isobel began to wail, her voice curling up from the depths of Sadie's elbows, and as outside the sleet turned to snow, and the snow began to settle, it seemed Domesday had at last arrived.

Fumbling in her pocket for a tissue to wipe Isobel's creasing eyes, Sadie found one of the cockleshells the taxi-driver at Heathrow had given back to her that morning, and she held it to her mouth, blowing gently.

'See this,' she whispered, easing Isobel upright and pushing the tiny crust into her hand. 'My daddy always told us that on the Day of Judgement the whole sea would be fitting in one of these, so it would, hiding to get away from God, isn't that the truth? Are you thinking it's there yet, sure?' Sadie held Isobel's palm to her ear. 'Are you hearing its roar, tell me now, are you?'

Isobel gazed at her grandmother, her face dappled mackerel with her drizzling tears, and stilled as the distant hum of the sea filled her head.

'Are you hearing it?' Sadie mouthed softly. 'Are you ready for the counting, sure now, for it'll not be long if the sea's in that shell, so it won't. We'll all be looking for hiding, so we will. 'S'good thing I brought so many, sure it is!'

Sadie smiled wistfully, and continued to pass the shell

from Isobel's ear to her own. Behind her a door opened unnoticed, and an oldish man wearing slippers and a stationguard's cap stepped out, shaking the dregs of a tea cup on to the concrete of the waiting hall.

'You're not after a train, are you, for there'll be no more engines out of here till the morning now . . .'

Sadie turned, gazing at the brown plaid feet of her questioner, and shook her head. She was waiting for a bus home or eternal judgement, depending upon which arrived first.

'You've missed the last buses as well,' he added.

Sadie shrugged. Looked like it would be the eternal judgement then.

'Where're you wanting to get to, is it? For you can't be sitting there all night, and there's a cold coming in that'd freeze hell over, honest to Her Blessed Self, it would.'

Sadie offered the name of her village, and Isobel crooned in recognition, but the man simply shook his head. 'You'll not be getting up there tonight, so you won't, not unless you're catching the Boatman before he leaves, to be sure.'

Sadie nodded, assuming the 'Boatman' to be some oblique reference to her doomed fate, and stared at the swinging door of the exit, where the snow could be seen to be deepening.

'Would you be having me call him, would you, 's'no trouble, and it'll save you a night in a guesthouse, so it will, surely to God, if he's still for leaving, which is not to be reckoned on, aye that the truth it isna . . .?'

Sadie watched his racing mouth chew and spit out the unconnected phrases, and tried to make sense of them. But by then he had disappeared again, back into the dark of the door, and she was left with only the flash of his tobacco-stained teeth and the pad of his slippers for explanation.

Minutes later, however, he was back. 'Now will you tell me, are you blessed or are you blessed? To be sure, he's leaving, but he hasn't gone yet, but he's still to be going, and he'd be glad to be taking you, that he would, glad.' He grinned at her excitedly. If this *was* the Day of Reckoning, then he was straight up to Peter for this one. And as if to make sure, he invited the girl and her scrap of baby into his two-bar-electric-fired office, where they might await their deliverance.

The 'Boatman', contrary to Sadie's expectation, was the mere mortal who ran the weekend ferry to the islands further up the Connemara coast, but spent his weeks in Galway doing a desk job for the Sea Fisheries Board. She never learned his name, although he chattered incessantly from the moment they climbed into the front of his rusted Ford van, but she was as grateful for the company as he clearly was, so such formalities seemed inconsequent. As the snow fell in an ever-thickening blur, and the road became increasingly indistinguishable from the ditches at one side and the intermittent glimpses of sea at the other, Sadie held tight to both dashboard and hope, with Isobel rocking on the seat at her side, and remembered that she was going home.

Joseph was beside himself. He was at the very edge of his oh-so-controlled temper and unsure where to turn, and Elisabeth, sitting next to him and repeatedly telling him she knew they should have called the police earlier, was not helping matters. How could he have known Sadie was going to do something like this? She never had before, or at least, not on this scale. So why should he have thought to notify anyone? Besides, he really did not think it wise to make this any more of an official 'interest' than it already was. If they could deal with it themselves, within the family, it would be better all round, for everyone. He told her so.

'For heaven's sake, will you please stop thinking about my

mother's reputation or your half-dead patients! Both can rot in hell as far as I'm concerned. My daughter is out there somewhere! Your granddaughter. Can you think about that?'

'Elisabeth, will you calm down? You know as well as I do that no harm will come to Isobel. Your mother dotes on her. Dotes. Let's just try and be rational, shall we?'

'Rational! Hah!'

More 'Hah!'s. That was all Joseph seemed to incite these days. Hah!s and Ho!s and occasionally outright laughter. It was as if, without anyone telling him of the change, he had woken up one morning, and he was a joke. No longer to be taken seriously. A clown, with painted sad eyes and a downmouth. Joseph shook his head, peering at his reflection in the circling brown of his tea, but all he saw were shadows, curving towards the rim. He would have to look further than a teacup for truth.

The world was white as the Boatman's rankling Ford van negotiated the last corner of Sadie's homecoming, and even the ghost-pale sea was veiled. All around them trees hung heavy with snow and hedges bowed deep, but any voices were lost beneath the dull thud of the sky, and their welcome was a silent one. Urging forwards, Sadie pressed her nose to the cold of the windscreen, searching for a face she might recognise, a name she might guess, but the road was deserted. She sat back, rubbing her bitten knuckles.

'They expecting you, are they?'

Sadie hesitated. 'No.'

'No, Jeezus, you're coming a fair way, honest to God, not to be expected. Sure someone'll be there, waiting, for it's no night to be out of a bed, surely it's not.' He stared at her, one hand balanced upon the steering wheel, the other drawing patterns in the air between them. 'You're welcome to come on up with me, till the morning, to be sure, if you're fretting . . .' It was a lonely life being a ferryman.

Sadie shook her head. ''S'kind of you, but I'm wanting …' She broke off, suddenly catching sight of the pooling yellow windows of O'Kearns' bar, 'You can drop me here, so you can. Just here.'

He slowed the van, and Sadie bundled out, pulling the sleeping Isobel after her, and slamming the door with a distracted wave. Isobel, thus rudely awakened, immediately began to squall, her habitually tranquil features whipping into a storm as she buffeted against Sadie's hip.

'Hush now, will you? You'll have to wait a bit, so you will. We're there now, so we are, so would you be saving your mawking yet, Issie?'

Issie, placated, hushed. Sadie looked around her, waving once again as the Boatman rumbled away, and slid her suitcase along his departing tyre tracks until she was outside O'Kearns. The snow beneath the bar windows was almost blue, stark and undisturbed, and any customers had clearly been there a long time. Sadie glanced back at the wavering trail of her own footprints. She was home.

She walked on past the bar, for the moment avoiding the explanations she knew her arrival would require, and followed the sea wall down to the quay. The harbour was in darkness, the only illumination a single beam from one of the houses which skirted its edge, the only sound a gentle slap-slap as the boats tipped against the full tide. She watched for a while, ignoring the damp wet that was seeping her shoes, willing one of the fishermen she knew to be tucked in O'Kearns to come out, to start the chug of engine and wheel out into the wide sea beyond. She wanted to hear the muffled roar, the deep-bellied grumble of night water she had dreamt of all these years, but instead there was only a windless hum. The windless hum of so many such watchings.

Isobel shifted, and in the darkness behind them something crashed loudly, followed by a chorus of giggled curses and a sudden still. The first of the footprints to leave O'Kearns, and by the sound of it, adding other parts of their anatomy to the record. Sadie smiled, looking down upon the mooning face of Isobel, and shrugged her deeper within the shawl as the snow continued to fall. Picking up her suitcase, she continued down the road, turning with the squared edge of the sea on to the flat of the harbour front. And then there she was.

The house was smaller than she remembered, huddled low behind the reaching arms of the quay wall, and worn somehow, as if the elements were finally gaining the foothold they had always sought. The windows were dark, and as she neared she saw a thick crust of salt had covered each one. Curtains hung wasted in peeling ribbons, and the paintwork was long since rotten, crackling beneath her touch. Wetting her finger, Sadie smudged a clearing in the salt, and pressed her eye to the glass. She could just make out the faded outline of a door on the opposite wall, beneath which a thin pencil of light dragged a lazy horizontal. Sadie frowned.

'In the name of God, what kind of a thing is this?' she demanded, glaring at the accommodatingly silent Isobel. 'What the bejeezus is going down, do you know?'

Isobel was not knowing. Nor was she particularly caring, it seemed, for she defiantly clamped her eyes shut upon her grandmother and began to wriggle irritably, pulling at the corners of the binding shawl and arching her back.

'Okay, Issie, would you stop fidgeting one second would you? Let me be trying the door, for I can't be believing they'd all be gone and left, to be sure I can't.'

Sadie sighed. The effort of such faith was draining. She moved to the door, hand upon the rusted lock, and studied it closely. It had clearly not been opened for some time, but nevertheless she put her elbow to the wood and leaned into the frame with as much effort as her long day and waning energies allowed. Nothing. Not even the satisfaction of a groan. Sadie kicked the door in disgust. And then she kicked it again in disappointment. And then she kicked it again simply because she did not know what else to do.

'What the divil are you . . .' A window above Sadie's head swung open and a woman's head burst through, fists like claws upon the ledge. 'Be off with you, in the Name of God, go on, before I take a bucket of water to you, so help me, be off!'

Sadie huddled against the doorframe, out of sight, watching as the woman craned left and right, muttering loudly, and wondering if she knew what bad luck it was to throw water from a window. She was about to inform her of the fact when a man appeared alongside, hands waving irritably and pointing towards the sea. 'Jeezus,' it grumbled, in a voice hoary with sleep, 'you and your bleeding fairies,' and pushing the first face back, began to close the window. 'Little feckers' might have been the last Sadie heard of both of them, had not the sight of the waving hand suddenly placed itself, and she leapt forwards, into the fading light of the shuttered window.

'Sweet Jeezus, is that Seamus, is it?' she whispered. 'Is that my Seamus, honest to God?'

'It is, aye . . .' The window slowly widened, and a chin, bristled and jowling, lowered itself suspiciously to the sill. 'And who is it that's wanting . . .?'

'It's Sadie, you great lump!'

'Sadie? Wee, scratty, Englishman Sadie?'

She nodded.

'Holy Mary mother of God, and there was I shouting me gob off, and it's our Sadie! Dear *Chroist* woman!' He shouldered the woman at his side. 'It's our bleeding Sadie, so it is!'

There was a scramble of toothy welcomes, and then a slamming of hands and windows, and Sadie hovered uncertainly as both faces withdrew into the isolating haze she had first seen fit to kick. But not for long. A bellow from the side of the house, and a barefooted hop to meet her, hurried her around the back, and into the stove-lit kitchen she had recently given up on ever seeing again. Falling into a chair, she unwrapped the sulking Isobel and laid her upon the hearth, before twisting towards the violet-toed Seamus who stood fascinated at her side and demanding.

'In the name of God, Seamus, would you tell me what's passing here, would you? I was thinking you were all dead and gone, so I was, and not a soul telling me, to be sure.'

Seamus crouched upon the chair opposite her, idly tickling the slowly warming Isobel with his forefinger, and nodded. 'Well, 'tis the truth that things are changing, so it is, but's been a while since you were here, Sade, God help us all. With the weather threatening these past years, they're all moving up in the village, leaving us here, rattling around this windy old place, surely to God, not living in the half of it, and slowly waiting for the sea to swallow us up good and all, that's the truth.'

His sandy head rose and fell as he spoke, the once raging mop of his hair now almost burnt out, and when he lifted his fist to bless God's help, Sadie noticed the mottle of freckles had been usurped by liver spots. He was an old man.

'But the others can't all be gone up, Shay . . . What about Ma . . .?' Sadie fingered the bottle she had untangled from Isobel's shawl, and stared around her hopefully. But everything had changed, and only the walls themselves, still damp, still crumbling, held any memories.

Seamus shrugged. 'The others being our lot, d'you mean? Well, they's mostly around, as is your mammy, never you fear. There's Devlin who's gone, and is living in Dublin, honest to God, of all places on this earth, and whose shaming the lot of us with his carry on, so he is. And there's Denis, who only this last month followed him, the fecker, leaving me with the nets to do, and Jesus knows what . . . And there's Lar, who's been gone a good few years now, to New York, he is, driving a taxi cab and married to a yank, for Christsake. And then Paul, who took off with a Wicklow girl one time he went to visit our Devlin, bless his soul, and is now living like Paddy's pig on some farm, with cows and hens, and God help us, He knows what else. And then the rest of us is here.' He grinned helpfully. 'Except Tommy,' he added. 'Tommy, scrap that he was, taken himself off to France – can you reckon it? *Frairnce!* Jesus take me if I tell a lie, and if he isn't sending us natty little postcards with "Bon Shure!" leeching all over them, honest to God it's the truth. Fancy he's getting an education, but get a cop on, I say, he was always a bleeding dreamer, to be sure he was, with his head in the clouds and his backside in the muck, honest to God it's the truth! Jeezus, I'm wondering what the divil the bit of harm it'd be doing . . .'

But Sadie was not listening to the devil and his harm, for she was counting her fingers and discovering that, where once she had had to add her big toes to make up the number of her brothers, now she had half a hand left over.

'Jesus, Shay, there's only the seven of yous, is that the truth. I'm not losing five, surely to God, I'm not.'

'Well, no, you're not,' Seamus fumbled, and when Sadie's hopeful smile began to lift, he shook his head sadly. 'There's Sean too, God bless him, for you were not hearing, I'm seeing . . . The sea got him going on Whitsuntide four years ago, for the love of God it did, fetching up a storm the likes of which you've never seen, and he's turning in the clay yet for going out in it, so he is. Honest to God, the man that goes out at Whit is fair asking for the drowning, to be sure he is . . .'

'Jeezus . . .' Sadie dropped her eyes from Seamus' growling frown, and gazed at the chuntering Isobel.

'I'm wishing it were diff'rent, Sade,' Seamus offered, 'but

feck it, you can't stop the sea, surely to the Blessed Virgin, you can't stop the sea.'

'Here.' The woman Sadie had seen earlier bent towards her and handed her a cup of tea. 'Get yourself warm, and then you can be staying upstairs for tonight, as your ma's living up in the village now, and it's too far for you to be going on a night like this, so help us.'

Sadie smiled obediently, gazing at her host.

'Maggie O'Connor,' she grinned, her hand to her breast, 'Post Office Maggie, remember me? Your lump of a brother here gave me four children, so he did, before he bothered to marry me, but he's not so bad now. See,' she pointed at him where he slumped by the fire, 'Friday night, sure enough, and he's home, would you reckon it, 'stead of boozing himself mad likes most of them, surely to God, and I'm grateful.'

Sadie shrugged. She could not have begged Joseph *into* a pub, never mind out.

The woman, Maggie, sat down on the arm of the chair, and began to play with Sadie's hair, teasing it through her fingers with childlike concentration. Sadie glanced at her, and slowly began to relax.

'I was thinking you were a mermaid, so I was, when I saw yous standing beneath the window like that, with all your hair and your eyes like candles,' she confided, softly. 'I thought you were after troubling us, honest to God, I did.'

Seamus flicked his thumb at her. 'You mad streel,' he muttered, 'with all your mermaids and spells, you're as bad as Sadie, so y'are. Were you thinking I'd been fooling with a lady of the waves, were you? To be sure, knocking at the door and coming to take me back, so she was!' He leaned forwards and tickled Isobel. 'It's this one that's got the eyes like candles, so it is,' he chuckled. 'It's this one you're wanting to be watching, you mark me now, it's this one.'

18

Sadie slept in her old room that night, slithering beneath the newly turned sheets, Isobel pressed to her stomach like a hot water bottle. The snow had eased off in recent hours, and was now a vague flutter somewhere beyond the salty panes. She wondered if knowing about Sean, about any of them who'd since cast themselves across the waves, would have stopped her coming, made staying in England easier. But she knew it would not. She had to come back here, to this house, to this bed. Whatever.

Whatever, whenever, however, forever. When Sadie awoke the next morning to find herself floating above a window full of sea, the sun, like a sail, lifting her up and away, she thought she could never be anywhere else again. She took considerable persuasion even to descend for breakfast, and were it not for the hungry wails of Isobel, most likely would not have done. Seven children, all of course Seamus', although not necessarily legitimately, hurtling around a kitchen, was not Sadie's preferred way of starting the day. Even Isobel was becoming rather tiresome, clearly having decided she was bored of playing second fiddle to Sadie's dreams, and already effecting a more demanding stance. She would be glad to get away to her mother's house for a few hours, and leave them all, including Isobel, behind. It was far too early for such confrontations.

But early for Sadie, living in London for twenty years and rising when she felt like it, did not crack the same dawn as it did for the rest of civilisation, and by the time she blew out of the door at just gone nine-thirty, she was at a considerable disadvantage. The news that the flighty redhead was back, arriving in the midnight hours with a baby of all things, had been scandalous revelation, tittle-tattled gossip, and old hat, before she had even opened her eyes, and if she expected to surprise anyone then she was going to be disappointed. By none more so than the very woman she had set off so punctually to visit.

Sadie's mother suffered few delusions when it came to any of her children, but in the case of Sadie, she was particularly circumspect. Thirteenth born and hell-bent from the first, she had always known her daughter would be trouble, but with a dozen sons to keep her occupied, the fact rather slipped her mind. Packing her off to London with the Englishman had been a timely saving all round, and although she had always suspected that would not be the end of it, she could hope. For it is simpler with boys. As children they fight their battles with one another, and then as men, with the sea, and there is little one can do for them but be waiting when they return. Girls are left with only the standing around, the letting go and taking hold, suppressing any conflicts they themselves might wage beneath the bloodier demands of brothers, fathers, husbands, and, eventually, sons. Only Sadie had never understood this. Never comprehended the secrets women silently share, the burdens they pass on, one to the next. She had always needed to be told, her brow wrinkling, a frown ready to pounce, and even then she had flung herself off before it could begin to make sense. And now she was back.

Outside the snow was falling once again, growing heavier by the ever-whitening minute. Seamus reported a flock of seagulls hiding out in one of the church buildings beyond the hill, always a sure sign of worsening weather, and he warned Sadie to dress warmly if she was to be going out. Handing her a pair of size fourteen boots – the same ones in which he had dug up Joseph's garden all those years before, and which had since been considered suitable only for special occasions – and a couple of fishing sweaters, he sighed loudly, lamenting the fact that she had not seen the country at its best. Sadie smiled at his melancholy, telling him it was this kind of wildness she so missed, and handed him back the second sweater. It was only later, struggling up the stone steps of the harbour that she realised he had offered the sentiment as an apology, a formality one might exchange with any passing tourist in the hope they will not think badly. Seamus, it occurred to her, had forgotten this was her home.

It was Maggie who called the Hill House, taking the number from the scrap of paper Seamus kept tucked inside his bible, and introducing herself as 'a friend'. She had known something was wrong, she insisted, from the minute she set eyes upon Sadie, a certain look, a brightness, 'candles', Joseph thought she had said. When Elisabeth came on the line, she was able to hold Isobel to the receiver and reassure her that she was fine, 'lickety split' so to speak, and offer her own consolation as to what it meant to be a mother. And then Maggie gave Joseph precise directions of how to find them, 'for you're maybe forgetting us after these years, to be sure,' assuring him there was no need to phone first, for this was a call box she was ringing from, 'and I'm not often up this way'. In short, she let the cat out of the bag, set it upon the pigeons, and then killed it with a sharpness of instinct (derived from too many years reading other people's post) which had long ago made curiosity but an excuse. As she said, she just had a feeling something was wrong.

* * *

Four others who shared that 'feeling' took the first flight out of Heathrow, landing in Dublin at nine o'clock that night to find, tomorrow being Sunday, there would not be a train to Galway until Tuesday. The car rental offices were all closed for the weekend, and a bus was out of the question. And so Joseph called upon an old college acquaintance he had heard was now lecturing at Trinity, and, pulling on the network, pulling out the stops, he borrowed the University minibus and saved the day. Or at least, saved tomorrow. For it was too late to be leaving that night, and the weather forecast for snow moving across from the west was not good. Hence, they booked into a small hotel, hoped for rain, and planned to leave in the morning. Still keeping it all in the family.

But Joseph missed her. He could not pretend otherwise, despite his awareness of her irresponsibility, his open denunciation of her wrong. He simply missed her. And when he had asked Maggie if she was all right, and Maggie had said she was 'lickety split' and offered to let Isobel tell her mother herself, it wasn't what he meant at all. For all her faults, it was Sadie who would always be central to his concerns, Sadie he would keep running after, much as he had guessed that very first day he saw her on the beach. Some things, even to a man of Joseph's rational philosophy, were just meant to be.

'Up the village', rather than the several miles Seamus' boot-and-sweatered survival attire had suggested, was a two minute walk across the harbour, and Sadie reached the door to her mother's new house with barely an icicle to show for it. She hesitated, the aluminium window frames, glass-panelled door and general order of the place, nothing like the scenes she had so frequently returned to all these years, and she almost turned back. Her preference for illusion was still her strongest defence. But a twitch of a curtain, and a double-glazed rap, put paid to such instincts, and barely had her foot risen in its boot to flee, than the door swung open, and her mother was standing, shorter and noticeably greyer, on the nylon-matted threshold before her.

'Bad pennies,' she muttered, flicking a cursory wrist of welcome and nodding Sadie inside. 'I should have known it, so help me God, I should have known it.'

Sadie sidled past, discarding her various layers upon the appointed newspaper, and twiddling her fingers nervously.

'Will you get off, honest to God,' her mother grumbled, swiping Sadie's knitting hands irritably, 'you've a fidgit on you to itch the devil, honest to God you do.'

Sadie 'got off', and hurried forwards, propelled by a bony knuckle pressed to her shoulder, and found herself in front of a bay window filled with porcelain figures, looking out upon the street.

'Would you sit down, now?' A spindled pine dining chair was nudged against her knees, 'And let me get a look, would you?'

As Sadie hovered upon the purple tongue of cushion, her mother slowly shook her head, lowered herself into an armchair opposite, the one piece of furniture Sadie recognised, and then smiled, softly. 'You're not changing, are you, honest to God, not changing one jot?'

It was a curious observation, considering the twenty years which had passed and the many battles Sadie had fought during the course of them, but sitting there, surrounded by potted plants and polyester cushion covers, she might have been right. Perhaps Sadie was the only one for whom nothing ever changed. She had certainly intended it to be so.

'Bit baggier round the ...' croning fingers pulled at her cheeks, 'and not so glinty, to be sure,' as she nodded to Sadie's hair, 'but ever the like in the eyes, I'm seeing that, surely to God, ever the wicked in the eyes.'

Sadie rolled her head backwards, uncomfortable before such an exacting study, and scratched her neck.

'But time waits for no man, oh no,' her accuser suddenly declared, 'and I'm sure there's changing after going on, so I am. That's why you're here, I don't doubt, am I right? That's for what you're doing picking yourself up and landing back here?'

Sadie was silent, and her mother moved closer, her ringless fingers gripping Sadie's knee, her voice barely a croak. 'Listen, Sadie, you were always a flighty thing, so help me God you were, but if you're after skedaddling back here just for badness, for I'm sure now that's what you're at, well you can skedaddle yourself back again, honest to God you can.'

Sadie pushed her away, turning towards the window and glaring out at the jigsawed stones of the church wall which fronted it.

'There's a reason in the way things are, sure there is,' her mother offered quietly. 'You can't always be fighting it, for the love of God, you can't.'

Sadie continued to watch the wall, daring the stones to move and add their own weight to such wisdom, but they remained motionless, huddled together and safe in their number.

'I'm not always fighting,' Sadie murmured, the first words she had spoken since her arrival.

'Honest to God, sure you are,' her mother nodded. 'Else what'd you be doing here, will you tell me that?'

Sadie left soon after, wading into Seamus' boots and plunging from the house with much the same desperation as she had thrown herself out of arms and beneath the waves as a child. Hucking her collar against the rising, snow-heavy wind, she gritted her teeth and chuntered angrily as she made her way back down the harbour towards the quay. The tide was on the ebb, and the boats rocked lifelessly on a muddy, seaweeded bed, their ropes stretched taut. She loved it when it was like this, when she could walk the sea floor, sink herself in its flooded waste, and imagine it was at her command that the waters would return. How many times she had stood upon the shell-speckled rock by the harbour end and screeched at the sea that it could come back now, that it was forgiven. A history's worth. But today, somehow, she did not feel like it. Today, she was afraid the sea just might not listen.

Maggie was in the kitchen when she got back to the house, boiling eggs and buttering toast soldiers, enough to feed an army, while the multitude of her offspring clamoured about her legs. Isobel was propped in an old pushchair, gazing contentedly on, and Seamus was rocking her back and forth from his sunken lookout by the fire.

'You're not fishing?' Sadie demanded, wondering that his stay-at-home husbanding should extend to the days as well.

'It's a bit airy for the going out,' he shrugged.

'Will you be taking me up to me brothers then, Shay, for I don't want to be missing them, sure I don't?'

'They'll be as soon coming down,' he nodded. 'They knows as you're here, right they does.'

''S'that why my mammy was not surprised to see me, is it? I was thinking I'd be surprising her, so I was, but she was fair sorry with the fact, so she was. Proper telling she gave me, so she did.' Sadie laughed, dismissing her earlier despondency, and Maggie looked up from her knifing recruitment.

'Word gets around, so it does. You're not keeping secrets for long, isn't that the truth.' If there was a hint of apology in her tone, Sadie mistook it for mere generalisation, and she nodded in acknowledgement.

'For sure, I'm forgetting how even the wind's gossiping, so I am. The English have to be shaken to find the news, don't you know, honest to God, they do.'

Maggie smiled. 'And are you for shaking your own Englishman then, Sadie?' she asked, glancing towards Isobel.

Sadie was silent for a moment. And then, picking Isobel from the chair and resting her against her hip, she replied softly, 'There's not much for shaking that one, Maggie, not much 't'all.'

She spent the rest of the day in her bedroom, unpacking her shells, and planning her future. With Seamus and Maggie only using the back half of the house, she could quite easily take over the front, and she'd have no difficulty getting one or other of her brothers to do whatever reparations were needed. There was a fireplace in both the front room and the bedroom above, so heating wouldn't be a problem, and she'd have no end of babysitters for Isobel. She'd miss having her old bedroom, but it would not matter really, for she only needed to walk outside and she'd see just the same view. Every day. And there would be no leaving this time. No. This time she was here to stay, whatever her mother thought of her.

At no point in her ruminations did Sadie dwell, or even dwindle, upon Joseph, and Elisabeth was wished quite out of existence. It was as if she had decided upon a world, peopled at her discrimination, which had no place for the inconsistencies such as they offered. Only Isobel was allowed to remain, bridging the innumerable gaps between old and new, and ever open to interpretation: mother, daughter, sister, grandmother, in the shrinking family of Sadie, she played them all. And while the fishermen on the quay hauled in their boats, their distrust of redheads only confirmed by the rising storms, Sadie handed Isobel her bottle and the thunder rolled.

The minibus left Dublin at eight o'clock the following morning, with the wished-for rain giving its all to their cause, but by the time they neared Galway some five and a half hours later, little less than a tidal wave would have cleared the banks of snow building up at every side. Freak

February winds blowing across the Atlantic were causing chaos both on land and sea, and as they neared the coast road, it was debatable if they would make it through. But Joseph battled on, buttressed over the steering wheel as if his life depended upon it, the twins and Elisabeth clattering around behind, and had it not been for one careless turn, they would have been home and dry.

Joseph never could say what it was that distracted him. He thought it might have been a bird suddenly flying up out of the bush, or perhaps snow falling from the trees above; Sadie thought it was more likely a *shee gaoithe*, or 'fairy-blast', kicked up from the heels of dancing fairies who were notorious along that road, and at the time Joseph did not dismiss it. But whatever its source, the brief second for which he looked away was enough to allow a tree to jump out from the verge and position itself directly before the bus, and any braking was already too late. Elisabeth screamed, the twins hollered, and Joseph quietly ducked as one of its lower branches came straight through the windscreen and took a chunk out of the top of his left ear.

Somewhat shaken, they staggered on to the roadside and surveyed the damage, not least to the side of Joseph's head, and it was rapidly apparent that neither bus nor driver would be going very far in the near future. They remembered a garage some miles back, but having spun several circles after hitting the tree, and the blizzard all around now blinding beyond the length of an arm, which way was back and which forwards was a matter unto itself. Seamus offered to walk in one direction, suggesting Joe and Elisabeth take the other, and Joseph was left propped against the passenger seat until either or both returned with help. It was not the way he had planned it.

'This bloody country,' he cursed as he watched their backs disappear into the fog, 'every time it gets me. Every time.'

* * *

It was almost an hour before the truck arrived, crawling along the road with every light blazing, and Joseph had almost given up hope. When the driver jumped out and ran around to his door, he was shivering so much he could barely speak, and it was not until he had allowed himself to be levered across the man's shoulder and into the front of his van that he realised neither the twins nor Elisabeth were there.

'Wal-king . . . fe-fetch . . . help,' was as much as he could stutter, squinting at his rescuer through icicled lashes.

'You'll be grand, don't you fret, just sit back there and we'll get you some looking at with a doctor, sure in no time.'

And although Joseph would have liked to tell him he himself was a doctor, that his three children had disappeared into a blizzard to find a mechanic in this godforsaken land, and that his wife had run off with his granddaughter two days before which was why they were here in the first place, he simply did not have the energy.

Doctors, however, are not always the easiest thing to find in the depths of rural Ireland, on a coast road in a snowstorm (unless they're half-frozen and sitting next to you), and hence the driver decided to leave at least two of the three conditions behind and, turning a sharp right on to an invisible farmtrack, took a short cut. By boat. Joseph still shuddering in the front of the van, he unhooked the currach he was towing behind, and eased it on to the beach. It was low tide and the sand was a deep rust, freckled by the drifting winds, and as he led Joseph to the boat, lying him along its base and resting several oilskin sheets above him, even the silence was muffled. Joseph closed his eyes, his senses filled with the pungent smell of tar, and offered no resistance. His chilled bones sank lower in the boat, and his defences sank with them, defeated. The exhaustive emotion of the past few days, combined with the bitter cold and the nick to his ear, had rendered him passive to the most ludicrous of schemes. (And taking a canvas-covered wicker rowing boat out in a storm must rank amongst these.) As his companion patted the top of the oilskin with an 'Okay there, are you?', and began to push them out on to the kicking ocean, Joseph thought neither to respond nor to argue. From here on in, he was a passenger.

The wind seemed to have dropped slightly as the boat edged across the shallow waters, the natural shelter of the coastline throwing the brunt of it on to the land beyond, and for a time it was almost calm. The waves rocked the sides of the boat, more than once sending it skidding on to the sand, and the beach held them close. But as they moved out into the bay, the sea appeared suddenly to lift, throwing off the trailing fingers of the land, and they were cast up and across amidst a furious bray of crashing water. From where he lay Joseph could just make out the bending back and struggling oars of his one-time rescuer, but any more pertinent view was impossible. He huddled lower. Walls of green-black bucked at either side, cutting the boat into a hundred flooding pieces as they swept Joseph's scrabbled sights, and the wind bit hard. His hand to his face, covering his salt-stinging eyes, Joseph listened to the whistling surge of the waves as they sliced above his head, and thought of Sadie. 'Carry a fish with you,' she had advised, all those years ago. Where was his fish now?

The beach was deserted. Wrapped in Seamus' outsized souwester, her hands lost somewhere around the elbows, Sadie crouched on the crumpled sand and stared out towards the thrashing ocean. She had taken off her shoes, and her feet were buried to the ankles in the surf-soaked wastes, anchored. Seaweed lay in ribbons around her, their deep blood reds speckled with salt and snow, and a broken buoy spun drunken circles as it was caught, thrown back, caught, thrown back, by the fickle sea. In her pocket she could feel the hard edge of a fisherman's knife, cutting against her hip, but she left it there, its sharpness comforting in the midst of such indecision, and gave herself up to the sway.

She did not see the boat. Nor did she hear it, for the grizzling wind had her rapt. But when the belly of the seabed rose up and the waves fell back to reveal the blackened shapes of two figures balancing above the water, she was waiting. She was waiting as they tumbled beneath the surf, hanging to the side of the currach like trailing lobster pots, and she was waiting when they found the rocks beneath their feet and dragged themselves to the shore. Her hair streaming green-red, her body rocking with the floating sands, she dropped the tent of Seamus' souwester, and moved towards them. She saw the taller of the men fall back, begin to search his pockets frantically for the same knife Seamus carried in his, but he was prevented by the second. This was no mermaid. Or if it was, then her seduction had already been accomplished, and any knives, stakes, holy waters, holy prayers, were twenty years too late.

Joseph rested his back against the bow of the currach and shunted it the last few yards up the beach, dropping his arms to the side and trailing them in the wash of shells which crackled beneath. Behind him the sea pounded angry fists, and the sky cursed ever whiter, but when he straightened up and walked towards the watching silhouette, his was the only voice audible. Without a word, without a whisper, he faced her, and his stare was deafening. The waves quieted, the snow held its tongue, and Sadie stepped towards him, mute. Perhaps she remembered what she had felt all those years before, or perhaps she discovered it once again anew. But as she lifted her head and closed her eyes, unravelling inside the reaching arms of his gaze, Sadie knew she would not forget its sound. It is the silences of an English accent which so intimidate.

Taking his hand, Sadie led him across the rocks and up on to the harbour road, her dress clinging sodden, her feet deep in snow. She wiped her sleeve across the bloody trickle of his ear, and then kissed him gently, her lips to his neck. Joseph smiled. He did not notice the man waving from the beach as he nudged his boat back into the water, nor did he see the cloaked and oiled crowd of onlookers who had gathered the length of their houses and were tutting about the state of Sadie's dress. He simply allowed himself to be taken.

'*Jeezus Chroist*, is that the Englishman I'm seeing?' Seamus exclaimed as he opened the door and ushered them into the kitchen. 'A fine state you're in, dear God, if it isn't.'

Maggie appeared from the stairs, Isobel hovering in her arms, but when she saw them, two drizzled ghosts by the fire, she put the child down and flustered to help. Sending Seamus out to find the souwester, 'for it cost a pretty penny, so it did', she set to licking and flicking as she cleaned Joseph's face and netted him to his chair with blankets and tea. Sadie looked on, glancing from Joseph to the window, and then back again, as if watching for some half-remembered arrival, and then sat down next to him. Squeezing her skirts upon the hearth, ignoring Maggie's disapproving frown, Sadie leant back against Joseph's shoulder, turned her mouth to his ear, and whispered gently.

'Were you coming to fetch me Jose, were you?'

He nodded.

'Coming across the sea to fetch me? For you knew I was waiting?'

He nodded once again.

'Good,' Sadie murmured, closing her eyes. 'That's as I was thinking.'

Joseph was put to bed in Sadie's old room, the poor child who slept there once again getting ousted, and for the remainder of the day he slept. When he next woke it was the early hours of Monday morning. The snow had ceased, and the sun cast a violet haze across the drifting surface of the sea, drowning his window in iridescent light. He sat up, for a brief second imagining he was still in the boat, but when his outflung hand felt only the soft froth of the nylon carpet, he was reassured. He was on dry land, he knew that much. Scratching his head, he caught the edge of the bandage Maggie had so conscientiously wound about his crown and ear, although an elastoplast would have been just as effective, and he groaned loudly. A shuffling on the floor beneath the bed responded in kind.

'What . . .?' He pushed back the mound of rugs and covers, and levered himself over the edge of the mattress. His upside down position threw him for a moment, but as the world turned around to meet him, he saw Sadie, bright-eyed and scaley-tailed, staring back at him. 'What are you doing under there?' he asked, bewildered. 'Why have you been sleeping under my bed?'

'I was looking out for you,' she smiled, 'in case you needed something in the night. But you slept like a baby, so you did, so I just lay here listening anyway.'

'But you . . .'

'I didn't want to disturb you,' she interrupted, shaking her head at his gesturing hand. 'You were real bushed, so you were. Was a long way you came, honest to God.'

Joseph sat back up, trying to piece together the few fragmented memories of the day before. The boat he remembered, and something before with a bus . . . And then it all came flooding back, knocking him sidewards on to the bank of pillows, and leaving him gasping for breath.

'Sadie . . .' he mumbled, his fist paddling against the leg of the bed, 'Sadie . . .'

She wriggled out, kicking free of the green quilted eiderdown, and appeared at his head.

'What's your problem?' she offered, anxious to help. And

then noticing his pale features as they sunk lower into the sheets. 'Are you sickening, Jose? Tell me now?'

'Where's Isobel?' he croaked, twiddling a strand of Sadie's woven hair between his fingers. 'Isobel?'

'O, she's here too, so she is,' Sadie assured, breezily.

Joseph dipped once again beneath the bed. 'Where?' he demanded, his voice lost in springs and duckdown.

'With Maggie. Over there.' She nodded towards the wall. 'Safe,' she added, mindful of her responsibility.

'Darling . . . come sit here.' Joseph once again patted the bed, and smiled as Sadie struggled to his side. She pulled the sheets across their folding bodies, and leant back against the wall. He continued. 'I didn't come alone, Sadie, you must know that.' He spoke quietly, each word rounded and smoothed, like clay cupped between palms. 'I came with Elisabeth and the twins as well.'

Sadie frowned, her eyes creasing as she considered his statement. 'Elisabeth?' she repeated, as if trying to place the name.

'They'll be here any time, Sadie. The bus broke down, and they went for help, but they'll be on their way this morning, I'm sure. Especially since the weather's turned.'

'Mmmm.' Sadie stared at the window, at the empty sky and the still, still waters, and knew she should have kept Isobel with her. 'Mmmm.'

'What do you want to do, Sadie?' He took her hand, dancing on the flattened edge of the sheet. 'Tell me.'

She gazed past him, her eyes still full of sky and sea, and shrugged. 'Stay . . .?' she murmured, almost inaudible. And then, as the idea embedded itself, she repeated it, louder. 'Stay.'

Joseph's mouth twitched, and he pulled at his bandaged ear thoughtfully. 'All right,' he agreed softly. 'All right.'

19

The minibus, complete with shattered windscreen and a fluttering of stubborn leaves, pulled into the village just after breakfast. Joe at the wheel, his inherent diffidence infinitely better suited to the Irish roads than his brother's more domineering character, steering a steady path around the lakes of melting snow, once pot-holes. Parking outside O'Kearns, they tumbled on to the street, Seamus searching his pockets for Maggie's instructions, and Elisabeth pacing to and fro nervously. She had already made up her mind about Ireland, and as soon as she found her daughter, she intended to put thought into action, and take the first plane out of it.

'Do you have any idea where we are, Seamus?' she snapped, turning towards her fumbling brother, 'or are we going to end up spending yet another day wandering around this hellhole of a country?'

'Nope ... nope ... it's here!' Seamus waved the scrap of paper triumphantly, hurriedly smoothing it legible as Elisabeth bore down upon him. 'Hey! And so are we! This is it, folks.'

The twins grinned at each other excitedly, glancing about them as they sought to identify the myriad of treasures their mother had shared with them. The inn where the man fell out of the sky; the harbour, where the seal women come to find fathers for their children; the rock where the mermaids wait to catch their sailor; the hedges where the leprechauns hide and the fairies dance; and there, beyond the wall, those must be the hills she was always talking about.

'Well come on then.' Elisabeth had no interest in memory games, and only wished to get this present farce over and done with. 'Hadn't we better find them? And hope to God that Daddy is with them, else that's another wild goose chase we're going to be on. Honestly, he's no better than she is.'

Jumping down from the wall where he had climbed to look for the seals, Seamus waved them all in the direction of the quay. 'It's the big one right on the end, according to this,' he declared, and they shambled down the steps towards it.

As they did so they met five remarkably similar looking men approaching from the other side of the village, hands thrust deep in pockets, heads burning in varying degrees of red. Five clumsy fingers raised in silent salute, before all eyes returned to the ground, all hands to coats. The twins nodded, while Elisabeth merely scowled. They walked alongside in silence, boots clattering brashly against the stone steps, until they reached the house, where Seamus, looking up from his directions, declared, 'This is it,' and glanced towards their five companions for confirmation. Nods all round. And they might have remained unintroduced had not Liam, always the best with names, suddenly announced, 'Seamus and Joseph! So help me God, I knews I should be knowing you.'

The twins grinned, hitherto not wishing to presume, and held out their hands. Five equally broad, equally mollusced fists were produced in return.

'Liam.' A hefty shake.

'Paddy.' The same.

'Jerry.' No less.

'Joe.' Slightly less.

'And Mick.' Barely a flicker. Mick had never been one for crushing bones.

Elisabeth stood to one side, waiting for them to finish, before demanding, 'Well, can we go in now?'

'Round the back, so it is,' Liam declared, nodding her ahead. 'Round the back's where we're looking to find them all, so it is.'

'Fine.' Elisabeth strode ahead, irritated by the general lack of concern everyone seemed to be showing and, having first kicked several pairs of boots and a couple of bicycles into relief, flounced through the open door of the kitchen.

'Elisabeth, I'm guessing.' Maggie was on her feet, hurrying towards her, the first even vaguely hopeful sight Elisabeth had set eyes on in days.

'Yes. Is Isobel here?'

'Yes. You must be desperate, sure. Sit down, and I'll fetch her.'

Maggie disappeared up the stairs and Elisabeth remained standing by the door, listening to the rising gabble of the men outside. Only Mick had followed her inside, and as he sat now at the kitchen table and began to play with the wooden blocks and coloured bricks which covered its surface, he smiled sympathetically.

'Is the babby yours?' he asked softly. 'I was hearing our Sade had a little one with her, and I wasn't for thinking it would be hers.'

'No, Isobel is not my mother's,' Elisabeth replied, acidly, 'although Sadie doesn't seem aware of that fact as yet.'

Mick shrugged his eyebrows. He understood what it was to lose out continually to those higher up the ladder. Especially since he had lost the one brother to whom he had been able to return the favour, Tommy, now in France.

'You the youngest?' he asked, balancing a brick atop a tower of yellow cubes.

'As such.' She moved towards the table, her eyes still fixed upon the stairs. Her mother was the real child of the family.

'Not much fun is it . . .' He was interrupted as Maggie reappeared in the doorway, Isobel wafting against her shoulder, and Elisabeth launched towards them, arms flailing building blocks in all directions.

'Isobel!' she screeched, and Isobel twisted against Maggie's arms and gave her mother a glowing smile. 'Thank God you're all right.'

With a grimace at the overwashed, grey babygrow her daughter had been changed into, and a cursory wetted finger to remove a chocolate smudge upon her face, Elisabeth reclaimed her child and headed for the door.

'Will you not stay a while, no?' Maggie invited, as Elisabeth hurtled into her brothers ambling inside the same way.

'No, er, thank you. We have to be off.' She glared at the twins as they pulled out a couple of chairs and joined Mick at the table. 'Come on,' she urged. 'I want to go.'

Seamus looked up from his study of Mick's construction. 'What's the hurry, Liz? We've only just got here. Hiya Isobel!' Another glowing smile for Seamus.

'My name is Elisabeth, Seamus. And the hurry is I want to go. Joseph, will you please tell him?'

Joe squirmed apologetically. 'We just said we'd meet the uncles in the bar for lunch. They've gone up there now. We don't really have to be rushing off do we?'

'For God's sake you two. Why are you doing this?' Elisabeth looked around in desperation, but there was only Maggie, waving a teapot in the far corner, and a pile of wet clothes hanging on a rack by the fire. 'Is my father here?' she demanded, recognising one of the sweaters. 'Did he arrive?'

'Yesterday, in a proper mess, sure he did. He's upstairs with Sadie now, still sleeping, I don't wonder.'

'Well would you wake him and tell him we're here? And that I want to leave. Now.' Elisabeth's voice was rising higher with every thwarted sentence. 'Please.'

'If you like,' Maggie shrugged, 'and you can call me Maggie . . .' She reached out a hand in an attempt at welcome, presuming Elisabeth would now accept the need to wait a while, but Elisabeth turned away, distractedly patting Isobel's back, and stared longingly towards the road. Maggie headed for the stairs.

'I'll take you, if you like,' Mick offered, intent upon his tower. 'If you're wanting, I'd be chuffed to . . .'

Elisabeth turned towards the table, glancing from her brothers to her uncle, and nodded, slowly. 'Would you?' she asked, gentler now. 'Would you really? I'd appreciate it if you did.'

Mick stood up, and with what he hoped to be a chivalrous bow, but which in execution was more of a hobbled cough and a quick scratch of his shin, he fumbled towards the door.

'And thank you,' Elisabeth threw at her brothers, a sugary smile grazing their ducking heads.

'Oh, see ya then,' Seamus grinned, sheepishly. 'Bye Isobel. See ya soon!'

Isobel chuckled amiably, waving at the twins from her shouldered perch. And the three of them disappeared out of the door.

'See you Mick!' Joe added, as they faded past the window. 'Bye . . .'

By the time Joseph and Sadie descended some ten minutes later, Elisabeth was several, grateful, miles away, and the twins had built the Houses of Parliament. As Joseph tiptoed around the doorframe, preparing himself for Elisabeth's angry onslaught, Seamus had just given the word to 'Fire!' and a hundred wooden bricks were catapulted across the room in noisy greeting. Recognising such chaos as necessarily of her own making, Sadie hurled herself past him and seized her grinning sons excitedly, scrabbling their turfed heads and demanding to know what they thought of her home. She waltzed from wall to wall when they told her that, apart from the lack of seal women, they loved it, and with a mischievous glance at Joseph, who only blinked non-committally, she announced she intended to stay.

Maggie, at the time collecting the far flung remains of the Houses of Parliament, looked up, immediately wondering exactly where Sadie intended to stay, and hurried around the quay to find Seamus. The twins marched clockwise around the table to a stamping beat of 'Brilliants!' and 'Seals!' and Joseph, after checking to see his clothes were dry, went to the door to look for Elisabeth. Sadie danced through and around them all, until, breathless with the early morning exertion, she fell to the floor, and lay back against the foot of a chair, laughing.

'Where's Isobel?' she wheezed, resting her head against a cushion and rolling her eyes. 'Where's old Mother Earth for taking her this time?'

'She went with Liz,' Seamus replied from his buzzard-like position above a wobbling Tower of London.

'Where did they go?' Joseph demanded, returning from his fruitless vigil at the door.

'Home,' Joe answered, imagining their absence to be self-explanatory.

'London?' shrieked Sadie. 'But that's not home . . . sure we decided that, didn't we?'

Seamus put a finger in his mouth and popped his cheek loudly. ''Tis as far as she's concerned.'

'She's not driving that van herself, is she? Who took her? Was she terribly upset?' Joseph leapt into paternal action, darting back to the door and peering out as if hoping to find the answers for himself.

Joe sighed, stood up, and walked towards his mother as she lay, rug-bound in the middle of the floor, shaking her head dramatically. 'Mick took her, Uncle Mick. Said he'd put her on the plane, as we wanted to stay on a bit longer. She was all right, a bit mardy like usual, but fine. Glad to see Isobel, I s'pose.' Sadie moaned, adding kicking heels to the shuddering assemblage. Joe stroked her hair into a corn-like sheaf, and tugged it fondly. 'We met some of your brothers, coming down, Ma,' he announced, changing the subject. 'Five of them. We're going to meet them later. Will you come? O'Kearns, they said.'

Sadie sniffled. 'That's all my brothers now, bar Seamus, so it is. I haven't seen them myself yet.'

Joseph moved and stood beside his son. 'We have to sort out what we're doing exactly,' he advised. 'We'll have to make our arrangements.'

Three pairs of eyes turned listlessly towards him. 'Later,' they all implored. 'Not right now.'

O'Kearns was heaving when they eventually stumbled their way through the debris of tears and building blocks and wandered up to the main street, the clink of glasses and roar of 'Cheers!' audible even from the house. Joseph trailed behind reluctantly, his recollection of this bar surprisingly lucid, considering the inebriated haze which characterised the majority of his wedding memories, and it took a son on either elbow finally to lever him inside. Tucked into a corner table, he watched his wife's five remaining brothers throw her from one to the next in their habitual greeting, without a smile between them, declaring to all who cared to listen how good it was to see her, and what a boring gobshite old married Seamus had become.

Slamming towards the bar, Liam ordered drinks all round, while Joseph held his breath and cringed at the soaking he predicted for Sadie. But he need not have feared: while Ireland might be learning to accept women in its public houses, the brothers were not, and as Sadie was handed a lemonade and a packet of Tayto, Joseph breathed a sigh of relief for the old values.

But his respite was brief. The twins, inspired by their first ever taste of stout, would not be palmed off as lightly as their mother, and within minutes they were inciting argument and revolution from all sides, just, it appeared to Joseph, for the hell of it. Opinions upon the British government, the Republican Cause, the Pope, the IRA, and other such 'smalltalk' were thrown like grenades from pint to pint, some more articulate than others, and it was soon clear that they were going to be in for a long afternoon. Sadie sat quietly with her crisps, largely unhearing of their debate, sucking the salt from her fingers and watching the seagulls wheel in graceful circles outside the window. Joseph caught her eye and smiled.

'Do you want to go for a walk?' he mouthed, intending to suggest they visit her mother, whose disapproval of drinking he could remember almost word for word. 'Godforsaken' was her favourite complaint, he seemed to recall.

Sadie pondered her empty glass, and nodded, scrunching the cellophane crisp packet and dropping it into the ashtray. ''Long the beach ...' she agreed. 'I want to show you something.'

Joseph nudged himself around the edge of the table, passing the twins a handful of coins and raising his forefinger to their glasses to imply 'one more only', before leading Sadie through the swinging doors emblazoned with Guinness pelicans and fluorescent clover leaves, and on to the road.

The afternoon sun had melted the remaining snow, and the sky was the curious greeny-violet one only ever sees in Ireland. Taking his hand in hers, Sadie crossed to the sea wall, and leaned over, searching for signs of life in the harbour, but only Seamus, untangling nets at the far side, was visible. She turned to point him out, but Joseph, the flat of his hand to his eyes, was looking past her towards a churning shadow just on the horizon.

''S'a boat coming in!' she declared excitedly, following his gaze. 'He would have been stuck somewhere 'cause of the storm. Can we wait for him?'

Joseph nodded. He was relieved simply to be outside, away from the rebel-risings of the bar, and welcomed the opportunity to be alone with her. 'We can talk about what we're going to do,' he suggested, hoping to sound more lighthearted than he felt. 'We do need to work it out.'

Sadie curled her fingers tightly around his palm, and flicked her head dismissively. 'We will, Jose, but not now. Can we not just sit for a moment, surely?'

They wandered along the quay, Sadie lifting up her skirts and vaulting the bundles of mussel-shelled nets which lay drying on the side, her legs purplishly pale from too many years spent drowning in sunless rooms.

'D'you know,' she began, waiting for Joseph to catch up, 'they used to salt the fish just . . . here!' and she stamped her foot on the alleged spot. He nodded. 'And do you know,' she continued, 'if you went outside after dusk with unsalted fish, you'd be walking all night long, so you would. Spirits,' she whispered, conspiratorially, 'don't like that, so they don't.'

'Don't like unsalted fish, or don't like you going outside?' Joseph enquired, kicking a roped buoy against the wall.

Sadie shrugged. 'That's what they say,' she aired, disinterested in such details.

They sat down upon the steep edge of the harbour wall, Joseph offering his jacket, but Sadie preferring the bare stones, and continued to watch the incoming boat.

'And do you know what the seagulls are shouting?' she began again. 'If you listen to them, can you hear it?'

They lay back, resting upon their elbows, and watched the gulls swooping overhead, scything the placid green waters and diving high again. Joseph, craning towards their hypnotic shrieks, shook his head in amusement. 'Nope. No idea.'

'Guess!' she teased.

Joseph listened. 'Ooops!' he offered lamely, as a particularly low-flying pair of wings cut the wall behind them.

Sadie laughed. 'Honest to God, man, you're useless, so y'are!' She sat up, her hand upon his leg. 'No, they're saying "*Iasc* ... *Iasc* ..." Can you hear it now?'

Joseph, enjoying her playfulness, raised his eyebrows. 'Oh,' he nodded, 'I thought you meant they were saying something comprehensible.'

Sadie glared at him. 'They are. It means "fish", to be sure. Not everyone has to speak English, you know.' She took her hand from his knee and tucked it beneath her skirt sulkily.

Joseph sat up hurriedly. 'I'm sorry, Sadie,' he implored, 'I didn't mean it like that. I just didn't understand what you meant.'

'You never do, Joseph,' she muttered, unusually acute. 'That's your problem.'

Joseph watched her as she tipped forwards, her shoulders resting upon her knees, and stared at the rippling water beneath their dangled feet. She looked as if she wanted to throw herself down, and his finger itched to hold her, to pull her back should she try, but he did not dare touch.

'Sadie,' he tried, tentatively, 'please don't be like this ...'

'Like what?' she accused. 'What am I like?'

Joseph sighed wearily. 'Sadie, it was only a seagull.'

'No, Joseph,' she returned. 'No it wasn't.'

They were silent then, she still fixed upon the swirling eddies of green water, he searching for the right words to cajole her with. But before he might offer them, she spoke.

'That's your problem, Joseph ...' Sitting upright, she turned sideways to look at him. 'You've never heard what I'm saying, have you?'

Joseph shifted uncomfortably, but said nothing.

'You've never understood, to be sure. Because you never listened properly, honest to God, you never did.'

She was staring past him now, watching the fishing boat as it made its final arc before entering the harbour, and the sunlight on her face shimmered its last strains. She was crying, colourless tears which washed her almost transparent, and her eyes were closed. And it was all there now, splashed upon her features like cold morning water, running down her neck, flooding. The desperation, and the silence, and the fear, were all there, mirrored as they had never been before.

'Sadie, please . . .' Joseph reached towards her helplessly, but she pulled back from him. 'You have to tell me, Sadie,' he insisted. 'Sometimes things aren't always obvious. Sometimes you have to explain.'

She shook her head, wiping a hand across her streaming cheek, and looked beyond. Beyond, to where the gulls were screeching, and the waves lolled, and the fishermen threw ropes around the stone bollards of the quay.

'Sometimes, Sadie,' he repeated, 'you have to explain.'

Lifting her skirt to her face, Sadie buried herself in its jangling folds, the bell shells of her very first green dress having adorned every hem since, and took a salty breath. Bringing her feet underneath her, she shakily stood up, Joseph at her elbow, and stepped towards the wall.

'I'm going for a walk . . .' she mumbled, her hands fanning her tear-stained cheeks.

'Can I come with you?' Joseph asked, afraid to lose her again when, after all these years, they had seemed briefly so close.

'No, I want to be on my own, Jose.'

'Where will you go?'

Sadie waved her arm indiscriminately. 'Just walking . . .' And she moved away from him down the quay.

Joseph watched her, his hands dug low in his trouser pockets, his eyes creased against the sun, until she had disappeared out of sight, and he was alone there. Turning back towards the fishing boat, now moored on the opposite side of the harbour, he saw three men jump across the thin divide of water and on to the quay, where they pulled at the mooring ropes, and grumbled softly to one another in unheard voices. Their boots echoed around the bay, clomping distantly like hooves in wet sand, and their hands worked quickly to secure the boat, their livelihood. He dropped his head, nodding towards his polished shoes. She was right. It was another world to him.

20

Sadie followed the harbour end down towards the beach, and made her way across the litter of rocks and gorse down on to the sand. Barefoot, she pulled her skirt into hoops around her waist, and walked towards the water's edge, swollen with the full tide. The ground was shifting with every wave, and each time she took a step, her foot was sucked deeper, drawn towards the looser sand further out. Shells spun and flickered in the dusty shallows, but when she tried to catch one, plunging her arm into the icy water, they faded from her touch. She bent her knees, lifted her feet, and kicked the spray higher and higher, till her eyes stung and her tear-stained face was washed clean, washed free. And then, her hands clamped behind her neck, her skirts fallen and trailing in the waves like a bridal train, she kept on walking.

She wanted to walk until she could walk no further. She wanted to keep going until she reached the edge of the earth and there was nowhere else to go. She wanted to go so far that coming back was just another part of the circle, and not this great, unassailable wall which it seemed now. Sadie waded deeper, feeling the current tugging at her thighs, the wet seeping her upper body, and she dropped her arms to her side and began to paddle them in moons around her, pulling herself on. She arched her neck and allowed her hair to tangle, wisp, flood, as the necklacing waves yielded lower, and as she dissolved into the shining depths, there was nothing else but this.

Joseph leant against the sea wall, skimming stones across the surface of the bay, and counting as each one bounced its descent into the still water. Sometimes five, sometimes as many as six, it hurled itself back, refusing to be taken under, but when at last it gave in, the spreading circles of its grave were a fitting tribute. Outwards from the centre, growing, reaching, one ripple always pushing further than the next. Joseph watched, held by the simplicity of it all. Stones and water. Water and stones. Blood need not even come into it . . . And so why all this heartache?

For a brief few seconds of insight, Joseph understood what it was to live this. He saw the trembling beyond the smooth, the current beneath the reflection, and he bowed to it, tightening his fingers around the chalky pebbles he had collected in his pocket, breathing hard. Every muscle, every bone, every restriction, seemed to yearn forwards, into the shadows of the water, and he felt himself falling, dropping, lost.

He turned away. The sea slapped back, refuted, and the boats across the harbour tipped disappointedly, yawning on their ropes as the stones stood firm, unrelenting. Today was no day for drowning. Joseph glanced at the sky. It was barely day at all.

Sadie sank back upon the rock. It was almost dark now, and the sky was a luminous mauve, unfurling above her like some oversized bath towel, wrapping her warm. She had always loved to swim out here, cutting beneath the tide and diving deeper until the drag was behind her, and the sea floor was way, way, below. Further than even her longest breath, her most reaching fingers. This rock was where the mermaids sang on summer evenings, waiting for the fishermen to pass in their boats so they might call to them, seduce them into the blue, blue waters. But it was February now, and there were neither mermaids nor fishermen to keep her company tonight. Only the rock itself, barnacled and black, and the ever moving, ever seeping sea.

Sadie rubbed her arms fiercely, watching as the blood rushed to the surface and the icy pale was flushed again. She was goose-pimpled, her skin tight with the salt, and her hair hung heavy and knotted across her shoulders like worn rope. She turned her face into the musk of granite, inhaling its dampness, its ancient breath, and she wondered how many times it had sat here, watching the tide ebb and flood, ebb and flood, every day allowing a little more of itself to be carried in with it. How tall, how grand, it must once have been, rising above the flats of the mainland like a wakeful god, overseeing its sleeping minions. Only they had betrayed him, let the sea sneak up when he wasn't looking, exiled him to here, where the waves crashed and the sun burnt, and daily he was worn a little lower, a little softer, as the water dripped through the stone.

She would stay here just a while longer, until the tide had begun to go out. It would be shallower then, and the shore not quite so far. Sadie smiled, turning back towards the beach, where the gorse prickled at the sky with its gleaming yellow pins, and the moon had begun its slow climb above the roofs of the village, to where it would hang, just above the gold and green flag of the church, and mock them with its many changing faces. Yes, she would wait until then. And Sadie closed her eyes, flooding into the rock beneath her, and lulled to the soft lap-lap of the waves.

She was not in O'Kearns, as Joseph had expected, nor at her mother's house just up the street, which was the second place he tried. She must have gone along the beach, but when he stood on the end of the wall, he couldn't see her there either. Joseph wandered along the lane which led out of the village, his chin thrust deep into his collar, his head low. So much for making arrangements. The twins were still huddled around innumerable empty glasses in O'Kearns, disputing rights, wrongs, and even the occasional maybes, and Sadie had disappeared off the face of the earth. Elisabeth was on a road somewhere in a borrowed minibus which could break down at any time, and Isobel? He hadn't seen Isobel in days, her capacity to slip from one state to the next, one cradling arm to another, was clearly as refined as her grandmother's. What was happening to this family?

Shrugging his arms around him like slings, Joseph sat down upon a rubbled ledge of the sea wall, and stared out across the Atlantic. The breeze hummed gently through the gorse bushes, and two magpies flirted back and forth in the trees above his head. So peaceful. Perhaps it would be good to stay for a little while, to gather themselves together before work and London and bathtimes divided them into their own distinct corners. And Elisabeth could have some time to calm down, to forgive the antics of the last few days. It might be better for all of them.

Fingering the cuff of his sleeve, Joseph remembered the first time he had sat upon this sea wall, filled with hope by a creature he was not even sure existed, filled with promises. So easily forgotten. He shook his head, folding back the sleeve of his jacket, and watching the blue of his veins pulse softly from hand to wrist to elbow . . . He'd often thought of dying like this, of watching his pulse grow slower and slower, until it simply faded into nothing. It made him feel safe, to know that as long as it was still moving, he was alive, in control, striding on. Only tonight, sitting here, he wondered if that was not just another way of forgetting. If he could concentrate hard enough upon this, he could deny everything else; if life was reduced to this single, telling vein, and all other lines and deviations put aside, he could survive untouched.

But was that living? Watching the white of the surf break upon the sand, hearing the dripping shells kick and clutter beneath, it occurred to him he was simply watching himself die.

Sadie shivered. It was cold now, the light having gradually slipped into blackness, and only the luminous shard of the new moon offering any warmth to the dark waters swilling around her. She sat up, hugging her knees, rubbing her cramping feet, and listened to the breaking waves grow closer. She thought of her brothers, flushed and drunken in O'Kearns, and her sons roasting before them. She thought of her other brothers, scattered around the world, far away from this scrap of land they had called home, exiles across this great wash of ocean. Would they be returning, as she had done, or was that it now? Were they gone for good?

For good? Had she herself gone for good when she climbed into that bus all those years ago? Or had she simply gone for adventure, for curiosity? And all the drowning, shouting, deafening, shrinking since then? Had that been for the good? She sighed, lifting her fists to her knees, and peering through the cliffs of her knuckles out across the rising Atlantic. Perhaps her mother was right; perhaps she had always wanted too much, fought too hard . . . But what else was there? Better to keep thrashing, in and out, lift and fall, than to be still and wearied like this rock. Better to wear oneself down, to corrode one's own edges, than to wait for life to do it first. She dropped her head, telescoped against her fists. These were the real rolling hills, these bony mountainous knuckles, that rushing, vaulting sea. Sadie smiled, rubbing the backs of her hands against her skirt. And they had been here all along.

But now she must go back. The moon was high and the

beach only a few lazy strokes away. If she waited any longer, the tide would be turning and she was too tired to swim all that way again. She lowered her legs over the side of the rock, preparing herself for the bracing icy water, and then with a flick and a splash, she was in, cutting across the waves and pushing for the shore. It was time.

At the sound of the splash, Joseph stood up, feeling his way along the shifting rocks, and down on to the sand. His legs were stiff from sitting, and his mind ached. And then, across the black lines of sea and sky, he saw her, flapping towards him, her arms arcing as she lifted herself up and through. Stepping into the dragging tide, he waded to meet her, salt water soaking his shoes and trousers, sand filling and dredging with every move. Reaching into the water, he caught her arm, steadying her as she gasped for breath, fumbled to stand, and he pulled her close. She struggled, thrusting his hands back, blinking her eyes rapidly, but when she saw it was Joseph she relaxed. He ran his thumbs across her lids, cheeks, lips, and she gazed at him.

'Where have you been?' he might have asked, although he did not hear the words.

'Swimming,' she replied, or may have done.

And then he picked her up, bunched wetly against his sodden shirt front, and carried her the last few yards to the shore. Taking off his jacket, he wrapped it around her shoulders and rubbed her gently, arms, back, legs.

'Better?' he asked, as she straightened her neck, and uncurled against his chafing palms.

She nodded. The moon was high now, hovering over their heads like a knife blade.

'Better,' she murmured.

'You know, I've been thinking,' Joseph declared, as he drew her towards him and they began the slow climb up the beach, 'it makes sense that the seagulls are shouting "fish!"'

'*Iasc!*' Sadie corrected.

'*Iasc!* then. Because that's what they spend all their time looking for, isn't it? That's what they eat.'

'Course,' Sadie smiled. 'What else would they be after sayin'? They're not eejits, you know, these Irish birds, sure they're not.'

The seagulls were flown now, back to wherever it is seagulls fly, and the air was quiet. Elisabeth and Isobel were in a cold departure lounge hundreds of miles away waiting for take-off, and the twins were higher than they had ever been, potent with politics and stout. Only Sadie and Joseph were fixed, leaning into one another as they wandered up the beach, feet heavy in the shifting sands, minds sure. It was as if the last twenty years had been washed away, and they were back to that first night of shirt tails and promises, when it had all been so simple. Joseph ran his hand across Sadie's splashing features, and pulled her closer. Still holding on, still chasing.

And up above them the bells for evening Mass began to chime, and slowly, doors opened, lights flooded, and the village began to muddle on to the lane and up the hill to the church.

'Who would that be, in the name of God?' someone muttered, glancing beyond the wall at the two shadows flickering upon the sand.

'It's that Sadie, for sure, a proper odd fish if ever I saw one.'

Another head nodded knowingly towards the beach.

'And that'll be her Englishman.'